WITH MY LITTLE EYE

BOOK ONE of the MIA SERIES

by

TESS MARSET

1 LONE CROW MEDIA

Front cover photography:
© 2010, 2019 Zachary Martzke

Book & Cover Design: Vladimir Verano, Vertvolta Design

PUBLISHED BY

1 Lone Crow Media

www.1LoneCrowMedia.com

ISBN: 978-1-7333609-0-6

Revised Edition

To my mother who hoped for me,
My sons who cheered for me,
And my husband who indulged me,
Your love made me believe in myself.

PROLOGUE
PROLOGUE

THE HEAT BORE DOWN UPON THE TWO LITTLE GIRLS as the sun climbed higher in the sky, turning the sidewalk the color of bleached bones. Yet they played on under the oppressive warmth of the sun, beads of sweat mingling on their small upturned noses.

"I spy, hmmm. I spy…. Okay, I got it. I spy, with my little eye, a ladybug on that leaf," Mia, the brown haired one, said.

Not to be outdone, Robin laid her finger alongside her freckled cheek as her hand cupped her chin.

"Okay, okay. Hmmmm." Her eyes narrowed as she searched for something that began with 'M.'

Spotting her prize, she shouted excitedly, "All right, got it! I spy, with my little eye, a moth in the mud! Ha! Let's see YOU top THAT one."

The alarm rang at the station and the men jumped into action, leaving their unfinished sandwiches on the kitchen table. They scrambled for their gear and their positions on the trucks. The great door opened and the big machines lumbered out onto the roadway. The sound of the siren grew to a high-pitched cry. The firefighters fastened their helmets and scanned the horizon for that telltale sign.

Mia wiped her brow, and then puffed out her cheeks, letting her escaping breath whistle up to her bangs. It was the first week of August and summer had been played out. The neighboring girls were bored and feeling feisty as the heat wave hung on. They had been through numerous rounds of Barbies and coloring books. And it was just too hot for jump rope and skating. As a result, they sat in the cool grass and resorted to their old preschool game of 'I spy.' But finding things that began with 'N' was going to be tough.

Holding her hand like a visor to block out the glaring sun, Mia scanned everything in sight. She had to find something before her friend could jump in and claim victory. Robin sensed her faltering and moved in for the kill.

"Give up? I got one already. I spy, with my lit—"

"No, wait. Give me just one more minute."

She looked at the street, the swings in the playground, the mothers walking by with strollers. Nothing began with N. She didn't want to have to concede so easily.

"C'mon. Give up already. I spy, with my little—" Robin gloated triumphantly.

"Ispywithmylittleeye," Mia said quickly, "a naked bird in a nest!"

"What? Where? Hey! You can't do that!" Her friend's face flushed up to her freckles.

"Why not? Naked and nest begin with N," Mia said defensively.

"But BIRD doesn't. And besides, where do you see it? I don't see anything."

The pumper truck followed the hook and ladder as they rounded the tight corner. By now they could see the huge clouds of black smoke rising above the second story rooftop. They pulled alongside a parked car that blocked the fire hydrant. The driver had to honk the horn of the great truck to get the gathering crowd of spectators to clear a spot in the street for them. People pointed and shouted. A woman screamed.

"Ummm—up there!" She pointed to a clump in the branches of a tall tree.

"Where? I still don't see it.

"There! You see that big branch going that away? Well, right next to that little branch beside it— see that nest? It's on the lowest branch. You can see the baby bird –"

"I don't see a thing! You're cheating!"

Robin jumped up and squared her fists on her hips. Her eyes joined forces with the sun's rays beating down on Mia.

"I am not! There's a baby bird right there!" Mia was on her feet in an instant pointing to the tree.

"You're such a cheater. Cheater! Cheater!"

"I'm not! You are! And I don't want to play this stupid game anymore if you're going to be a sore loser."

"Cheater! Cheater! Take a stick and beat her!" the girl sing-songed, leaning into Mia's face.

"No I'm not! I can't help it if you can't see the bird with your silly little piggy eyes!"

"Cheater! Cheater! Take a stick and beat her! Cheater! Cheater! Take a stick and beat her!"

"If you don't stop, I'm going to beat you with a stick in a minute!"

"Oh yeah? I'd like to see you try, Cheeeeeater."

As the firemen gathered in front of the house and prepared to go in, they could see the flames and smoke billowing from the first story windows. A man, clothed only in boxer shorts and tee shirt, bolted out the front door, gasping and coughing. His legs swaggered beneath him for a moment, and then dropped him to the lawn. Paramedics ran to his side with oxygen. When they rolled him over, he smelled strongly of gin.

The relentless sun witnessed the standoff as sweat beaded upon their top lips and across their brows. Robin stood almost a half a head taller than Mia. They locked stares and gritted teeth at each other. But within a few seconds, Mia's eyes betrayed her by darting away.

Sensing that split second of meekness, Robin gave Mia a shove and growled, "I said, I'd like to see you try it, *Cheater.*"

Mia swallowed the hard knot in her throat as she tried her best to scowl back. But a spark of fear ignited in her despite her attempt at being brave. Her adversary was bigger and tougher. Mia's eyes became wells of tears. She swiped angrily at them, streaking dirt across her cheeks.

"What's the matter, crybaby? Scared?"

Her nose began to run and she couldn't help but sniff loudly. Round, fat teardrops crested the rims of her eyes and rolled two wet stripes down her cheeks.

"Oooo, lookit the little crybaby cheater! Let's make her cry some more!" Robin grabbed a handful of Mia's long hair and yanked it hard.

"Oww! Stop it!" she squealed in defeat.

The other girl's eyes lit up as she reached for another yank. "Why? What are you going to do about it?"

Crying and holding her hair, Mia sobbed, "I hate you! I don't ever want to be your friend again! I hope you get cooties and die!"

The words spat out like venom and her chest heaved. Then all of a sudden, like a cloud moving in front of the sun, a calm fell over her and her skin crawled with goose bumps despite the heat of the day. She locked eyes with her friend once again. Any trace of fear had evaporated, replaced by a new sense of knowing.

"I bet you'll even die today!" she blurted out, but stopped short, dumbfounded at what had escaped her lips.

Robin stepped back and gasped, "What did you say?"

"You... you are going to die today in your own house... In your own room..." Mia murmured, as if in a trance.

Wanting it to stop, she clapped her hands over her mouth. Her stomach lurched from the poison of her words.

"T-that's not funny. Take it back."

Mia, still holding her mouth tight, could only give her head a little shake.

"I said, t-take it back, or I'm gonna tell..." Robin grew quiet, all of her bravado gone.

"I can't," Mia whispered.

She watched as Robin ran off, her eyes tracking her until she saw the red braids clear the corner. A few minutes later, all alone, she slowly followed.

The firefighters tried to turn back the flames that leapt out of the side windows as screams flew from within the house. One firefighter emerged with a half conscious woman draped around his neck. She coughed violently and fell to her knees clutching her throat. The engineer darted from the controls at side of the truck and joined by a paramedic, rushed to move her away from the house. Her head flopped backward, allowing her to draw in a deep breath that brought on another heavy bout of hacking. Immediately, she became alive again and started to scream and reach for the house.

"My daughter's in there!"

Mia did not know why she had said it. It was the cruelest thing she had ever said in her whole life, yet she wasn't able to stop. Although she disliked Robin at that moment, she knew the words she had spoken were not hers. She did not know where they had come from or what made her say them. Making her way home, she dragged her feet over the pavement, her stomach squirming with shame. The relentless heat made the air feel thick.

When she reached home, she peered around the side yard to the neighboring house that stood catty-corner to hers in the back. Mia could see the pink curtains of Robin's room fluttering out of the second-story window. She knew Robin would be inside right now telling her mother of all the evil things that her friend had said.

Thinking back, maybe she *had* cheated just a little. But she imagined that naked little bird in that perilous nest, its neck outstretched and wobbling. It was Robin's own fault that she couldn't see it. However she was right, bird does not begin with N. Still, it couldn't erase all those horrible words that were said....

She climbed the stoop and opened the screen door to the cool dark sanctuary of her home. She tiptoed through the foyer past her mom who was conducting bible study with several other ladies in the living room. Mia took a peek to make sure no one was watching, then crept past to the kitchen to sneak a cookie. She climbed the stairs and followed the hallway to her room. There, she decided to make a tea party with teacups of water, the cookie, and her dolls. She knew they wouldn't call her a cheater.

The afternoon heat eventually broke as the sun slowly dipped beyond the horizon. Downstairs, the ladies were closing their bibles and tucking away their rosaries. Every last 'God Bless' and goodbye faded with the sound of their footsteps on the walk outside. Within a few minutes, Mia could hear her mother chopping vegetables and filling pots in the kitchen sink below, getting dinner ready. Her father would be home soon.

Like the shush of water through a garden hose, the growing noise of city traffic wafted in through her open window. A distant siren sliced through this gray noise. As it grew closer and closer, the sound forced its way to the forefront, drowning out everything else.

Scrambling up the attic stairs to get a better view from the dormer window, Mia saw two fire trucks pull around to the street directly behind her house. Looking to her left, she sucked her breath in sharply when she saw smoke and flames pouring out of Robin's house. Spying over the narrow yard and between the houses, she could see people gathered in the street. She jumped to her feet and ran downstairs to her mother.

"Mom! Mom!" she shrieked, "Robin's house is on fire!"

"Mia?"

Hearing her child in distress, her mother set down the dish she was washing in the sink and ran to the stairwell, her hands dripping bits of soapy foam on the waxed parquet floors.

Tugging her arm, Mia insisted, "Come! Look! Robin's house! It's on fire!"

Mia reached the dormer window first and sunk to her knees to watch while her mother caught up, wiping her hands on her apron.

"Oh, merciful Father!"

"Is there anything we can do, Mommy?" the little girl cried.

"No, Mia. It looks like the fire department has already been called," her mother said, her face creased with worry.

"Can't we go down there?"

"No, it's better to stay here out of the way. The last thing the firemen need is more people crowding around. The only thing that can help right now is prayer, child."

Mother and daughter held hands and whispered prayers as they watched the chaos from their haven across the yards. Shouts and screams and the roar of the fire reached its way up to them through their open window. They spotted paramedics hovering over two people lying upon the lawn and other firefighters running to and fro.

A couple of them climbed onto the steep roof. With axes and a large hook, they punched a hole through the shingles and stood back as flames flew up through the gap. Suddenly there was a shout, sending them scrambling off their post. Just then, a large portion of the roof caved in.

Mia turned and hid her face as her mother pulled her close. But a moment later in an impulse of grotesque curiosity, she peeked out, feeling the need to watch the tragedy playing out before them. Her last glimpse was that of Robin's pink curtains, fluttering out of the open window as flames consumed them before her mother made her look away.

About fifteen minutes later, they could hear Mia's father come in through the front door below them. They ran downstairs to tell him the news, but as he entered, they could smell the fire's smoke clinging to his clothes. Seeing the commotion on his way home from work, he had stopped to see if there was anything he could do to help.

"What happened? Is everyone all right?" Mia's mother asked.

"From what I was told, it seems that McCane was drunk again. He was smoking and watching TV on the sofa when he fell asleep and dropped his cigarette on the cushion. When he came to, the sofa was already on fire. But he ran out without telling anyone. They said that Katherine was washing clothes in the basement when she smelled the smoke. She tried making it upstairs to fetch their daughter, but the fire was too great and she couldn't see anything. Poor woman was overcome with smoke. She barely made it out alive."

"But what about Robin? Is she okay?" Mia held her father's hand and looked up at him.

Her dad got down on his knee to face her, "I'm sorry, honey…they weren't able to save her," he said quietly.

Mia gasped for air, feeling as if someone had punched her hard in the stomach. Her father went to put his arms around her to comfort her, but she squirmed and fought against him.

"NO! She can't be! She can't be! I didn't mean it! I didn't mean it!" Mia screamed.

She turned and fled to her room. Perplexed, both husband and wife stared at each other, not knowing what to make of her strange statement. When they sought her, she was curled up in the small corner between her bed and the wall. "I didn't mean it, I didn't mean it," she kept repeating.

Her mother took her by the shoulders and made her face them. "Why do you keep saying that, child? What are you talking about?"

"I knew it was going to happen! I caused her to die!"

"Now Mia, calm down. Exactly what do you mean?" her father asked.

Her sobs came out in ragged gasps. She struggled hard to make herself talk while her head filled with the noise of swarming bees.

"Young lady, you are to tell us what happened this instant!" her mother said, gripping her and giving her little shakes.

"We-we were in the playground, and she called me a cheater, then she yanked my hair. But I didn't cheat! I saw the bird!" She broke into sobs again, and continued, "We got into a fight and she called me a crybaby and wanted to beat me up. But I-I told her that I wish that she would d-die."

"But you were angry! It's perfectly natural to lose your temper and say things you don't mean," her father tried to console her. "It doesn't mean that you made the fire happen."

Her voice was a hoarse whisper, "But I saw it. I *knew* she was going to die."

"Of course we saw the fire through the attic window child, but it doesn't mean –" her mother started.

"No! I saw it! I saw it in the playground when we were fighting *before* the fire. She wanted to make me cry, but I wouldn't. I told her I hated her. Then all of a sudden I saw it. It was like a dream. Robin wasn't in the playground anymore. She was in a dark place—her closet. And there was smoke—it was so thick. And she couldn't see…"

"But you couldn't have possibly known that."

"But I did, Mommy. She was coughing and it was so hot, but she was afraid to leave."

"Stop this nonsense at once! There is no possible way you could have seen that. It is only for our Lord in Heaven to know what will happen to us."

"But I did."

Her mother's face grew red. "I said stop it! Not another word!"

Her dad stepped in. "Why don't you let the girl finish, Margaret? She's obviously upset over her friend."

"No, I will not have blasphemy in this house!" her mother said. She pushed Mia down by her shoulder, forcing her to kneel in place. "Pray child for forgiveness for your words and actions, and to have mercy on that poor girl's soul."

"Do you really think that's necessary? She feels bad enough today without—"

"Steve, don't you undermine me. I don't want her turning out like Lydia with all that unholy voodoo sacrilege. Now Mia, pray."

Mia did as she was told and as she had done many times before when she had been tempted to stray. She laced her small fingers together, bowed her head and started, "The Lord is my Shepherd, I shall not want…"

As soon as the flames died down and the smoke let up, the firefighters did a sweep of the house. Upstairs in the north bedroom, they revealed a heartbreaking scene they had witnessed many times before in a number of their runs. Behind the charred closet door was the lifeless body of a little red-haired girl, huddled in the corner. Her head cradled in her arms, she apparently had died of smoke inhalation—the only victim of the fire.

ONE

THE PILE OF FRESHLY LAUNDERED CLOTHES sat in front of her on the sofa, an insurmountable mountain waiting to be conquered. Mia wondered how two people who weren't home all day could generate so much laundry. She plucked another shirt off the summit, laid it in her lap and started folding.

If they were house painters or auto mechanics or worked with wild animals, she could understand it. But as adults both working at desk jobs, she should only be looking at a handful of work outfits, 'grubbies' for the weekend, underwear, a few changes of nightwear, plus various odds and ends, times two.

She imagined what a family complete with kids' laundry must look like and raised her eyebrows at the calculations. She smoothed out another pair of trousers and hung them on a hanger, envisioning mountains and mountains of clothes and even more folding.

All the assorted sizes of underwear and pants, socks and pajamas. Not to mention the linens. And all of those little baby shirts....

She forced herself to stop immediately. She was backsliding again. No matter what she set out to do, whether a diversion or mundane household task, she always wound up in that same place time and again. Mia sighed and choked back emerging tears. She tried to continue folding, but the clothes became big and dark and heavy all of a sudden. Dropping the jeans she held in her hands, she wandered listlessly into the kitchen.

She opened the refrigerator door and half-heartedly looked about, trying to get ideas of what to cook for dinner. Dan would be home soon and he usually arrived with a healthy appetite. She considered making a hearty meal of roast and potatoes. He always loved it when she cooked like that.

But looking at the clock, she thought otherwise; time had run out again. Surveying what remained in the near-empty refrigerator, she spied leftover pizza from last night and leftover Chinese takeout from the night before. There was only the two of them. It should be enough.

Feeling achy, Mia made her way to her darkened bedroom and sat down on the bed. She felt weighted down and tired. Even breathing required too much energy. Everything seemed to take so much effort lately.

The breakdown pervaded every waking minute and dominated her dreams at night. Going over it in her mind, she knew she had done everything correctly—the scheduled checkups, the prenatal vitamins, a nutritious diet, plenty of rest, and an exercise plan for pregnant women. She and Dan had started preparing and decorating the nursery, choosing the color swatches and themes, and looking for furniture.

Why can't I have a baby?

After almost two years of trying to conceive, they had finally succeeded. They had planned so carefully. Money was set aside in the bank to cover the birthing costs. Her maternity leave was submitted early at work. She did her homework on various birthing techniques and positions, and had enrolled in their HMO's birthing class. CDs of *Mozart for Baby* and *World Lullabies* among others sat gathering dust beside stuffed animals on the shelves that Dan had already hung in the room.

What did I do wrong?

She recalled every detail, every misstep she took, every object that might have been a bit too heavy for her to lift. Maybe she should have quit work. Maybe she should have had a more positive attitude. There had to be *something* she overlooked. She should've seen the doctor immediately when she experienced her first cramp. But everything she had read told her it was perfectly normal. Even the triage nurse on the phone had told her it was nothing to worry about.

Squeezing her eyes shut, Mia tried to push away the memory of that evening that took place seventy-four days ago. But a haphazard jumble of events and their sensations paraded before her, displayed against her closed eyelids: the intensely bright light above the exam table; the feeling of the cold metal stirrups against her bare skin; masked nurses hovering about; Dan's face, concerned and caring, telling her to take it easy and breathe; the internal exam; excruciating cramps; a burning sting from a needle.

After a round of sudden heavy contractions, all that was left was a wee bloody body on a blue surgical cloth; a boy; her husband's eyes, full of tears. "It's all over now, honey," he had whispered. She had only caught a glimpse of a tiny fist no bigger than a hand on the dolls she used to play with as a child, but when she tried to get a better view of her baby, the nurse had covered him with a cloth. If she held that precious little hand in her own right now, it would be no bigger than the tip of her pinky finger....

"Babe? Are you okay?" Dan stood in the doorway.

Mia hadn't heard his key in the lock or the front door closing. She dove for the tissue box on her nightstand and fumbled with trying to pull a tissue out. It tore into shreds. Helplessly, she wiped her eyes and nose with the back of her hand but wouldn't face him. He wasn't supposed to catch her like this again.

Dan sat down next to her on the bed and held her. Then he took a tissue out of the box and handed it to her.

"Had one of those days?" he asked gently.

"It didn't start out like that, but yes. I have."

"Well have you gotten out today? Call anyone?"

"No," she answered a little defensively.

"Okay, but you know you can't keep doing this to yourself. You've got to start letting it go."

"That's easy for you to say."

"I know, I know." Dan hugged her and rested his chin on her head for a moment. "It's just that you've been through some tough times before, and you've always been able to bounce back."

"They weren't like this. This is different and you know it. We are talking about our child's life. This is not the same as those stupid ruts I fall into. This isn't the blues or a funk that I am in, we—I…" The pain in her chest grew sharp. "I *lost* our baby. I've been going over it. It had to be something that I did."

Dan put his hand to her chin and made her face at him. "Get this straight, Murphy, you didn't do anything wrong. Do you understand that? I don't ever want you to think that."

"But why couldn't I carry him? Why did this stupid body fail me? You know that's why I'm an only child. My mother lost three more after I was born, two miscarriages and the last was stillborn. What if I'm like her?"

"Hey! Why does anything happen in this crazy world?" He continued more carefully, "We can't explain it. But please, Mia, don't give up. You know the doctor said that we could try again. You just need to take it easy for now."

"He could be wrong."

"We've been through this. Your prenatal exam said that you could have children, and your post exam said that everything was okay, so we're going to have to trust that and be patient."

She mumbled under her breath, only half-convinced, "I did trust. And I have been patient."

He shook his head. "You know, if you are going to be so negative all the time, maybe that's why you can't shake this thing."

"You're right. It is my fault."

"Aw c'mon! You know I'm not saying that! You're hearing what you want to hear. All I'm saying is that we can try for another in the future."

"You don't get it do you? We *had* a baby and I lost him! And we'll never know what he'll be like or what he was going to grow to be. And I didn't even get a chance to hold him." She broke down again. "He was depending on me... I failed him...."

"We've gone around and around with all of this for more than a couple of months now, Mia. It's not good for you. You know your dad would have said—"

"Leave my father out of this!"

"Okay... But you're going to have to start pulling yourself together." He grew quiet. "You think that I don't give a damn about any of this. But I do. I really do. You don't seem to realize that I also had to let it go and get on with my life."

"Listen - just leave, okay? I want to be by myself right now," Mia snapped and turned to the wall.

"C'mon, Hon, don't shut me out. I want to help you through this." Dan laid his hand on her shoulder, "Murph—"

She shrugged it off.

He pulled his hand back. "Suit yourself. You can't beat this if you don't want to even try," he said, rising.

She remained silent, her back rigid to him. Her tears fell leaving wet spots on her faded sweatpants. On his way out, he hit the light switch, bathing the darkened room in bright light. There she sat, vulnerable, exposed under its cold white circle that illuminated her shame. She gasped turning her tearstained face up.

"Please turn that off."

"No. If you want it off, you are going to have to get yourself out of that hole that you are in and turn it off yourself," he said as he headed out of the bedroom.

"Dan? Please? Please—"

◊ ◊ ◊

Too many times before he had turned back around to apologize and couldn't help but wonder if he were only making matters worse. In the kitchen he grabbed the slice of cold pizza and a beer. Plunking down in the armchair in the living room next to the pile of half-folded clothes, he turned on the TV and pretended to watch. Through the corner of his eye, he could see the light switch off in the bedroom. Next, the door slammed shut and within seconds, he heard her sobbing bitterly.

Losing his appetite, he threw down the pizza and picked up the beer instead. He hated what had just happened, but was at a loss for what else he could have done. In the past, before the miscarriage, they would have reached out to each other to comfort and console. Now she kept pushing him away. All they seemed to do anymore was argue.

Whatever happened to the person he married just a few years ago? He surfed listlessly through the channels although nothing held his attention. Finally he left it on a sitcom, but its one-liners and canned laughter did not reach his ears.

He understood the loss of the baby devastated her, leading to this heavy bout of depression, but her obstetrician had reassured him that in time she would get back on track. But her depression was getting worse. Her father's death last year was quite a blow to her. She seemed to have recovered, especially with all the excitement of the pregnancy. But maybe she hadn't recovered as fully as he had previously thought.

Whenever he mentioned her father in trying to help her through her grief, she became upset. He eventually dropped it. He missed him too. It was as close to knowing what it would be like to lose his own father. Stephanos was a warm-hearted, generous, and easy person to talk to. And if it weren't for "Poppa Pappas" he would have never met Mia.

Although tension from their fallout hung heavy in the air, the memory of the obvious setup that had brought them together made him smile inwardly, in spite of himself. His father and Pop worked side by side for over eleven years as aircraft mechanics for a small private airline. Together, throughout the workweek, the two close friends would plot their retirements, plan joint travels for RVs they wanted to buy, and schemed to match their kids together. Eventually they had waited and conspired long enough until the time was right. Once Dan came home from his tour of duty with the Navy, the two old connivers set upon him and Mia.

Within hours of his call to tell them of his arrival at homeport, the senior Labonts held a cookout in his honor and invited the Pappases as their guests with very obvious intentions. It worked. Despite feeling a bit intimidated by her scrutinizing mother, Dan couldn't help but fall head over heels for the spunky girl that nothing ever seemed to keep down.

Overcome with fatigue from putting in long hours at work, he started to doze in the armchair, dreaming about San Diego and when they were first married. He saw them on that lonely wild beach filled with craggy rocks and secret coves. Mia was wearing her bikini with the ugly flowers on it, but she made it look great. He could see her laughing and running before him on that summer's day, her slender legs covered with sand and her long wet hair clinging to her back. They had made love on the beach later in the evening after the sun had gone down with nothing but the sound of the waves, the light of a small campfire and the warmth of their bodies. After minutes of dreaming, Dan was deep asleep.

At work the next day, echoes of their fight from the night before resounded in his head. He knew she would be depressed again today and hated being at odds with her, especially when she was down. He also didn't want to give her the impression that he was upset with *her* since he didn't climb into bed until the early hours of the morning and had left for work before she had awaken. Tossing it about for a while, he finally conceded and picked up the phone.

"Babe? Listen, I'm sorry about last night. I know I said some things that were out of line. You don't deserve that. But it seemed that when I tried to cheer you up, I only made things worse. I want to understand what is going on and I want to be there for you," he explained, "But it made me feel like nothing I said made any difference."

There was silence on the other end. Then she said quietly, "No... you did make a difference. I am feeling better. Thanks for trying."

She sounded distant as if she were focusing on everything else but their conversation. Still, he was relieved to hear that she wasn't angry with him.

"Are you sure you're okay? You seem, I don't know—distracted or something."

"No, I'm okay. Really. Don't worry. I'm not mad at you ... in fact, I'm sorry for putting you through all of this... I'm sorry for a lot of things...."

"Hey, you don't have to apologize for anything, okay? We'll see this through together. Just like we have everything else, all right? You know, if I can finish up these last few edits, I think I can make it home earlier tonight. Maybe we could go out to dinner or something. How 'bout that Greek restaurant at the plaza that you wanted to try?"

"Sure... I'll see you then."

Her abruptness seemed odd, but not wanting to over-analyze every one of her actions, he turned to the editing board and cued up the feed. Maybe he would have another chance at patching things up between them after all. Their phone conversation had hinted at the possibility of things resembling some normalcy tonight, so he was anxious to get home to spend some time with her. He didn't realize how much he missed her.

Dan wasn't able to leave Pryus Productions as early as he had planned. His partner had to leave because of a dental appointment. And the hard drive started acting up, just as his supervisor came in with a few last minute changes to a clip. On the drive home, each delay in traffic felt like points deducted off a big timecard.

The house was dark when he drove up. Dan felt a twinge of disappointment in realizing that she may not even be there, but her Hyundai parked along the side yard confirmed her presence somewhere close by. The front door was unlocked when he tried his key and it swung open to a living room with no one in it.

"Babe?" he called to let her know he was home.

He wanted to remind her to lock the doors when she was home by herself, but something didn't feel right. He went directly to the bedroom where she had been spending a lot of time recently, but didn't see her there either. As he returned to kitchen, he switched on lights as he went.

"Mia?"

There were four unchecked messages on the answering machine and a half-gallon of milk left opened on the counter beside an unused glass. Feeling its sides as he put it away, the milk was at room temperature indicating that it had been out for a while. Perplexed, he headed back to the bedroom to change his clothes.

Maybe she's out back or talking to Mrs. Lopez next door.

His foot struck against something that rattled and spun across the wood floor. Picking it up, he was startled to see that it was an open box of ammunition. When he slid out the plastic tray, a round of bullets was gone. The box was full the last time he had checked it.

"Mia?!" he called as he started to search frantically throughout the house.

He took a quick glance to the backyard, and then in every room, but she was nowhere to be found. He returned to their bedroom once more, preparing to tear apart the house room by room if he had to. As he came around to his side of the bed, he discovered her in her nightgown, huddled in the corner between the bed and the wall. She was trembling and dazed but wouldn't face him. In her hand she held his old .38 service revolver that he kept up on the shelf in their closet.

"Oh my god! Mia?" He knelt by her side, fighting back panic.

"I didn't mean it... I didn't mean it...." she whispered.

"Are you okay? Are you hurt?"

He looked her over quickly and seeing no blood anywhere, he carefully placed his hand on the weapon. "What happened? What are you doing with the gun? Mia? Did someone come into the house?"

When he tried to take it from her, she gripped it firmly.

"I didn't mean it... I didn't... I didn't mean it...." she repeated with more agitation, not seeming to be aware that he was beside her.

"Honey, give me the gun," he said slowly and deliberately, trying to remain calm as he pried her fingers from it. "C'mon—let it go, Mia."

She continued to stare beyond him not responding to his voice or touch. When he finally freed the weapon, he promptly opened the cylinder, shook out the bullets and put them in his pocket. Then he took the empty revolver and slid it across the floor, away from them.

Trembling himself, he gathered her in his arms and held her tight. "That's my girl," he said weakly. With her out of harm's way, only then did he allow a sigh of relief to escape. "Was someone here? Tell me what happened."

She broke down in ragged sobs. "I didn't mean it. I didn't mean it. I didn't mean it."

"I know, Honey. It's okay...I know," he whispered hoarsely as he stroked her hair. He held her in his arms and rocked her gently.

If there had been an intruder, he could have dealt with it. But the realization of what she was attempting to do struck a hard blow. He racked his brain over what could have driven her to this point. She had been depressed about the miscarriage, but he never thought she was capable of something like this. Not Mia. She cherished life and everything associated with it.

After about an hour, he felt her tense body slip into a fitful sleep. Then he placed her in their bed and covered her. It took him another hour to make his own body relinquish the terror that gripped him. For the rest of the night, he kept a sleepless, anxious vigil in a chair by her side.

Dan knew she couldn't continue on this way. What if he had been delayed even longer at work? An overwhelming pain engulfed him as he imagined finding her lifeless body sprawled out on the floor. What could she end up doing tomorrow or the day after that? He couldn't be with her every minute. He had never been enthusiastic about psychiatry, but Mia couldn't keep fighting this alone.

By nine-thirty the next morning, he had already spoken to two receptionists, a triage nurse, and an insurance representative liaison but was nowhere near to talking to a doctor. Pacing up and down the living room floor with the phone, his voice rose in frustration.

"Goddamnit! You people are just not getting this, are you? Haven't you heard what I've been saying? My wife tried to shoot herself last night! What the hell does a person have to do to talk with a psychiatrist over there? What? No, I did not check her into a hospital. I've been watching her like a hawk all night. Listen, we have to get in to see a shrink *today!*"

He did not realize that Mia had gotten up and with the blanket from the bed wrapped around her shoulders, was watching him from the hallway like a shy animal.

"No, I want to speak to your supervi—"

Suddenly aware of her presence, he spun around to face her. Except for her eyes being puffy, the rest of her face looked calm and expressionless.

"Never mind. What? Okay, I'll hold." With the sound of recorded violins scratching in his ear, he turned to Mia, still holding the phone. "Hey - how are you doing?"

"Okay, I guess. I just feel wiped out."

"I'm sure you do, Babe. You need to take it easy. How about sitting down here on the sofa instead of standing? Or do you want to go back to bed? Can I get you anything?"

Choosing to sit down, she replied, "Some tea, please?"

She looked as if at any moment, she could shatter into a million pieces.

Dan nodded and took off to the kitchen. Within minutes he reentered the room with a steaming mug and placed it on the coffee table in exchange for a medical insurance card amongst all the forms, pamphlets and physicians' directories strewn about.

"Okay, got it right here…Yes, ma'am, the medical record number is 53295L-02 and her primary care physician is Dr. Ong. All right. Okay. Thank you." He hit the off button and shook his head. "Goddam HMO's."

"Please don't use that word," she asked. "What's going on? Why are you home from work?"

He sat down next to her and looked at her perplexed. "Don't you remember last night?"

"Yeah… I mean no. Well, some of it. It's strange, but I haven't thought of Robin McCane in years and this morning I woke up with her on my mind." Then cautiously she added, "I - I didn't do anything crazy, did I?"

"No, but thank god I got home when I did."

They both sat in silence for the next few seconds.

"So, I hope you don't mind, but I made arrangements for you to see someone. You have an appointment at four-thirty this afternoon." Dan tried to present it as delicately as possible.

"*You* want me to see a psychiatrist?"

"All right, I know what I've said about them in the past. But this is beyond you and way beyond me too. I'll admit it, I am scared, Mia." He took her hand in his, "I don't ever want anything to happen to you. So please, Babe, tell me that you'll go."

Seeing the concern in his eyes, she took a deep breath. "Okay, Murph. I'll go."

◊ ◊ ◊

Their old Jeep Cherokee rambled up the freeway onramp. Threatening rain, the Seattle sky was the color of dirty mop water and a light drizzle had begun to fall on the increasing rush hour traffic. Mia and Dan had endured a quiet, wary day at home together, both avoiding any in-depth talk about what had happened the night before or its implications.

Watching scenery and cars stream past her eyes, Mia couldn't help but consider the recent events and persistent question that was now crowding her thoughts. *Am I going crazy?* She didn't have a death wish, yet she couldn't remember how a loaded gun ever got into her hands. She knew she was depressed, but who wouldn't be after losing a—

Shifting her thoughts, Mia pulled her jacket a little more tightly about herself and crossed her arms. She must have really freaked Dan out for him to insist on her seeing a "head doctor" as he liked to put it. But how was she going to be able to talk to anyone about this? What if the doctor agreed that she *was* going insane? She found little comfort in believing there had to be some reasonable explanation to her actions. The trees, exit signs, and other cars fell past them in a blur as the Jeep picked up speed.

"What is the psychiatrist's name anyway?" she asked.

"Actually, with this cheapass HMO, all they will provide is a counselor. His name is Gerald Monroe. I'm sorry that Pryus ever switched to PartnersHealth."

"So I'm not seeing a psychiatrist? Is Mr. Monroe a psychologist then?"

"Well, he may or may not be. They told me that some of their counselors have psychology degrees while others have sociology degrees. But they all answer to a couple of staff psychiatrists who oversee all the patients." With his voice laden with guilt, he added, "I'm sorry, Mia. It's the only thing we have."

At the center, it took another fifteen minutes for Dan to argue with the receptionist that they indeed had an appointment. It was then they found out that PartnersHealth had double-booked appointments but was willing to make a concession given her circumstances. The misunderstanding and the wait made her feel even more anxious. It looked like any other medical doctor's office. *But,* she reminded herself, *this wing is for people who need psychiatric help.*

They waited a half-hour more in the waiting room. Dan kept his eye fixed on the Health Watch closed-circuit TV that repeated health and medical related news every ten minutes. She knew that after the first loop, his eye would turn critical as he studied the camera angles, scripting, and editing of the programming, finding flaws and thinking of ways he would improve them. She wished that he could have pursued that studio producer position he had applied for.

She rose to get a drink of water and returning to her seat, realized this was the first time that she had been out of the house in more than a week. Mia spied upon the other patients about the room from behind a dog-eared gardening magazine. As she studied their faces, she wondered what each of them was here for. The man in the business suit looked edgy as he chewed his thumbnail. Down the row from him was seated a young woman with a gaunt, haggard face and a case of the shakes. There was also an older couple whose wife refused to face her husband and body language kept her leaning away from him.

With her mind's eye peeling away the strangers' exteriors to expose their frailties, Mia was suddenly overcome with shame and self-consciousness. Could someone look at her and ever guess that she had flipped out with a loaded gun just the night before?

"Mia Labont?"

They followed the medical assistant down a corridor decorated with cheery prints of doe-eyed children and colorful landscapes and were shown to a small room with a desk and three chairs. The large window behind the desk overlooked the soggy parking lot below. The bright sport memorabilia that adorned the shelves, walls, and desktop looked oddly out of place and clashed with the institutional colors of the room. It felt as if they had been taken to the wrong office.

"If you'd just fill out this questionnaire, Gerry will be with you in a moment," said the medical assistant with a pasted on smile as she handed over a clipboard. Mia took up the pen and paused to read the questions. The ones about smoking, drinking alcohol and taking illegal or prescription drugs were easy enough to get through. She couldn't remember when her last menstrual cycle was—it seemed so long ago.

But as she went on, the questions seemed to take a more accusatory tone. Sensing Dan over her shoulder, she pivoted to stare directly at him. That was enough for him to recoil and get up to look out the window instead. She knew he felt just as uncomfortable as she in this place where therapists could only screw with your mind.

She turned back to face the print that was reproaching her:

Have you ever been pregnant? If so, how many live births?
Do you have any children living with you at present?
When was the last time you had an intimate encounter?
Have you ever been diagnosed with any mental health problems?

She drew her breath sharply and held back the pen. Just then the door swung open and in stepped a smiling bearded man in his mid-forties.

"Hello! You must be Mia." He swooped down, extended his hand, and shook hers, his other hand pinning back a bright green tie swimming with tiny goldfish to his chest. Quickly turning, he thrust his hand towards Dan. "And you are?"

"Dan Labont, sir. Her husband."

"Hi, I'm Gerald Monroe, but please, call me Gerry."

He shook Dan's hand heartily and then threw down a file on his desk. Nodding towards the clipboard he asked, "And are you finished with that?"

Mia tipped her head slightly. He plucked the board from her and then took up his post in the swivel chair behind the desk.

"Let me see… Mia, Mia…" he said absently as he slipped on his reading glasses and scanned the questionnaire. "That's a pretty name."

She blushed a little then answered, "Thank you." Her hand reached out to find Dan's.

"And what do you do, Mia?"

"I work as an assistant copyeditor for a local magazine publisher."

"Um, hmm. Sounds interesting. Do you like it?"

"Yes. Most of the time."

Gerry picked up a pencil and started tapping it on the desk, whistling a quick tune between his teeth as he continued reading. The whistling stopped.

"Uh oh. Looks like you didn't get to finish these last questions."

"Uh—no."

"Do you need a few more minutes to complete the questionnaire?" He peered at her over his half-glasses.

"No, not really."

"I see. Well, okay. But it's helpful when we have a full profile on you," he said.

She could feel her face flush. Nervous sensations raced through her. Now even Dan was looking at her.

"I just didn't feel the need to. Not now. But if you need an immediate answer, you can answer 'no' to all of them. Does that help any?" she said, trying to reign in her composure.

Gerry held his fix on her for a moment more, then smiled broadly and leaned back in his chair. The once-tapping pencil became a fluttering blur between his fingers at the end of his propped up arm.

"Okay. Well, is there anything that you'd like to tell me?"

"About what?"

Dan shifted uneasily, but he gave Mia's hand a little squeeze of encouragement.

"About yourself perhaps. For starters, how would you describe yourself?"

"Me? Uh, average. Quiet, I guess, in a way...."

"Nothing else you'd like to add to that?"

"No, not right off."

She suddenly felt very thirsty and her hands turned cold despite being held in the warmth of Dan's.

"Uh huh, and how about your life?"

"I guess about the same."

The therapist continued, "Well then, how would you describe your childhood?"

Mia thought for a moment and then said, "I had a normal childhood. Nothing extraordinary, by any means."

"Really? Nothing? No major traumas or setbacks?"

"No. Actually, it was pretty uneventful when I think about it."

"Uh huh. And your parents? Did you live with both of them?"

"Yes. Yes I did. My parents were good people. They loved me. I was an only child, so I never wanted for anything."

She watched him open the file and made a quick note on a paper within. Then the pencil went back to fluttering, a blurred yellow moth hovering anxiously about. He waited for her to go on, but she didn't.

"Would you like to continue?"

"No, that's about it."

"Nothing else about your parents or your relationship with them?"

"I told you, I had a good relationship with my parents."

"You told me your parents were good people."

She was starting to feel cornered. "They were. And I had a good relationship with them."

He scribbled down some more notes. Mia tried to peek at what he had written, but wasn't able to read his writing upside down. At the sake of appearing obvious, she stopped.

Dan leaned in close to her and whispered, "Don't you want to tell him about your dad?"

"No. I don't," she whispered back.

"Hey! No keeping secrets from old Gerry now," he said as he winked. "Is there something you care to share?"

She disliked being put on the spot at anytime, but this was feeling more like interrogation than counseling.

"Not right now."

"Are you deliberately being evasive?"

"No."

He leaned forward, "Okay then, how about last night?"

"What do you mean?"

"Well, from what I understand, you ran into a little trouble. Talk to me about this," he said as he tugged at his bearded chin.

Her cool composure melted away in a flash from the blood rushing to her head. Oddly enough, her mother came to mind. *The Lord is my Shepherd…*

"I—I was just a little mixed up. I don't know what happened. I mean, I've been feeling depressed lately, but—"

He looked her directly in the eye and said, "I heard that you suffered a miscarriage a couple of months ago. How are you feeling about that?"

Mia quickly faced Dan, her eyes blinking betrayal. He swallowed hard and avoided her gaze. She could see the muscle from his clenched jaw bulging in his cheek.

Coolly slipping her hand out from under his, she turned back to Monroe who was studying her as if she were a microorganism under a glass.

"I'm okay. What I mean is, I *was* upset, but I feel okay now. Like I said, I think I just got a little mixed up... I wasn't trying to—to kill myself or anything...." She hated the way her voice shook out of her control.

He leadeth me beside still waters....

The therapist added more notes to the paper as she stumbled through her words. Mia stared at the graying wavy hair on the top of his head as he wrote and wondered if he was even listening to her. She could feel a stifled scream growing in her chest.

Gerry returned his stare. "Dan here found you with a gun, Mia. What did you intend on doing with it?" he insisted.

"Nothing. It's not like I was going to—"

"To what? Hurt yourself? Or perhaps your husband?"

"What? No! Never."

"Then what exactly? You had a loaded gun in your hand. It just didn't get there by mistake."

"You don't understand... I don't want to hurt anyone. I didn't want to hurt my... I loved my baby. Yes, *my baby*. It wasn't just a fetus or a group of indiscriminate cells. He was my son! I know that is hard for a man to understand. *Any* man." She shot an inclusive glare at Dan. "Everyone keeps telling me that I can have another and I should forget all about him and get on with my life. But I can't! I can't replace my child that was lost. He is lost forever! You don't know what it's like to have a life growing inside of you and then know that it has died inside of you. And it was your own body that murdered that life! How can I ever get over that?" By now she was perched at the edge of her seat, shaking and indignant.

The prayer went silent in her head. Her bitter tears flowed once more. Dan put his arm around her but she pushed away from him, still feeling the sting of his betrayal. She never intended to share her guilt with anyone besides him, but especially not with a total stranger.

Dan looked to Monroe for validation. The therapist responded with a slight nod.

"Now Mia," Gerry said sympathetically, expertly, "I'm very sorry for your loss. It has been a tragic turn of events and I know you must be grieving."

She didn't want to face him. *How could **you** ever know?* she thought.

"But it's time for you to work through your grief, instead of letting it build up inside of you. It's normal to feel angry, but the important thing here is not to blame yourself. You have to realize you had nothing to do with this. Things just happen. Things that are beyond your control."

Her silent thoughts screamed back her condemnation, *You son of a bitch. Of course I had everything to do with this.*

"Regardless if you wanted to or not, you told me a lot about yourself today. And from what I can see, you've been really really hard on yourself. In fact, I think last night's episode was an attempt at some kind of punishment."

Mia caught him sneaking a look at the wall clock hanging behind them.

"Do you understand what I mean?" he asked as rose and moved around to the front of the desk where he sat down on the edge facing them.

Mia had grown weary. She wanted to bolt from this office with its veneered desktop, mauve chairs, and clashing team banners. It felt as if she had been looking at that goldfish tie, the dusty silk plant, and the book with the title on its spine that read *Smiles Count!* in the shelf for an eternity already. Training her eyes to her lap instead, she studied the white rows of knuckles under the tightened skin of her fists. But when Monroe sat down in front of her, she was forced to look up at him.

"So I'm going to give you a little homework. I know that you are saying to yourself, 'Homework? I left that behind just a few years ago.'" He gave her a sly wink and a charming smile crept onto his face. "Are you willing to do that for me?"

Anything to get out of here. She sighed. "Okay."

"Good. First thing I'd like for you to do is to write everyday in a journal. Did you ever keep one when you were young? I can take one look at you and know that you probably did. You can write about anything. Your feelings, your frustrations, your anxieties, your fears. It doesn't have to be a fancy diary, just a regular notebook will do. You might not think anything of it now, but eventually you'll see the importance of it.

"What I also suggest is that you write an actual letter to your baby, explaining how you felt about him or her. It's also very important that you write an apology to your baby and ask forgiveness. Keep the letter somewhere special or perhaps burn it and spread the ashes in a place that gives you peace. It is very cathartic, I assure you.

"And last," He leaned back across the desktop, reached into the side drawer file, and withdrew a paper. "This is a page of affirmations. I want you to pick at least three different ones to say to yourself everyday in the mirror. You might feel silly at first, but I want you to stick with it. They'll help you feel a ton better about yourself and start moving you away from the destructive pattern you're in. Have you heard of these?"

Mia stared ahead.

"Good. They really work, so give them a try." He handed the sheet to her then picked up a notepad. She glanced at the copy-weary page of affirmations with its fuzzy print and happy face border.

"Okay, last, I want you to take this note to Dr. Gamez right down the hall. You should still be able to catch him if he hasn't left already. He is the psychiatrist who will oversee our progress. I'm making a recommendation for him to prescribe some diazepam and sertraline for you. He will explain to you what they are for and how to take them. I think they will help take the edge off of things for you until you get back on your feet."

She reached up to receive the prescription, but Gerry handed it to Dan instead. She let her hand fall back into her lap.

"Any questions?" The therapist looked back and forth between husband and wife, the charming smile now a little broader.

Dan shook his head and said, "No, not from me. Honey?" He looked towards her. Mia gave her head a small shake.

"Okay. If there isn't anything else I can do for you today, I expect to see you in about seven to ten days so we can talk some more, so be sure to see the girls at the reception desk to schedule another appointment." He stood up and extended his hand once more. "Dan, it's been a pleasure."

Then, turning to Mia, he said solemnly and slowly as if talking to a small child, "Mia, take care of yourself and do what I say, okay? We can win this game, but you have to be a willing player. Do you think you can you do that?" He clasped her hand in both of his and gave it a squeeze. "All righty. It's been a pleasure." With that, he walked around them to the door, stepped outside, and popped his head in for one last "See ya" and a wink.

They could hear him place her chart in the rack on the door and call down to the assistant, "Is my five o'clock still here? Go get him, we're running into overtime already."

The rain had picked up outside. The lights in the parking lot were sputtering on, splashing their tungsten yellow patches of light upon the cars below. The small room was silent except for the sound of rain striking against the windowpane.

Dan turned to Mia, "I'm sorry, Hon. I didn't think that he—"

"I'm fine. C'mon," she answered in monotone.

Curiously, she felt as if she had just been sideswiped by a freight train. Numb and empty, she got up and retrieved her jacket from the chair. "We better try to catch Gamez."

They caught Dr. Reuben Gamez, Ph.D., in a dark room illuminated only by a desk lamp. The small balding man with a no nonsense air seemed to be very busy dictating into a recorder. Although she expected more, Mia was relieved when he only asked her a few medical related questions concerning interaction with other prescription drugs she may be taking and her overall medical health. She answered briefly and to her surprise, he scribbled out her prescription and handed it to her. With as little verbiage as necessary, he explained that she needed to take the antidepressant on a daily basis and to only take the sleeping pill if she was feeling overly tense or couldn't sleep. When she said thank you, he grunted a little and nodded. He then dismissed them promptly by resuming his dictation.

◊ ◊ ◊

Heading home through the wet streets, Dan expected to hear a commentary of some sort on the afternoon's events especially after her outburst in the office, but so far, none was forthcoming. She didn't say a word at the clinic's pharmacy and continued her stony silence throughout the drive.

Although Monroe seemed a little too "happy" for him and rushed through things a bit, his advice seemed plausible enough. Maybe it would be just the thing to get Mia back on track. But in the meantime, she volunteered nothing, keeping her gaze fixed out of the rain-streaked window.

"Everything okay?" He realized he had been asking that question a lot, but it didn't hurt to ask once more.

"Yeah. Just tired."

He knew she was lying. He reached over to give her shoulder a rub. "What did you think of that goldfish tie? Maybe I should get one?" A remark like that would have at least won a smile from her before, but not tonight.

"I could imagine that," she answered flatly.

They drove on for another mile, the sound of the windshield wipers slicing through the thick silence.

"Listen Mia, I'm sorry I had to tell them about the miscarriage. I know that's why you're upset with me. They had asked me over the phone if I could think of any reason why you did what you did. I honestly couldn't except for what had happened. That's all I could come up with. Unless… Are there other things that are bugging you that you haven't told me about?" He hesitated for a moment, and then went on, "I mean, I think you are happy with our life together, aren't you?"

There was an uncomfortable pause.

"'Cause if you're not, I hope that you wouldn't be afraid to come right out and tell me. I don't ever want you to be miserable, stuck in a situation with someone you don't love anymore."

"No, Dan," she said slowly and determinedly, "I do love you and I always will. And I am happy in our marriage. I can understand why you wanted me to talk to Gerry about what happened last night. But I'm still trying to understand exactly what happened myself. And I didn't feel like sharing my miscarr—," She swallowed and forced herself to complete the word, "—miscarriage with anyone. I felt that it was something private between you and me."

"I only thought that maybe if you got it out in the open, it would help. They are always saying about how you're supposed to talk about everything."

More silence.

"So, are you going to at least give it a try?" He glanced over at her.

"Give what a try?"

"Well, the affirmation thing and the journal. The medication. All the stuff that he talked about. It doesn't seem half-bad. Remember, I'm the guy who doesn't like shrinks, but I don't think it would hurt to at least give it a try."

"I guess," she said resignedly, "If you think it would help." She returned to looking out the window.

He had already pushed her as far as he would while trying to avoid a fight. There was always that fine line with Mia. When things didn't go right, she'd dig her heels in further. And with the past couple of months, he knew that fine line had grown so narrow and taut between them that it was liable to break at any moment. Her present silence wouldn't go on forever and pretty soon after taking the medication and following Monroe's directions, she should be back to normal in no time.

They would just have to wait and see.

TWO

"I AM WORTHWHILE. I AM LOVEABLE. I feel like a total idiot for doing this," Mia said as she forced herself to stare into the mirror, "but... I am filled with positive thoughts."

Muttering affirmation number seventeen under her breath with some uncertainty, she looked down again at the wrinkled photocopy with the happy face border for the next set. She had to retrieve the paper from the trash for the third time since the therapist placed it in her hands over a week and a half ago. But the tedium of repeating the sentences over and over was at least something to keep her mind off of 'It.'

"I am intelligent. I am capable. I am a thinking person... I am thinking that that jerk was right that I would feel silly doing this."

With a sigh, she decided that she had affirmed herself enough for the day. She took one last look in the mirror and was relieved to see that the deep shadows under her eyes were fading. And she needed a haircut.

Dan had stayed home to be by her side for the first couple of days after that terrifying evening. Yet they did not discuss what had happened. She knew he tried to venture into that territory a couple of times but she had successfully shut him out. She wasn't even sure as to why she had the gun in her hand. The implications of it all frightened her just as much as him.

To her relief, he eventually dropped it. What Dan did instead was make sure she took her medication. He also dug up a notebook and pen and put it on her nightstand, but so far, she couldn't bring herself to write in it. Not just yet.

But she had to admit that she was feeling better every day. Slowly the antidepressant was turning the tide, making her feel a little more relaxed and free, while the sleeping pill permitted her the sleep she had been starving for. As the days passed, their house gradually morphed itself back into home again, casting off the cold sterility that had pervaded it for the past few months.

Each day, as her depression receded, she felt herself regaining ground. Food started to resume its taste. Colors and sights caught her attention once more. As if she had rediscovered an old friend, laughter erupted from her as she and Dan worked in the backyard on Sunday.

She had finished spraying water on her wilting plants when she accidentally dropped the hose. It fell on its handle, setting the lock, and sending a stinging spray of icy water directly at Dan who had just walked up. The hose wriggled about wildly as he grappled to get it. She knew she should have turned off the faucet, but she was doubled up and holding her stomach from laughing so much.

Although he was thoroughly soaked, she looked so beautiful to him at that moment, that he couldn't resist planting a wet kiss on her. Her lips yielded to his and she kissed him back. Feeling the cold water from his shirt soak through to hers, she pulled away and gasped, starting another round of giggles between them.

What Mia thought was the most unusual aspect in her healing was what she had repressed. Memories of her father that had been bottled up were now surfacing. Affection, tinged with regret, guided her recollections for she realized she hadn't thought much about him since the pregnancy. She missed him terribly, but what had seemed too painful to think about before was now mercifully tempered by the antidepressant. Finding comfort in her memories now, she granted herself the leisure to take time with each of them, sorting through and turning them over in her mind like photographs in an album.

Stephanos Pappas was a kind man who doted over his only child as much as his busy work schedule and her mother would allow. Oftentimes it was just the two of them running errands or fixing things about the house since Mia's mother was frequently involved in her bible studies and prayer groups.

Margaret Pappas had tried to make her young daughter take an active part in her groups, but if Stephanos was home, he rescued the child from the religious regiment by asking Mia to help him with one thing or another. He would never tell Margaret directly to leave her be. Instead, he would shift the focus off of Mia onto whatever task was at hand and insisted that he needed assistance. Mia learned early never to question his motives.

Away from her mother, she could share with her father the smallest of problems or the funniest of jokes she had heard at school. His laugh came easily and was often so infectious she would join in laughing too, even if the joke wasn't that funny.

Their biggest secret was sneaking a slice of pizza at Gino's Pizzeria on the corner of the street where the hardware store stood, even though dinner time might be only a couple of hours away. The two of them would fix their eyes on the cook twirling the dough high above his head as they perched on the tall counter stools, sipping forbidden sodas and inhaling the spicy scent of fresh pizza bubbling in the ovens.

One time when she was still young, as they drove to the auto parts store, she couldn't remember why but she asked him why Mommy prayed so much. Her father stopped the song he was singing with to the radio and kept his eyes fixed on the road ahead. He took a few moments before responding while she agonized over the possibility that she had angered him.

Carefully choosing each word he answered, "She wasn't always like that Mia, but she has come to rely on her faith to see her through everything in her life, both good and bad. It comes from having to endure just too many things."

Mia could not figure out what it meant. She wanted him to go on, to explain it patiently and thoroughly like he did everything else. She wanted to know why she was an only child, or why Mommy never joined in on any of their fun, or a whole bunch of other questions about her parents and their life—if only he would continue.

But he stopped there, not saying another word. Through the years she always wondered what made an easy going, simple man like her dad fall for someone like her mother, but it was a question she decided never to ask.

As she grew older, her friendships gradually took priority in her life and her father spent more and more time running errands by himself. Mia always felt sorry for him as she left the house to go out with friends, leaving her mother fervently praying over her rosary in the kitchen while he sat in the living room alone watching the TV. He always called out to his daughter to have a good time. In retrospect, she wished she had spent more time at home with him instead.

She didn't even get a chance to tell him goodbye. His heart attack last year was sudden and massive. By the time she reached the hospital, he had been pronounced dead by three minutes. She stood there, clutching his hand, feeling the fading warmth as the nurses unhooked the monitors and cords from his body that lie twisted and contorted as if the life had been wrung out of it. His eyes that beheld only her when she was in the room, now stared past her, through her, searching beyond.

Before, such memories were so upsetting that Mia thought her own heart was going into arrest. But as her thoughts flicked from scene to scene, just when she began to feel the familiar sharp pang in her chest, the medication graciously stepped in and dulled the razor edge of grief away.

On the morning of her next counseling session, the receptionist from PartnersHealth called to say that Gerry Monroe was out of town on an emergency. She could either reschedule two weeks from now or talk to another therapist if she wanted to keep her appointment for today.

Mia politely put the receptionist on hold to give herself a moment to think. Things did seem better than they were before. She had even tried a few practice entries in the notebook. What was Monroe going to do for her anyway? Quiz her on how many affirmations she memorized? It was obviously a deep depression that she had been in, and now things were beginning to right themselves, just as she had hoped.

She wasn't sure how Dan would react, but with a smile she told the woman on the other line that she would wait to reschedule.

◊ ◊ ◊

After sitting at the edge of the runway for forty-five minutes, the Boeing 737 was finally cleared for takeoff. Monroe slammed his eyes shut and repeated his mantra silently in his head while beads of sweat broke out across his forehead and under his moustache. He gripped the armrests tightly and tried to breathe deeply as the plane rumbled down the concrete. He could feel it accelerating as he was slowly pushed back into his seat by the g-forces. This was the worst part and he knew it. As the plane reached top speed, he gritted his teeth and held his breath, abandoning all of the deep breathing relaxation techniques he knew and embracing sheer panic.

Just when he certain they would run out of tarmac and be instantly hurled across the dirt field into the chain-link fence to explode in a fireball, there was a slight bump and the whine of rubber against pavement fell away. This sixty-six ton mass of metal, glass, and plastic was now jetting through space. His stomach lurched and he swallowed hard trying to make the greasy bratwurst he ate at the terminal go back down. The plane rolled slightly to the left, then what seemed like an eternity to him, finally leveled out.

His eyes opened automatically at the chime of the "fasten seatbelts" light shutting off. He had survived. And, he told himself encouragingly, he had seven hours to recoup before going through the terror all over again with landing. With a deep cleansing breath, he took a crumpled tissue from his pocket and dabbed at his forehead, destroying any evidence of fear and hoping no one had noticed.

Monroe was looking forward to his time in Orlando. When his friend Everett called and told him that he had two tickets up for grabs for tomorrow's game, courtside, and absolutely free, he couldn't resist. It was also a good way to spend some time catching up with his thirteen-year-old son, Austin, since his girlfriend Amy couldn't get time off of work to go. Things worked out just right. His bitch of an ex-wife even agreed to let him pick up Austin from Kissimmee to spend the night. She must have some hot date that she had planned on to be so agreeable.

Humming a little tune to himself, he decided to check his smartphone to see which appointments he had skipped out on. This always gave him a little thrill, as if he were reckless enough to throw away the rest of the world on a whim. There was Mrs. Lattimer, the demure elderly woman who believed that she had been reincarnated from a Roman chariot driver. Next was Bob Bowles, the whiner who didn't have the balls to stand up to his shrew of a wife. After lunch, there was the anorexic teenager Ashley Childress, who had both of her overindulgent parents wrapped around her skinny little pinky. Then Hien Long, some new patient he hadn't met yet, and last Mia Labont. Oh yeah, she was the hostile woman with the sad-looking eyes who had lost her baby and her cool.

Oh well. He was confident that all of his patients were in capable hands and would survive until he got back. Thank God for meds.

◊ ◊ ◊

Dan left work a little earlier than usual so they wouldn't be late to her appointment. Mia had been doing well and he wanted to make sure there was nothing to derail her positive track. Maybe this visit with Monroe wouldn't be as tense as the last time when it was such a fiasco.

He had never seen Mia so tight-lipped before in his life. For the past months, all she had wanted to talk about was the miscarriage. Then, when she finally got a chance to really open up to a professional, she clamed up. He hoped Gerry would get to know the real Mia, so they could get down to the bottom of things once and for all.

As he pulled into their driveway and shut down the Jeep, he couldn't help but notice, once again, that their house looked unusually still and dark. Instantly it didn't feel right, making the hairs on the back of his neck crawl.

Oh no, she couldn't have....

His heart flew to his throat as he imagined her lifeless on the floor with the gun in her hand. Without stopping to close the car door, he raced to the front of the house. He was so nervous fumbling to find the right key that he dropped them all. Swearing under his breath in frustration, he picked up the keys with trembling fingers, opened the lock and bolted in.

A little prayer raced through his head, *Please God, let her be all right.…*

He sprinted directly to the bedroom where he immediately switched on the light and ran to that place between the bed and the wall where he had found her last. To his relief but confusion, no one was there.

She must be in another room. He turned, wild-eyed, wondering where she was.

"Oh, hi Honey."

Mia casually stepped out of the bathroom, clipping on a back to her earring. She straightened up and smoothed out her dress, but then noticed the look of alarm on his face and his rapid breathing.

"What's the matter? I'm sorry, did I startle you?"

"Uh, no. I, I just.…"

Not being able to speak, he grabbed her up in fierce hug instead. His fear slowly abated as he felt the warmth of her skin and the pulse of her heart against his chest.

"Wow. I should get dressed up more often if I'm going to get a reaction like that," she said.

"Huh? Oh, right."

He released her from his grip, feeling sheepish. Then he cleared his throat and took a step back, trying to regain his composure.

"Are you sure you're okay?"

"Yeah, yeah. I'm fine *now*… Hey! Look at you—you look great, lady," he said noticing her attire for the first time. She beamed at him and gave a little sway while looking down at her dress. "But isn't it a little dressy for a doctor's appointment?"

"Monroe's office called to cancel."

"I mean, unless you feel you want to get all dressed up for 'Ol' Gerry,'" he teased, still trying to cover for what had been going through his mind. If for a second, she knew what he had been thinking, it would ruin everything.

"Stop," she smiled. "They said he had some kind of emergency out of town and he wouldn't be back in until next week. I could see someone else," she decided to tease back, "but no one else does it for me like 'Ol' Gerry,' so I rescheduled."

At this news, Dan grew serious again. "Are you sure you want to go that long?"

"I think so. I've been feeling a lot better lately. I mean, I still think about 'it,' but it's a lot easier to deal with. The medication is really kicking in. And at least I can finally sleep again."

"Okay," he said hesitantly, "As long as you are sure."

"Yes. I'll be fine. But anyway, I figured that since you would be home early for the appointment, we never did get to try out that new Greek restaurant. And you know me and Greek food," Mia said brightly.

"All right, Murph, let's go. Just give me a moment to change out of these work clothes."

As Dan stepped into the walk-in closet, he took a few minutes to gather his thoughts. He guessed that if she felt comfortable enough to skip a session, it should be okay. He didn't want to force her into doing anything, especially after her last reaction in therapy. But as he was about to slip into his jeans and a pullover sweater, he heard a muffled noise coming from the other side of the wall. He froze. It sounded like crying.

Straining to hear, he was pleasantly surprised to discover that she was singing instead. *Maybe she is doing better*, he decided. As he pulled the sweater over his head and smoothed back his hair, he began to feel a mix of anticipation and excitement in knowing that he would be spending time with her. It had been a while since he had felt like that, and he welcomed it eagerly.

◊ ◊ ◊

The weekend slipped by before they knew it. Watching her husband get ready for work on Monday morning, Mia knew that she should consider going back to work, herself. She had taken sick leave during the miscarriage, but not being able to pull herself together afterwards, opted for a leave of absence.

Her copy editor Loren understood, having suffered through a miscarriage herself. But Mia didn't want to wear out Loren's generosity either. The temps who were called in for editing and research were never able to catch everything in the sometimes-confusing proofs and manuscripts. Although she had bailed Loren out of many deadline binds before, she was going to end up owing her big for this one. She made a mental note to call her boss later to see what was going on.

For now, Mia sat on the edge of the tub and studied Dan as he finished shaving. She loved the way he scraped through the cloud of foam that hid his square jaw, leaving a clear swath of skin behind. She hadn't talked much to him during her depression, but this weekend had given them the chance to catch up. It seemed they did nothing but talk constantly for the entire two days, enjoying each other's company as they had once before.

Dan stopped mid-shave to wink at her then returned to his task, his neck outstretched as he made the last few passes. At that moment, she realized how much she loved him. She had never intended to shut him out of any aspect of her life. Letting her eyes wander over his muscular bare chest and biceps, she was overcome with a strong desire for him.

Obviously there are other areas we have to catch up on as well, she told herself.

Unfortunately, it was Monday. She considered persuading him to stay home again, but he had missed quite a few days already. She knew that if she asked him to, he would. But she also knew truthfully, that it would be taking advantage of the situation. Whereas Loren understood, Dan's boss, Mr. Greenlee, did not. It wouldn't be fair.

Giving in to reality, she rose up, planted a kiss on the middle of his back as he bent over the sink, and then resignedly padded barefoot to the kitchen to prepare a quick breakfast for him. The morning sun was breaking over the horizon and steadily filled the room with light. Usually on workdays Dan only downed a glass of milk or orange juice before heading out, but Mia wanted to pamper him today.

She took out a pan to boil eggs and held it under the running tap. While it filled, she looked at herself in its curved chrome sides. Her nose appeared ten times bigger than it should. She noted how everything looked so bent and misshapen, reminding her of the mirrors in a fun house she used to go to when she was a kid. She tilted the pot a bit to see the whole of her kitchen in convex and caught the twisted figure of her husband standing in the doorway behind her. Just then the water overflowed and she realized that she had been goofing off.

Feeling foolish, she turned around to explain, "Whoops. I don't think I need that much water to boil a few—"

The doorway was empty. She looked over her other shoulder, but she was alone. The advancing morning light cast shadows about, playing in corners and illuminating the cabinet doors. She knew she had gotten up too early.

With the pan filled with eggs and water heating on the burner, she opened the refrigerator to retrieve leftover breakfast sausages from their Sunday morning pig-out and placed them in the microwave. Punching in the time on the keypad, Mia was faced with another "looking glass" version of her kitchen in the surface of the microwave's black plastic door. She examined the reflection and the angles of the room carefully to see how she could have possibly mistaken Dan at the doorway.

Oddly, by the edge of the microwave's door, she caught the reflected image of someone's hand and leg swinging in stride toward the table, but the appliance started and its interior light came on, canceling out the reflection.

What the...? she questioned.

While the microwave hummed, she looked back at the kitchen table, puzzling over what she thought she had just seen.

A voice at her side startled her. "Mmmm, smells good," Dan said buttoning up the last button on his shirt. He kissed her on her neck. "Honestly, you spoil me too much. You better be prepared to love a whole lot more of me if you keep feeding me like this."

"Huh? Yeah," Mia said distractedly, still pondering.

She opened her mouth to mention it to him, but thought otherwise. He didn't need to worry about her all day. *Did I take my meds this morning?* She was obviously still half-asleep and her eyes weren't working right yet. Robotically, she poured orange juice for him, made toast, and set out the rest of his meal.

"Boy, Greenlee's gonna be a bear this morning. The client's breathing down his neck and Ho and I are having a hellluva time getting those final edits down. When I left on Friday afternoon, he was fishing around for me to stay late, but I had made it clear to him that I had to leave early. I bet he's there right now, and more than likely, he's made a mess of everything. I only hope Ho is there to head him off. It'll be a nightmare if he gets in there and starts messing with things. He'll only screw it up worse," Dan rambled on as he ate.

Mia sat down next to him. She realized that she hadn't been paying much attention to what he had just said, so she nodded her head in agreement and smiled, hoping that it would be the correct response.

"So, do you have any plans for today?" he asked.

"I'm not sure yet. I think I'll give this house a good cleaning. Then I'm going to call Loren and see how things are going at the mag."

"Great! Do you feel ready to go back?"

"Yeah, it's time. Poor Loren is probably going crazy with those temps they keep sending her."

"Okay, but take your time if you have to. I'm sure Loren and *Home and Life* aren't going anywhere."

"Well they're most certainly not if I'm not there," she quipped.

He smiled fondly at her. "That's my girl." He ate some more then asked, "Hey, have you heard from your mom lately?"

"I didn't show you? She sent a postcard from the Mosque in Bethlehem the other day. It came on Saturday, I think. I have it somewhere. Can you believe it? She actually saw the site where Christ was born. I worry about her with all that fighting going on over there." Mia sorted through the stack of mail on the counter and produced the card. She handed it to Dan.

"Your mom? Huh. I don't think you have anything to worry about. She can definitely handle herself. But I sure hope God is on the side of the residents there," he laughed as he looked at the photograph on the front and then flipped it over. On the back he read out loud, "'The Jordan was absolutely beautiful. Wish you were here for Rapture. It should happen any day now. Brother Bill promises by the next new moon. Love you and Miss you, Your Mother.' Hmm. Your mom has always been an *interesting* lady, I'll say that."

"Funny. That's not what you use to say about her."

"Aw, she's okay. Just interesting, that's all," he smirked, biting into his toast. "I don't know who's more *interesting*, your mom or your Aunt Lydia. Man, what a pair."

"Uh huh. And it sure would be *interesting* to see how you are going to explain being late to work to Greenlee," she said, giving the clock a nod.

"Aw shoot." He jumped up, gave her a kiss and shoved the rest of the toast into his mouth. "Bye! Love you!" he said with stuffed cheeks.

Just beginning to enjoy their little dialogue, she sadly watched him leave for work. When he disappeared out the door, she looked back at the empty kitchen. The morning light completely filled it now, muting the shadows and sharpening the images. It was calm and still. Her mind returned to the odd figure she had seen in the reflection, but decided to dismiss it as nothing but a bit of a latent dream leftover from the night before.

The remainder of the day unfolded quickly as Mia became immersed in housework. With a new sense of purpose and energy, she evaluated each room as she went about her tasks, fresh ideas of rearranging and decorating blossoming in her head. A little later she called Loren and they chatted a bit. Her boss was indeed babysitting the temps and was relieved to hear Mia on the other line. Mia reassured her that she would be in by the following Monday, giving herself the remainder of the week to wrap up things at home.

That afternoon, she decided to indulge herself by taking a break. She tried a couple of entries in her journal and practiced enough affirmations to feel foolish. After idly browsing through her *J. Jill* catalogue, she decided to walk, instead of drive, to the market to pick up some groceries for the week.

The day was cool but mild. It was refreshing to be outside again. It had been a few ages since she had taken a stroll outdoors and it felt good to inhale the fragrances of grass, air, and water. She let the sun's rays warm and nourish her, feeling it on her skin as a reptile would emerging from a winter's hibernation.

On impulse, she changed direction deciding to go to the food store later. Within a few blocks, she knew that she was headed to the memorial arboretum where her father's ashes rested. When she and Dan had first moved to the Pacific Northwest, she knew this would be the place for her father to be. Inside of the forty-acre private park, friends and families were invited to plant a tree in someone's memory and even mix the ashes with the soil.

She quickly found her father's nameplate upholstered on the plush green lawn under the dogwood tree she had planted there almost two years ago. Regretting that she hadn't stopped for flowers, she knelt down to run her hand over the bold capital letters stamped in the smooth brass. "In Memory of Stephanos Pappas, Loving Husband and Father, 1948-2010" was all it read.

She considered how sad it was to have an entire lifetime of loves, dislikes, losses, dreams, and accomplishments reduced to forty-three characters of Bodoni Bold font. If it weren't for her recollections, hardly anyone would know what he was like.

Her thoughts returned to her infant son that never was and realized that he didn't have any marker at all to show he had ever been. His abbreviated life and her father's legacy lived only in Mia's memory. She imagined the two of them together, her dad holding up her little boy, that smile of his made even brighter with grandfatherly pride. She longed to see them both. A cool wind shook her from her reverie and, after placing a kiss on her fingertips to place onto the brass plate, she rose slowly and left.

What started out as a day of promise, slipped into an afternoon of pensiveness and yearning. Maybe it was a mistake for her to visit her father after all. She wasn't ready. The sun suddenly turned mocking and the street looked unfamiliar and threatening as she walked on. Instead of continuing on to the market, Mia turned and headed straight home. The oncoming depression was strong this time and she struggled against it, not wanting to return to that dismal place.

Previously, she would've fallen completely over the edge into the deep, cold void that engulfed her many times before. The medication running through her veins was indeed working; this time it felt as if a heavy net kept her from plunging headlong into the abyss. However, it was not enough.

When she arrived home, she was completely fatigued. She knew her overwhelming desire to escape her emotional state could only be found in the form of sleep. But instead of waiting for it to arrive on its own, she hurried it along by putting the tiny sleeping pill on her tongue. As she lay down on the sofa, she prayed that the depression would be gone by the time she awakened. She had come so far this past week only to be frustratingly thrown right back to where she had left off.

Hours later she awoke in the dark to the sound of the Jeep pulling into the driveway. Sitting up on the sofa, she groggily reached for the switch on the table lamp, nearly knocking it over. She was a little embarrassed to have Dan find her sleeping so early in evening, so she reached for a magazine and pretended to be reading when he came in.

As they ate a hastily prepared dinner of franks and beans, she struggled to concentrate on his one-sided conversation. It was mostly about Greenlee, an incompetent production crew, and the IT guy's comments about why the edit program was acting up. These were subjects that she had to strive to pay attention to on a good day, let alone in the groggy mind swamp that she was wading in now.

After washing the dinner dishes, they took up their usual posts in the living room: she on the sofa, and he in the armchair. It had been some time since they had watched TV together and they easily resumed their abandoned routine. While waiting for their favorite show to begin, Dan browsed through *Popular Science* while Mia tried to occupy herself with the TV guide, hoping the Hollywood gossip would get her mind off of the afternoon. The depression was still lingering, but she didn't want it to spoil their evening as it had in the past.

Flipping through the pages, she suddenly found herself compelled, as if someone were beckoning her, to look at the darkened screen of the television. It was an old set, one that they had put off replacing with a flat screen while Mia was not working. Looking at the reflection, she saw Dan and herself posed like players on a stage in a distorted miniature of their living room. Just as she was returning to her reading, a movement on the screen caught her eye and brought her attention back. It was only Dan dropping one leg and crossing the other over.

She sighed. Reminiscent of the fleeting images in the reflections on the saucepan and microwave door this morning, it gave her the creeps. To force them out of her head, she concentrated on the Q&A Celebrities Corner before her. When she turned the page, she made herself look at the screen again, proving to herself that this was reality. The sightings were all her imagination. *Things like that certainly don't happen for real,* she reassured herself. She glanced at the reflected setting that was her living room, identifying herself on the sofa and Dan in his chair.

She counted a third figure in the room.

The discovery made her jump. In the corner, behind Dan's left shoulder, a shadowy outline stood. She squinted hard and leaned closer to the thirty-six-inch screen for a better look.

"Don't you think you'd see more if you turn it on?" Dan chuckled.

"What?!"

Startled, she whipped around to face him. He laughed until he noticed her eyes were not on him but instead searching for something behind him. He turned around in his seat to see what she was riveted on.

"What are you looking at? Hmmm…Looks like I'm going to have to do a better job in hiding the stereo speaker wires," he said, absent-mindedly.

When he faced her, her gaze was intent on the screen. It shifted to the corner, and then back to the screen again; her head oscillating as if she were watching some kind of imaginary tennis match.

There was no one there, yet Mia could see something *or was it a someone?* in the reflection cast upon the glass of the TV. She couldn't make out any details, for the figure was too recessed in the corner of the distorted image. She gasped and held her hand up to her mouth. The 'it' had moved.

"Babe? What's the matter? What are you looking at?" her husband asked, puzzled by her behavior.

She squeezed her eyes shut, then open them slowly to view the black glass, hoping that it was only her eyes playing tricks. But the figure lurked there in the reflection. "Dan, oh my God. Look—on the screen." She pointed a trembling finger at the TV, but stayed upright and stock-still on the sofa.

"What? Something up with the set? One of these days we're going to have to replace this old thing."

Dan rose from his chair and started to approach the TV. His reflection advanced slowly and grew in size on the screen, yet the figure remained in the corner. It appeared to shift weight from one leg to another.

"There - in that corner behind your chair," she whispered.

"Behind the chair? Wha-?" he stopped in his tracks to turn back in the direction he came from. "Wait a minute - what are you talking about?"

"No, no. On the screen. Look at the TV screen, in the reflection. Okay now at that corner *behind* your chair on the screen," she hissed through clenched teeth. Her heart felt as if it were beating a hole out of her chest. "Look! There's *someone* standing there. See it?"

He turned once again and stared hard at the glass. "Okay…I dunno, Mia. I can see you and me. But I'm not catching anyone else."

"C'mon. Don't you see it? Right there. Behind your chair in the corner," she spoke slowly and carefully in fear of setting it off.

He looked again. This time he let his eyes rest for a second on each item in the reflection. "And I'm supposed to be looking for…?"

"I don't know—it looks like a person. You have to see it! In the corner?" her voice pleaded.

"No… I see you and me and the furniture, but no one else. I don't know what you are looking at." He let his eyes move across the reflected scene one more time, checking each corner carefully. "Nope, nothing else there. Are you sure?"

Obviously, he couldn't see it. She gave one last look at the empty corner behind his chair, and then returned her eye to the reticent figure on the screen. It was there all right, whatever it was. And staring straight at her, patiently waiting.

"Hon? I can take another look if you want." He crouched down in front of her and put his hand on her knee, then asked cautiously, "It's not that I don't believe that you are seeing something, but are you feeling okay?"

There was that question again. It was enough to draw her attention away from the image for a moment. *Could it be starting all over?*

When she looked at him, his face was creased with that familiar concern again. If she persisted on whatever that was in the corner, he was going to think that she was slipping. He would insist that she go in for an appointment the very next day. She didn't know what was going on, but she knew if she continued acting bizarre, he and Gerry would consider the possibility of insanity.

But it's only depression, she told herself. She knew that now. And she was going to fight it. She tried to think of what to do. An instant decision was made in her head.

She took a deep breath and feigned confusion though her heart continued to pound out of control. "Huh? Yeah, I'm fine. I'm sorry. I just thought I saw something. It was nothing." Her eyes darted back to the screen, but she forced them to train on Dan instead.

"Do you still see it? What was it? I looked, but I couldn't see any—"

"No. It must be my eyes. I'm kind of tired. There was a shadow - probably the lighting. You know, weird." She tried her best to sound calm hoping to convince him that everything was okay. She had to convince herself of the same.

"A shadow? I don't understand. Do you want me to turn on the overhead?"

"No. It's *okay*," she stressed. "Really. It's probably just my medication or something," she said impulsively. It did sound plausible as she recalled the sleeping pill she had taken this afternoon.

He raised an eyebrow. "Your medication? You should have that checked. Are you sure you're okay? We could skip watching the tube tonight and just get some sleep if you're tired." He gave her leg a pat.

"*No*. Really, I'm fine. We're going to miss the show." Her voice was small and weak.

Breaking eye contact with Dan, she glanced around for the remote. Finding it on the coffee table, she pushed the power button, but not before her eyes returned directly to the shadowy figure that stood stubbornly in the corner. The screen lit up.

She held her breath as her husband returned to his seat. There was no way of telling him *not* to go there. What explanation could she possibly give him? She swallowed hard to stifle a scream when Dan sat back down, knowing that whatever it was loomed directly behind him.

If there is something. Maybe it's those pills I took.

Mia plucked a throw pillow off the sofa and held it close. She tried in vain to recall an article that she had proofread a while back about the effects of overdosing on diazepam, but her mind drew a blank. Instead, she pretended to watch the crime drama on the screen as it plodded through its formulaic pace of murder and car chases. A chill coursed through her veins at the thought of that "thing" being in the room with them.

As the hour went on, Dan commented off and on about the show, but it was difficult for her to concentrate on anything but the figure. She attempted to spy nonchalantly at the area over her husband's shoulder but found him surveying her, so she stopped.

When she heard the music build as a car chase erupted, she stole another quick glance. There was absolutely nothing in the corner. Dan's gaze shifted from the screen to her immediately. He looked perplex, but she ignored him and returned her attention to the TV.

"Did you see something again?" he asked.

"No! Will you just watch the show and quit watching me, okay?" she snapped. "Wasn't Agent Broyhill in the hospital the last time we saw this?" she asked, hoping to make him believe that she was occupied with the show. He didn't answer, keeping an analytical eye on her instead.

But soon, his attention shifted to the screen once more. For the rest of the evening, Mia didn't dare look to the corner behind him for fear of scrutiny and another round of questions.

It's got to be my medication. It's got to be my medication, she repeated, clinging to the hopefulness of the words.

She couldn't bring herself to venture off of the sofa, seeking the security of her husband and fearful of having to walk past that area.

After what seemed an interminable amount of time, the show and then the eleven o'clock news were finally over. Usually, it was their cue to shut everything down and head off to bed. Since she showed no signs of reaching for the remote, Dan rose from his chair yawning and stretching, took the control and flicked the set off. Mia tensed as her eyes adjusted to the dark screen.

To her immense relief, the figure was gone.

She scanned the rest of the reflected room and counted only the two of them. *It was those pills I took,* she deducted. Exhaustion washed over her, leaving her feeling more drained than she had felt this afternoon.

Seeing her continuing to stare at the TV, Dan said, "I'm sorry, did you want to watch something else? I didn't think—"

"No. I'm heading off to bed. I'm beat," she responded as she got up from the sofa and walked directly back to the bedroom before he became suspicious again.

While in the shower, thoughts of the phantom figure raced through her mind, making her shiver. Goosebumps popped up on her arms even under the warm stream of water. Not being able to shake the eerie feeling that came over her, she made sure her eyes weren't closed for any length of time under the spray. She felt very vulnerable in her own bathroom and suddenly wished she had locked the door. Knowing that Dan was right outside in the bedroom did not allay her growing fear. He was only human, after all, and with her imagination going wild, that was not enough.

The glass shower door had fogged clouding her view of the room. *This is just like in the movies,* she thought anxiously. *As soon as I wipe the steam away, I'll see 'IT' standing there, waiting for me.* She argued inwardly with herself trying her best at reason. Rationale finally won out. Mustering up whatever courage she had left, she reached a quivering hand up to the glass, and gave it a quick swipe.

She remained the only occupant in the bathroom. Her confidence surged a little. *It was my medication,* she reminded herself.

Stepping out of the shower, she faced the fogged mirror and relapsed into fear once more. She knew 'IT' could be waiting there for her as well, as she recalled the saucepan and microwave door reflections from this morning. But this time, she decided that she was just too weak to force herself to clear the steam a second time. It was too grueling to go through the suspense again .

Not wanting to be alone one minute longer, without drying off she slipped her nightgown over her damp body and quickly rubbed her dripping hair with a towel. She walked out into the bedroom where Dan was showered and already under the blankets. He was dozing, but roused when she climbed into bed.

Sleepily, he asked her one more time, "Everything okay, Murph?"

"Yeah, I'm…all right," she said hesitantly.

His eyes were closing when he mumbled, "Are you sure? We could talk about it if you want…"

She appreciated his effort, but seeing him so tired she knew it would be selfish on her part if she made him wake up fully to discuss this.

"No, it's fine, Hon. Go to sleep." Giving him a small peck, her wet hair left a cool trail across his face. After turning off the light, she scooted closer to him. She slipped her hands around his arm and clung on to him if he was going somewhere without her. With it being quiet and still, he immediately fell asleep, leaving her awake and wide-eyed in the dark.

◊ ◊ ◊

"This is the third message Mr. Labont has left you," Marcia said, holding out the slip.

"Who?"

"Dan Labont. He's been calling about his wife."

"Labont… Labont…Oh yeah, quiet dude with the sad lady. Yeah, I saw them a few weeks ago. What does he want?"

"Well, he's been calling since last week."

"Since last week? Why didn't anyone tell me?"

Marcia's face flushed and her eyebrows drew together. She answered indignantly, "I've been leaving the messages on your desk. You must've seen them."

Gerry shrugged his shoulders and pouted out his bottom lip in exaggeration. After giving a few half-hearted shuffles through the piles of papers on his desk, he looked up with a patronizing grin.

"Nope, nothing here. Do you suppose the cleaning crew's up to their old tricks again?"

His medical assistant stood with her hand on her hip anh a look on her face that shriveled most people. He knew she was pissed.

Redirecting, he asked in a more professional tone, "So, what does this guy want anyway?"

"He wants to know about his wife's prognosis and wants you to call him back as soon as possible."

"ASAP? Why? Is his wife teetering up on a ledge somewhere?" he quipped.

Again, Marcia glared at him, clenching her jaw. "I don't know. He didn't say. He wants you to call him back. That's all," she finally answered.

"Yeah, well people in hell want ice water. I'll get to him tomorrow. I'm still catching up on a backlog of work here since I've been gone."

"Okey-dokey," the MA said, with a slow, gritted determination, "But what should I tell him if he calls again?"

"Just take a message."

At that moment, his phone rang and line two lit up. He waved a dismissal to the assistant and took up his swivel chair behind the desk. He hoped it was the call back on the season tickets at center court that he had seen for sale on Craigslist.

"Hello, Monroe here," he chimed into the receiver.

"Mr. Monroe? This is Dan Labont. Hi- we were in to see you some time back?"

Gerry sat straight up in his chair and looked towards the doorway but Marcia had already left.

He said quickly, "Mr. Labont! Hey bud, I heard you've been calling, but will you please hold for just a moment?" Before Dan could answer, he pressed the hold button. Laying the receiver down on the desk, Gerry craned his neck to see if he could catch a glimpse of anyone in the hallway.

"Marcia!"

No response. He couldn't figure out how this Labont character got ahold of his direct line. All outside calls were answered by the front desk or redirected to the MA's center. Someone must have intentionally given out his phone number. And he had a good idea whom. He viciously jabbed at the buttons to ring her extension.

"Veronica," the voice at the MA center answered.

"Ronnie? Where's Marcia?" he tried to ask calmly, despite the fact that she was answering Marcia's line. They all covered each other's asses over there.

"She just went on break." Then, with saccharin dripping from each syllable she asked, "Is there anything I can help you with Gerry?"

"Who the hell gave out this number? Now I've got that Labont asshole on my personal line! The minute she gets her fat ass back in here, tell her I want to see her immediately!" he roared.

The sweetness oozed on, "Okay *Gerry*, I'll let her know." The phone clicked in his ear.

In the span of the next few seconds, he rapidly thought of several ways to get Marcia and her friend fired, then remembered Labont was still holding on the line. Why couldn't these people ask questions during the session times instead of plaguing his life every frickin' moment?

"Dan! Hey, how's it going? How's..." He took the slightest pause to think of her name, "...Maria?"

"Mia?"

"Mia! Right. I'm sorry, I was right in the middle of a difficult case when you called."

"Uh, I'm sorry. I didn't know. Did you need me to call back at a better time?" Dan apologized.

It was too easy, but even Gerry knew that if he didn't talk to him now, he eventually would have to sooner or later. "No, man. I can take a few minutes to help you out. Tell me, how's it going? Is Mia doing any better?" he asked pinning the phone to his ear with his shoulder as he searched the piles of charts on his desk. Spying her name on one of them he opened it up and scanned through it quickly. "Is she taking her sertraline like she's suppose to?"

"Yes sir, it looks like she's doing better. The med seems to be helping her out."

"Good! Good."

Gerry waited for Labont's next question or statement, but none was forthcoming. He hated when he had to spoon-feed people conversation especially when they called *him*. He prompted, "So, my MA tells me that you've left three messages. Would you believe that I didn't get any of them? I'm sorry for the screw-up. What's up?"

"Oh, I was just wondering if, uh, you thought that Mia was, you know— all right."

"Exactly what do you mean, all right?"

"Well, I mean, she was really upset. I was worried that she might.... You know she wasn't all that happy with me telling you about the miscarriage."

"That's understandable. Many women feel it is a private, personal grief."

"Uh huh."

It went silent again. Gerry rolled his eyes and snatched up a pencil. The fluttering began.

"Well, is she still upset?" he asked.

"I don't think so."

"*Welll*...." He tried to think of a way to pry information out of this guy, "You said that you were worried about...."

More silence. Feeling his pressure rising, he took a deep breath and hoisted his feet up onto his desk. This apparently was going to take all day.

Finally, Dan spoke up hesitatingly, "I was worried that she might still try to, you know, attempt something. It's like, she's okay one minute, then the next, she's not. I've taken off as many days as I could with the miscarriage and all and it's not that I don't want to help her, but I've got to go to work. But I couldn't live with myself if she was left alone and decided to..." his words trailed off.

Gerry realized what he was getting at. He could handle this one.

"Has she seemed depressed, melancholy? Doing anything out of the ordinary? For example, not eating or sleeping?"

"No sir. Actually, she's acting more like her old self every day. At times, she's still a little jittery, but not like before. And she seems to be eating and sleeping fine now."

"Has she been working on her affirmations? Getting out of the house? Talking and interacting with other people?"

"Yeah, it seems like it. In fact, she was talking about returning to work."

"Good, good. And you say that she *is* taking her medication?"

"As far as I can tell."

Gerry was going to put this one away. He lined up for the shot. "Well, I don't think you have anything to worry about. I think what she did wasn't so much of a suicide attempt, as much as it was a suicide *ideation*. Get what I mean?"

"Uh, not exactly," Dan answered, sounding perplexed.

"Okay, let me see if I can explain. She probably entertained thoughts about what it would be like, but I don't think she was serious. I think it was a cry for help and you caught it in time. If she had really wanted to go through with it, she would have. And now her medication should be enough to get her back on track and stop her from going that route again.

"I see we had a session that was canceled when I was out of town and she didn't opt to talk to another therapist. She must be feeling better. I have people who can't go one week without having to check in with me. But she sounds like she's doing well from what you've been telling me. I wouldn't worry."

"Okay," Dan breathed out a sigh of relief, "I just wanted to be sure."

It was a slam-dunk. If only everyone was this easy. "Nope, man, everything's on track. In fact, I'll be seeing her on… let me see-the twenty-fourth. Perfect."

"Thanks. I'm sorry for wasting your time, I just wanted to be sure," he repeated.

"No problem, Dan. Any time. See ya."

Gerry put the phone back in its cradle and took a few minutes to massage his temples. As he rubbed, his eyes went to the five by seven picture on his desk. It was a shot of him taken with Yao Min at a lucky moment at Madison Square Garden. He seriously regretted not going into sports therapy. Amy had tried to push him in that direction after they had started living together. But it would have meant him having to return to school, strapping himself financially because of all the goddam child support he was paying, and a whole bag of other excuses that he didn't want to fish around in.

All in all, PartnersHealth was not a bad place to work. Of course he had to put up with all the whackos he saw and the moronic M's up front, but the pay was decent, and it was worlds better than the crisis hotline center he had worked at when he first got his degree in Sociology. And it especially looked good to have a steady income when gearing up to fight the queen bitch in a child custody battle.

Line two lit up again. He hesitated for a moment before picking it up. When he heard the voice on the other line, a broad smile came across his face and he leaned back in his chair.

"Yes, about those season tickets…."

THREE

THE HOUSE HAD REMINDED THEM OF AN AGING STARLET who was beautiful once, but after years of people, coats of paint, and hard living, had started to sag and peel. Yet for being a seventy-five-year-old fixer upper, its foundation was solid, the framework was sound and the original copper plumbing had yet to spring a leak. What's more, it had a large front yard and an even bigger backyard. The mature trees and the promise of a safe play area for their future family cinched the deal.

Dan and Mia had shopped through numerous model homes and master planned communities before deciding on the resale rambler. The surrounding community was filled with house-proud neighbors who groomed their yards and kept close vigilance with a strong neighborhood association. The Labonts were some of the youngest residents on a street where original owners were slowly relinquishing their homes to the new blood reviving an old neighborhood.

Joining the revival by renovating the small house, they removed some existing walls to open up living spaces, tore out shag carpets to reveal wood floors, and extended the back porch. The only things they decided to leave in place were the ornate ceiling fans, thinking they might come in handy when summer arrived. Slowly, and with effort, they brought the fixer-upper into the twenty-first century. Dan wired it for stereo surround sound, Internet access, and satellite, while Mia painted and wallpapered. She spent her Saturday mornings pouring through flea markets, yard sales and consignment shops to find furniture, decorations, and trinkets to accessorize their new home.

Within a year of weekends and countless hours of labor, their efforts had paid off. The old layers of harvest gold, avocado green, and metallic floral prints gave way to an eclectic blend of the natural colors and textures that Mia sought mixed with Dan's stainless steel and techno tastes. To add a crowning touch, a large mirror with a mosaic tile frame brightened the living room of their simply but tastefully furnished home.

But the renovation stopped abruptly a little over two months ago. The only thing that remained unfinished was the nursery. There, the drop cloths covered the floor and masking tape framed the areas prepped for painting and borders. A large, cracked dressing mirror from the previous owner was still affixed to one wall, waiting to be removed. Boxes of books and odds and ends sat undisturbed in a corner. After the miscarriage, Mia had tried unsuccessfully on several occasions to finish the room. Many of those times ended miserably in crying bouts and wistful longing. And on most days, she never entered the room at all, lacking the will to put herself through the pain of it all again.

It was morning. As the sun peeked through the curtains, her eyes fluttered open and slowly focused on the blades of the ceiling fan above. Her head felt as if it were wrapped in cotton batting. Contemplating the feel of the fabric against her toes, she stretched and moved her feet slowly under the blankets. She was having a hard time waking up.

The eerie surrealistic image of the figure she had seen on the TV screen three days ago, played before her eyes every night whenever she tried to sleep. Last night at two in the morning, after lying awake for hours, she had conceded to take a sleeping pill, desperate for rest. Perhaps she was not taking enough of the medication? Or maybe it wat the medication that was generating the tricks being played on her eyes? She couldn't be sure.

While she lay there, she became acutely aware of being alone in the house. Dan had left for work over an hour ago. She vaguely recalled the sensation of him getting out of bed and kissing her goodbye.

What if I see 'IT' again?

The thought pushed its way into her consciousness. She wondered if she could possibly stay in bed all day, where she felt safe. But a few minutes later, her full bladder started to nag her. She pulled back the blankets, cautiously looked about the room, and then got up. When she entered the bathroom, she glanced nervously into the mirror, but her own reflection stared back complete with rumpled nightgown and tangled hair. She couldn't help but inspect every corner and crack of the room that was reflected in the mirror searching for any other sinister figures.

Like a victim fearing a sniper on a rooftop, her morning was spent warily eyeing all the reflective surfaces about the house. The microwave door, polished chrome work, the brass doorknobs, the large mirror in the living room were all a constant source of vexation to her. She tried to distract herself by reading the newspaper and doing laundry. But she was paranoid, feeling as if someone's eyes were constantly on her.

There were a few times she thought she caught a fleeting shadow over her shoulder and whipped around, only to find an empty room. She knew she was carrying things too far and had to come to grips before she lost it all together. *I'm an idiot. A complete and total idiot,* she scolded herself each time she jumped at the slightest change in light or noise.

She tried to find something to do to get her mind off of it. Spying a plant on the kitchen windowsill that had outgrown its confining container, she made it an objective to go outside to the shed for potting soil and a bigger pot. It was a small task, bur fear held her captive. She wasn't capable of much else at the moment.

She opened the back screen door and stepped into the warm sunshine, breathing out a sigh of relief. *Whatever was in there can't reach me out here,* she reassured herself. As she looked about her, a new appreciation for the outdoors, its brightness and openness, and most of all, its lack of shiny surfaces—encouraged her.

After the plant was settled in its new pot, she lingered a bit on the back porch swing enjoying the lack of stress the outdoors provided her. She knew, unfortunately, that she couldn't stay there all day. She decided to form some resolutions in her mind. Although she hadn't had much control over her life for the past few months, she knew she couldn't allow herself to backslide again. She had to overcome this. Determination, tinged with hesitation, forced her slowly to her feet. With one last look at her peaceful, sunny backyard, she allowed herself to be swallowed up once more into the dark confines of her house.

For the rest of the morning she sought refuge on the phone with Dan, Lauren, and anyone else she could think of to call. Although the sound of their voices comforted her, she couldn't help but feel envious. Everyone was at work, being productive, and contributing to society. She longed to be back in step with the rest of the world and realized how much she missed working at the magazine.

Finding more objectives to engage her, she went to her closet to see what clothes she would wear for her first week back to work. Then she made a list of all the unfinished house projects. She wanted to stock the kitchen fully; their supplies had been pretty meager lately. She also needed to trim back and tend the plants in the yard. Finally, she determined that, once and for all, she was going to finish the nursery.

By staying occupied, she successfully dismissed the memory of the phantom image to the TV screen just as she had found it—another errant, distorted reflection, along with all the other inanimate objects in her living room. In the late afternoon, she jotted a few notes in her journal and remembered to take up the dog-eared affirmation sheet once more, squaring off with the bathroom mirror for a few minutes.

"I will only allow positive thoughts… I like who I am… I can…" Mia trailed off, her eyes drawn to something small and red by the corner of the mirror. Leaning closer, she was perplexed to see it was blood. The drop had apparently run, trailing a crooked course almost to the edge of the frame. *Dan must've cut himself while shaving this morning,* she thought as she reached into the cabinet beneath the sink for a cleaning rag they stored there.

The blood looked dried so she wet a corner of the rag under the running faucet. The drop wiped easily off the glass. But as she opened the rag to rinse it out, it appeared to be untouched. She turned the rag over and over to search for the spot. Oddly, there was none to be found. *Maybe the water diluted it?* Her mind questioned with amazement.

Stepping back to examine the entire mirror, she became aware on more spots of blood, looking as if they had been splattered on with a paintbrush. It surprised her that she hadn't caught them before and wondered where all of it had come from. Before her very eyes, the spots seemed to multiply, and run, leaving serpentine trails down the surface of the glass. With a wide sweeping motion of her arm, she wiped vigorously across the mirror with the rag, hoping to erase the marks. They only smeared, leaving a bloody swath that clouded the glass. She opened the rag to refold it for another pass. It was clean.

Mia gasped and dropped the wet cloth. She stared in horror at its crumpled form upon the bathroom floor. Then, slowly turning her eyes towards the mirror again, her mouth fell open in a silent scream framed by her trembling hands. The glass was completely clear of any and all blood. Only her pale face and frightened eyes stared back at her. Her lungs heaved and gulped for air as the sound of the running water dominated the stillness of the room.

◊ ◊ ◊

When he arrived home from work that evening, Dan found his wife sitting alone on the swing on the back porch. The sun was already dipping beyond the horizon and a cool breeze blew across their yard. The warm, spicy smells of neighborhood dinners mingled with the cold air while the kids next door played a screaming game of war in their yard.

Mia sat, clad only in a tee shirt and old jeans, with her thin arms folded tightly about herself. As he sat down beside her, he could see that her arms were covered in goosebumps. She glanced up briefly at him with a faint smile, then returned her gaze to the cracks in the cement beneath their feet.

"Hey. What are you doing, sitting out here freezing? You should've brought out a sweater or something," he said concerned. His arms went immediately around her trying to erase the chill.

"I'm okay. I was just…watching the sunset. Waiting for you to come home."

His eyes followed hers to their fix on the cement, and then he said, "Well, I just can't let you sit out here in the cold. Let me get you something to cover up with, okay? Hold on, I'll be right back." As he opened the screen door, he took another look at her staring at the ground and added, "I'll join you in watching the, uh, sunset."

While he searched around inside, Mia thought about how she was going to explain what had happened with the mirror this afternoon. At first she considered not telling him at all. She wasn't sure how he was going to react, but she knew it wouldn't be good. There would be all those same old questions. After having wrestled with it all afternoon she decided, against her better judgment, that it would probably be better if she shared the incident with him. The trick now would be to find the right time and words to describe it.

He emerged about ten minutes later, clutching her sweater in one hand while holding a glass of wine and pinning a can of beer to his chest with the other.

"I think you forgot something inside," he chuckled as he gave her the sweater.

She knew he must have had to look all over because even though it was her favorite sweater, she had put it away because it was out of style. She accepted the sweater and he waited patiently for her to put it on.

"Thanks for bringing this out."

"No, I mean the water. It was running in the bathroom sink," he said as he handed her the chardonnay.

Looking at the drink, she started, "Oh Honey, I'm sorry, but I don't think I'm suppose to…." she said, remembering the prescription warning against any alcohol while taking her meds. Thinking about her upcoming explanation though, she retracted. "Never mind," she said and took the glass.

They sat and swung, watching the changing hues of the sun's rays against the clouds while Dan told her of his day at work. Pryus Productions just installed a new digital editing board, and there was a chance he might have to do some production work on location in one of their remote broadcast trucks.

Mia listened and sipped away, waiting for the wine to kick in and give her courage. Typically she was sensitive to effects of both alcohol and medication. A regular "teetotaler" Dan often teased her.

Within a few minutes, sooner than she had expected, a familiar tingling about her face and throat signaled that the wine had begun its magic. She gratefully welcomed it. While he continued to talk, she felt the buzz enter her head and settle somewhere behind her knees below. Now all there was left to do was take a deep breath and…

"I experienced something strange today," she blurted out interrupting him.

He stopped short and looked at her. It wasn't exactly the lead-in she had been groping for all afternoon.

He's going to grow tired of me and all of this bizarre shit, she thought. She gulped down the remainder of the wine in her glass.

He held up his hand, motioning her to hold on, as his head turned toward the sound of a wailing child next door. "Uh huh. You knew *that* was going to happen. I don't think those kids know how to play without maiming someone." He shook his head, chuckled, and took another sip of beer.

She felt she could tell him anything at this point. The antidepressants and depressants in her system mixed and mingled and spilled out from her mouth in the form of words before she could stop them.

"I said, I experienced something strange today," she said a little too loudly.

"Huh? Oh yeah. How so?"

She certainly had his attention at this point. Mia looked at his quizzical expression and was reminded of when she would make squeaking noises at her friend's dog, just to see it perk its ears and cock its head in curiosity.

She pressed on, "I don't know how to explain it… it was just something weird." Inwardly she embraced the warm fuzzy feeling engulfing her and moving her lips.

"Okay, I'll play your game. Weird in what way?"

There was that crooked grin of his. Suddenly Mia had the urge to kiss him. And she did, deeply, not wanting the moment to end. She knew, even in her buzzed state, that after she described to him what she had seen, they would definitely lose all the ground they had gained and be dumped back to the same place they were just a few weeks ago.

The kiss took him by surprise, but he kissed her back.

"Wow, Murph. Where did that come from?" he asked softly as she pulled away. He looked deep into her eyes and smiled.

"I just love you. That's all. And I hope that you will continue to love me and have patience with me even though I might act a little strange or tell you about strange things," she said, hoping for some reassurance from him.

Hearing this, his smile faded. "Okay, what's up? Tell me what happened already."

"It's just that, *arrgh!* How can I explain this?"

She sighed, rolling her eyes upwards and biting her lip. The wine was having too much affect now, swirling the words that she had so carefully rehearsed.

"Well, you're not doing a very good job of it yet."

"Okay! I," she took a deep breath and went on, though she couldn't face him. "I was in the bathroom, saying my affirmations in the mirror."

"And?" He wasn't going to let her off the hook.

"Well, I thought I saw some blood in the corner of the mirror. Did you cut yourself this morning?" she asked looking up at him. She bobbled a little and tried to steady herself.

"Yeah, just a little nick, nothing serious. Go on."

Her eyes locked on the small scab by the curve of his throat. "Well, that's what I thought. But when I wiped it off with a wet rag, the rag was clean."

Finally it was out. She waited for him to catch on.

"Okay, the rag was clean. And...?" He scanned her anxious face and waited for the punch line to this oddball joke.

"Didn't you hear me? *The rag was CLEAN.* I unfolded it and looked it all over, but I couldn't find any blood on it."

"Okay, well, maybe it washed out with the water?" he offered.

"No, that's what I thought at first. But that's not all. When I looked up again, the mirror had streaks of blood all over it. And they weren't there before! I wiped at them again and they smeared all over the place. Yet when I looked at the rag, it was still clean. And when I looked back at the mirror, there was no more blood on it. It was as if nothing had happened."

"And you say *streaks?* All over?"

"Yes!"

She knew by the look on his face that he was fishing through all his logical reasons, trying to hook the right one that would explain it all away.

"I didn't want to ask, but have you been taking your medication lately? I don't mean to keep after you all the time but—"

"Of course I've been taking it. Every day and night. That's why things have been getting back to normal. Or at least they were. Until this… Listen, it's what I saw. I told you it was strange."

He shifted on the bench away from her, looking to the sky as if he could find the answer hidden in the darkening orange and red clouds.

"What's going on Mia? It seemed that you were getting back on track, and everything was going great, now it's this. First that thing with the TV screen the other night and now you say you're seeing imaginary streaks of blood on the mirror? You know, maybe you should talk to someone about your dosage. It could be off or something."

"Well, it's not like I want to see this stuff. What if it's not my medication? What if it's something else? I'd like to know what is going on just as much as you do."

She hated the wine-induced slur in her voice. It didn't do much for her argument.

"I know, I know…" he answered distractedly.

After a few moments, he stood up.

"You know, maybe you should lay off the wine too. I forgot all about your meds and shouldn't have given it to you in the first place. Me? I think I need another beer," he mumbled as he vanished inside, letting the screen door bang loudly behind him.

She listened for him in the kitchen, but there was no sound. Long minutes passed until she finally heard the television turn on.

As the last cold rays of the sun dimmed beyond the rooftops, she thought sadly of their kiss. Why didn't she just let the conversation end with it? They would have watched the sunset together and then go inside to have dinner. Things between them would have continued on course. She would've figured this out on her own and everything would have been better. Much better.

There were times in the four short years of their marriage in which they had had disagreements. But they had always discussed everything with neither of them walking out on the other.

Now he was inside and she was out here by herself. She knew she had made a big mistake in ever mentioning anything to him about seeing things. She promised herself never to make that mistake again.

Four

THERE WAS A PERSON IN THE DOORKNOB.

Lurking within the curve of shiny brass, a figure was watching her. Mia gasped and reflexively stepped back, retreating slowly until she backed up against the frame of the doorway. With her hand over her mouth and nowhere to go, she continued to stare in horror and amazement. The screwdriver she held in her other hand slipped past her outstretched fingers and clamored to the wood floor. Its impact made her shriek in fright.

She shouldn't have been seeing anything, anywhere. Her medication had since been readjusted and her appointment still stood to see Gerry by the end of this week. Things had been quiet since the mirror sighting and everything was under control.

Or so she thought.

With her alternating depression, suicide attempt, and delusions, she never knew how she had made it this far without someone wanting to throw her into a padded room already. That alone, was no small feat.

"I need to speak to Gerry Monroe, please," the phone call earlier in the week had started.

Dan's new tactic of passive resistance to her hallucinations prompted her to make the call. He had barely held a normal conversation with her in the days following their sitting on the back porch swing when she had told him about the rag and the blood.

"Are you a patient of his? What is your name and medical record number?"

"Mia Labont. And yes, I am a patient of his. May I speak to him please?"

"Your medical record number?"

After rummaging through her purse for her insurance card, she produced the number.

"Just a moment…" the bored voice on the other line responded followed by a click.

The sound of light rock filled the receiver. The brief interlude was immediately interrupted by a pleasant masculine voice, talking over the doubts that were filling her mind.

"At PartnersHealth, we give our patients the ultimate in quality, friendly care…"

Mia almost hung up. How was she going to explain this to Gerry? She remembered uncomfortably how Dan had reacted when she told him.

The music played in her ear again for a few minutes more until the recorded voice returned, "PartnersHealth has several locations to serve you, staffed with experts in the fields of internal medicine, pediatrics, dentistry, and psychiatry.…"

"Ma'am?"

"Yes?" She snapped back to attention.

"You are going to have to speak to our triage nurse. She will relay your message to Mr. Monroe unless she feels it is necessary for you to come in. Please hold while I try her line." It was obvious the receptionist had recited these lines to the point of monotony.

"…now has three new facilities to accommodate our growing population of satisfied customers. At PartnersHealth, we are partners in your health," finished the pleasant voice.

More light rock tunes played on. She could scream at the top of her lungs at this end and no one on that side of the line would be the wiser. On a whim, she opened her mouth, preparing to give it a try.

"Mia Labont? This is Barb, the triage nurse. What can I do for you?"

She swallowed hard and tried to steady the shakiness that instantly flared up inside of her. This wasn't going to be easy.

"Ah, yes. I've been in to see Gerry for depression."

"Yes, shug, we have that all down here in your file."

"Well, it's sort of difficult to explain. After I was in… I'm, um, I mean lately I have been, ah— seeing things." Her breath was held captive in her throat as her heart hammered away.

"You have? Well that can't be too fun for you now, could it?" Barb soothed cheerily in her soft southern accent. "What kind of things, hon?"

"I don't know… how I can describe them? Just—things."

"Well are you seeing spots, flashes, or floaties? Strange splashy colors or any kind of auras?"

"No, nothing like that. It's hard to explain. I saw… drips on my mirror. They uh, looked like blood. One minute they're there, and the next minute, they're not. And, I have also seen, well, like an outline of a person. At least I *think* that it's a person. I don't know. It's kind of hard to make it out."

"All right." There was a pause on the other end. "And is this 'person' doing anything to you, hon? Saying anything?" Barb asked, matter-of-factly.

"Uh, no. Just standing there. Reflected in my TV screen…. Oh, and the TV was off at the time."

"Uh huh. The strong, silent type," she said. "Hmm, and I see here that Gerry prescribed you sertraline and diazepam. Are you still taking them?"

Could it have been the medication? Mia jumped at the possibility.

She answered anxiously, "Yes. Should I stop?"

"No, no. I want you to keep taking them. He has you listed here at twenty milligrams. I am going to increase it to forty milligrams. That means that you will take one pill twice a day, okay hon? Stay with your same dose of the sleeping pill unless you are feeling agitated or cannot sleep at night. Then you can call our office and we can adjust the dosage. I'll make a note right here on your chart about what I've told you. Now you haven't been consuming any alcohol while you've been taking these meds, have you?"

"No. I mean, yes. A little wine. Only every now and then."

"Well you've been a naughty girl and are going to have to stop that. No alcohol at all while you are taking this prescription, understand? Okay, looks like you have an appointment with Gerry on the twenty-fourth. Great. Now is there anything else I can do for you, hon?" the nurse started to sound impatient to get off the phone.

Mia was confused by the turn of questioning. "That's it? Am I supposed to be doing anything else? Is this normal?"

"That's it. Nope, nothing else. It's perfectly normal. Sometimes it just takes a little more umpf to get things going, but I wouldn't worry about it. Thanks for calling, shug. Bye-bye now."

Barb, the triage nurse, hung up.

Mia kept the handset pressed to her ear until the dial tone signaled that the conversation was indeed over. Then she slowly rested the phone back in its cradle. Looking at the clock, she calculated she had been on hold for about fifteen minutes and had spoken to Barb for a total of two.

That was over six days ago. She had been taking the new dosage and hadn't seen anything since the streaks on the mirror. Her life had returned to its usual pace. Or as close to normal as it could get.

Her world—her and Dan's world—had changed so much in the past year. The memories of exactly what used to be normal were being erased, one by one.

As if the answers to their demise lie in the house, Mia had thrown herself into finishing their forgotten home improvement projects. The jobs kept her mind busy and her energy focused. Although Dan had been treating her gingerly for the past couple of weeks, it gave them something to talk about at the end of the day when they found themselves in the cautious presence of the other. Her latest job was to replace the last of the old, cracked, and stained doorknobs about the house.

However, there was a *someone* in this doorknob.

This was no shadowy outline on a darkened screen or a fleeting distorted image on the side of a pot. He, or she, or whatever the hell it was, could clearly be seen standing, reflected from the doorway of the nursery.

The figure was dressed in dark clothes and cloaked in a hood. There appeared to be some kind of dark red stain that started from its face and ran down its neck to its jacket, deepening the front of its garment an even darker hue.

Mia shut her eyes, held her breath, and slowly pivoted to where the figure should be standing in the doorway. In a scant whisper, she counted to three, and with more courage than she ever thought she possessed, she opened her eyes to face it.

The doorway stood vacant. When she spun around to search the doorknob, the figure was gone. Timidly, she approached the knob to inspect it carefully, studying the twisted reflections of her face and the hallway within it. There was no one looking back but herself. She held her head and fell back against the wall, trying to catch her breath.

I'm really losing it. There shouldn't have been anything there... There **wasn't** *anything...*

It took her a few minutes to finally compose herself. Shaken and drained of all energy, she decided to put everything away for the day. She picked up the fallen screwdriver. The only thing she could think of doing was lying down with a cool rag at her forehead and another sleeping pill on her tongue. Regardless of what Barb had advised, she would welcome some wine as well. Abandoning the loose knob on the door, she turned on her heel and headed for the garage.

Not being able to recall where the screwdriver was usually stored, Mia opened up each subsequent drawer on the tool chest. She concentrated on making her trembling fingers wrap around the pulls moving her way down the drawers.

There is no end in sight to this madness, is there? But it has to end sometime. It just doesn't make any sense. It's going to take a little more umpf, Barb said. I'm just going have to wait and get a hold of myself...

In a corner of the third drawer down some neatly folded papers caught her eye. She hesitated for a moment, and then picked up the packet and unfolded it to find pages cut from a *Woodworking Projects* magazine. She wondered where her husband had gotten them. Dan had always worked on electronic and electrical systems, and occasionally some simple home repair. This rare detour to carpentry was enough to distract her momentarily.

When she inspected the pages, she realized they were plans for building a wooden cradle. Her eyes welled instantly with tears as she studied the details and handicraft he was prepared to try. She slowly folded up the plans and returned them to where they had been carefully stored. Wiping away her tears with the back of her hand and closing the drawer, she looked up.

"It" stared back at her.

A life-size reflection of the ominous specter cast itself boldly upon the tinted glass of a stereo cabinet door perched on Dan's worktable. Her own reflection meshed with the apparition's causing a blood red stain to appear at her own throat and searing the blazon image into her mind.

A ragged scream tore past her lips as she raced out of the garage, slamming the door shut behind her. With her back against it, she panted wildly, feeling as if she was being hunted.

Her mouth formed words instinctively into prayer, *Our Father, who art in heaven, hallowed be thy name...*

Panic stricken, she turned around to lock the door. But her fingers, crippled with terror, couldn't manage the simple lock on the doorknob. When she looked down to see what was holding it up, the hooded visage glared back at her from the curved metal. Averting her eyes, she bolted to the kitchen and snatched up the medications on the counter by the sink.

Hastily reaching for a glass in the cabinet, she knocked it out of the shelf. The glass exploded upon the tile floor, sending thick fragments in every direction. With shaking hands she coaxed the pills from their vials, turned on the water and filled another glass.

The "thing" suddenly lurched out on the faucet in a grotesque sideshow image, its body, and hooded face contorted in the curved chrome, leering at her. The drinking glass and pills tumbled into the sink as she screamed again.

Sobbing uncontrollably, Mia fled into the living room. No matter which way she turned, every reflective surface in the house harbored the sinister phantom. It surrounded her from all angles, invading her home. It was on the TV screen, lamps, and framed pictures on the wall.

She needed to escape, to get out into the open where reality waited for her and this bizarre nightmare would end. Heading for the front door, not seeing, she crashed against the wood and glass coffee table, causing her to tumble upon it, and spill onto the floor. A sharp pain radiated up her shin as she clutched her leg and rolled onto her back. Her fingers became wet and slimy with her own blood.

Pinned down by fear and pain, she was more paralyzed by the idea that *It* was there in the room with her right now, watching her. Whatever it was could get to her. She was vulnerable, exposed, helpless. Animal instincts took over, making her believe that if she remained motionless and quiet, she was safe. All the while, her thoughts twisted and writhed about like snakes, nothing making sense.

This can't be happening. Pray child, pray… There's got to be a logical explanation for all of this. Tiny fist… My meds not working, needing more umpf… I didn't mean too…I didn't mean to…

The house was enveloped in a silence that permeated every room. Mia timidly curled up on her side weeping like a child, with the throbbing hot pain in her leg. Her mind filled with images of her father. She longed to be a little girl being lifted by his strong arms into his lap where she could hide her face in his shirt while he made everything right again.

Daddy, why? Why did you leave me? Please, if you can hear me, help me…

She could see her father's loving face smiling at her. It comforted her, but it lasted only for a few moments. His memory quickly mutated into the face of the sinister apparition. Stricken with fear, she coiled up even tighter and continued to weep. She felt completely abandoned and utterly alone.

Within time, the slant of the late afternoon sun pierced through the back window and stretched a bright finger towards her, making her turn her tearstained face aside. Moments, then minutes passed. She was aware of them slipping by one by one, but couldn't keep track of how many she had lost. Her leg continued to throb and the skin grew tight with swelling.

Mia would have laid there indefinitely had it not been for the sounds of the living beckoning her from outside her window. A car without a muffler coughed and belched its way up the street. Children called out to each other on their way home from school. A large truck pulled up into the driveway next door with a couple of short blasts of its nasally horn.

Is he still here in the room with me? This is the real world I am in. This is reality, she reminded herself. *There are living, breathing people right outside my door.*

It was a mental struggle to gain control once again. Rising slowly from the floor to a sitting position, she peered around cautiously. From her place down low, she couldn't see any reflections. As she pulled her legs up, a whimper escaped her lips. The pain in her leg certainly was real. She checked it over to find that the blood had run, drying in a crooked circle about her calf. Wincing, she carefully examined the torn back flap of skin that exposed the moist pink flesh underneath.

Two of her neighbors started up a conversation outside. A distant weed trimmer buzzed to life. A siren blared in the distance, reminding her of the urgency of the world and its other occupants.

There's no one in this room but me. I can do this.

Mia rose unsteadily to her feet. Brushing back her hair away from her face, she looked directly across to the large mirror on the living room wall, and braced herself for what might be there.

According to the reflection in the glass, she was the only person present.

The lonely sight surprised her. She checked all of the other reflective objects and doorknobs about her. They too, were clear. Mia felt puzzled at first.

There isn't anybody here with me… Maybe there never was?

She couldn't tell what she had seen or whether she had imagined it all. Her cheeks flushed red with embarrassment. Her neighbors talking outside suddenly made her feel self-conscious.

Could they hear me scream before?

She looked about the living room. Blood spots—her blood—puddled in irregular patterns on the hardwood floor. The coffee table lay broken and pushed against the sofa. When Mia hastily righted it, it wobbled pitifully on its cracked leg. Turning her attention to the drying spots, she went to the kitchen for paper towels, only to come upon the broken glass scattered on the floor and running water still streaming away in the kitchen sink.

There was no way she could ever explain this event to Dan. She didn't understand what had just happened; he surely would not. Although he was intelligent and gentle, he was practical and clear-cut, the here and now of the situation. It wasn't that he couldn't comprehend fantasy, he just did not believe in it.

Mia always wondered if there was an element of fear of the unknown in him. It certainly was safer to stay rooted in his concrete world of reality where he could confront issues face to face or turn them off with the flick of a switch. Beyond that, in the realms of the psyche or psychic, he flat out refused to accept any of it as truth.

In the past, whenever she had tried to talk about anything outside of his pragmatic realm, he ceased to listen. Like the time she tried to explain the rift between her mother and Aunt Lydia. He listened patiently up to the point in which she tried to describe the differences of her mother's fundamental Christian values versus her aunt's belief in the paranormal. He insisted that it was none of his business and refused to discuss it any further.

And so she found herself thinking of him and his practical sensibilities, picking up shards of broken glass from the floor and sink, all the while making sure she avoided the reflections in the spout.

◊ ◊ ◊

The doorknob felt different.

Inspecting it, he noticed that the once smooth and shiny brass had been sanded and scratched to a rough dull finish. When he opened the door and entered the house, he found all was quiet inside except for a radio playing softly in another room. As he passed through the living room, his eyes were immediately drawn to the mirror. There, he stopped in his tracks, not being able to make sense of what he was seeing.

A checkered throw blanket was carefully fitted around the mirror, covering it completely. Perplexed, he looked about him. All large prints and pictures in the room were similarly dressed out in assorted wardrobes of towels, sheets, and pillowcases. Smaller frames were taken down and sat on the floor, facing the wall.

"Murph?" he called out.

A faint scraping noise started up, and then stopped again, coming from the end of the hallway. He followed it to discover Mia on her knees at the door of their home office. The scraping noise ensued as she vigorously sanded its doorknob with a piece of coarse sandpaper. The radio played and she hummed along, not looking up.

"Something up with the doorknobs?"

Mia screeched with fright and fell back. From her place on the ground, she looked up at him with wide eyes, panting and clutching the crumpled piece of sandpaper to her heart.

"I'm sorry, Honey! Did I startle you? I thought you heard me come in," Dan apologized as he gave her a hand up.

He noticed that she was visibly shaking as she scooped her hair back behind her ears and looked away. She only managed a weak smile and her lips felt cool as he gave her a quick kiss.

"I'm really sorry. Are you okay? You still look shaken up."

"No, I'm okay—now. I thought for a minute that you were the… It's just that you scared… um, never mind."

She bit her lower lip then focused on straightening out the crumpled fifty grit paper in her hand.

He looked around and let out a low whistle through his teeth.

"Boy! Are you preparing to hold a Jewish wake here or something?" he asked with a laugh in his voice.

"What?" Mia snapped to attention.

"A Jewish wake. You know, mirrors covered up with blankets and stuff…? Uh, never mind," he stopped when he saw the puzzled look on her face. "But what's going on with the sandpaper?"

"Oh I, um, got tired of the shiny look. Yeah, I decided to see how it would look with a, uh, matte finish instead," she fumbled. Then she quickly added, "And the sun, well any light for that matter, has been, mmmm… bugging my eyes lately. They must be sensitive from the medication or something. You know, the sun. When it reflects off the mirrors and glass, it uh, bothers me. So I covered everything up."

Dan studied her for a few moments, and then decided to agree by nodding his head. She was definitely off again today, but some things were better left alone. They hadn't been having much luck in communicating lately and he didn't want to get into another hassle of misunderstandings.

As he went to their bedroom to change out of his work clothes, he was met by more wall hangings covered with various dishcloths and towels. Some other home decor had been removed from shelves entirely. When he entered the kitchen, he encountered a sanded and gouged kitchen faucet as well.

Some of this change in decorating is getting quite costly, he mused to himself.

Grabbing a soda, he headed back to the living room. He set his drink down on the coffee table that suddenly seemed to move on its own. It pitched and wobbled as he gently rocked it back and forth. When he rotated it around to examine it more closely, Mia entered the room. She perched on the arm of the recliner, viewing him with guilty eyes.

"Wow, what happened here? Have you been holding wrestling meets while I'm at work?" he tried another joke as he wiggled the cracked leg.

"Um, no. It was an accident. I tripped over it while I was—sweeping. It was a, a freak thing."

She seemed edgy again.

"Did you hurt yourself?"

"Well, yeah. Kinda."

Mia tugged at the leg of her sweatpants, pulling it up high enough to expose the deep cut on her bruised and swollen shin.

"Holy smokes! Are you all right?" He winced at the sight of her wound.

"It hurts a little, but I'm okay. Nothing broken." She gingerly pulled down her pant leg.

"Are you sure? It looks really swollen. You could have a slight fracture—"

"It's fine," she cut in.

It became apparent to Dan that she was a little embarrassed.

She continued, "Are you hungry right now? I didn't get a chance to make dinner. How about we grab a pizza or something?"

He studied his wife again, trying to figure out what was going on. She was distracted, almost agitated. Her eyes kept darting about as if she were expecting something to jump out at her at any moment. He debated whether or not to get her to elaborate, but she didn't appear to want to divulge anything. The ensuing tension wouldn't be good, for either one of them.

"Yeah, sure Murph. If that's what you want, we can do that."

◊ ◊ ◊

The two red colon dots dividing minutes and seconds on the digital clock pulsed relentlessly like a heartbeat, pacing the passage of time. Once again the couple were seated in the small office where team pennants screamed over their heads in cheerleader colors. They shifted uncomfortably in the mauve chairs. He was fifteen minutes late already.

Just then, the door swung open wide and he burst into the room with a flurry of activity.

"Hello, hello. Hey! Sorry to keep you guys. I'm running so far behind today I don't think I'll catch up with myself until tomorrow. You ever have one of those days?" The chair creaked loudly as Gerry plopped himself down in it and rolled up to the desk. "Okay," he said as he glanced down at the file folder on his desk, "—Mia, Dan. Long time no see. How have you guys been?"

This time a tie printed with smiling bug-eyed frog faces hugged his neck.

Both simultaneously mumbled a quiet "okay" and "all right."

Mia had a feeling that today's talk wasn't going to work. Nevertheless she still couldn't help but feel somewhat curious. Maybe Gerry would have a logical explanation for her sightings.

The answer could easily lie in any one of those textbooks that lined his shelf. She was inclined to believe that some of his other patients had to have had episodes like this at one time or another. And perhaps, his explanation would be plausible enough for even Dan to accept without complaint.

"Hey, how are those affirmations working out for you? They're great, aren't they?"

She found herself nodding yes, although she didn't agree.

"And are you keeping up with your meds? Whoops! I see here that Barb has upped you. How are you doing with that?"

Mia could feel Dan's eyes on her. At that moment it occurred to her that she hadn't mention anything to him about the increase in medication. If she didn't acknowledge his stare, she might be able to avoid his barrage of questions later. She regretted having asked him to accompany her this time.

"Uh, okay, I guess."

"Um huh. And it says here that you've been seeing 'things.' Let's talk about that for a moment."

What she had so carefully concealed was out. But to her relief, the therapist didn't seem surprised or shocked. Instead, he smiled his most patient smile.

"Well, I was, um, seeing something."

"Can you describe what, exactly? Colors? Flashing lights? Catching something out of the corner of your eye perhaps?"

"Well, it seems to change. Sometimes it's like, I don't know, an indiscriminate shape of something. And then it disappears," she stammered feeling self-conscious in front of her husband. This was all news to him, and she wondered how he was taking it. She continued, "Other times, it was sort of a person. At least it looked like a person."

The words tasted awkward and funny on her tongue.

"And where did you see this person? Was he or she standing in front of you?"

Gerry's yellow fluttering pencil moth had returned.

"It was…" Mia hesitated.

She knew that Dan would now discover what she had seen the other night on the TV screen and in the doorknobs. Everything that she had kept hidden from him thus far would now be revealed. As far as he was concerned it would seem that she had been deceiving him all along. She began to fear that their trusting relationship in which they had so carefully built was being taken apart, bit-by-bit. Realizing her tenuous position, she chose her words with care.

"…Well I should say that I see It from time to time, in different places."

The fluttering moth landed on the legal pad on the desk and scratched out a few notes.

"Go on."

"I don't see it all the time. Just a few places here and there," she reiterated.

She observed that her husband had not budged at all in his seat.

"Yes, you've said that. Now is there a time when you notice it more? Like when you're tired or hungry? Or how about when you're under stress?"

"Uh, yeah…*Yes*," she answered more definitively.

Now this was a logical explanation, one that Dan would surely understand. Gerry had inadvertently thrown her a life ring and she grabbed at it.

"All of those times. In fact, it has been when I am feeling more stressed out."

"And how about places? Inside or outside? Dark corners or right out in the open?"

"I guess I've only seen It indoors. And mostly in dark corners. Like I said, I really can't make it out."

"Uh huh. And in any particular rooms? The kitchen, the nursery, or," his eyes shifted momentarily to Dan then back to her, "your bedroom perhaps?" he asked.

"Yes, all of those places."

"Okay," Gerry replied decisively.

The top of his wavy head was all they could see for a moment as he furiously scribbled down a few more lines of notation. As they waited, Mia stole a peek at Dan but he kept his stare forward. His square jaw was clenched and he had since pushed back in his seat and crossed his arms.

The therapist continued, "What it sounds like to me is a stress-related problem. Different people handle stress in different ways. Some eat uncontrollably, others get abusive, while others, like you, think that they are seeing things. I bet you are a visual person, am I right?"

"Well, yes, come to think of it, I am, I guess," she agreed.

"Thought so. You've been through a traumatic event in your life and you are pretty fragile. You might be feeling a little undue pressure to start all over again. Maybe it's self-imposed, or perhaps from other people, to make things normal. The two of you might even be trying to start a family again.

"I say, back off. Take your time. Don't rush to produce another baby right now. You have to heal emotionally before you want to take on that responsibility. Right now the only thing you should concentrate on is making yourself better. No one else matters, understand? Remember, the team must be strong before we can win the game. Right?"

Mia let out a sigh of relief. What he said made sense. She wasn't going crazy. She just needed to slow down. Thinking back, the memory of lying, panic stricken, on the living room floor, paranoid that there was some kind of Boogie Man out to kill her, suddenly filled her with embarrassment and shame. She was glad she didn't divulge any of *those* details.

However, what was she going to do should she returned home and still find *it* there, staring back at her?

"Okay, but what if I see It or any other weird things again? Should I call you or...?" she trailed off, hoping he would finish her sentence.

"No, I don't think that will be necessary because as you relieve your stress and recover, I think you will be seeing 'things' less and less. You already know that you are dealing with stressed-induced figments of your imagination, so they shouldn't shake you up so badly anymore. But if you think you need more help in learning how to get rid of stress," he fished around in his desk drawer, "call this number here for member services, and ask for their stress-management courses that they offer. I hear that they are super."

He produced a refrigerator magnet bearing the familiar PartnersHealth logo and phone numbers and slid it across the faux wood desktop at her.

"And should I continue with the dosage that I'm taking right now?" she asked.

This whole matter couldn't be *this* simple, could it?

"Of course. It takes a little time for things to kick in and your body to adjust to the new levels of serotonin in your brain. I assure you that when it does and you learn to relax, you probably won't be seeing any more creepy crawlies. Okay then, is there anything else that I can do for either one of you today?" Gerry folded his hands and leaned across his desk.

Mia thought for a second then gave her head a shake. When she looked at Dan, he remained unmoving and stiff, his arms still firmly planted across his chest. Seeing him like that, she immediately felt unsettled. She knew she was going to have to answer a lot of questions on the ride home.

"All righty! Well I hate to run, kids, but I have a killer schedule today and like I told you when I came in, I'm running behind as it is. Mia?" He jutted his hand at her. When she accepted it, he pumped it firmly. "Dan?"

The gesture was lost when Dan refused to acknowledge him. Gerry quickly converted his rejected hand to the shape of a gun and fired off an imaginary round, clicking his tongue, and winking his eye.

"Okay, I'll catch you next time." He started heading for the door.

"Which will be?" Mia asked as she turned to watch him leave.

"Why don't you call and make an appointment with one of the girls at the desk, 'kay?"

Gerry and his frog tie were gone. As with their previous visit, it seemed as if he had sucked all of the noise out of the room with his departure, leaving Dan and Mia in a vacuum.

They quietly gathered themselves and made their way out to the parking lot. There was something really up with Dan. He had never been that rude to a person since Mia had known him. Her happy relief in the easy solutions provided by today's session was short lived as she thought about the fact that he had been hurt by her deceit. She never meant to keep so much from him. It all got so hard to explain.

She decided that she would tell him everything from the beginning, then face the possibility of his disbelief or worse yet, his rejection. In a way, she would accept it as payback. But for now it would only be fair for her to start the exchange instead of letting him initiate an already strained communication.

"Honey? Is everything all right?" she ventured, and then braced for the interrogation.

She picked up her pace to keep up with his long-legged stride, but limped as her bruised shin complained with pain.

He remained stony as he opened the door for her on the Jeep. With growing dread, she watched as he crossed around the front and then entered in on his side. He slammed his door hard, making the vehicle rock from the impact. Then he sat for few moments, clenching and unclenching his jaw. Finally he turned to her, his dark eyes shining with anger.

"I can't believe what just went on in there!"

By the volume of his voice, she was grateful that he waited until they were inside the Jeep before he answered her question.

"I-I know, but I—" was all she could reply.

"Son of a bitch!" he swore and shook his head. "I think I've been pretty understanding through all of this, haven't I?"

She nodded.

"I mean, I've listened to you, worried about you, tried to get through all of this mess."

She nodded again, and then lowered her eyes in shame.

"I haven't put any demands on you and have done everything I possibly could think of. I mean, I don't know what else I could have done... I just can't believe this shit!"

Mia fished around in her head for the right reasons for having kept things from him. In all their marriage, they had always been open with each other. None was forthcoming.

"Answer me, have I asked you for anything?"

"No, no you haven't," she agreed quietly.

"And you've got to admit, it's been a while. First your dad, then the baby, and now these episodes. There was no way I was going to try anything. I wanted to give you some space. Hell, I know a lot of other guys who can't go that long."

Huh? She thought. *What is he talking about?*

"When that asshole in there insinuated that I was forcing you to do something you weren't ready for, I could have reached across his desk and choke the living shit out of him with his own goddamn tie. Son of a bitch!"

She looked up at him and then suddenly it became perfectly clear. Relieved, she reached over and took his hand that was balled in a fist on his knee.

"Didn't you see his eyes? He practically stood up and accused *me*, like I was causing this or something. I love you. And believe me, I won't ask you to make love until you are totally ready. I hope you understand that."

She smiled inwardly knowing how conscientious he had always been of her feelings. He was definitely one of the good guys.

"I do, Honey," she reassured him.

He sat for a few minutes more, grinding his jaw, probably thinking of a few more ways to dismantle Gerry. She remained quiet. It was usually better if she didn't try to talk through everything. Talking had already gotten her into too much trouble.

With the anger slowly ebbing in his voice he said, "Hey, I'm sorry for blowing up. You don't need all of this. How about we go so we aren't siting in this parking lot all evening." He started the engine.

Mia knew that she would explain everything to him eventually, but not until she could find the right time and words. In the meantime she was thankful for the reprieve she was just granted. Thinking over these past few weeks' events and their obvious solutions: the medication, the talk with Gerry, and Dan's patience, she wondered if she had been making things out to be more complicated than what they actually were.

Maybe it could be this simple, if she would only let it.

FIVE

MIA REMEMBERED HOW BRIGHT THE DAY had started out with clear skies and the scent of ocean salt on the breeze. It held a promise of something more, something exciting. The sun seemed to shine with an extra intensity buoyed upon a feeling of optimism. She sensed—even knew—something was going to change for her that day.

Although the day was perfect, she couldn't help but feel nervous and agitated. Her dad had told her what he knew of the young man. What kind of things he liked to do, what college he had attended, his warrant officer commission with the Navy. But he wouldn't answer one of her most pressing questions: what did he look like? At least the weather had cooperated.

She had begged her father for weeks to elaborate. But all Stephanos Pappas would do was shrug his shoulders and say something like, "I don't know. He looks like any other boy. Last time I saw him, he didn't have three heads or anything, if that's what you are asking."

"Dad! You know what I mean. Is he tall? What color hair does he have? Does he have a nice smile?"

Fathers seemed to miss all the important details.

"Like I said, I don't know! He was in his uniform in a small picture that Dick carries in his wallet. You can't tell anything from that. He looks, okay, I guess. Very militant. Is that what you want to hear?"

Her father was teasing again, but it was getting frustrating. She knew it was shallow of her, but still she wanted to know if her blind date had more than a nice personality and a future.

"C'mon, Dad! You had to at least see the color of his hair! How about his eyes?"

"How could I? He was wearing a hat, like all good sailors do."

For Mia, if she was going to allow herself to be set up to meet someone, especially by her father, it might prove to be disappointing, if not disastrous. Although she understood that he would make sure the suitor was responsible and intelligent, there were, after all, other things that had to be considered and she had better get some clarification.

"Well, how about his uniform? His buttons weren't gaping any, like around his gut, or anything… were they?"

"Of course not, Honey. Don't you know those uniforms are tailor made for each person?"

"Daddy! You can be positively infuriating!" she wailed in exasperation. Her father chuckled at his daughter's antics. They both stopped short when Margaret Pappas walked in, carrying scissors, and the small misting can she used on her African Violets.

"I don't know what all the fuss is about in this room. I can only hope the young man is suitable enough for your daughter to be introduced to, Steve."

"I think he is, Margaret. From what Dick tells me, he earned the highest grades in school. And he's already made Warrant Officer Second Class in the Navy. He's supposed to be some kind of technical wiz with electronics and video production."

"That's what Dick tells you. He's his father, what do you expect? But does the boy have a sound moral upbringing? Which church does he attend and how often?"

"I don't know. I can always ask if you—"

"There seems to be a lot of things you don't know about him." Her lips pursed together in a stubborn thin line as she started to snip at the withered blooms. "I don't like it. There's absolutely no reason why Mia can't go out with someone we do know more about. Take Jon for example. He's a boy with a solid Christian upbringing."

"Jon? Jon who?" Mia asked.

"Jonathon Thompson. Delilah's son," Margaret Pappas said with impatience growing in her voice. "He's a perfectly nice young man, brought up well and with good manners too."

"Oh. Him," Mia answered contemptuously.

With his wife's back turned to them for a few moments, Stephanos looked over at his daughter for more on this particular suitor. She answered by making an ugly cross-eyed face, clutching her throat, and sticking out her tongue while pretending to gag.

"Yes, him. Remember we all went to the Pancake Charity Breakfast last June? We had a perfectly lovely time," her mother asked over her shoulder.

"I remember him, all right," Mia said blandly as if she had a bad taste in her mouth.

She thought about his pasty complexion, white eyebrows, and widely gapped teeth, all topped off with orange curly hair. He had dripped blueberry syrup across her new sandals, without as much as a "pardon me." To top it off, after the breakfast, he had followed her out to the parking lot and tried to feel her up when she bent over to get something out of the trunk of her car.

"Well, how about it? There's going to be a Fish Fry in the Hall next week. I'll be seeing Delilah at Stations of the Cross tomorrow. If you like, we'll have him call on you."

"Uh, no!" Mia exclaimed, and then realized she had said it a little too loudly. She continued, trying to sound as calm as possible, "That's okay. You know, Daddy and Mr. Labont went through a lot of trouble for me to meet his son. I mean, wouldn't it be discourteous to not attend their barbecue and, uh, at least say hi?"

She tried a bright smile, but Margaret's narrowing eyes extinguished it. Usually that meant her mother was not the least bit amused.

"Fine. Have it your way. Your father is not even remotely concerned with who or what you go out with."

She turned her full scorn upon her husband. "A sailor! Heaven knows what he might expose your daughter to. You have no idea who he has been with or the places he's been in. I can only imagine lots of bars and those foreign ports of call that are just crawling with diseases and immorality."

Margaret slammed down her misting can and walked away in disgust. From the kitchen they could hear her plea, "Merciful Father, You know I have tried my best to raise a daughter who was chaste and pure. Please let her not be tempted by the ways of the wicked and the vain. Help me to bear this cross…"

Father and daughter looked to the kitchen, then back at each other. Stephanos picked up his newspaper while Mia leaned in closer to him and whispered, "So Dad, *what does he look like?*"

By early afternoon, they were among the other thirty or so guests, mostly relatives and neighbors, who had turned out to welcome Dan Labont home from his tour of duty. While Mia anxiously awaited his arrival, she enjoyed the view of the San Diego Bay from his parents' hilltop backyard. Earlier, one of his uncles had pointed out the tiny gray shape in the distance indicating that it was the battleship Dan was stationed on. She looked along the city skyline and surrounding hills and imagined what it would be like driving to this place he called home after being away at sea for months.

As the day waned on, the conversation amongst the relatives, neighbors and friends eventually turned from excited anticipation, to the weather, to complaints about the pesky flies buzzing around the food. There apparently had been some kind of delay in his leaving ship.

Jenna, the Labont's youngest child, tried desperately to mingle from table to table only to be hindered by her ample body and shy tendencies. Her mother kept a watchful eye on her teenage protégé, all the while trailing out platter after platter of food for her son's homecoming.

Mia shifted uncomfortably in the plastic lawn chair and pulled at the caved-in bodice of her dress. She never had enough bust to properly fill out any of the dresses with built in bras. Her self-consciousness caused her to fidget with the straps of her dress. She would have much rather donned the silk blouse and denim skirt she had selected from amongst her clothes, but her mother insisted on her wearing this dress because she said it was more "appropriate." Mia knew it was one of her more matronly-looking dresses. Even thinking of her mother's pet phrase made Mia roll her eyes and sigh, making her question her motives.

Watching her squirm, Margaret Pappas hissed, "Stop that. You look fine. There is nothing wrong with that dress. Honestly! The way you carry on about meeting this young man. You know, your father with his hair-brained schemes in setting you up. I've told him time and time again never to-"

Much to her relief, her mother's words seemed to fade away as an ocean breeze blew in from the bay and resuscitated Mia with its cool breath. She glanced over to where her father stood, talking with Dick Labont, co-workers, and mutual friends. They seemed to be having a fun and lively conversation. She envied them, but her mother would not let her join in the men's discussion. Maybe her mother was right. This might have been a mistake to come after all.

Within time, there was a flurry of excitement by the tables closest to the back door of the house. Some of the young cousins ran inside and soon they erupted, hugging, towing, and pushing a smiling young man in a dark uniform out the back door and onto the lawn.

Without trying to look too curious, Mia craned her neck to get a better look, but the sailor was engulfed by a noisy huddle of people, pressing about to hug him, pat him on the back, or shake his hand. At that moment, she felt out of place, as if she were intruding on a family affair. She settled back into her chair and waited, watching the ice cubes melt in her glass.

After the initial commotion, she could see him moving from table to table with the confident ease of someone amongst family and friends. From what she could tell from the limited view of him that she had been afforded so far, he was tall and broad shouldered. Finally she saw Dick Labont go up and mumble something in his son's ear causing the young man to straighten up and peer around cautiously. Then his father led him to her table.

As he approached, a dozen thoughts raced through Mia's head, *What if he thinks that I'm a frump? Why did I ever wear this stupid dress?*

Her thoughts stopped abruptly when he came into view. His dark eyes locked onto hers as he reached out his hand. He looked so serious at first, all business until he removed his hat and offered a charming lopsided grin that completely disarmed her. For a moment, she felt as if she were in a vacuum, hearing her name in the introduction somewhere off in a distance.

She stammered, "Hullo, uh, ah, nice to meet you."

She kicked herself inwardly for sounding like an idiot. Yet, his hand was warm and strong and if she weren't mistaken, it lingered a few seconds longer than it should have in hers. While Dan was being introduced to her mother, she peeked over at her dad. He raised an eyebrow and tossed his head as if to ask, "What do you think?" She beamed back. The dirty rat had been holding out on her all along.

Dan had to continue on with his obligatory greetings and reunions. In the meantime, Mia excused herself to the bathroom. There, she took a good look in the mirror and studied every hair out of place, every blemish on her skin. She checked her teeth and pulled at the loose strings on her dress, then tried to center the seams on this horrible dress that had a mind of its own. She stared hopelessly at the flattened cups in the front. If only she had some kind of cleavage. For a fleeting moment, she panicked and thought about stuffing her bra with toilet paper, but she regained her composure, blushing at her juvenile attempt to be attractive.

Get a hold of yourself girl. He might not even like you. And if he does, he'll just have to like what he sees here.

With that, she smoothed back her hair one more time, gave her dress a resolute tug upwards, and returned to the homecoming.

"I was beginning to think that you went AWOL or something."

The voice coming from behind her was deep, but kind. Her heart flew back into her throat, all of her bra-tugging resolution gone.

"Oh hi. I was just in the—"

She stopped, realizing this was going to be the first real sentence she was going to say to him. She certainly didn't want the word, "bathroom," in it.

"—Um, admiring your house. You really have a beautiful view here."

He had since changed out of his uniform and into a pair of faded Levi's and a polo shirt. Without his uniform, he looked less formidable, but still handsome. Mia found herself breathless.

"Thanks, I've always loved it here. It's one of the things I look forward to when I get leave." His eyes scanned the ocean in the horizon.

"I can see why," Mia replied.

While he looked out over the view, she racked her brain trying to think of something witty or intelligent to say, but her head wouldn't cooperate. Her racing heart didn't help matters either. The next few speechless minutes grew agonizing. Was he going through this too?

No, she determined, *he looks too calm*.

Thankfully, Jenna approached.

"Hey Dan, Mom wants you to make sure that Mia gets something to eat."

"Okay, Kiddo. Hey, by the way, I haven't been able to ask you yet—are you still making moony eyes over that guy in your chemistry class?"

He grabbed her in a playful hug and tickled her. Mia could tell that the siblings missed each other while apart.

"Dan! You're like, such an idiot! Stop!" She giggled as she squirmed her way out of his grip. "No, I'm not making MOONY eyes over any boy."

"Oh, I know," he teased, "He's making moony eyes at you. You better let me know if he is because I'll take him around back, work him over and throw him in the dumpster for looking at my sister. Wait a minute. I'll take him around back and throw him in the dumpster if he ISN'T looking at my sister."

"Ugh! You're impossible!" she giggled again as she rolled her eyes in feigned exasperation. "Anyway, come eat, before Mom comes and seeks you out," she said, pointing a menacing finger at him.

He pretended to cower. Then Jenna smiled happily at Mia, called out to a cousin crossing the yard, and left.

"You two look like you have a lot of fun," Mia offered.

"Yeah. She's a good kid. I love it when she's happy. You know, sometimes she has it rough, with her size and all. Some of the other kids tease the hell out of her." He watched her with concern as she ambled across the lawn.

"I understand that other kids can get pretty cruel."

"They do. That's why I worry about her when I'm gone. Mom and Dad just think that it's something that she needs to find her own way to solve, as if she has control over the situation. It's not that they don't love her or feel for her, but they think that it's part of growing up. Something that will make her a stronger person in the long run."

"Hmmm. That's a shame," she replied, holding her tongue from prying into family business.

"Yeah, well anyway… Hey, I'm sorry about my manners. Would you like something to eat? We better go before my mom ships me back out."

She was surprised when he took her by the hand and started leading her to the buffet table. She liked the feel of his hand and let hers stay where it was.

Now that the ice had been broken, Mia found that she fell into an easy conversation with the young man. They stood side by side in the long food line exchanging various views, finding themselves instantly compatible with each other. Within minutes, they were completely engaged in their conversation not noticing anybody or anything else, until they were prompted by his Uncle Bert to move up.

Mia liked Dan's gentle manners and his quick wit. And she was pretty sure she caught him stealing glances at her whenever she looked away. As they approached the buffet, he picked up a plate and handed it to her.

She pushed it back to him and said, "Thank you, but no, you go ahead. This party is for you. I'm sure that you can't wait to get some home cooking again after all of that mess hall stuff they've been feeding you on ship. Everything here looks delicious."

"No way. By all means, you are my guest." He tried handing her the plate again.

"Well, technically, I'm your parents' guest," she parlayed.

"Okay, well, girls first."

"Nah uh. Whatever happened to being politically correct?"

"Okay, we'll do it by alphabetical order, like they do in the Navy."

"All right *Dan.*" She laughed, thoroughly enjoying the exchange.

"No, not by first names," he tried.

"All righty then, Warrant Officer *Labont.*"

He clutched his heart in pretend agony. "Oh! Zing! She got me again. Hey, you're pretty good."

Uncle Bert pushed passed them and snatched up a plate, mumbling something under his breath about "having some consideration for starving people," and started helping himself to the food on the table.

"Well, someone with a pretty name like 'Mia' should always have first dibs."

"Oh? And if I had a name like, let's see…Murphy? You'd boot me to the back of the line?"

"I think I'd make an exception in your case, Miss Murphy," he said, slowly and distractedly while looking deep into her eyes.

Mia couldn't help but blush, then look away with a shy smile.

"So by all means, Miss Murphy," he said again, but this time he deposited a spoonful of potato salad onto her plate.

She giggled, and then countered with a spoonful of macaroni salad dumped onto his plate.

"No, no. After *you*, Mr. Murphy. I insist."

He added chicken to hers, "No really, Miss Murphy, after *you*."

They were surprised by how fast the moon had risen to a high position in the sky, even more amazed to find that it was already ten o'clock at night. They had spent the last four hours sitting on a bench in a forgotten corner of the yard, overlooking the lights on the bay and casually exchanging their thoughts on just about everything.

Their conversation wove and interlaced effortlessly in the cool night air. Mia couldn't believe how much she enjoyed talking with Dan. There were too many times that she had met athletic, good-looking guys like him who were either stuck on themselves, inarticulate, or both. To her satisfaction, he was neither. And she found that they shared the same viewpoint and feelings on so many things that there was something immediately comfortable and familiar about him. She sensed it was more than just a mere attraction to each other. It was as if she had met him before, some place and time long ago.

She had dated a couple of guys in high school, but never seriously, only going out with friends on group outings. Then in college, she immersed herself into her journalism and editing studies and didn't really take the time to meet anyone new.

She blamed it partly on her mother's control over her social life. Whenever her mother could, she would bring her to church get-togethers in efforts to match her with "suitable young men." "Suitable" usually meant getting stuck with someone who mirrored her mother's own religious fanaticism.

Mia also knew that it would be unfair to place the blame solely on her. She had held off from actively seeking someone, almost intentionally. There was always this feeling of expectation; she knew she was going to find *him* someday. And although she had just met Dan, she knew, almost intuitively, that he was the one.

While he talked about his tour of duty, she watched as a returning dinner cruise ship made its way on the dark waters below. He stopped in mid-sentence, catching her attention. He studied her face in the moonlight for a few seconds, then let his fingers gently caress down the smooth curve of her cheek.

He leaned close. "I know we've just met, but may I have your permission to kiss…you…?" he murmured, and then impulsively kissed her.

It was soft, but lingering, his lips barely brushing against hers. Her lips tingled and it was as if he had stolen her breath away once more. When she opened her eyes, his were searching hers, asking. Her smile said yes and he kissed her again, this time slowly and passionately. She felt hopelessly, happily lost in his embrace with his scent, his warmth, the strength of his arms, the feel of his lips against hers. She wanted to freeze time to stay there forever.

"Mia! I think it is well past time we went home," Margaret Pappas's voice snapped from the dimly lit yard behind them.

They broke apart and quickly sat up straight on the bench. Her mother marched around to the front of them. Mia could tell by the weak light cast on her mother's face from the porch that her eyes were narrowing again. Margaret sniffed disdainfully as she looked from her daughter to the sailor.

"Don't you have consideration for anyone? I've been looking all over for you. And here you both are, in this dark corner alone. I can't believe that you purposely sneaked off to—"

"Mia, honey, let's go." Stephanos Pappas stepped in swiftly to bail them out. "Dan, it's good to see you again, son. Welcome home."

Dan stood up and gratefully shook his hand. "Thank you, Sir. It's good to be back."

"I can see that," Steve chuckled and patted him on the shoulder.

"Good night Mrs. Pappas. Thank you for coming," Dan said politely as he tried to smooth the older woman's ruffled feathers.

She scowled at him and turned on her heel to stalk off. Mia hesitated, not wanting her time with him to end, and unwilling to part.

He must have felt the same because he took her hand and whispered to her, "Good night Miss Murphy."

She quietly giggled back, "No, good night to you Mr. Murphy."

She gave him one last smile, then scampered off to catch up with her father, who had stopped to offer his arm. She took it and squeezed it in excitement, then turned to look at Dan standing with the lights of the bay behind him, watching her intently as she walked off. It was as if she couldn't feel the ground beneath her. If she hadn't been holding onto her father's arm, she would have floated away.

They passed Jenna on her way towards her brother. And before they left the yard, Mia could hear his sister taking a turn at teasing him, saying, "Moony eyes, huh?"

"Wha'dya say?" he answered absentmindedly.

Mia sighed happily to herself as she recalled the day they had first met. It started off well enough in any case—who could ask for anything better than "love at first sight"? From that day on, they were hardly ever apart and had become best of friends, and eventually lovers. They had never had anything much past a disagreement up until recently. But this past year or so had really tested them. Hurt feelings and misunderstandings had been getting harder and harder to repair. And then there was the whole ordeal with her moods: the crying, the arguments, the "seeing things."

The gun. It was any wonder to her that he still kept his cool and hadn't left her already. With each passing hurdle, she felt as if they were being pulled further and further apart. She resolved that this turmoil in their lives had to end. They had to get back to where they were before. She wanted her marriage to survive more than anything.

Rolling onto her side, she watched her husband as he slept. His alarm clock would be waking him in another five more minutes or so for work. She gazed upon his features, letting her eyes stroll over the contours of his face and the shadow of a beard waiting for a morning shave. He still kept his hair Navy-short, and while he hadn't changed much in his looks, she could see where a few more lines had settled on his once smooth cheeks and around his eyes. He looked so peaceful at the moment, that it was odd to think these past two years had been hard on him as well. She knew how much her father had meant to him. And their son....

He had lost his baby too.

Guilt crept under her skin, spreading like a rash. She watched as he murmured a little in his sleep and turned onto his back. Suddenly, she was upon him, kissing him softly on his cheeks, lips, and eyelids. He awoke, looked at her sleepily, and smiled. When he pulled away the blankets to get up, she held onto him, forcing him to lie back down. Her eyes beseeched him with a look that they both knew and understood. He cocked his head quizzically, silently asking, "Are you sure?" And like she did that summer evening long ago, she smiled, "Yes."

In a moment they were intertwined, the two of them desperately tugging and peeling away each other's clothing, embracing, clutching. She hungered for the feel of his body against hers. It had been much too long of a time they had been apart and she missed him intensely. Their brief interval of passionate, consuming intimacy was interrupted once again, as it had been back then, but this time by his clock radio going off. Both reached out their hands, frantically groping at the air to hit the off button. Mia knew that he would be late to work, but she didn't want to stop. Not this time.

◊ ◊ ◊

"Here are all the case files for this month, Rueben." Gerry Monroe entered the dimly lit office and set a short stack of manila folders on the corner of the mahogany desk. Dr. Gamez peered up at him over the top of his reading glasses for a moment, his face half lit by the small desk lamp that seemed to be forever burning. Saying nothing, he took another minute to write a few more notes in the chart he was reading and closed the folder.

"So, how's it going?" Gerry asked casually as he settled into the chair across the desk from the small serious man. He leaned back, stretched and yawned, crossing his leg in front of him and folding his hands behind his head. Gamez considered him briefly, then reached into his side drawer and extracted a binder thick with forms. Paging to the appropriate place, he reached over and plucked the first file from the stack of folders, took up a pen and sat poised. Gerry didn't budge.

"You know the procedure for PMR's, Mr. Monroe. Let's get this over with."

Patient Monthly Reviews were one of the numerous aspects Gerry hated about his job. In fact, he wasn't sure which he liked least, these or those insipid office parties complete with ptomaine potluck. As far as he was concerned, he was a licensed therapist and felt this answering to some PhD was not only demeaning, but also a bunch of bullshit. A total waste of his already overtaxed time.

Gamez cleared his throat and started again. "Childress, Ashley. Sixteen years old. Anorexia Nervosa," he read off her chart in the same monotone reserved for inventories. "You are aware, Mr. Monroe, that Miss Childress had to be hospitalized over the weekend? She was found unconscious on the floor of a public restroom. Apparently she was dehydrated and severely malnourished."

"Yeah. I think I received a memo about that. It's somewhere on my desk." He shook his head and added, "Bummer."

"*I* sent you the memo, Mr. Monroe," Gamez said as he looked up from the file. "It seems her parents are quite upset and are questioning her treatment here. They demanded her records and are going to admit her to St. Joseph's instead."

Oh great, Gerry thought to himself, *that's all I need to get my ass in a sling over that manipulative little twig.*

"Well, you know, Rueben, that kid has a lot of issues going on at home. I believe the majority of her problems stem from her parents projecting a lot of their anxieties and fears onto her." He was reaching for it, but he didn't care as long as it got him off the hook.

"Your notes state here that you felt she was making progress."

"She WAS. I mean, she was opening up to *me,* and even her parents were beginning to disclose. I felt that we made some big leaps."

Gamez stopped and glared at him again. It was a steady fix that lasted for some undeterminable length of time. Gerry almost wanted to reach out to feel for a pulse, when Gamez broke his gaze to make a few careful notes on the PMR form.

"We *will* be discussing this further, Mr. Monroe. Legal is waiting to see if the Childress's are going to go through with their lawsuit. I suggest you prepare. Let's move on… Next, Bowles, Robert. Forty-nine-year old. Clinical depressive. Tell me about him."

"Oh, Mr. Bowles is doing very well. In fact, he requested that our sessions start tapering down. I feel he is much stronger and should continue on with his quest to become more autonomous."

Gamez continued to make more notes as he methodically ticked each patient off the stack, one by one.

"Lattimer, Alice, eighty-one-years old. Delusional."

"Well, at least she's progressed to the eighteenth century right now. Let me tell you, it's a helluva improvement from the toga and sandals." Gerry laughed a tight, dry laugh, but Gamez continued without so much as a hint of a smile.

"Labont, Mia, twenty-eight-years old. Post partum depressive. Her dosage was increased. Why?"

"She was stressing out and couldn't seem to get a handle on her miscarriage. Her stress was starting to manifest itself into mild hallucinatory visualizations. Nothing serious, and she seems to be responding to her meds. She assured me that she will be taking a stress management class in the meantime."

Gerry looked down at his watch. They were only halfway through the stack. The Lakers were playing the Sixers tonight and he had just missed the tip off. Crap, he also meant to call Austin, but had to take into account the three-hour time difference for Florida. His son would probably be long asleep by the time he got a chance to call tonight.

He studied the man who was responsible for detaining him and ruining his personal life. Gamez didn't look like he had a life, stuck here in this miserable hole, dictating his youth and career into his dictaphone. The thick gold band he wore around his finger probably didn't account for much. More than likely he went home to an equally dim house every night complete with a little dower wife and a reheated dinner in the microwave. He inwardly smirked at the thought of his supervisor's plight.

"Jackson, Leticia. Thirty-five-years old. General anxiety disorder...." Gamez droned on.

◊ ◊ ◊

While shopping through the aisles of the department store, Mia smiled inwardly to herself, thinking of the morning's lovemaking. Remnants of guilt still remained, but more in knowing that Dan was definitely late to work, probably to be chewed out by Greenlee and on an empty stomach to boot. After this morning, she also knew he probably didn't mind one bit.

She decided that since she was shopping for his upcoming birthday, she might as well go all out and really surprise him. Clutching the shirt she had already picked out for him, she changed directions and headed to the electronics department.

After a half-hour of sorting through potential gifts, she had finally decided on the digital video camera. She knew that Dan had been eyeing one of them since they had come out. Although things were a little tight since she hadn't been working, she was going back to the mag next week. She could make up the cost in no time. It would be totally unexpected and she thought about the look on his face when he opened the wrapping. She smiled extra warmly at the cashier and held the bag with his gifts close to her.

It had been a while since she had been to this store. Looking about her, she had to admit it had been some time since she had been to *any* store. Her bout with depression had kept her well away from almost everything. It was a quiet weekday morning, and she encountered only a few people in the aisles as she took her time browsing through the jewelry and shoes.

Then with much wrestling of her conscious, she made up her mind to go for broke and buy a new outfit to return to work in. As she passed through the furnishings department, she came upon a mirror and lamp sale display. A tiffany style lamp caught her eye. They were always her favorite. She stopped long enough to read the price tag. It was way too much. There was no way she would be able to talk this one into the budget.

Just as she dropped the tag and raised her eyes to look over the other lamps, she saw It.

Reflected in the multiple mirrors displayed on the salesroom wall, a dozen dark gray phantoms stood menacingly before her.

He was back.

She didn't think it was possible. How could it be? She was here. In a store.

However, in the clear unmistakable detail of mirror reflection, *he*—a man —stared back at her with sunken, lifeless eyes. His face, partially cloaked by a drawn up hood, was an unnatural gray pallor as if the flesh were cold and stiff. The crimson swath that led from the top of his mouth, down his throat and staining his dirty jacket clearly was blood, and it continued to flow, drop by drop onto the floor about his mud caked boots. His cracked lips opened slightly, and seemed to be forming silent words, over and over again. His arms remained at his sides, though his long tapered fingers were clenched and stiffened like frozen claws.

His appearance pulsed a shock through her. Mia cried out in horrified anguish. Her knees felt like an electrical charge had coursed through them, leaving them weak and rubbery and giving out beneath her. She crumpled to the floor, shaking uncontrollably. In panic, her eyes searched around for where he might be standing, but found she was the only person on the aisle.

When she looked back, he was indeed there forming the silent words as if he were beckoning her, his face still in the partial shadow of his hood. This wasn't a stress-induced hallucination. This was real and now. He was *stalking* her. The thought terrorized her as everything came crashing back. She hadn't escaped him after all.

Hysterics flooded her brain and she shrieked, "Who are you? What do you want? Stay away from me!!"

She scrambled to get up, but her legs wouldn't obey as they slid and spilled out from under her on the smooth floor. That face in the mirror, the dozen faces in the mirrors, watching her, condemning her, seeking her all at the same time but yet saw past her, dead eyes unseeing. Mia let out another cry of mortal terror and complete and total despair.

A saleswoman rushed over from the next department to see what the commotion was about. Seeing Mia on the floor, she immediately asked her if she was okay and started to help her up. At the sensation of hands upon her, Mia flailed and kicked out defensively, the packages in her arms sent spinning down the aisle.

"Oh God! Leave me alone! LEAVE ME ALONE!" she screamed at the images in the mirrors, then collapsed into a huddle of wild desperate crying.

The saleswoman backed off, seeing the mad woman, and immediately went to phone security, then helplessly stood by and watched as Mia sobbed and heaved. Other customers gathered, pointing and whispering, holding back small children, but stubbornly staying on to witness the bizarre scene. Within a half a minute, two security guards arrived, huffing and clutching their walkie-talkies. They pushed back the spectators and cautiously approached her.

"Hey miss, are you okay?"

The sinister phantom remained, blood dropping to the floor, splashing onto his boots. The fingertips on his clawed hands looked as if they had been torn off and were bloodied as well. His stained lips formed the words over and over again. Two dozen piercing eyes watched her every move.

The image before her was real. In the other reflections at home, there was always the possibility that they were merely plays of light, optical illusions. Here, down to every last detail was a real person, waiting for her. It didn't matter whether she was alone or in a roomful of people.

The two guards hoisted her up onto her unsteady feet. She clung to one of them and asked, her voice choked and tight within her throat, "D-do you s-s-see him?"

"Excuse me?" the guard asked perplexed.

"Him! That man. There!" The words struggled to get out beyond a harsh whisper. "Do you see him? Tell me that you can see him!"

"Who?"

"THERE!" she screamed, pointing a trembling finger at the mirror display.

All eyes went to the mirrors. All that was reflected back to any of the witnesses present were two confused guards and a hysterically sobbing woman.

"Listen miss, I don't know—"

But she didn't hear the rest. Her head was overcome by a loud buzzing noise that drowned out everything about her. She felt her body go limp. The walls of the store closed in around her and she was falling, tumbling headlong into a never-ending blackness. The last thing her eyes saw was something not different than the static snow across the screen of an un-tuned TV.

◊ ◊ ◊

Slicing its way through the dark, the acrid smell of cigarette smoke stung her nostrils. She also became aware of a cold wet sensation on her forehead. And, as if a volume knob was being turned up, the noise of her surroundings became increasingly clearer. She could make out continuous transmissions of calls on a two-way radio. A paging bell. Two voices talking to each other about a phone call.

Mia forced her eyes open and sat up on the couch, its stiff Nauga-hyde squeaking beneath her. The cold wet feeling left her forehead and plopped down onto her upturned hands in her lap. As she focused through her hazy headache, she could see that it was a soaked and folded paper towel, hastily torn from a public restroom dispenser. The two voices immediately hushed as they noticed her coming to.

"Uh, Ms. Labont, why don't you take it easy? You fainted out there on the sales floor. We called an ambulance and they should be here any minute. So why don't you lay back down okay?"

The security guard talked to her as if she were a bomb set to go off with the slightest movement. She recognized him as the guard from the aisle. The younger guard sat bolt upright in his swivel chair, gripping the armrests, all the while keeping his eyes trained on her and slowly chewing his gum.

"No, I'm—I'm okay" she said groggily as she rubbed the side of her face. "How do you know my name?"

"The salesclerk. She got it off your receipt after you..." he paused, "you know, fainted. We carried you back here and called 911. John here looked you up in the phone book, but all we got was the answering machine at your house. Is there anyone you need us to call for you?"

Her head started to spin. She knew that they were only trying to be kind, but she was desperate to leave the claustrophobic stale-smelling security office. There was no telling when It was going to show up again. She eyed the row of surveillance monitors behind them warily. Luckily, they were all televising different angles of the store, so they were incapable of reflecting anything at the moment.

"Ms. Labont? I asked you if there was anyone you needed me to call for you," the guard said again, slowly emphasizing each word. "Huh? No. It's okay. But is there, uh, a restroom I can use? I think I'm going to be sick," she stood up clutching her stomach.

The overwhelming smell was caught in her throat and her legs felt shaky beneath her. The older guard jumped to his feet to brace her, while the younger guard cringed and pushed back even further, trying to allow the most space possible between them.

"My- my purse," she reached out a trembling hand.

"Sure, here it is. Need some help?"

She teetered a little, and then let herself be guided out into the hallway. Forgetting herself, she involuntarily looked at the mirror when she entered the employee's restroom. She froze with uncertainty. With a sigh of relief, she saw that she was alone. But the relief was only momentary as her stomach lurched again. In the stall, she doubled over and vomited, continuing to retch until there was nothing left. Oddly, after the heaving subsided, she felt a bit better.

As she rinsed her mouth and splashed water on her face, she heard a knock on the restroom door. It opened a crack as the guard called in, "Ms. Labont? Are you okay in there? I think I hear the ambulance guys down the way. I don't think John is in the office, so I'm going to bring them on back. Will you be okay?"

"Yes, I'm doing better now," she answered, thinking about what to do next.

She didn't want to be taken to the hospital. Someone there would end up calling Dan, and there wouldn't be any way that she could explain what had happened to him. He would become unglued just by the fact that she had been taken to ER. No, it would be better to wait and explain this to him privately, in their own home, in her own time. She had to find a way to get out of there.

Mia pushed open the door and looked down the hallway from where she came. She could hear the older security guard talking to the EMTs as they approached. This was her chance. She turned and ran the other way, the sound of her footsteps echoing off the long gray walls. The service hallway took one more turn where she spotted an exit at the end. The door opened out into the back parking lot, the bright sun blinding her for a few seconds. It took her a few seconds to get orientated to where she was at the rear of the mall. She knew she had to get away quickly. The security guards and ambulance techs were close behind.

She made her way around to the south side of the store where she had parked. An ambulance was positioned by the entrance, its white and blue strobe lights flickering, drawing the curiosity of some shoppers. At first Mia broke into a run towards her Hyundai, and then realized she would call too much attention to herself. With her panic held in check, she straightened up, kept her face down, and tried her best at a normal gait.

"What's going on here?" a startled voice asked.

She froze once again. When she raised her eyes, they came upon two elderly women approaching her on their way to the store. She managed a weak smile at them when she realized they weren't talking to her.

"Goodness. I hope it's not another armed robbery. You know last week, the convenience store down the street from me was held up by two men with guns and everything, and they made the clerk get down on the floor, and...." The pair continued on, their feeble voices growing fainter with each step.

Mia reached her car and quickly got in. Slamming the door shut, she immediately locked it. For a moment she sat there, letting the warmth of the sun penetrate through the windshield and heat her chilled body.

What am I going to do? Who in their right mind is going to believe this?

She sat gripping and releasing her steering wheel, trying to remember when she last took her medication, wanting to flee but not knowing where to go.

By the mall entrance, she could see the two security guards and EMTs searching for her. She hunkered down low in her seat, and waited for a few minutes. Seeing them go back into the mall, she let her breath escape, and sat up straight once more. She felt like some kind of fugitive. But she knew she was running from something more than just the security guards.

Everything was out of control again. Trying to sort it out, she decided that the only place she wanted to be was home. She sought the solace and seclusion of her bed, surrounded by her own things, and more medication to make it all go away. Starting the car, Mia looked over her shoulder as she backed out of the parking space. Drive followed reverse as she switched gears and drove down the parking lane, picking up speed. She gave a quick glance into her rearview mirror to check if the ambulance was still there.

A pair of lifeless bloodshot eyes stared back.

The Hyundai's tires shrieked in protest as the car nose-dived to a sudden stop. She gasped and locked stares as the accusing eyes pierced hers and then rolled back into their sockets, showing blood red and white. A car behind Mia screeched to a halt inches from her bumper. His eyes rolled back to fix once again onto hers, but then looked away as if in a dreamlike state. His mouth continued to make the motions of words, but in deathly silence.

A blast of a car horn behind her made her jump, shaking her from her trance-like fix on the mirror and the sinister image it harbored. She knew she had to get her foot off the brake, but panic had frozen it in place. The impatient driver behind her aggressively squeezed by on the right, just narrowly missing her door, and laying on his horn the entire time. She could see his angry scowling face and his finger flipping her off, but it played like a silent movie set in slow motion. Her focus flicked from the snarling motorist back to the grisly phantom in her rearview.

Why am I seeing this? I must be insane. Oh God. What am I going to do? I've got to get home...

She twisted around to find the back seat of her car devoid of anyone. She returned her stare once again to the mirror. He grimaced back, his teeth outlined in blood that coursed down and around his lips.

A faint whisper from long ago began to fill her head, *The Lord is my shepherd, I shall not want...*

With her leg jogging up and down uncontrollably, she slipped her foot off the brake. The car crept along at idle speed.

Am I really going insane? He maketh me lie down in green pastures... Got to get home. Go to bed...

The thought of home beckoned her like a beacon light through a storm. Mia's hands were clenched in dead white knuckles around the steering wheel as her eyes nervously switched from the road to the gruesome visage in the mirror.

And though I may walk through the valley of the shadow of death.... Get me home. I didn't mean it... I didn't mean it... Home.

Her view of the road became blurry and out of focus as her eyes flooded with tears. At a few stoplights she broke down and wept openly helpless, frightened cries. Her Hyundai wove dangerously between lanes, ran red lights, and then failed to go on the green. Other motorists must have noticed her desperate state, but hurried on past her to their homes, jobs, errands, and lives. Mia had never felt so alone and vulnerable in her life.

As soon as she entered her house, she slammed the door shut behind her and locked it. She peered warily about her living room. She was safe here. Any possibility of "him" appearing was hidden away, cloaked behind the assorted blankets and linens that still enshrouded all the reflective surfaces of her house. After that last meeting with Gerry, Mia had intended on removing all the cover-ups. She was relieved now that she had never found the nerve to do so.

Still feeling shaky, she went directly to the kitchen counter where her diazepam vial stood and shook out the last three pills. She seized a bottle of wine from the refrigerator and downed the tiny pills, greedily gulping straight from the bottle. Mia had time only to cork the remaining wine, return it to the refrigerator and change out of her clothes before the room started to reel and the floor rolled beneath her feet.

The last thing she did before slipping off into a respite of unconsciousness was to grab Dan's pillow. It was his and gave her comfort. She curled up into a tight ball on her side and allowed herself to fall off the edge into the ensuing darkness.

I fear no evil for thou art with me....

◊ ◊ ◊

His eyes followed the monitors, searching through the segments for edit points, but his mind kept wandering back to her; the softness of her skin, the smooth curves of her body. He snapped to attention when he realized he had missed yet another edit point. With growing annoyance, he slapped at the computer mouse and flicked the scene back frame by frame, trying to concentrate on the pulse count to see where he had lost it.

Although this edit job was already taking twice as long as it should have because of his mind's detours, Dan decided to indulge himself some more by allowing his focus to drift back to thoughts of his wife. He missed her, even craved her, and this morning's lovemaking had open up a floodgate of desire that he had tried to keep stowed away through these long months of her grief and depression. Just the memory of feeling her body once more against his started to arouse him and he felt an erection coming on.

He immediately forced himself to focus on the balding interviewer on the screen and the elderly interviewee, trying to get his mind off of Mia. It had been a constant battle all day and he kept a watchful eye on the clock as the minutes gruelingly dragged on.

He sped all the way home, only stopping to buy flowers from a corner vendor. The house was dark and quiet when he entered and he was amazed to find her sleeping so early in the evening, somewhere under a mound of blankets piled upon the bed. Deciding to surprise her, he put the flowers in a vase with water and set them on her nightstand. Then he eagerly undressed and slipped in under the covers behind her.

When he pulled her close, he noticed she felt cool. He smelled her hair and then let his lips glide down the curve of her neck. She continued to lie still. Puzzled by her behavior, he rolled her onto her back. She softly murmured something, and then was quiet again.

Dan slid on top of her and studied her face for a few seconds. She looked so out of it that he debated whether or not to just let her sleep. He caressed her cheek with the back of his hand causing her to smile and nuzzle against it, so he kissed her, waiting for her lips to respond to his. They started to move against his own, but then rounded out into a scream.

Her eyes opened wide, staring at him, first in shock, then in horror. She pushed against him and fought hard, her arms flailing and clawing. He reflexively pulled back, trying to avoid her swings. She struck him across his jaw. At first, he was perplexed at her fearful reaction, then realized that she must be having a nightmare.

"Babe! Babe, shhh! It's all right! It's me," he tried to console, but she screeched and fought back even harder.

Her outstretched hand caught the vase of flowers at the edge of the nightstand and sent it crashing onto the hardwood floor. He scrambled to switch on the light while she continued to kick and tear at him with all of her might.

"Mia! Honey, wake up! You are only dreaming. C'mon Babe, you're all right." Pining her down by her shoulders, he was finally able to restrain her. "Hey, it's only me."

Through her tangled mass of hair, she finally recognized him and settled back onto the pillow. She lie there, trying to catch her breath, and looking up at him with terrified eyes.

"Are you okay, Honey? What were you dreaming? Man, you were fighting like a wildcat," he asked.

"I thought that you were…that you…."

"Huh? I was what?" he asked, concerned.

"That you were… Him. Nothing. I don't know anymore," she mumbled in a bewildered voice.

"Him? Him who? What are you talking about?"

Did someone do something to her? his mind questioned immediately.

"I can't explain, I don't think you'd understand. It's just too weird," she blurted out, then ashamedly averted her eyes.

"Tell me, what happened."

"No, it's okay. I feel better now."

Remembering what she had disclosed at her last session with Gerry, he knew he needed to pry. She could be stressing out again.

"Go ahead, try me. Were you seeing things again?"

She grew quiet. Then looking directly at him, she answered definitively, "Yes. I was."

He knew he had to handle this very carefully while trying to avoid setting her off into another one of her moods.

"Okay, now we're getting somewhere. What did you see?"

"I saw this thing. A man. And he was bleeding. He kept staring at me and saying something, but I couldn't make out what he wanted."

"Was he here? In the house?"

Her face turned dark, scowling. "No. At the store."

"So what was he doing? Was he following you? He didn't threaten you or anything, did he?"

"No, he just—just stared at me. And he kept saying something, over and over again. But I didn't know what it was."

"And this is what you were dreaming?"

Could she possibly be getting her dreams mixed up with reality? he wondered.

"Yes, I mean, no. I mean, I *saw* him at the store today. I came home, took my medication, and went to sleep. When you were on top of me, I thought that you were him."

"I'm sorry Murph, you're right, I don't understand. Okay, he was *just standing there*? In front of you?" Dan had tried to follow along, but it threw him.

"Yes. I mean, he was reflected at me, in the mirror display at the store. Then he appeared in my rearview mirror. And he kept looking at me with those dead eyes, but it was like he was seeing right through me. And he kept bleeding and bleeding all over the floor... I don't know. I was so frightened."

At that moment, she looked like a little girl. He instinctively wanted to protect and shelter her, but from *what*? He felt powerless. The feeling left him agitated and restless.

"Well, can you show him to me?"

"No, I don't think I can," she said tearfully.

He sucked up his patience, and then chose his words with care. "I don't know what I can do for you Mia. I want to help. Believe me, I really do, but I don't know what to do."

He pushed the pieces around in his head, but couldn't make them fit.

"So you said you *did* take your medication today?"

She nodded her head determinedly. "Yes I did. But this wasn't a hallucination. He was actually standing right in front—"

He cut her off. "Are you feeling stressed about something? I mean, this morning, you did want to fool around, didn't you? At least that's what it seemed."

"Now you're starting to sound like Gerry. Yes. Yes I did want to make love to you. But that's not the problem. I think this 'thing,' whatever it is, is following me."

The situation confused him. He had never experienced anything like this or even knew anyone who had. She persisted in personifying her stress and depression, and now it was "someone" stalking her.

"Babe, listen to yourself. You're taking this to a whole other level. Why don't you just try to relax and back off a bit? Don't worry about doing anything. Don't even worry about going back to work just yet. You're still recovering. Take all the time you need. I'm sure Loren will understand and if she doesn't, there's twenty zillion other magazines out there who would be happy to have you. Have you called about any of those stress management classes?"

"I don't need any damn classes!" she hissed through clenched teeth. "You are not listening to me. This thing is after me and whether or not I take any stupid classes will not stop him!" Her cheeks flushed and her eyes were shining with anger.

He knew he had better put on the brakes. The last thing he wanted to do was fight with her. Besides, all this additional stress would probably make matters worse.

"Mia…" he started, but was at a loss for words. What could he say to get her to come around? "I love you, Honey. I just want things to be better for you. For us. This morning made me realize how much we've missed. If we can only work together to get back to where we used to be."

"I don't want this any more than you do. I hate this! I hate being apart. I hate us fighting," she cried. Then looking into his eyes, she touched his face and implored, "But this is *real*. It's not stress. I know it isn't. It is as real as you and I. You have to understand that. I just don't know what to do to stop it."

Breaking away from her imploring gaze that always had to ability to capture his heart, he rolled onto his back and sighed. He realized there wasn't going to be any way to convince her. But now wasn't the time to keep pushing.

He figured that after she took her next round of medication, he would try to approach her once more about this. Maybe by then she could look at things more realistically. He rose from the bed and pulled his pants back on.

"Well, I'm going to get the broom and mop. If you're getting up, watch your feet. There's a big mess on your side. If you need anything, I'll be right back."

She peered over the side of the bed at the shattered vase upon the floor. Then she slipped out from the other side of the bed and walked around to the bright flowers lying scattered in a puddle of water. "Oh—did you get these for me? I'm sorry. They're beautiful," she said sadly as she crouched down and started to retrieve the flowers one by one, gathering them out of the water and shaking the jagged shards of glass from their petals.

While he rummaged around the broom closet for the bucket, he could hear a short stifled scream from their bedroom. Throwing down the mop in his hand, he bolted across the house, a few long strides getting him there in an instant. He found her huddled up against the dresser with her knees pulled up to her chest.

She whispered in a trembling voice, "He's there. Under the bed."

He knelt down on the floor and peered under the bed, but couldn't see anything but some boxes and suitcases stored there and a stray flower she was probably after. As he inched closer, his knees became wet from the water as he lifted the bed skirt to get a better look. For a second, something moved and caught his eye.

Could there really be something under here? he asked himself.

As he crawled in even closer, it continued to move. He squeezed himself under the bed until he came face to face with a twisted looking visage glaring back at him.

Then he reached for it.

Mia scrunched herself up even tighter and shook with fright as he dragged something out, working his way out from under the bed.

"Is this what you saw?" he asked as he placed a smoke-black plastic turntable cover by her feet.

It was from a retro component stereo system he had wanted to put back together. When she looked down at it, only her face mirrored back, bent and misshapen in the contours of the plastic. She studied it for a few moments.

With her eyes welling up with tears, she faced him, then rose and left the room. A stray carnation that had been caught in her lap tumbled to the floor and landed back in the water.

Dan watched her go. He wanted to call out to her but couldn't find the words.

Holy Shit. How could that have gone so wrong? he wondered. *Just what the hell is going on here?*

He thought that she was doing okay. This morning, it certainly didn't seem like anything was wrong. Was she having some sort of relapse? Or was this how things were going to continue to be?

This was way beyond him. He was confused and torn. His eyes drifted from the doorway where she had left to the top of their dresser where a framed, glassless photograph showed a happy, young couple honeymooning in Kauai. It was taken four years ago.

Back then, filled with the hope of sharing their lives together, their whole future lay open and bright before them. They hadn't any need for anyone or anything. And it seemed that back then, when they were madly in love, they believed that as long as they were together, they could face anything.

SIX

"HELLO? AUNT LYDIA?"

"Mia? Mia Pappas? Is that you darling?"

"Yes it is."

"Mia! How are you? It's been so long! Oh, this is wonderful!"

"I'm okay, Aunt Lydia. How are you?"

"Oh fine, dear. Fine. Just moving a little slower these days, you know what I mean? My bursitis is acting up in my shoulder and the corn on my right foot needs to be removed, but it's the same old thing. Anyway, you don't want to hear about all of that, I want to talk about you. How is everything? How is that handsome sailor of yours?"

"He's—uh, fine."

"You two look so beautiful in your wedding picture. I never did get to thank you for sending it to me. I have it hanging right here on my living room wall so I can look at it every day. Ever since you and your parents moved to the West Coast when you were little, I always think about you and wonder how you all are getting along."

"Oh, well, you're welcome. I'm glad that you enjoy it."

"My Little Potatoes. Remember when I use to call you that? You were just a little thing. I'd say 'Mia Pappas? My Potatoes?' And you'd laugh and laugh. You were cuter than a button."

"Yes, I remember that now. You use to call me that whenever I'd climb up into your lap...Uh, how's Evelyn and Bobby?"

"Evelyn's doing wonderful! She's a teacher up north and loves it. She teaches English to high schoolers and a writing course at the community college too! This past summer, she just completed the rest of her Master's degree at Oxford, can you imagine? And I guess Robert's doing fine. He's some big hoo-hah lawyer in Vegas now working for one of the casinos—the Mirage? The MGM? I don't know. I get them all mixed up. No, he hardly calls anymore. I get a phone call from him a couple of times a year. He's too busy making money! But that's just Robert... And your mother's doing well, I presume?"

"Yes, she's doing fine. Currently, she's on a pilgrimage to the Holy Land. Her gr—"

"Uh huh, and how's your dad?"

There was an audible gasp. "What do you mean?"

"Your poppa. Did he go with Margaret too? Or is he just hanging out at home by himself enjoying the peace and quiet? He probably needs a little break from her, eh?" she chuckled.

There was silence on the line.

And then, "You mean, you don't know? I don't know how to tell you this.... I thought you knew.... H-he's dead, Aunt Lydia. He died last February of a heart attack. I'm sorry. I thought that Mom had contacted you..."

"Stephanos! Dead? Ohmigod.... I'm sorry Mia...Oh, Stephanos... You know, I should've known. Whenever I looked at his and your mother's picture, I just wasn't sensing an energy force from him lately. A heart attack! Oh blessed man... I'll miss him ..."

"I'm so sorry you had to hear about him like this, Aunt Lydia. Honestly, I thought you knew."

"It's okay, darling, it's okay.... He was such a good man. Decent, gentle... always kind. Tell me, did he journey well?"

"Uh, yes. He did."

"Thank God. It's always comforting to know when someone you love has left this world on good terms. He certainly was a good man. There are not too many people out there like him... No, they're a rare few. I'm going to miss him. Yes, I'm really going to miss him...."

There was a small cry heard over the line, followed by some sniffling.

"Aunt Lydia? I'm sorry..."

"Damn it all! You know, I never knew what he saw in my sister. They were not made for each other. At all." Pause. Then, "But I know what he meant to you. How are you holding up, Honey?"

"It's been hard. I miss him so much. There are days in which I go to talk to him, as if he were still there."

"And you always will. It's perfectly understandable. I still miss my Benny and it's been eighteen years already."

More silence on the line.

"Are you okay, Auntie?"

"Yes, Honey. I'm okay now. When you get to my age, you get use to people you know checking out of this world on a regular basis and you always keep your hanky handy. Now child, tell me what's really the matter. Why did you call Auntie? I love to hear from you, but I can sense something is not right. I had a dream just the other night that you were tumbling down through the earth. Down into some dark place. I couldn't make it out—it was some kind of pit or tunnel. You were lost and couldn't find your way out. I wanted to pick up the phone and call you, but I didn't want you to get a scare from an old kook like me."

"You're not an 'old kook' Aunt Lydia! But...I'm fine. Really."

"Come on, this is your aunt that you are talking to. I appreciate you calling to say hi, but I know there's a bigger reason at hand."

"It's sort of hard to explain."

"You know, there are some things in life that can never be explained. They just happen and we have to find the best way to deal with them. Now, what is going on, Mia?"

"Well, I've been under a lot of stress lately, and I've been seeing a therapist and- "

"Don't *explain* to me darling, *tell* me."

Silence, and then, "I called you because you've always seemed to know about these kinds of things and I think you would understand. I—I've been seeing, I don't know... some kind of presence? But it's EVERYWHERE. No matter where I go, it seems to find me. But it looks more like a someone, I guess. I don't know..."

"You *have?* Go on dear, I'm listening."

"It's a, a man, I think. At first he showed up in reflections about my house, on anything with a shiny surface like glass and metal. It was hard to make him out and I thought it was just my eyes playing tricks on me. But a couple of days ago, he showed up at the department store while I was shopping. He appeared in a bunch of mirrors that were on display."

"Really! That *is* unusual. And have you seen him since?"

"No. I've locked myself in my house. I haven't gone anywhere. I keep all of my mirrors and other things covered up so I won't see him. I don't *want* to see him. I don't know what else to do. Dan and I have been fighting because I can't make him understand what is happening. I even tried to show him, but of course he doesn't see this thing. No one does, Aunt Lydia. I think I might be going insane or something...I don't know what to do or who to turn to anymore."

"Don't cry, Mia, sh, sh, don't cry. It's all right, Honey. You've called the right person. Auntie will always be here for you, okay? Hmmm, let me see… It's a person you say? A man?"

"Yes. I don't know why I see that. I don't even know if I'm just imagining it. Everyone tells me I'm hallucinating, but this is too real to be a hallucination."

"I have to ask you, Mia, do you trust your old aunt?"

"Why, yes, Aunt Lydia. I do."

"Well, you're going to have to trust what I tell you then. I've been in this business a long time. So I've seen quite a few, let's say, strange phenomenon. And what I have found is, after all these years, if you say it is so, then it is. Forget about what others are telling you what you are seeing or what you should be feeling. They don't have the right to tell you that because they are not in your shoes. Right off, you need to accept what you are seeing. Let yourself believe, okay? That's the first step. I know these occurrences can be upsetting at first, but in time you'll get use to them. It's really not so hard once you learn to let yourself go. Can you do that, Honey?"

"I- I guess…"

"Now tell me, how does this man appear to you?"

"My therapist was saying that it's probably happening when I'm under a lot of stress. I'm just manifesting my-"

"No, not when, *how*. Does he look like anything in particular? What is he wearing?"

"Oh…He's wearing some kind of black jacket or coat. It has a hood that he keeps up, so I can't see his face really well. There's blood on his face and all down the front of him, and dirt and mud. And he has cold lifeless eyes. … It's all so horrible and bizarre. He frightens me."

"Can you tell me, does he appear light or dark, Mia? What I mean is that when you see him, does he have any kind of bright aura surrounding him or a darkness about him?"

"Dark, I think. Yes, I'm pretty sure…"

"Mmmmm. All right. Yes."

"Does that mean something? Is it important?"

"Very important. It sounds like you are dealing with an oppressed and unhappy source, child. The soul is probably trapped somehow or on its way to being lost."

"A lost soul? I don't understand. What does he want with *me*?"

"Why, he's reaching out to you, Mia. Yes. For some reason he has selected you. Maybe you are sensitive, or perhaps you are linked to him through some sort of emotion or feeling. But somehow or another you have connected with him on his plane. There are some of us in this world who can only sense these beings. Other people are so blunt, they don't sense them at all. You, my dear, are one of the lucky ones. You can actually *see* one!"

"Lucky? No, I'm sorry. I can't consider myself lucky to go through this. And linked through some kind of feeling? The only feeling I have is sheer terror and revulsion whenever I see him. I can't accept this, it can't be happening! Spirits don't exist."

"I know it's hard to believe at first, but they do."

"But this is pretend stuff—ghosts, evil spirits, the boogey man! No wonder my husband thinks I'm cracked."

"Open your mind, Mia. Just as we are alive and walking about this earth, there are beings not of this physical world walking right alongside of us every day in their own spiritual dimension. Their energy that they used for living is still being held together somehow, instead of being freed into the universe where it can be reused again. I'm sure your mother taught you about the Holy Spirit, didn't she?"

"Aunt Lydia! That's completely different! You can't expect me to—"

"Is it now? Other spirits may not be as powerful as the Holy Ghost, but they exist just the same."

"It sounds almost blasphemous…"

"Now I hear your mother talking. You know, she could never open her mind enough to crawl out of her bible. Not even for you or your father."

"But I don't know about *this*…"

"You will and in time you will come to understand. Let yourself free, child, and accept what is. Embrace this wonderful gift that has been given you."

"But what am I going to do? Will he continue to stalk me?"

"Yes. I believe he will, until he makes contact with you. He's desperate because his soul must be in terrible danger. He might be eternally lost for good. Damned to Hell or some other God forsaken place."

"Until he makes contact? With me? What kind of contact? And why should I let him? He's horrible and frightening. Wouldn't it be better if he were lost?"

"No, darling. We, as the living, cannot turn our backs on the nonliving. We are the only ones to help them get to where they need to go. Why do you think we pray so much for the departed? We still hold the life force, they don't. You are the only hope in saving his soul and you've been given an incredible challenge. It will be hard, but you have to keep in mind that you will be *saving* someone, someone who probably doesn't have anyone out there who cares enough about him. Someone who will be doomed perhaps, for an eternity."

"No. No, I can't believe this. This sounds like something out of a horror movie. Besides, what if I don't want to do this? I can't deal with all of this right now. I really can't! My life is out of control, Aunt Lydia. I don't know how much I can put Dan through. First it was Daddy, and then I… we lost our baby a few months ago. I had a miscarriage."

"Oh Mia. My dear, dear Mia…. I am so sorry."

"So you see why I can't handle this. Even if this person was real, I couldn't help him anyway. I can hardly save myself right now."

"Well child, do as you must. But I believe dealing with him directly and as soon as possible will be the only way you can get it to stop. Should you ever want to try, all you would have to do is relax and open your mind. Let him communicate with you."

"Communicate? How?"

"You'll know when you see it. Each one has their own individual way of going about it."

"No. There's got to be some other way to deal with all of this. Maybe I'll call my therapist about adjusting my dosage again. It's probably just that. I think I'm getting stressed out again, that's all."

"Are you sure that you don't want to at least make contact? It'll be the only way."

"No. This is crazy. If I go that route, I don't know if I'll ever make it back from the deep end. And Dan will never understand it. He'll really think I'm insane, and I couldn't blame him. I'll just call my therapist. I'm sure it's a dosage problem again, come to think of it… I'm really sorry to have laid this all on you. I just wasn't thinking clearly."

"All right then. But please call me and let me know how you are doing either way, okay dear?"

"I will." Silence, and then after a brief moment, "Aunt Lydia, I hope you don't mind me asking, but have you ever experienced anything like this before?"

"Like what?"

"Seeing 'ghosts' or 'visions' in mirrors or anything like that?"

"Well I have communicated with many spirits through my channeling and power séances. But, no, unfortunately. Truthfully, I haven't ever gotten to see one. I only wish I could."

"Have you ever known anyone who has?"

"No, not really. Although Mother had mentioned seeing things before her Episode. When we were young, Margaret and I always thought she had an active imagination. And now, in retrospect, I've got to wonder. Maybe you got your gift from your grandma. I wish you could have met her."

"Oh. Well, it um, has really helped to talk to you but I've got to get going. Thank you for listening to me."

"Anytime dear, anytime. It was so good to hear your voice again. Please send Dan my love."

"I will."

The telephone repairman unclipped his portable unit from the connection in the box. Running the line checks for polarity feedback in new installations often were boring and tedious, but occasionally he hit upon some interesting calls or better yet, really hot ones. There's nothing like eavesdropping on a little phone sex to make for an interesting lunch break.

"What a bunch of whackos," he said out loud to himself while packing up his equipment and going over everything he had just heard in his mind.

This weird ass conversation on "spirits" and "the unliving" he just overheard really took the prize. He wanted to make sure he got all the details right to tell his wife. Joanne was never going to believe this one.

Although he was still feeling a little creepy over what he had overheard, surprisingly, he found himself feeling sorry for the young woman on the line. She sounded like she needed a one-way ticket to the peanut farm, not encouragement from some crackpot who was not all there herself. That old bat was only confusing her and filling her head with all that spiritualism new age crap. It just wasn't healthy.

As he climbed into his service truck in the alleyway behind the old lady's house, he decided to step up on the doorjamb of the truck, curiosity egging him on to peek into her yard. Through the golden haze of the afternoon sun, he could see at least two dozen assorted wind chimes and sun catchers fringing the sagging back porch, each errant breeze setting off a concert of chimes. Several overweight cats loitered about the herb garden and yard overgrown with weeds and uncut grass. Her cracked rear window sparkled and twinkled with the refraction of a hundred or more crystal pendants catching the sunlight.

"Um hmm, just what I thought. Bunch of whackos," he muttered disgustedly under his breath. With that, he lowered himself back into the truck, slammed the door shut and drove off down the alley leaving nothing behind but a spray of rock and dust.

◊ ◊ ◊

The rectangular hallway lights overhead zipped by in rapid succession, much like the passing white stripes on the freeway whenever she drove too fast. She tried to lift her head to look forward, but as soon as she did, another cramp would grip her, causing her to recoil in pain. A cool hand took up hers, and when she glanced over, there was Dan, pale and concerned. His jacket and hair were dripping from the rain outside.

"It's gonna be all right, Honey, just hang in there. I'm right here. I'm right here," he said as if the words themselves could protect her.

She watched him running alongside her gurney, keeping pace with the medical team while trying to keep his eye on her to make sure she was all right. She was on the verge of saying something to reassure him, when another contraction hit. This one radiated from her back, making her clutch his hand with such force she wondered how his bones didn't break. She gritted her teeth trying to hold back the groan that escaped past her lips.

"Remember to breathe, Mia. Breathe!" he reminded her, seeming to ignore the death grip she had on his hand.

But Mia didn't want to breathe. To willfully start all those deep-breathing exercises would mean that she was in labor. And she couldn't possibly be in labor because it was too early. Way too early. At only nineteen weeks into her pregnancy, the baby didn't have any possible chance of surviving. She held her breath and clenched her bottom, trying to force herself to sustain a Kegel hold. She was going to keep this baby in with all her of her will and strength, with every fiber of her being.

She had little control of much else. Next she was lifted and settled onto the table in the delivery room; a pelvic exam; being hooked up to monitors; Dan's continual coaching.

Slicing through all the commotion, the nurse's voice at the door was telling someone outside the room, "This one's coming on fast. She's already nine centimeters and one hundred percent effaced. Uh huh, there's some vaginal bleeding too… Yeah, looks like she's about to abort…"

But how could that be? Despite her daylong cramping and bleeding, the baby was doing fine. Twenty-seven minutes ago, she had just seen an active and very vital little boy on the ultrasound monitor. Oh, how she wanted her husband to be there to see their son. The ultrasound tech had patiently waited as long as she could until Dan phoned to say he had been delayed by a traffic accident. They had to give up the room and she had to be wheeled to OBGYN, stat.

No. She was determined to hold this baby in. Next, a sharp sting of a needle and a burning sensation - an IV had been inserted, opaque adhesive tape forming an "X" on the back of her wrist.

"I want to keep my baby," she panted, though no one seemed to be listening to her through all the activity. "Please help me keep my baby... please!"

The technician stared at her, not responding, and then checked the IV line. Mia clenched even tighter and curled up on her left side, feeling the burn of the IV line in her vein as she pulled against it. Another contraction encircled her middle like a noose and started to slowly squeeze the tiny new life out of her body. She felt hands roll her onto her back, pull up her legs and guide her feet into cold metal stirrups.

"NO!" she cried out in panic.

Dan hovered over her in an instant, brushing back her bangs from her sweaty brow and clinging to her hand repeating, "Hang in there, Mia. Hang in there..."

She moved her mouth to speak again, but all she could manage was a squeal of pain.

Instead, her thoughts screamed, *My baby is alive! He is staying with me. Stop! Can't you see that you will kill him?*

Mia grabbed her husband's arm and struggled to get up off the delivery table, her instincts begging her to flee. She could see herself running out in her bare feet, clothed only in the hospital gown, and carrying her baby away to safety. The contractions were continuous now, and another heavy one paralyzed her, keeping her down. Within the next moment, a warm watery feeling flowed from between her legs. At first she thought she had lost control of her bladder, and then realized that her water had broke.

The obstetrician produced a needle and swiftly injected her with a local anesthetic. Then he rubbed and patted the inside of her bare thigh trying to get her to relax. The nurse stood ready with a blue surgical cloth stretched out between her two hands like a net. Mia gritted her teeth as she clenched down, a desperate feeling of knowing this was her last chance of holding on, of saving her child. A powerful sustained contraction ensued, her own muscles betraying her. Her body went rigid and a burning sensation flared up in her crotch. A sudden feeling of mass rushed from within her.

Oh God, the baby is out.

Breathing heavily, she brought her chin to her chest and hoisted herself up on her elbows to peer down between her legs. All she could see was a tiny lifeless body, white and slippery, and a purplish, spiral umbilical cord still trailing back to its life source.

She could hear Dan's voice softly saying, "It's all over now, Honey…"

The figures in the room suddenly seemed motionless causing alarm to plant itself deep within her heaving chest. They needed to be working on the infant, but they weren't.

"What are you doing? Why aren't you doing anything to save my baby? Please help him!" she sobbed.

The world instantly slowed to a crawl while her head filling with the intense buzzing sound of a thousand flies. She looked towards the doctor, pleading with him to save her son. When he pulled his mask down and stared back, his face went gaunt, gray and haggard. Then his eyes turned glassy and red, rolling back in his head. Blood started to pour out of his nose, running crimson rivulets around the corners of his mouth and coursing down upon his mud caked boots.

She saw him snatch up her son, still covered in mucus and blood, holding him carelessly by his tiny ankle. The doctor bared his stained teeth at the infant as if he would bite and tear at him at any moment. Mia lunged forward to take back her baby, but the IV had become a cable, strapped across her body, holding her wrists tight against the rails.

She screamed and looked to Dan, but as he leaned close, his face became bent and misshapen, distorted beyond recognition. The nurse started to pray out loud in a high sing-song voice like a siren, lifting her hands upwards to heaven, while the surgical cloth caught on fire in her arms, its fiery ashes dropping to the floor, unnoticed.

Mia screamed and grappled towards the doctor, but he fixed his dead eyes upon her, mouthing silent words over and over again, tentatively holding onto her baby boy slick with afterbirth, swinging him like a pendulum. Threatening to drop the helpless child at any moment.…

Mia sprung up in bed, sobbing uncontrollably and trying to catch her breath. Her adrenaline pumping, she looked about, prepared to fight anything. Residual images of the nightmare continued to flash before her eyes against the darkness of their bedroom. It took a few minutes for every last one of the grisly scenes to slowly fade away and her racing heart to finally slow down.

This was her fourth night of nightmares and fitful sleep. Her renewed prescription of sleeping pills seemed to hardly have any affect at all unless she took double doses of it downed with wine. Every morning, it was getting harder to wake up, yet every evening, it was harder to get to sleep. She looked over at Dan, sleeping heavily and undisturbed. How she longed to return to that state of peace.

But It was on her mind constantly. The frightening image invaded her thoughts throughout all times of the day and night, during any task she undertook, whether she was trying to cook a simple meal, or watch a TV show, or take a shower. She continued to keep everything covered about the house, hiding away from his accusing eyes. Perhaps she was obsessing about the phantom. No, she knew this was different. It was as if he pushed his way into the recesses of her mind, forcing her to think about him against her will.

The reflection distracted her so much she didn't go anywhere, call anyone, or have anyone over for visits. It was no use anyway. Whom could she talk to about this aside from Aunt Lydia? Everyone else was leading normal sane lives. Her two closest friends had moved to other states years ago and were busy having babies and raising families. Jenna was away at college, and the senior Labonts were taking their cross-country RV trip. Her own mother remained in the Holy Land. Besides, who out of all of them would listen to her bizarre stories without trying to commit her?

She considered calling PartnersHealth to see about adjusting her dosage once more. But each time she picked up the phone, she promptly returned it to its cradle. She knew they were only going to tell her what they've been telling her all along: let the medication take its time. Undoubtedly, they wouldn't be much help.

"Do what you must. But remember this will be the only way you can get it to stop..."

As much as the idea repulsed her, she considered her aunt's advice. What if she did try to make contact? If it *was* just a hallucination as everyone said, maybe she could make herself somehow not to see it anymore. And if it *wasn't* a hallucination, but truly a spirit? It troubled her to consider that possibility. All in all, she knew she couldn't tolerate her imprisonment much longer.

As she lay sleepless in her bed, she fervently recited Hail Mary's over and over again and waited for the morning light to arrive, hours yet away. Her eyes peered through the darkness and fixed upon the covered items hanging on her bedroom wall. She knew that he was lurking behind each one, biding his time to get to her. There was no one to turn to and help her out of all of this. There was nothing else she could do but the inevitable and the insane....

The next morning after Dan had gone to work, she stood across from the mirror in her living room. Contemplating its large square shape, she remembered how happy she had been when she discovered the glass in an out-of-the-way flea market in San Diego when she and Dan were first married. Now it hung ominous and foreboding, shrouded under an old quilt, harboring one of her worst fears. She didn't have to do this. Once she started on this odyssey, there would be no turning back.

But where am I now?

Bracing herself, Mia took a deep breath and gingerly tugged at the quilt. As it slipped away from the frame and crumpled to the floor, she let her eyes follow its descent not wanting to face what she expected in the glass. She choked back her fear, and with her heart trying to beat a hole in her chest, she determinedly raised her eyes and looked directly into the mirror.

Her own face stared back, catching her off guard. Anxiously, she searched the reflection of the room in every inch of the mirror's surface, looking at each corner, studying every shadow. But there was no one else present but her. How could that be? She was so sure that after all this time, he would be waiting there, ready to pounce and terrify once more.

Mustering up more courage, she timidly removed a few more cover-ups about the room. With each subsequent unveiling, she discovered no one there but herself. Pushing herself, she continued.

The minutes passed. Oddly, as she revealed each surface, she felt nothing short of a small victory and a growing feeling of control—the first time she had felt that way in months. The tables were being turned back in her favor. She was now seeking *him* out to confront him. She was no longer the prey. Her confidence mounting, she tore off the rest of the cover-ups about the house.

"Where are you? Where *are you*, you son of a bitch…?" she grumbled angrily as she searched for the elusive specter. "Why won't you show yourself now!" she screamed out loud in the empty house, as her sense of power surged.

For the remainder of the day, nothing could keep her from scrutinizing and searching all reflections, keeping a wary eye open for his reappearance. She considered leaving the house, just to take a break, but decided that should he show up outside somewhere, there was no way she could be prepared. Although she was victorious in her own home, she didn't feel quite brave enough yet to encounter him anywhere else in the real world. At home, she maintained some control with blankets on hand to hold off any appearance.

However, no image appeared before her anywhere throughout the house. A strange mix of relief yet disappointment overcame her, though she wondered how long her confidence would hold out should he reappear again.

When Dan came home, he noticed everything uncovered once again, but he kept silent. He seemed to be playing his own watching game and Mia knew she was his subject. Many times out of the corner of her eye, she would catch him studying her, making her feel as if she were some kind of microbe on a slide. She also knew by his manner of speaking, that he had been hedging a lot of questions lately, being sure to stick to safe topics and saying nothing to set her off. So, the remainder of the week passed in the same quiet manner for husband and wife, both living day to day in anxious but separate vigilance.

◊ ◊ ◊

The last dish was rinsed free of food and stacked in the dishwasher with the others. Thinking of her next chore to do, she fished her cleaning tote out of the storage closet and moved on to the bathroom. Another week had trickled by without any more sightings, yet she couldn't relax, always wondering if and when 'he' was going to ever come back. Her nightmares continued almost on a nightly basis. Fatigue and worry started to line her face and a drop in weight showed on her already lean frame.

During her session with Gerry, Mia alluded to the fact that things still were off-kilter, but since nothing had appeared since that time at the store, she didn't mention anything to him about it. The therapist wasn't astute enough to sense any other problems, although she was relieved he didn't. The more she formulated an explanation of the specter in her head, the sillier it sounded. She was ready to give up and discount her previous episodes as mini-breakdowns of sorts.

Life continued with its endless routine of chores and tasks, and today was no different. First it was cleaning the bathroom; after that mopping the kitchen floor. She was grateful to keep busy. On her way through the living room, she glanced up at the mirror as she had gotten into the habit of doing.

All at once he *was there*, menacing and horrid, looking directly at her. Her tote slipped away from her outstretched fingers and crashed to the floor, tumbling supplies and cleaning tools in all directions. No matter how much she had rehearsed exactly what she would do if she ever saw him again, he still held the power to terrify her.

He looked like he had before, when he had appeared at the store—sinister and wretched. The difference now was that he had succeeded in invading her home completely, standing life-sized before her, with unbelievable and undeniable clarity in her own safe haven. Her only instinct was to scream, but this time she stifled it by swallowing hard, getting her rapid breath under control. She forced herself to focus on what she needed to do next.

Determination spoke to her. *It's now. I've got to make contact now.*

Her body broke out in a cold sweat all over. Trembling, she reigned in her terror, stood her ground, and then raised her eyes to meet his.

At this show of unexpected defiance from her, he bared his teeth, while blood flowed into and around his mouth. His eyes rolled upward, showing their bloodshot whites, closed, and then refocused on his subject. He lunged suddenly at her. Mia gasped and reflexively stepped back, her stomach wrenching and twisting with fear and panic. But her own will halted her retreat. She steadfastly stared him down once more. He scowled in return, his brow creasing with rage. His sneering mouth started moving in the now familiar patterns, cracked and bleeding lips shaping the same muted syllables over and over again.

Seconds ticked by and she held her stance, shaking uncontrollably but keeping her gaze trained on the image in the mirror. It was a battle of the wills between them. Mia tried to keep her eyes locked with his, but for a sheer moment, her courage slipped, making her unable to maintain a steady fix on the gruesome face. His red-rimmed eyes seemed to penetrate to her very soul. Feeling vulnerable and exposed, she lowered her stare.

In that moment of timidness, her gaze fell upon his chest. There, she noticed something odd—a bit of yellow showing through the grayness and dirt on his jacket. Above his right breast, she could barely make out what looked like Roman block letters, silk-screened in yellow: WI—OL. A black patch of blood-caked dirt blocked the middle portion of the words, making the rest illegible. Dumbfounded by what she had spied, she studied the insignia even harder, trying to make out the rest of it. This "ghost" had lettering printed on his jacket!

With her discovery, her eyes crept back to his. He still held his countenance, but he had lost the scowl. Instead, his eyes were wide and bewildered as apprehension found its way onto his own face. Her curiosity edging out fear, she contemplated him for a minute longer, puzzled by his change in reaction.

She went to study the letters once more, but he suddenly vanished, his disappearance jarring her as if she had been awakened by the snap of a hypnotist's fingers. She put her hand to her forehead and stepped back, reeling. The room felt like it was spinning and she was filled with a heady relief. Looking back at the mirror, all she saw was herself, searching for something that wasn't there.

Feeling slightly disorientated, she found that her knees ached. She let them fold under her as she sunk to the floor amidst the scattered cleansers. She took a deep breath and her eyes watered, reacting from the release. It took her a couple of minutes to get her frenzied thoughts in order.

Did she just make contact with a spirit? The idea astounded her. Aunt Lydia could be right. All this time, Mia never entertained the notion that spirits actually existed. It was the stuff of horror movies and fairy tales.

But he was real. There was no denying it now. The idea that she was dealing with some sort of supernatural being was the only thing that made sense out of all of this madness now. The only other alternative would be to believe she was losing her mind.

This paranormal business is true, she deduced. *I've seen it myself!*

What's more, Mia couldn't believe she had stuck it out. She never knew she had that sort of strength. And, amazingly, he *couldn't do anything back*. No matter how horrible and terrorizing he was, he couldn't touch her.

The realization intrigued her. Recalling Aunt Lydia's words, the thought of saving a lost soul flashed through her mind. Mia took a few moments to wrestle with this dilemma. If, indeed, what she was experiencing was true and not some hallucinogenic breakdown, she reasoned that she could get on with her life if she saved him. And in turn, once he was saved, it would prove that she was not crazy at all. Although a baffling conundrum, she decided to take a chance. She would continue. It was her only hope of surviving this nightmare.

This newfound sense of direction gave her fresh courage and in return, sparked more of her curiosity. Just who was that person in the reflection? What did he want? How did he wind up there? And what about those letters on his jacket? What did they mean? Hundreds of questions popped into her head about the phantom. She continued to toss them around while she gathered her cleaning supplies and headed back to the kitchen.

A quick glance at the clock reminded her it was time to take her medication. A small part of her wasn't completely convinced that she was seeing ghosts and she knew had better continue her treatment regardless of what she saw. All the while, she considered her next step in conquering her new adversary. She shook the tablets from their vials and popped them into her mouth, rolling them around on her tongue before they finally slipped down her throat.

◊ ◊ ◊

On Saturday morning, the toaster popped up two burnt pieces of toast just as Mia went to receive them on a plate. It was apparent she had forgotten to adjust the setting.

"Oh shoot," she said to herself as she examined them. Snatching up the blackened pieces of bread, she hoped to chuck them into the trash before Dan noticed.

He did. "Here, Honey. Let me get that. I can do the toast if you want."

"No, it's okay. I got it. You're already making the eggs, and, well, everything else," she said as she surveyed the fried bacon, cut fruit, and set table.

"Are you sure? I don't mind," he said, eyebrow raised.

"Of course I'm sure. I think I can at least handle toast," she snapped defensively, and then regretted it.

Her period was still off track from the miscarriage, so she wasn't sure how much of this was PMS or Dan just getting on her nerves with his watchdog approach. He hadn't let up for the past couple of weeks. He alternated between being immensely concerned with her—trying to make her eat more, turning up the heat in the house, and covering her with blankets—to being aloof and silent whenever she tried to discuss what she had been experiencing.

"I'm not saying that you can't. I was just trying to give you a hand. Listen, forget it."

He jerked open the refrigerator door and took out the orange juice. His own mood didn't seem much better. They avoided each other as they prepared breakfast, moving stiffly about the other. When they sat down to eat, there was an awkward silence after she said grace.

"So, what are you planning on doing today?" he finally ventured after a minute or two, breaking the ice.

"I don't know yet. Some things about the house, I guess. Why?"

"Nothing, I was just wondering, that's all."

They continued to eat, the sound of their forks scraping their plates filling the void between them.

"Why? What do you have planned?"

He tried a smile and raised his eyebrows. "Well, I was hoping that maybe we could do something, I dunno. Do you want to see a movie? Or maybe we could even take a drive somewhere. How about the beach? Or the trail? You know, make a day of it. It's been a while since we've picked a day to goof off."

"Oh, I don't know, Murph. How about some other time? I really need to catch up on some of the things I've started around here," she lied.

Two more days had passed since the break through. She hung around waiting anxiously for another appearance, determined to make contact again. Dan being home on the weekend came at a bad time.

"Okay," he said, his eyes dulling with disappointment. "I guess I have things that I need to get done around here myself."

She watched him as he ate his breakfast, his eyes fixed on his plate. If only there was a way she could discuss her attempts at communicating with the spirit in the mirror, it could might clear the air between them. But since that afternoon when she tried to explain the hallucination at the store to him, he never asked her again about her sightings. Once more, they had slipped back to the strained and evasive conversations from before.

"Uh, how about next weekend? I'm right in the middle of what I am doing and just want to finish what I've started. I'm on a roll of sorts," she offered. "You know how that is?"

"Sure. Whatever."

Mia could tell by the way he pushed his food about his plate that he was put out. Trying not to resent his reaction, she finally conceded. If that thing showed up again, it would just have to wait for her.

"I guess we can go play today. What do you want to do?" She feigned interest, complete with a smile.

"Never mind. It doesn't matter. You've got your stuff to do and I've got plenty I can do," he said, standing up and taking his unfinished breakfast to the sink.

"Aw, c'mon, Murph. Don't be like that. Let's go out. I hear that movie, *Hunting For Shadows* is supposed to be good. It sounds like your kind of film, with lots of action."

She came up behind him and hugged him, laying her head against his back. He remained rigid.

"No. I said forget it. I've got to get going."

He pulled out of her arms and stalked off to the other room. She hated when he acted like this.

"Well, where are you going? Hey —what's up with you?" she called after him and then decided to follow.

"The hardware store, okay? And why are you asking *me* what's up? What's been up with you?"

"Huh? What do you mean?"

He fished out a shirt and jeans from the chest of drawers, slamming each drawer as he went.

"You've been so damned moody lately, I can hardly talk to you. You know, for a minute there, I thought that maybe things were getting better, but I guess I was wrong."

"I'm sorry that I've been moody, but I've got a lot of things on my mind lately."

He turned to her. "Like what? Geez, Mia, if you never tell me, how the hell am I supposed to know? I'm not clairvoyant, in case you've been too busy to notice."

"I've tried to tell you a few times, but you don't want to hear anything about it," she said defensively.

"What, you mean like 'scary things' in mirrors and blood on wash rags, and all of that? I thought you were taking your medication and everything was getting straightened out."

"I *am* taking my medication, but I'm still… seeing things."

"Uh huh. Like the stereo dust cover under the bed," he grumbled sarcastically.

Her cheeks flushed red. "That's not fair."

"Yeah, like you've been treating *me* fairly. I can understand with the miscarriage and all why you were depressed. But then things started looking up. The next I know, you're jumping me for sex. And then crying and moping again. And now you're back to your silent treatment. Anymore, I don't know what to expect from you. I can't keep up. You know, this whole situation is shit but I can't do a damned thing about it.

"I've tried to be as supportive as I could. I've listened to you and tried to console you. I was the one who made the appointment for you to see the shrink, for Chrissakes. Listen, I swore to myself that I would never bring this up, but what the hell? We could've been back in San Diego right now earning more money if I didn't have to pass on that technical producer position last spring. But I wanted to give you a chance to get through all of this instead of dragging you back down the Coast and disrupting your life even more. I've made concessions and sacrifices.

"So, I give up. Okay? I'm tired of all the ups and downs. I figure that when you are ready to help yourself and ready to turn this whole thing around once and for all, you'll do it. In the meantime, I'll just do what I have to do." He yanked on his trekkers and pulled the laces tight, tying them with short angry strokes.

She was shocked by his reply. Did he really think that she held the power to stop this?

"It's not that easy!" she said in defense. "If it were, this whole ordeal would have been over and done with a long time ago. Do you think I *like* what this is doing to us? I know you've been supportive and I've told you before how sorry I am that you let that position go. But I'm just asking you to be a little more patient and try to understand that I hate this more than you do. And I have to live it every day!"

"Then quit already! Put your mind to it and make yourself quit. Don't you get it? You are the person in control of this situation. You are the only one who can make it happen. Not me. Not Monroe. *You,*" he emphasized, pointing a finger at her.

"I can't. Believe me, I've tried! But apparently it's not up to me," she answered, exasperated.

"Then who? And don't tell me it's up to that 'whatever-it-is' in the reflections."

She couldn't answer.

"All right then. I'm out of here."

"No, you're not listening. That's what I'm talking about. I've tried to explain this all to you, but it doesn't fit your nice neat logic. Instead, you insist on it being what you believe it to be instead of trying to be more open-minded and seeing it from my perspective. You're hearing only what you want to hear, and when that doesn't agree with you, you stop listening," Mia insisted. She found this conversation with him to be maddening.

"I *have* listened, but you keep shutting me out. You talk about fairness? Why wouldn't you tell me what you were seeing that night on the TV screen, or the real reason you ruined all the doorknobs and fixtures in this house, or your need to increase your medication? I had to find it all out when you told that asshole at PartnersHealth. Now where does that leave me? You know, I'm beginning to wonder if you don't mind this little fantasy world that you're in."

Hearing this accusation, her face flushed with anger. "Fantasy world! And what do you mean, 'I'm shutting you out'? I've told you everything! The problem is you can't accept it! You'd rather believe that I'm going nuts and somehow place the fault on me then to think that for just one minute, there *could actually* be something there."

He stopped short, his eyes wide with disbelief.

Then he smirked, "What? In the reflections? No. That's totally asinine! You really expect me to believe that there's some kind of goddam spook lurking in our house, following you around, hiding in mirrors, and showing up on shiny jars and other shit?"

She looked him square in the eye, challenging him. "Yes I do. What is so hard to believe?"

He shook his head, then pulled his fleece pullover on and headed out of the bedroom with long strides. She had to scurry to keep up with him, but he did not slow down.

"Why aren't you listening to me now? There *is* someone in the reflections! I have seen him several times already and I expect to see him again, soon. When I do, I'm going to try to communicate with him. I *have* to."

Dan grabbed up his keys and opened the door. "I'm outta here."

She called after him as he walked down the sidewalk. He didn't answer as he hopped into the Jeep, started it, and backed out, the tires chirping on the street as he accelerated. Mia watched him speed off. She slowly closed the door, feeling angry and frustrated at his words.

Why can't he believe? He wanted an explanation. Why isn't my answer good enough?

She wanted to shake him, or scream, or throw something. He had the ability, with his cool reasoning and smug remarks, to make her doubt herself.

Could he be right?

She recalled the sight of the jeep as he sped away. He wanted—no, needed—to get away from her. Never before were they intentionally apart from each other, even when they had disagreements. A sudden fear sparked inside her. For the first time since she had known him, she was forced to think, *What if he doesn't want to return?*

The phone ringing made her jump. She automatically went to the kitchen to where it sat on their countertop, but ended up staring at it, too lost in thought to answer. Their argument replayed, word for word in her mind. Frustration left her trembling and teary. The answering machine picked up.

A familiar happy voice sang over the speaker, "Happy Birthday to you! Happy Birthday to you! Dan, honey? If you're home, pick up! It's Mom! Oh darn, I wanted to wish you well, sweetheart and see how your day was going. We're in Wyoming today at Yellowstone. It's breathtaking up here. You kids must see it sometime. Dad's doing fine. Oh, he says Happy Birthday too! Hope you have something special planned! Tell Mia we said hi and we'll try to reach you later. We love you! Bye-bye!"

The phone call ended. Mia stared numbly at the red number one that appeared on the panel. His birthday! How could she have forgotten? Dumbstruck at her negligence, a realization over what she had done produced instant guilt.

Oh God, I've really screwed up this time.

Her heart went out to him. Now she knew why he was so insistent on spending the day together. Instead, they had this major blowout. His day was ruined. Just when she wanted so much for something to be right between them, everything turned out so wrong.

Why didn't she just make time for him? That thing in the mirror could have waited. It hadn't even been around for the last few days.

She closed her eyes and swore under her breath. Remembering the digital video camera, her first thought was to get it out of their walk-in bedroom closet where she usually stowed gifts until she could wrap them. It would be a nice surprise. He certainly wasn't expecting one and maybe it would serve as some kind of peace offering. She searched around her usual hiding places on the shelf but couldn't find anything under the blankets, comforters, and boxes stored there.

Aggravated, she tore everything down onto the floor and faced the empty shelf. It was then that she remembered with a cold assurance that she had left his gifts back at the store's security office. A faint memory reminded her of an erased message from the store some days ago, asking her to call. She struck her forehead hard with the heel of her hand. How could she have been so stupid?

First his birthday... now this.

She rummaged through her desk drawer looking for the generic greeting cards she kept in the event of an overlooked occasion. The card she found was plain and impersonal, but it would have to do since she hadn't bought a birthday card for him. Fretting over what she could do to make this morning right, she picked up a pen and tried to gather her thoughts.

Murph, I will make this up to you. I never meant to hurt you. Please see it in your heart to be patient with me just a little longer. I promise you things will get better. Soon!

I love you, more than ever.

Me

She placed the card on the bookshelf in the living room so he would see it as soon as he came in. Trying to salvage any part of his birthday, Mia raced back to the kitchen and opened the pantry. Dan never liked store bought cakes, always preferring ones she made at home. To her dismay, she found only an old box of cake mix and a few odds and ends. Looking through their cupboards, she ashamedly recognized that she hadn't done much food shopping lately.

Even more determined, she rounded up the last two eggs, quickly mixed the batter, set the oven's auto timer, and put the cake to bake. The clock indicated that if she kept moving, she should be able to swing by the department store's security office to see if they were still holding her purchases, and then continue on for frosting and decorations at the food store. With any luck at all, she would be back before he returned and really surprise him. Maybe she would make a nice dinner for him or take him to his favorite restaurant. Most of all, she wanted to apologize.

That was *if* Dan returned.

The troublesome thought gnawed at her as she picked up the cake mix box for one last check of the temperature. As she adjusted the dial on the wall oven, a now familiar figure appeared clearly in the black glass of its door.

The phantom was contemplating her, the same way he had at the store and in her car. Spying him, she jumped, and then slowly backed away. She saw the reflection of herself standing in front of the oven with the kitchen backdrop, but she could also see *him* right beside her looking down at her, standing at least six inches taller than she. Looking about the room, there wasn't anyone or anything she could see or even sense.

Instincts made her flee the kitchen. But his face displayed itself in every reflective object she passed, bending and distorting itself upon the different shapes and contours of various surfaces. He definitely was pursuing her, beckoning. When she reached the living room mirror, he abruptly stepped into full view, making her gasp against her will. His image fully eclipsed hers.

Fighting against fear once more, she knew she had to act. She couldn't back down now. The time had come to communicate.

Swallowing hard, she started, "W-who are you? Are you trying to tell me something? I - I want to talk with you…"

Looking sinister, he grimaced and scowled, flashing his stained teeth.

She pressed on, "Please. Who are you? If you'd tell me, I might be able to help you."

He began to pant and his eyes rolled back in his head. Blood shot from his nose, splattered the mirror, and coursed down the glass. He threw his head back and screamed silently. Mia flinched. She was going to get through this, no matter what.

She continued, "Where are you from? How did you get there? I want to help you."

From within the shadow of his hood, she could see his cracked lips part. His eyelids fluttered and then opened, revealing a gaze that was cold and stone-like.

She wouldn't back down. "Can you speak? What are you trying to tell me?"

Through the jagged lines of his blood flowing down the glass, she saw his eyelids quiver and close while his mouth formed words. A night in her childhood flashed through her mind: a sleepover at her cousin's house. The two cousins had watched Evelyn's brother Bobby as he slept walked through Aunt Lydia's kitchen. She remembered the eerie way his eyes never seemed to focus, fleeting emotions shaped his brows, and his lips murmured incoherent sentences.

It was as if this thing in the mirror was sleepwalking....

Summoning up more courage than she thought she had, Mia drew nearer to the mirror. Hesitatingly, she reached out to touch the long streaks of blood coursing down it. The cool dry smoothness of the surface caught her off guard. She had anticipated feeling the wetness from the lines of fluid. When she pulled her hand back and examined her fingertips, they were clean, much like the rag in the bathroom.

But when she returned her gaze to the looking glass, it too, was suddenly free of any blood. Remarkably, there was no trace left on him, either. His new appearance shocked Mia. With his eyes closed and the absence of the crimson stains, she could make out that he, in fact, was quite human.

"Tell me. Who are you? Can you speak?" she asked again with amazement.

Jerking suddenly, his eyes opened and he came alive, looking around as if he had just awoken and was noticing her for the first time. He started immediately into his silent babbling and shaking his head, as if he were pleading in an almost apologetic way. His torn hands went up against the mirror, making feeble clawing motions.

"If only I could understand what you are trying to tell me," she muttered out loud to herself.

His face was still in partial shadow from his jacket hood that remained up, masking parts of his expression that could hold clues to his message.

"And I wish your hood was down so I could at least see what you look like..."

To her astonishment, he obediently reached up for his hood and pulled it down. She gasped again and trembled while he stood there with an expectant look on his face. She had *communicated* with him and he had *responded*. He wasn't just an illusion.

For the first time, with the full light on his face, she was able to clearly scrutinize the person in the mirror. Mia realized that he was young, a teenage boy of about eighteen to nineteen years old. His ordinariness shocked her. This was a kid she would expect to see at a school, or skateboard park, or any other place where kids hung out.

What was he doing here?

His short brown spiked hair and gold earring looked completely out of place against the gray pallor of his skin. And his blue-green eyes stood out in stark contrast set against deep black circles that ringed them and the angry red vessels that intersected them. His face remained dirty and unshaven under a layer of dust and mud.

"Okay, let me see if I can try this again. First of all, do you understand me?" Mia asked carefully.

He contemplated her for a long moment, and then slowly tipped his head in a brief nod. His response proved to her that they, indeed, were communicating. There was no doubt about it now.

"Okay, okay, this is good," she replied excitedly. "Well, um...How about your name? What is your name?" she repeated.

His face turned sullen and after a little hesitancy, he just barely moved his lips.

"What was that? I'm sorry, I didn't catch that."

His eyes narrowed as he stared at her again. She wondered if he trusted her or not. Then, through clenched teeth, he mouthed a single syllable word.

"Please, is there any other way you can tell me? I can't hear you on this side.... I don't know how we are going to do this."

He turned his back to her. *I must've really ticked him off,* Mia thought with a twinge of apprehension. She wasn't sure whether he was going to appear savage towards her again or simply vanish.

Instead, he retreated into the depths of the reflection, away from her. Going to the bookcase, he picked up something and wrote on it. She craned her neck to see what it was, when suddenly it occurred to her to look back to where he would be if he were in her actual living room.

The paper upon her bookcase that he wrote on was the envelope of Dan's birthday card that she had placed there. Her head snapped back to watch him approaching the mirror, carrying the envelope. But when she looked back to the bookcase for verification, the envelope mysteriously remained there, apparently still resting upon the top shelf.

The teen was now in front of the mirror once again. When he held the blue envelope up with his mangled fingers, she could see he had written H T E S in a jagged scrawl that was barely legible. Her brain tried to decipher what it meant.

"Are those your initials?"

His eyes closed briefly and reopened in a dark scowl. His shoulders rose and fell from a deep sigh.

She continued to guess. "Are there letters missing? Or does that stand for something?"

He closed his eyes again and hung his head. When he lifted it, she could see a thin line of blood seeping from his nostril.

"Please, you've got to help me out here. Can you write some more?"

His head rolled back and slightly off to the side, then oddly, a fleeting sly smile crept across his face. His lips started to move, but Mia recognized it as the same pattern of babble from before. The youth slowly shook his head as if he were disagreeing with someone.

In the next moment, he was gone. She was left with only her own likeness in the mirror, wide-eyed and with her mouth gaping. An ice-cold sensation ran through her veins making the hairs on the back of her neck stand straight up.

This can't be happening.

She had asked him questions and he responded. Did she actually communicate with a spirit? A lost soul looking for help? It was an inconceivable thought that felt foreign and uncomfortable to her. She forced herself back into reality. Perhaps it was a self-fulfilling hallucination. She was simply seeing what her mind told her to see. She looked about her and reminded herself that she was standing in her living room in her own house in a suburb of a city. She was not in the middle of a movie script or between the pages of a novel.

The sound of keys in the front door lock shook her from her thoughts. Dan came in carrying a few bags. He eyed her warily, averted his eyes, and continued on his way to the back door. Mia was so relieved to see his return that she followed him outside. She wanted to share what she had just experienced so badly with him.

"What's up with you?" he asked as he unpacked odds and ends onto the patio table. "You look like you've just run a marathon."

She jumped at the opportunity he had given her. "You won't believe it if I tell you, but I saw—"

"I hope you are not going to start in with all of that seeing ghosts in reflections stuff, okay? I'm not in the mood for it."

"But he—"

She ceased abruptly when he held up his hand and shook his head.

"I told you, I am not in the mood."

She bit her lip and watched silently as he gathered up the bags to put in the recycle can and stow supplies away on the garden bench.

"Listen Hon, I'm really sorry about this morning. I don't know how I could have forgotten that today was your birthday but—"

"You think that's it? That I'm pissed about you missing my birthday? C'mon Mia, I'm a big boy now. I think you and I both know we have a bigger problem here."

"Okay, I don't want to get into that again. But would you at least let me give you something?"

She turned on her heel and marched inside, determined to give him his card and work things out between them. She snatched it off of the bookcase. Although the blue of the envelope in the mirror caught her eye as she walked back towards the kitchen, another sight stopped her cold.

A series of dark black lines marred its once clean surface. There in the reflection, she could see the name, "SETH" in a black, spidery, handwritten scrawl.

Astonished she reread the name in the mirror. Then she looked down at the envelope. Clearly, there was no mistake that they were the same ragged lines of ink that had formed the letters he had written: H T E S . She stifled a shriek and dropped the card as if it had burned her. There it lay face up on the wood planked floor and looking as if at any minute, those spidery lines could take hold of her and carry her off to where she wouldn't be found again.

◊ ◊ ◊

"Okay, I'll admit that I was a little put out about her missing my birthday last weekend, but this whole deal is getting serious. I really don't know what to do anymore, Ho," Dan said as he pushed away from the editing board and leaned back in his chair. Absorbed in thought, he nibbled absentmindedly on his thumbnail.

"Is she still seeing the shrink?" Hoason Ng asked as he gingerly tested the hot coffee that was brimming over the edge of the Styrofoam cup.

"Yeah, she's seen him a few times already but I'm not sure how much of it is doing any good. I mean, I don't know if I'm reading this right, but it seems that her condition is WAY out of that asshole's league."

"Oh yeah? How so?"

"Well, to be completely honest, it doesn't seem like he knows what he is doing. He gives her these affirmations to say to herself in the mirror and he refills her medication, but it all seems like chicken shit. There's got to be more than that! All he does is ask her a lot of questions that only make her more upset, then goes on with some explanations that sounds like he's been watching way too much Dr. Phil. And did I tell you about the time the sucker tried to shift the blame of all of this unto me?"

"Really? Aw man, that's just wrong. All I know is that my cousin went through this post partum depression stuff and it hit her pretty hard. One day they found her kid, butt naked, by the side of the driveway in winter. No clothes, no blanket, no anything. I'm talking *Chicago* winter with all the snow and ice and crap. She had laid him outside on the ground and forgot all about him. And he was little too, I don't know, maybe two or three months old?"

"No shit. Was he okay?"

"Yeah, he was suffering from some hypothermia, and I think he lost one of his toes to frostbite. But the crazy thing is when the cops asked Fran why she did it, she told them that she was trying to keep her baby safe," Hoason answered, while attempting another sip. He recoiled from the scalding liquid, then wiped his mouth with the back of his hand, swearing softly under his breath.

"Safe? Safe from what?"

"We don't know man. Hell, Fran didn't even know. And these days, she is so embarrassed by it all, she still doesn't talk about it."

"Yeah, but Mia didn't even have the baby. Do you suppose she could get that messed up from only five months of pregnancy?"

"I don't know. That hormone stuff is pretty weird. Look at that lady in Texas who drowned all five of her kids in the bathtub. They said that she was probably losing her marbles, a few each year with each pregnancy until finally it got to be too much."

"I remember hearing about that. And I sure as hell, don't want to be like her husband and be that clueless about my wife. I guess it's good in a way that Mia *is* seeing Monroe and taking care of this early, even though I think he is an asshole." He picked up a pen and pretended to study it, trying to ignore the flush of heat rising to his face. "I just wish a real psychiatrist could treat her."

"Yeah right, on our insurance? And with what shrinks charge? You've got to be kidding. You're lucky that PartnersHealth isn't trying to treat her online or over the phone or something. At least she is seeing a living human being."

"Yeah, I guess." Dan threw down the pen and sighed.

"Hey man, do you want to grab a beer after work? I'll buy. I never did get to take you out for your birthday last week with Greenlee riding our asses to get those videos out. Aw shit!"

Hoason shook the spilled coffee off his hand, and then looked down at the spot on his pants.

"Thanks Ho, but maybe some other time. I need to be with Mia at home. Although she's stubborn, I hate to leave her alone for any length of time while she's going through all of this, if I can help it. It's bad enough with us pulling all of this overtime lately."

"I hear you. Okay, some other time," his coworker responded. Then Ho's face grew solemn. "Hey Dan, I've been meaning to tell you… I hope Mia is going to be, you know, all right. She's a beautiful lady and tops in my book. You're lucky to have someone like that."

"Thanks," Dan said as he turned back to the monitors, "I suppose I am."

WENT TO PICK UP SOME BURGERS FOR DINNER was the note hastily written on the message board in the kitchen when he came home later that evening. Looking around, Dan had to make space just to lay his keys down on the counter crowded with plates, papers, and other junk there. He immediately collected the dirty dishes off the countertops and table and added them to the ones piled in the sink. Seeing several messages waiting on the answering machine, he pressed the button.

"Mia? This is Loren. Where are you, girl? Haven't you been getting any of my messages? I've called, I dunno, at least FIVE times in the past two weeks, just in case you want to know. Listen, I can't hold your position any longer if you don't call by this afternoon. We miss you and I really want to help you out, but we're swamped here. Sorry. So, please, please, please, call me!"

The answering machine's electronic voice piped up, "Thursday, October second, eight-thirty-five, a.m."

Hearing Mia's old boss and seeing the calendar, Dan couldn't help but think, *I guess that job is gone.*

He put away the dry dishes from the dish rack and went to stow a tray in the oven. When he opened the door, his nose was hit with a strange sweet smell. He pulled out two cake pans filled with stale dry cake, looking shrunken and crusty.

The idea hit him, *maybe she was trying to do something for my birthday… but what happened?* If he recalled correctly, she hadn't mentioned a thing all that day about any cake in the oven. *Was her memory getting that bad or…?*

When he looked around him, it was evident that their once-tidy house was slowly being overrun with dirty clothes, dishes, newspapers, and fast food wrappers. With all the overtime at work and then having to deal with Mia's behavior at home, he was a little embarrassed that he hadn't noticed the mess until it was excessive. They hadn't talked much since their argument, and this past week, she had acted even more distracted than usual. He would definitely have to get her to open up tonight.

He decided to inspect the house inside and out. The mailbox by the curbside was stuffed full with periodicals, past due bills, and postcards from his parents and her mother. The garden and flowerbed were wilted and brown. Her houseplants that she had tended so carefully were yellowing or dead in their pots in the windowsills. Open cans of paint were filmed over and dried in both the nursery and the garage, used paintbrushes left to stick to the lids where they rested. The washing machine in the garage was filled with clothes, water and detergent, but had stopped midway because the lid had been left open. By the strange odor emanating from the gray water standing in it, he wondered how many days it had been left in this state.

Apprehension crept into his mind. *What was going on here?*

He had never known Mia to act like this. Words of their argument from last weekend replayed in his head and he remembered accusing her that she in control of her situation.

But was she really in control here?

As he went through the house, he picked up trash and put things away. Crossing through the living room he noticed her journal notebook lying open on the shelf by the large tile mirror. Curiosity forced him to pick it up. The first page was slightly wrinkled and puckered as if water had dripped on it, and was dated about a day or two after they had first seen Gerry. Written below the date were several beginning entries, but each was crossed out:

Dearest Baby of Mine,

~~My Dearest Little Son,~~
~~I am so sorry for what I have done. I never~~

~~Dearest Angel in Heaven,~~
~~I hope you know how much I love you and how sorry I am for what I have~~

The following pages only had a scant sentence or two on each:

Sept. 4th I have seen "it" again.

Sept. 11nd Dan doesn't believe me. I have no one to talk to about this Who would believe me anyway?

Sept. 19th He's back again.

Skipping ahead through several blank sheets, he came upon pages exploded with scribbles and notes all over them. Most of the writing appeared to be incomprehensible words and phrases. Almost all of the letters were illegible and written backwards. But the oddest thing was that they appeared to be written in a heavy sloppy print, a handwriting Dan didn't recognize as Mia's.

"What in the hell…?" he wondered out loud.

Below the lines of scrawl, he saw some uniformed and legible notes clearly in Mia's neat longhand:

-name is Seth

-seems to doze in and out of conversation

- It is very dark, cold, and damp

- gets angry very quickly—frustration? Confusion?

- sleepwalking?

The rest of the notebook was blank. Perplexed, he closed the cover and tried to figure out what he had just seen when his thoughts were interrupted by Mia's car pulling up the driveway. She carried in fast food bags heavy with food.

"Oh hi, Honey!" she said as she gave him a small kiss. "I'm glad you're not working late tonight. Now we can eat dinner together. You saw my message on the board? I put it there just in case you came home before I did. I hope you don't mind burgers again—"

She stopped abruptly when she spotted her notebook in his hand.

His voice was quiet and low when he spoke. "Mia, we've got to talk."

SEVEN

That stupid bitch. What was she up to now?

His eyes flicked over the document as his mind narrowed down the various possibilities. It had to be that guy she was seeing. That asshole had a way of getting into everything and swaying her mind. Before he came along, everything was fine.

Gerry Monroe threw down the summons with disgust. There was no way his ex-wife was going to get full custody over Austin. He barely saw the kid as it was. Although he had forfeited visitation throughout the remainder of the year, it was perfectly understood that Thanksgiving and four weeks out of the summer were *his*. And no skinny, greedy wench with a divorce attorney boyfriend was going to change that.

Jabbing on his computer's mouse, he pulled up his desktop address book and located his lawyer's number. Although Jack had dropped the ball in getting him lower child support payments, Monroe knew he would be an absolute animal when it came to battling for custody. Alysse would get a good fight, if anything. Hopefully an expensive fight on her part that would finally make her put up or shut up. And if she weren't careful, he'd submit a custody appeal of his own and get the kid full-time.

Time for a little offense.

Amy just moved in last week and if he pressed her, she'd probably help keep an eye on Austin. Besides, the kid was already a teenager. In another five years he'd be off to college, but in the meantime those support payments would kick into reverse and start rolling back to good old dad. Monroe thought about the football season tickets that he wanted to add to his basketball and baseball seats. Or maybe that classic '68 Corvette he had his eye on.

Marcia entered the office and without so much as a nod in Gerry's direction, threw down another paper upon his desk, turned on her heel, and left.

"Good morning to you too…" he called after her as he picked up the memo, and then added under his breath, "…fat ass."

As he read through the memo, his pressure rose and his stomach churned with acid. The Childresses were going through with their lawsuit. While PartnersHealth was listed as the primary defendant, his name showed up as the secondary. It was just what he needed as if he didn't have enough on his plate already. Between his custody case and this, it looked like he'd be spending the next couple of years of his life in court. For a brief moment, he considered whether all the fat and skinny bitches in the world were out to get him in some kind of feminist-unite-hate-the-white-male conspiracy.

Tossing the memo into his in-box, he leaned back in his chair and put his feet up. Gently massaging his temples, he closed his eyes and started into his deep breathing technique, trying to lower his pressure and settle his stomach.

This day was turning to crap already; I don't need much more stress, he mused to himself as he concentrated on shifting his focus to a little me time.

The rest of the world could go away as Gerry Monroe relocated his center, reciting his mantra over and over again in his head: *NBA PLAYOFFS. NBA PLAYOFFS.* Just as he drifted off into a light snooze, he was snapped awake by the beep of his intercom.

"*Gerrr-rry!* Your nine-twenty is here," a syrupy voice dripped.

He sat up straight and rubbed his face. Groggily, he pulled up his appointment screen. Mia Labont, post partum depression.

Oh great. Another skinny bitch out to bust his hump.

"And your prescriptions are working out all right for you?"

"Uh, no. Not exactly. That's why I'm here today. I was wondering if something was wrong. It's like I'm not responding to them anymore."

"And what leads you to believe that?" he asked, concentrating on making patience stick to his voice.

It was the same story with all of his clients. They always hoped to resolve all of their hang-ups and find ultimate happiness in the form of an easy-to-swallow pill. He watched her squirm in her chair before she sat back.

"I don't know…a lot of nightmares? My imagination running wild? I mean, I've reduced my stress as much as I can. I say the affirmations and write in my journal. There is no pressure from anyone, including myself, to start a family right now. I've even taken it easy and have let everything go, just like you said to do. Yet, I keep *seeing* things. I thought the medication was supposed to take that away."

"It will. But you've got to give it time. I've told you before that these are chemicals in your head that have to be turned around the other way. It's not a simple process. They didn't change overnight, so you can't expect the medication to correct them instantly either."

"I guess."

She clamed up and lowered her eyes. The room was silent for the next few seconds.

Oh great, she's getting moody and uncooperative, Gerry thought.

Now he had to get her to talk again.

Why on all days did I come to work today? I should have stayed home when I first picked up the envelope marked "Family Court."

"How's the hubby? He decided not to come today?"

Mrs. Labont sat quietly for a moment more while her mind seemed to be elsewhere. He eyed her enviously, wishing he had that luxury.

"Mia? I was asking about your husband," he repeated.

"Huh? Oh, Dan. He's not here because he had to work and couldn't take any more time off. But he's fine, thank you."

"That's good. You've talked to him about what you've been experiencing?" he asked, hoping to get more from her indirectly.

"Um, yes. In fact, it was he who suggested I come see you today."

They were back to square one. Time to shift gears.

"Well… it has been reported that about twelve percent of the people who take sertraline may experience a little insomnia or nervousness. The diazepam should help to counteract that."

"Okay, I can deal with that. But what about that person I keep seeing in the reflections? Just the other day he was—"

Line one on the phone lit up. It was probably Jack returning the hasty call Gerry had made just before she walked in.

"I'm *terribly sorry* to interrupt you Mia, but I have to take this call. It's really important. Excuse me just a sec," he said holding up a finger, and then swinging his chair around to face the window.

The news on the other line was not good. Jack could not make court. He was out indefinitely because of heart surgery and subsequent rehabilitation, and all they could do was provide a substitute. It figured. On any other day he would have been surprised. But not on this one.

No, not on this fucking day.

Exercising the greatest effort in control, he debated whether or not to fling the phone out the window as he hung up. Mrs. Labont looked up at him expectantly, opening her mouth to go on. At that moment, he really didn't want to hear it. He had had enough already. Someone complaining about how long her medication was taking to work just wasn't much of a priority for him at the moment.

"Mia! I'm really sorry about that. Thanks for being so patient. Hey listen, it sounds to me that what you are describing may be a dosage problem." He scanned her chart quickly. "Okay, you're on twenty milligrams twice a day now, am I right?"

She closed her mouth and gave her head a small nod.

"Yup, that's not enough. Okay, what I want you to do is start taking the sertraline three times a day instead, one pill every eight hours, and let's see how that goes. We may as well kick this thing in the butt and get you feeling better already, all righty? And keep taking your diazepam for any nervousness and insomnia, okay?"

"Okay… But what if I continue to—"

"You've got to give it time. It's as simple as that. I promise you it'll clear up if you'll just be patient. In the meantime, get your mind off of things. You like shopping? Going to the movies? Get out and do something positive and indulge yourself. Buy that dress that you've always wanted or eat the chocolate cake if you want to. Do what *you* want to do and don't let all these little nuisances in life bug you, okay? It'll keep you happy while you give your meds a chance to work." He looked directly at the clock, appearing very obvious and hoping she would take the hint. "I think that's all we have time for today."

She sat for a moment longer seeming to disregard his signal that their session was indeed over. *Why wasn't she leaving?* he thought tiredly.

Then she rose slowly, picked up her purse, and said, "Thanks Gerry. I guess I'll see you next time."

"Hey, not if I see you first!" he said, pointing his finger at her and giving her a wink. "You call me if you have any problems. I'm always here for you." He stood up from his desk and shook her hand. "See ya. Give Dan a shout for me, okay?"

Finally, the door shut behind her and he was alone. He immediately turned to the intercom and pushed the button.

"Marcia? Cancel the rest of my appointments for today. I'm not feeling well and I'm going home."

It was time for Gerry Monroe to take care of his own problems for a change.

◊ ◊ ◊

When she looked into her rearview mirror as she pulled out of the parking lot at PartnersHealth, her eyes fell immediately upon the phantom sitting in the rear seat of her Hyundai, pensively staring at her. Unprepared for his appearance in her car, her heart jumped, but she forced herself to calm down.

"H- hey, Seth, um, how are you doing today?"

He kept his hood down now but his face remained drawn and gray under the layer of dust and mud. He nodded listlessly and then leaned his head back on the headrest as if he was resting. All the while his eyes stayed on her.

She knew it was useless to engage in dialogue with him while she drove. The conversation would be pretty one-sided as there wasn't anything for him to write with. As she drove home, at every light she would steal a peek at him, only to meet his gaze.

Their few encounters over the past week proved that he did want to communicate with her, despite it being tedious. First, he wrote very slowly. It had taken almost an hour to get down only two pages of conversation. Also, his attention during these sessions often seemed to wander and he didn't divulge much out of lack of memory or unwillingness.

Once inside the house, Mia dropped her jacket, purse, and keys on the floor and went directly to the big mirror. Seth stepped into view, his hands in his pockets and his eyes bloodshot.

"Okay, we're home. I mean, we're at my house now. Do you feel like talking some more? There're so many questions I want to ask you. I hope that we can, uh, discuss some more today? Will that be okay with you?"

He nodded once more, but stood there, his hands shoved in his pockets. He appeared to be waiting for something although she couldn't quite figure out what it was. Suddenly it dawned on her as she jumped up to fetch a notebook and pen. She held them up to show him and then placed the items on top of the bookshelf that she had moved next to the mirror. There they sat, untouched.

"There you go. Unless—hey, wait a minute—do you have a phone? Maybe we can try texting. It'll be faster." Mia's heart started to race. "I don't know why I didn't think of it sooner, I'll go get my—"

She stopped abruptly as he shook his head no.

Of course. A ghost wouldn't have a cell phone.

He held up his cell phone to the mirror, jabbed at the buttons, and showed her the screen. Apparently, it was dead.

The teenager tossed down the phone and picked up the pen to write instead. She immediately looked at the undisturbed notebook on her side of the mirror and saw the spidery lines appearing instantly on the clean page just as they had a few days ago, although the pen rested where it lay.

When he wrote, the act looked painful. Mia studied him and wondered how he barely held the pen in his battered fingertips, all the while his face remaining somber and dark. She was ashamed to have ever asked him to attempt to text.

WONK OT TNAW U OD TAHW

When he held up the book to the glass for her to read, Mia found it frustrating to try to figure out what the backward scrawl said. In the reflection, as soon as he placed the notebook down, she picked it up on her side of the glass and held it up to the mirror to read,

WHAT DO U WANT TO KNOW

"Well…why are you—I mean, how did you get there?"

Again, he waited for her to return the notebook to the shelf. The routine repeated.

?EREHW

"In the reflection of my mirror? Don't you live somewhere?"

I DONT KNOW I WOKE UP HERE

"But where do you stay normally? Do you live with someone? Parents? Or family…? Do you live in a house?"

DONT REMEMBR

"Okay, then, maybe you can answer this: when you first appeared, you know, at the store and later in the garage, why were you making such frightening faces at me? It looked like you wanted to attack me," she asked cautiously, not knowing if she would offend him somehow or he would agree with her assessment.

His eyelids fluttered for a moment, and then he sighed.

DON'T KNOW WHY. CUDNT HELP IT

She wasn't sure how to phrase the next question, but she had to determine once and for all, if he was real indeed, and not merely a product of a vivid imagination.

"This might sound strange to you… I don't know how to put this… but are you some kind of illusion or a hallucination? You know, that only appears in my mirrors?"

It sounded stupid to her, once it passed her lips. Would a figment of her imagination admit that it was? How would she know? But there seemed to be no other way she could think of to find out.

He furrowed his brow, looking cross at her, and shook his head, mouthing the word NO. Then he wrote:

HUMAN—FLESH N BLOOD

LOOK AT UR NOTEBOOK

Again, in her excitement in talking with him, she was sorry she hadn't thought things through. How else could his handwriting have gotten there? Dan had even seen the writing. It was concrete proof that she wasn't delusional.

"Okay, so since you are real, are you appearing to me telepathically? Are you…" She hesitated, not knowing how he would respond. He waited patiently for her to finish. "…are you alive somewhere?"

He turned away from her. His shoulders rose and fell as he breathed deeply. Mia waited with some trepidation, wondering if he would transform himself back to the gruesome figure he was before. When he finally faced her, she was relieved to see that he hadn't, but she noticed blood forming at his nostrils again. Then he wrote out his reply.

DONT THINK SO

She gasped at his response. He was only a kid. What could have happened to him? It surprised her even more to find that she suddenly felt pity for this sullen apparition. Just then, the phone rang.

Mia ignored it and tried to press on, "Was there an accident? Did someone do something to you?"

By now the answering machine had picked up and she could hear Dan's voice over the phone saying, "Mia? I was hoping that you were home already. I was just calling to find out how everything went with Monroe today."

She knew she should pick it up. He would worry about her and she didn't want to bring any more strife between them. She looked imploringly at Seth.

"Could you please hang on for just one minute? Please, please stay there. Let me talk to my husband, I'll be right back, okay?"

Mia ran to the kitchen and with mild annoyance, snatched up the phone. "Dan?"

"Oh hi, Honey. I thought you weren't in so I was leaving a message."

"No, I'm here. Just busy. What's up?"

"Nothing. I was calling to see how your appointment went."

"It was okay. Fine."

"And did he say anything about, uh, what's been happening?"

Impatiently, she shifted her weight to her other foot, then lowered her voice and answered, "Uh, no. In fact, he said that it probably is my medication. He wants to change the dosage again. Something about taking time to shift my brain chemicals back." She sighed, anxiously wanting to get back to the mirror.

"Well, do you think that's going to work?"

"I guess it should. It made sense what he was saying. But listen, Honey, I've got to go. I, uh, promised Mrs. Lopez that I'd…help her with something," she stammered, knowing she made a poor liar.

"Oh, okay. Just calling to see how your day went."

"I did fine. I'll see you later. Love you, bye!"

He barely said goodbye before she hung up and raced back to the living room. But when she arrived at the mirror, Seth was gone. Disappointed, she looked down at the notebook still on the shelf. She ran her finger over the heavy black scrawl. He had been there.

Should I continue with this? she asked herself.

The arrangement was completely unusual and she didn't know where it would lead her. She wondered what would happen as she continued her course of medication. Would it make any difference? Now that Seth had confirmed it, the thought of her communicating with the Dead made her feel uneasy. Her thoughts flashed back to advice her mother had given her long ago: *Never start what you can't finish.*

But try as she might, she couldn't think of any other way to get this to end. It was an ominous journey she was about to embark on. Looking over his laborious lines in the notebook once more, she realized she hadn't asked him the one question that stood apart from all the rest:

Why are you here?

◊ ◊ ◊

Two gray wobbly heads peeked over the fringe of the nest, struggling for survival and gaping for nourishment. The mother bird held their breakfast in her gullet, as she cocked her head to view her demanding charges. She stuffed her beak down the open mouth of the more boisterous of the two, regurgitated, and then continued onto the other, producing less and less as she toggled between them.

Mia was sipping tea as she watched them through the kitchen window. She was thinking about Seth and what they would talk about when she saw him today, but the nest in the forked branch of the pyracantha bush diverted her attention for the time being. The house finch family was one of the few respites that she granted herself each day, allowing her to slip away from phantoms, medications, and the constant fear of insanity. She often worried about the little birds and threw bread crusts and birdseed out the window to them while they hid and surveyed her with wary eyes.

For no apparent reason, the mother bird suddenly took flight. The babies wobbled about a bit more, seeming to be just as surprised by her hasty departure. Seeing she wasn't returning, they settled back down below the rim of the nest. Just as Mia was about to return to her tea, a slight movement caught her eye. Quite unexpectedly, one of the baby birds was pitched out from its haven. It tumbled through the air and landed hard upon the ground, flopping, and wriggling about on undeveloped legs and wings.

From one of the sturdy middle branches of the bush, a large black cat appeared out his hiding place and gracefully dropped down onto the ground beside the bird. It studied the defenseless nestling for a moment and then reached out a tentative paw to swat at it. The baby bird gaped and beat its useless wings as the cat grew more intent on batting it about.

Mia stared in horror and rapped furiously at the window, shouting, "Hey you! Leave it alone! Leave it alone! Get out of there!"

The cat turned its big head up towards the noise and viewed Mia through the glass with startled eyes, dark pupil slits slicing through the yellow centers. With some disdain, he glared at her for a moment, licked his lips, and then returned to his sport. Mia dashed out the back door and took the corner around to the side of the house.

"Stop! Leave him alone!" she scolded loudly. "Get out of here! Shoo!"

She charged upon the cat, hoping to frighten it away. Instead, the feline crouched low, pinned his ears back, and hissed. Emitting a low moan, he immediately seized the baby in his fangs and scooted off. He moved so fast, Mia was only able to snatch at the cat's fluffy tail, but that too, slipped through her fingers.

"Nooo! Drop it! Damn you, drop it! DROP IT!!" she shrieked.

Jumping up to safety upon the wood fence that separated the two yards, he looked back at her with contempt, lashing his tail back and forth. The baby bird flailed and chirped feebly in his jaws, helpless in saving itself.

"Diablo! Déjalo! Déjalo!" Mrs. Lopez's voice commanded from the other side of the fence.

Apparently, she had been summoned from her house by Mia's cries. Surrounded on both sides now, Diablo rose up from his crouching position and delicately walked along the top rail, never missing a step until he reached where the corner of the roof hung down. Once there, he leapt up lightly and scurried across the rooftop to torment and play with his prize in peace. Mia stood there, feeling impotent and hopeless.

"Mia? Are you okay, mija? I'm sorry that he upset you so. My Diablo is fat and selfish. He's always going after those poor birds. No matter what I do, I can't get him to stop," Mrs. Lopez called to her through the fence slats, hoping to comfort her neighbor.

Mia swallowed hard and found her voice beyond the hot tears that threatened to come. "I'm all right Mrs. Lopez. Thanks, but I think I'm going to go back inside now."

"Are you sure you're okay?"

Mia didn't answer.

"Oh, okay, mija. You take care, okay? Again, I'm sorry my Diablo upset you so much. I won't give him any of his treats tonight, okay? That'll teach him!"

Standing by silently, Mia waited to hear the bang of Mrs. Lopez's back screen door, signaling that she was alone once more. Then she crept up to the pyracantha bush and peered in through the branches. There in the tidy nest, she could see the fluff of the remaining gray head. A bright serious eye looked back at her, as the rest of the bird remained completely still, his closed mouth turning down at the corners like a frown.

"Oh you poor little thing. I'm so sorry. You're all alone now. I promise I'll protect you, okay? I won't let anything happen to you. I promise," she whispered to the tiny bird.

Just then, big round drops splattered the sidewalk and Mia became aware of a faint rushing sound spreading over the neighborhood and tops of the trees. A cool breeze blew over the fence. The sky suddenly opened up and rain started to fall. Low heavy peals of thunder rolled somewhere in the distance. She flinched at each rumble, the threatening sound making her nervous.

She took one last look at the lonely nestling shivering in his nest without his sibling. The rain soaked through her clothes quickly and she felt a sudden chill to the bone. She knew his mother was out there somewhere, waiting for her to leave, but Mia couldn't help but wonder if she should scoop up the little bird and take it away from this world of predators, damp, and cold.

She didn't use to be afraid of thunder. As a child, she would often sit with her father on their enclosed front porch during rainstorms in the warm summer months, he with his newspaper in the rattan chair and she, propped up on her elbows on the outdoor carpet playing with her Colorform shapes.

When a bright flash illuminated the room, she would look up at her father and the two of them would count the seconds before the ensuing crash. Then they would calculate how many miles away the lightning had struck.

On the long rolling peals where it echoed over the neighborhood, sometimes he would wink at her and say, "Sounds like the angels are bowling again, Mia."

She would giggle and respond, "Yes! That angel had a strike!" On the smaller rumbles, her imagination ran wild as she called out, "That one had a split" or "That angel just picked up a spare."

It was on another rainy night that Mia had awakened from a crash of the heavens. As the thunder resounded, she could hear the frantic flutter of wings beating against the bars of a cage. Abraham, her parakeet, was a gift given to her from her Grandma Adara for her eighth birthday just the week before. At first, Margaret Pappas had objected to her mother-in-law's outrageous gift and insisted on giving it back, despite Mia's protests.

"Mia is too young to take care of a pet. I don't think it is a good idea or time for her to get involved with this," her mother asserted.

Stephanos and Aunt Lydia took up sides against Margaret; one posing the argument that a bird was easy to care for, while the other said it was a good lesson in responsibility.

What Mia had remembered most was her grandmother pulling her mother aside. Typically, the two women avoided each other and only regarded each other with polite civility. Even at her young age, Mia knew they disliked each other.

But now, they talked in hushed tones with Grandma Adara's arm around her daughter-in-law's stiff shoulders. It was such an unusual event that Mia was bursting with curiosity to overhear what was going on. Yiayia's words finally found her straining ears. "…and after what she has just been through with her little friend and the fire and everything else… This would be a good thing to take her mind off the tragedy."

Despite her argument, Margaret Pappas eventually relented, making Mia solemnly promise to clean and feed the bird every day.

Now, the little bird clung to the bars and chirped, his body quaking with fear.

"Shhh! Shhh! Abraham, it's okay. It's just the angels bowling up in heaven," the little girl recited her daddy's explanation to the frightened bird.

Just then, the room lit up with a bright flash followed by another crack of thunder reverberating throughout the house. The beating of wings and frantic chirps added to the din.

"Abraham! Quiet! It's okay. I am right here," she tried to reassure him.

"Mia?" She heard her mother's drowsy voice call to her from down the hall. "Mia, go back to sleep. This is no time to be playing with that bird."

She waited quietly for a few moments for her mother to fall back asleep. Next, she slipped out of bed and tiptoed to the cage. The parakeet chirped and fluttered crazily about.

In her faintest whisper possible, Mia pleaded with him, "*Please* Abraham, be quiet or you are going to get us both in trouble."

She took out a blouse from her dresser and placed it over the cage, then crept back to bed hoping the storm would be over soon. With each flash of lightning and following thunder, she feared for her bird's well being, whispering promises to him that she was right there and nothing would harm him.

Late the next morning, she awoke feeling groggy and thick-headed from the active night before. But to her relief, the storm was over. She happily went to the cage.

"See Abraham? Mr. Sun's out this morning. No more thunder and lightning!" she said as she pulled back the blouse.

The bird was dead. She stared in disbelief, hoping that it was only sleeping and feeling as tired as she. Timidly, she rocked the cage. The bright blue body rolled and pitched stiffly but its eyes did not open. Mia ran to get her father and soon her mother joined them, all three witnesses to the still bird lying on the floor of the cage.

"Didn't I tell you that she didn't need a pet, Steve? Didn't I? Now she has to suffer all this unnecessary heartache, especially after she just lost her—"

"Margaret, that's quite enough," Stephanos spoke over his shoulder to her in a low voice.

Mia studied the motionless bird. He looked like a stuffed toy. She felt a sharp tug at her heart. Refusing to cry in front of her mother, she bit her lower lip instead.

"Well, we're going to have to do something with it. I'll go get a paper bag. We can put it right in the trash," Margaret Pappas suggested practically.

"No Mommy! We can't just throw him away! He's not garbage. Abraham needs a funeral. Don't we need to pray for his soul to go to heaven? He's one of God's creatures isn't he? Please?"

Her mother sighed impatiently and pursed her lips. "I suppose."

Mia watched her father lift the tiny body out of the cage and place it in a shoebox she had carefully lined with a clean handkerchief. Then she tenderly stroked the soft speckled breast with her finger one last time and covered him up.

The small procession of two marched out to the backyard bearing the makeshift coffin. Her mother refused to go outside for any "foolish funeral for a bird," but Mia could see her spy at them from time to time through the kitchen curtains.

While her father dug a hole, she gathered petals off of her mother's rose bush and then stood solemnly by. When the hole was completed, she placed the shoebox in it, sprinkled the petals over it, and stepped back. She counted seventeen shovelfuls of dirt until the box was completely buried. Then she asked her father to say a prayer.

He looked uncertain for a moment, then with some thought he cleared his throat and finally spoke, "Father in heaven, watch over this little parakeet."

"Abraham."

"This parakeet, Abraham, who has gone to join You. May his soul be with You and all the other, um, creatures that have passed before him. Amen."

"Amen," Mia said earnestly, with her eyes squeezed shut and her small hands clasped tightly together.

When Stephanos looked down at her, she nodded back at him with approval.

"Do you want to talk about this, Honey?" he asked gently.

"Nah, uh."

She returned her stare to the fresh mound of damp earth. After a few more minutes, her father cleared his throat once more.

"Well, how about some lunch? Mom's probably fixing up something good in the kitchen right now. You missed breakfast this morning, sleepy head."

"No. I'm not hungry. I think I'm going to stay out here for a little while," she answered resolutely.

She went off to sit alone, silently dismissing him. A hollowness pervaded within her, not allowing tears to fall or thoughts to intervene. All she could feel was a sadness that sunk through to her insides, an overwhelming, encompassing grief.

A short time later, her mother came out carrying a glass of milk and a sandwich wrapped in a napkin to where Mia was posted on the bench.

"Mia, I want you to eat this. Afterwards, why don't you come inside and play with your toys? You can't be sitting out here all day looking at *that*."

The little girl took the sandwich and lowered her head, then resumed her stare. Her mother lingered a moment with her hand on her hip, then returned to the house. It was the end of August and a warm, humid day. The sky was still clouded over from the previous night's storm. The kitchen windows were open halfway to catch some air, and the cotton curtains swayed lazily in and out on the soft currents.

Mia opened the napkin to reveal her favorite sandwich—bologna and cheese. Taking a few nibbles, she settled back on the bench and ate, but she continued to watch over where Abraham lay. A short time later, she became aware of her parents' voices as they drifted out of the open windows and grew thin in the summertime air.

"I should have never let you do it. Holding a funeral for that bird! What was I thinking? I should have told her to stay in her room while you disposed of it. Have you seen her? She hasn't taken her eyes off of it yet! It isn't healthy."

"Give her time, Margaret. I'm sure she won't sit out there all day."

There was a faint rustle of newspapers.

"But why mislead her with this silliness? I've told you time and again, that she should've come with us to pay her last respects to the McCane child. She would've dealt with it then. Now there's this fantasy foolishness over a dead bird instead. And you had to let her keep that bird in the first place, didn't you? Against my wishes. You and my sister, always romanticizing everything. And who pays the price? Not you two. I didn't think she was strong enough Steve, not after what happened to her little friend. And now I see that I was right. I should have put a stop to it right there and then."

"No. She is way too young to have to deal with the death of another child. Could you imagine what kind of nightmares she would have had seeing Robin McCane laid out, and then buried in the ground? It's better that she goes through it this way. Let her build up an understanding with time."

"Yes, but dying is what happens in life, and she has to learn to deal with that. We put our faith in God and he will carry us through."

"Yeah, well try explaining faith to an eight-year-old."

"Try explaining death."

After that, no other words were said. Mia could hear the sound of dishes being washed and the occasional turn of another newspaper page. Her eyes left their fix on the little bird's grave and started moving upward over the fences, across the yards and to the darkened bedroom window that was visible from her backyard.

Robin's house looked gray and abandoned. Angry black scorch marks flared out past the planks of wood that had been nailed against the window frames and doorways to secure them. Robin's very window was boarded up tight, shut off from light and life. Mia had overheard conversations from her parents and neighbors about how after the fire, Robin's parents had split up and moved away. There was also some talk about the house being torn down or sold, but in the meantime, it stood neglected and forgotten.

She looked at her friend's window and remembered the pink curtains fluttering out on billows of deadly smoke. The memory of siren cries and shouts and voices filled her ears. Instantly she was there, inside the house, her eyes seeing everything clearly before her. It was just as she had witnessed in her mind's eye when she had forewarned her friend of her fate on that hot afternoon a few weeks ago.

Robin is lying across her bed, singing softly to a Beatles' song playing on the oldies station and matching the paper clothes and hats to the printed faces of her cutout dolls. She starts to cough, but ignores it, going on with her play. Soon her cough becomes insistent and she is suddenly aware of acrid smoke filling her room. She hears her mother scream from one of the floors below. When Robin flings open the door to run to her, huge clouds of smoke roll in. The house below is a growing, deafening roar as flames consume it, room by room.

Robin cries out for her mother. She starts to gasp as the toxic smoke fills her lungs and steals her breath. She backs into her room but trips over the leg of her bed and ends up sprawled out on her bedroom floor. Panic fills her and she crawls to her closet where she shuts the door and hides from the smoke and noise of the flames ravaging her house below.

The temperature is rising and she cannot stop coughing and gagging. In between, she cries out again and again for her mother who hasn't come. She huddles in the corner of the dark closet and drops her head onto her knees, crossing her arms in front of her, shielding her face. Within minutes her coughing subsides and her cries grow quiet. Her body goes limp.

A faint, almost undetectable noise caught Mia's ear, shaking her from her trance and instantly returning her to her own backyard. At first, she looked toward the bushes by the fence, thinking it was probably some squirrel or other animal. But the sound grew louder, drawing her attention away from the bushes and closer to herself. With increasing horror, she traced it back to the fresh mound of dirt. Dropping to her knees, she turned her head and put her ear close to the grave. The terrified chirps were muffled, but the sound was definitely coming from within. Mia started to dig with her hands, her fingers clawing away the black damp earth.

"Abraham! Abraham! Hold on! I'll get you out!" she cried.

Dirt packed under her fingernails and grit ground into her bare knees. The chirping rose in crescendo. The earth flew away and within minutes, the red lid to the shoebox started to appear. As she lifted the box out of the hole, she could clearly hear the din of frenzied chirping and flapping wings trapped by cardboard. The box shook with life under her fingertips.

"Hold on, I'm right here!"

Tearing off the lid, she lifted him out and threw down the box. She fumbled with the layers of the handkerchief. Her hands trembled so much it was difficult to part the folds. With great expectation, she finally she uncovered her parakeet.

"Here you go, Abraham... Abraham?" she questioned when she found him as cold and lifeless as before. Confused, she prodded him timidly with her finger, but he remained still.

The sounds of the backyard, her parents in the kitchen, and the busy neighborhood faded away as the world turned deafeningly silent, leaving Mia enshrouded in the stillness of death. Her mind flicked rapidly between images of Abraham's body in her hand and Robin's body slumped over in the corner of her closet.

"I didn't mean to," she whispered.

Time stood still, and she felt cold. She was overcome with a sensation of floating weightless, out of control.

A shriek from the kitchen window cut through the silence, jarring Mia, and sending the dead bird tumbling from her dirty hands onto the churned up earth below.

"Merciful Father in Heaven! What are you doing child?"

Margaret Pappas was outside in an instant. Mia could feel her mother's strong hands grip her shoulders tightly, but she kept her eyes fixed on Abraham, waiting to see if he would somehow come back to life again.

"Steve! Steve! Get out here! Immediately!" her mother ordered.

She forced Mia to turn away and steered her towards the house.

"Margaret? What in the world?"

Her father stopped short when he saw the parakeet on the ground.

"Didn't I tell you Steve? Didn't I? But would you listen to me? No! I told you she wasn't ready! You always think you know her better than anyone. Now *she* pays the price. Well I'm taking her inside. Meanwhile, you can take care of *this*," she said vehemently.

Mia let herself be guided into the coolness of the house. There, she awaited the scolding and punishment she was sure to receive. But she knew her mother's anger could not reach her. Her heart was numb and her head foggy, the feel of death permeating every muscle of her body. The sharpness of words was nothing compared to the shard of hurt she already felt. Despite her anticipation, surprisingly there was no penalty or angry complaints.

Instead, her mother gently pushed her up the stairs to the bathroom. While the water ran, they stood silently and watched as the tub filled. Words could not find a place in the small room. As she was undressed, all Mia could do was stare at the grains of black earth that had fallen from her clothes and peppered the clean white tile of the bathroom floor. Her mother lowered her into the bath, sending swirls of steam rising from the water. Oddly, Mia didn't perceive the warm water, feeling detached from her own body.

As she soaked, her mother withdrew a pretty blue bottle from the medicine cabinet. Mia recognized it as the one she wasn't ever allowed to touch. She stared in amazement as her mother opened the cap and emptied the sweet smelling bath oil into the steaming water. Margaret Pappas did not ask her daughter any questions. Her lips remained closed in a thin crooked line, but Mia could see a gentle sadness fill her eyes. It was an unusual sight and she couldn't keep from studying it.

The daughter sat very still in the scented water and let her arms and legs be lifted to be washed, one by one, treasuring her mother's touch. Not having been bathed by her mother since she was five years old, she watched as the dirt was scrubbed out from under her fingernails, and the dust was gently washed from her long dark hair. With each stroke, the warmth of the living began to trickle back through her skin and chase away the chill of death. She longed for her mother to speak to her, but nothing was said. Mia did not want to jeopardize the moment for anything, so she too, remained silent.

Afterwards, she was taken from her bath, dried, her hair braided, and her soft nightgown slipped over her head. She was put to bed even though the late afternoon sun had started to break through the thick clouds. Her mother disappeared downstairs for a bit and then returned with a glass of warm milk and honey that she set upon the nightstand. She carefully sat on the edge of the bed and laid her hand lightly on her daughter. Her lined face looked as if she were pondering something.

With that same sadness still present in her eyes, she finally said, "Give it up to God, Mia. All the pain in your heart, the grief that you are feeling. That's what I do when I can't bear it. Just give it all up to God. He sees you. He understands. He loves us all, regardless of what happens."

Impulsively, the little girl reached up to hug her and for a brief moment, her mother held her and hugged her back. All of a sudden, as if she caught herself, Margaret Pappas grew rigid and pulled away. Lying Mia back down, she drew the blankets up to her daughter's chin. Then without another word, she left the room and shut the door behind her.

Under the covers, although she finally felt comfortable and warm, Mia couldn't get her eyes to close. Her mind was swarming with questions.

When you die, are you all alone? Are all of Mommy's little unborn babies still waiting there in heaven if they never had a chance to be born? Were there people up in heaven that took care of you, or did you have to look after yourself?

She hoped that Robin was looking after Abraham in heaven. Things that young should never have to be alone.

◊ ◊ ◊

After the first half-dozen appearances, he didn't startle her any more when he came into view. Inside the house or out, he would be there in reflections, waiting, usually with a downcast look on his face. Eventually she came to count on his constant presence. Yet he came and went as he pleased. Some days he chose not to show himself at all. It was hard for her to determine any pattern or schedule of his arrivals, except to expect that there was always the possibility that he may show up at any time.

As their 'talks' became more frequent, in time, Seth grew more animated; his somnambulistic demeanor diminished. His increasing expressions whispered clues to his emotions. From time to time even a hint of a smile tugged at his lips. Aside from that, he certainly looked much cleaner than when she had first encountered him a few weeks ago. Each time he reappeared, the mud and dirt became less and less, although his complexion remained dull and gray.

During their first few encounters, he wasn't very cooperative, alternating between 'normal' and what she called 'fading out.' That was when he would choose only to sit and stare. His visits increased and lengthened, and he opened up and began to write more. Mia set out additional notebooks and pens about the house so they could communicate as he followed her from room to room in reflections.

Then there were times when he regressed; moody dark days when he brooded and wouldn't take part in their conversations at all. On those days, he often frightened Mia with his hostile appearance, reminding her that perhaps they had not come as far along as she had thought. In between sightings, she lit votive candles and prayed for him, hoping that soon, he would be set free to find peace.

Despite their talks, she still didn't know much about him. Seth had little recollection of his former life. He could not recall his last name, where he lived, his school, or much else beyond his current physical state. The insignia on his jacket that had the potential to reveal his identity remained stubbornly stained and unreadable, not divulging any answer to his past. But she pressed on, reasoning that as long as he continued to appear to her, he was still trapped and her task not yet finished.

She tried guessing at the possibilities of where he was. Based on the descriptions he gave her, she wondered if he was in some kind of pit or hole... or grave. At one point, she considered whether he could be in some version of Hell, but quickly changed her mind. It was hard enough to deal with the fact that she was communicating with a spirit, let alone that he might be suffering some eternal damnation.

"Do you know where you are yet?" she asked, initiating a conversation after he had followed her around the house for a half hour one day.

She was always sure to prompt him, hoping the repetition would make him recall more details and clues. Little by little she began to piece together bits of information from his life.

CANT TELL. TOO DARK.

"Anything else that you can tell?"

MUD. STRNGE SMELL

"Okay, this is new," she encouraged, "What kind of smell?"

STENCH—DNT KNOW

"Have you ever tried getting out of there? Climbing out?"

SMTHNG WRNG LEGS DONT WORK. SIDES TOO STEEP

"What's wrong with your legs? Are they just asleep? Or have you injured them in some way? Have you tried pulling yourself up...?"

The teenager held his hands up to the glass for her inspection. It was the first time he offered her a close look. She winced at the tatters of flesh and skin on his fingertips. Bone tips showed on some of his digits. It was obvious that he had tried many times, frantically. Feeling horrible in having asked him, she desperately switched subjects.

"Uh—what is it that you normally like to do?"

WHAT DO U MEAN

"I mean, when I was your age, what—eighteen or nineteen—I liked going out with my friends. You know, shopping, movies, whatever. Hey, how old are you anyway?"

He stared for a few moments before responding, seeming to have to concentrate on the questions. Then he answered,

18   HANG OUT. NOT MUCH ELSE TO DO WHR I LIV.

"Okay, well, where do you hang out? At the mall? The park? With your friends?"

WHREVR. JUST HANG OUT. FRIENDS –

His eyebrows furrowed and he stared off to the side, looking deep in thought. Then with a spark of recollection lighting his eyes, he began to write,

FRIENDS—JUSTIN MARCUS JOSE

"Hey! All right! That was good! Was that hard for you to remember?"

He nodded his head yes, but there was a look of satisfaction spreading across his slim face.

"And how about your parents? Do you remember anything about them yet?"

MTHER AND STEPDAD

When he held the notebook up this time, his expression suddenly turned dark. She noticed blood starting to seep from his nose again. She had begun to recognize it as a sign of stress for him.

"Seth? Are you okay? What's the matter?"

He remained still and only blinked, not responding.

"Did you want to talk some more about them? Can you remember?"

NO

Judging by his reactions, she had apparently and inadvertently hit upon something significant, but difficult for him. This was tricky, trying to navigate through his life. Mia shifted the focus again, before she lost him.

"How about a girlfriend? Do you have one?"

The sullen face perked up some when he picked up the pen and started writing.

SHAYLA

"Her name is Shayla? Okay, you remembered! And it seems to me that you might like her, just a little…huh?" She tried a tease, a wink, and a lively smile.

He shared a shy grin in return.

"Hey! Look at you! Anything else you'd like to confess?"

He shook his head but kept the small smile on his face. Then, without any notice, he vanished.

Mia blinked her eyes as if she had been dreaming. She picked up the notebook and immediately jotted down notes about their conversation, adding to this extraordinary puzzle. It was impossible to determine how long all of this was going to take to solve. However, it never ceased to amaze her that she was even attempting it at all.

While he was gone, she knew that she should get some things done before Dan got home. She decided to head over to the food store. It had been at least a few weeks since she had last shopped and her shelves were showing it. She could grab a few things quickly and be back in case Seth returned in the afternoon. She didn't want to miss out on an opportunity to talk with him some more.

◊ ◊ ◊

"He's not in? Again? Okay, will you tell him I called? Yes… I know. I'm sorry, I don't want to keep calling. I just need him to contact me. It's kind of urgent… Yes, it's still about my wife. You have her name down? Mia La—… Yes, ma'am. That's correct… Okay. Thanks," Dan said with polite restraint and then slammed down the phone.

He had waited on hold for over ten minutes only to be told no, again. He wasn't getting anywhere with this Monroe jerk or PartnersHealth.

Mia was just as frustrating in stonewalling him. When he had confronted her with the strange notations in her journal, she made all sorts of weird excuses, saying it was some kind of writing exercise that she was working on. She never was a good liar and he saw right through her halting speech and the tripping over her tongue.

Besides, neither the writing on the pages or her explanation made any sense. If it was a writing exercise, what did all the crazy words mean? Maybe it *was* something as simple as a dosage problem again. Although he found that he couldn't be completely assured of that possibility either. Not anymore.

His work schedule made it impossible to devote the time he needed to this situation. Pryus had lost a technical producer to another company, so his and Hoason's workload doubled. He would've complained, but he couldn't afford to lose this job, not with Mia unemployed.

Dan became aware of a slight odor rising from his shirt. With some embarrassment, he kept his arms down. There were only so many times he could re-wear a dirty shirt without it being noticeable. He knew the growing mound of laundry was just another thing he had to tend to at home after he prepared dinner and paid the bills.

Pulling into their driveway, he looked at the house. In an instant, a familiar fear arose in him—a recurring flashback of finding her lifeless on the floor. It was one he could never quell. What would he do without her? Would this be the day? He braced himself and entered their home.

Not finding her immediately, he was about to start searching when he heard her talking on the phone in another room. Taking a deep breath, he felt relieved and even a little hopeful. It seemed like ages since she had called anyone. With remorse, he remembered how he use to tease her about how much she talked on the phone, suggesting that one day she was going to need the device surgically removed from the side of her head. Now he wished they were back to those days. He would gladly welcome her talking to anyone for hours at a time or doing any of the other everyday things she use to like to do.

Without disturbing her, he quietly slipped into their bedroom to change out of his work clothes. He found the mirror covered up again in the bathroom, although the others around the rest of the house remained down, and made a mental note to ask her about it. He also prepared to rummage around in the kitchen to see if he could come up with anything for dinner. Trying to remain positive, he had to admit with a little pride, that their current situation had forced him to become more skilled at cooking.

As he was leaving the bedroom, he noticed their phone still in its cradle on their dresser. He wondered if she was on her cell phone in the nursery where he could clearly hear her talking animatedly. Then she paused. He started down the hall to ask about the bathroom mirror when she resumed talking. Trying not to interrupt her call but wanting to let her know he was home, he peered around the doorway and looked in.

Mia sat cross-legged on the floor, holding a notebook up to the cracked dressing mirror that hung on the nursery wall. She stared intently at the glass.

"Uh huh, so do you have any close relatives—you know, cousins, aunts, uncles?" she asked her reflection. It was obvious she hadn't noticed him standing there.

She placed the notebook down on the floor beside a pen and stared at it. From his place by the door, he could see scribbling all over its pages again. Dan was curious.

Why would she ask herself about her own relatives? Could this be one of those writing exercises she was talking about?

"What? Oh, c'mon. You mean you're not going to tell me? Why not? I thought we were getting a lot accomplished today. And your memory is starting to kick in! We have to work with it while it's here."

Dan watched as his wife carried on her monologue and then turn her eye once more to the notebook on the floor. She looked up to the mirror and pouted a little, then smiled. He stared in wonder at her unusual behavior.

"Okay. Well, be that way. You know, sometimes I don't understand why you get so tight-lipped all of a sudden. I bet you were one stubborn kid," she said.

"Murph? Honey? What are you doing?" Dan asked gently, hoping she couldn't hear the sorrow in his voice.

Mia looked up in surprise at her husband standing there. Immediately she grew excited.

"He's here Dan! Come look. Now you'll be able to see him! Quick! See?" she said, rising to her knees and anxiously pointing to the mirror.

Perplexed and curious, he approached the mirror and with one last look at her, surveyed it.

He saw his wife and himself.

"Wow! Look! He's staying this time! He hasn't vanished. Do you see him? You didn't believe me when I said there was a person in the reflections. Well there he is!" she said proudly, excitement bubbling over in her voice, as her hands gestured towards the mirror. "Can you see him? He's right there in front of you. Seth, wave! Do something so he can see you!"

He watched her wide eyes in the reflection. They toggled back and forth as if she were tracking something. Then she looked at her husband.

Noticing his expression, she exclaimed, "Come on, you've got to see him. He's right there!"

Dan squinted and stared hard at the glass. But he knew he was doing it more for her sake, than his.

"Hold on, Dan. Please Seth! You've got to show him! For some reason, he's not seeing you yet. Oh, I know! Here, write some more. Then he can at least see you write..." Mia said tapping on the notebook on the floor.

Dan looked at her incredulously.

"Wait a minute! You're not saying—don't tell me that whatever it is you see in the mirror is writing this stuff?"

He looked at the notebook, then back at their images in the mirror. She couldn't possibly be suggesting it.

"I thought you said that you—" he started, but her face began to crumple.

"Please Seth! Show him. He's not seeing you. All you've got to do is write something. Anything! He'll see your words! Please Seth…No, don't go. No, not now. Don't…"

Dan studied her anxious eyes, searching about the mirror.

"Mia…" he said quietly.

"He was right there! You *had* to have seen him. He was standing right in front of you, clear as day. Here! This is his handwriting! Look at what he wrote just before you came in."

She eagerly shoved the notebook into his hand. Dan viewed the page. Once again, he recognized two distinct handwritings just as he had earlier in the week, but he still couldn't make any sense of the bizarre sloppy print. He looked down at his wife, her expectant face anxious for his response. He couldn't. There wasn't anyone in the mirror talking to her, much less writing in her notebook.

"I'm sorry, Honey. I can't…"

"Please Dan, why can't you see him? He was standing *right there*. I'm *not* going crazy, if that's what you think. He really does exist. You've got to believe me…please…" she pleaded, her dark brown eyes tearing at him.

At that moment, his heart went out to her. He wanted so badly to make everything right for her—to believe what it was she so desperately wanted him to believe.

He sunk down onto the carpet beside her where she knelt. When she wrapped her arms tightly around his neck, he could feel her tears soaking into his shirt and her body shuddering as she drew a breath. He put his arms gingerly about her as if she would break with the slightest squeeze.

"Okay, Murph. Okay. I'll … I'll try," he quietly conceded.

However, taking one last glance into the mirror, he saw only their two reflections.

◊ ◊ ◊

"There have been seventeen messages left for Gerry already, Dr. G. We just don't know what to do with them anymore," Marcia explained, timidly holding out a stack of phone memos to her superior. "I mean, we always leave messages for him for call backs, but it's usually only a few. We normally wouldn't be bothering you with this. It's just that, well, it's *seventeen* messages. Us girls up front are worried that the patients are starting to get upset."

Dr. Rueben Gamez peered over his glasses from the reports piled on his desk. In the dimness of his office, he wasn't quite sure who was speaking to him until the woman stepped into the light of his desk lamp. He recognized her as Monroe's medical assistant. Without a word, he stuck out his hand to receive the slips of paper where she obediently placed them. He scanned through the batch quickly, noting the patients.

She started explaining rapidly, "Some of these people have called and left several messages already. Mr. Labont, alone, has called over six times. We don't know what else to do except to tell them that Gerry's out of the office. Lynne, the new receptionist up front, poor thing was nearly in tears after she got chewed out by Mrs. Lattimer on the phone. Mrs. Lattimer demanded to speak to Gerry and became very angry and verbally abusive. Lynne had to take all of her shi-, I mean the brunt of it. I would make his call backs for him, except that he didn't leave me any notes or instructions this time. I don't know what to tell the patients."

Gamez looked up quickly, "You make his call backs for him?"

"Uh, well, not all the time. Just when he gets backed up."

"You are not to *at all* unless it is to relay some routine information, do you understand?" he said, his voice tight.

He picked up a pen and immediately jotted something down on his pad.

Marcia rocked a little with uncertainty and then continued, "Okay, Dr. G. Like I said, it's not that we want to go over anybody's head; it's just that we don't want the patients to get upset with *us*. When they're angry, they start yelling. And everyone's got to take the heat because we cover the phones for each other while others are rooming patients. We just thought that you might want to know."

"Thank you for calling this matter to my attention. I will get down to the bottom of this and the problem will be corrected," The psychiatrist said tersely. When the medical assistant continued to stand there, he added, "Is there anything else I can do for you?"

"Well, yes. Um, what are we suppose to do with the messages?"

"Has Mr. Monroe given *any* indication as to when he plans on returning?"

"He's called in sick for the past three days. I'm not sure."

Gamez did not speak for the next few moments, making Marcia increasingly uncomfortable. Finally he handed back the slips.

"Pull these patients' files for me and leave them on my desk with these messages. I'll make the call backs myself."

Surprised, but relieved, she replied respectfully, "Yes Dr. G. Thank you. I'll get those for you right away."

Leaving the dark office, she was eager to get out into the bright hallway amongst the cheery posters again. She passed Doreen, another MA, who was on her way to the filing room.

"So did you talk to Dr. G about good old *Gerry*?" Doreen asked, smirking evilly and popping her gum.

Marcia smiled, a Cheshire cat full of satisfaction. "Why yes. Yes I did."

"And?"

"Oh, he's pissed all right. I have to pull the files right now. He's going to make the call backs *himself.*"

"No! Really?"

"Oh yes, really," Marcia laughed and patted her on the arm.

They giggled down the hallway, each imagining how nice it would be to see good old Gerry twisting in the breeze.

◊ ◊ ◊

Dan heard the phone ringing inside the kitchen from where he was working outside on the porch. By the fourth ring, he wondered why the machine wasn't picking up. He swore softly, put down the wrench and greasy power steering unit he was working on, and entered the house. He hoped by now Mia would answer it, but he didn't see her anywhere.

When he looked in the living room, she was talking to the mirror again and holding up her notebook, oblivious to everything else just as she had been for the remainder of the week. Shaking his head, he returned to the kitchen and tore off a paper towel to wipe the excess engine grease from his hands as the insistent ringing continued.

Using the paper towel, he picked up the phone, trying not to handle it while placing it on his shoulder. *Maybe it's that jackass Monroe, finally returning my call.*

"Hello?" he said.

"Dan? Is that you? Hello! It's Aunt Lydia! How are you sweetheart?"

"Uh, okay, Aunt Lydia. How are you?"

With impatience, he rolled his eyes, hoping the conversation would be short. The Jeep's power steering unit was in pieces on the patio table and without a lot of interruptions, he was planning on getting the seal replaced and put back together by the end of the weekend.

"Oh I'm fine dear. The power séances are a little slow around this time of year, but I'm making up for it with my herbal remedies. I've added three more, you know—elecampane, datura, and pigweed. People are buying my remedies for everything from psoriasis to constipation."

"That's... good. Hey, did you want to speak to Mia?"

"Yes darling, I wanted to see how she was doing with her visiting spirit and all."

"Visiting spirit? Excuse me?"

"Yes! Yes. She called me the other day. It was so nice to hear her voice. She told me all about the troubles you kids were having. I'm so sorry, dear."

Dan didn't quite know what to make of it, but he didn't have time or patience for explanations. It was obviously something that Mia knew about.

"Well, uh, thank you. I'll go see if I can find her. Will you hold on for just a moment?"

He picked the phone off his shoulder carefully with two fingers, used a corner of the paper towel to hit the hold button, and then went to the living room.

"Hon? It's your Aunt Lydia."

She was fully engaged in talking to her reflection, so she waved him away.

"Mia, she wants to talk to you."

"Tell her I'll call her back. Can't you see that I'm busy right now?" she said without looking at him.

He held up his hands in defense. "All right, all right. So sorry to *bother* you," he said sarcastically.

This time he didn't care about getting greasy handprints all over the phone.

"Aunt Lydia, she can't come to the phone right now. Can she call you back?"

"Ohhh. Is the spirit visiting her right now?" she cooed.

"Huh? Yeah. I mean, no. What exactly are you talking about?"

"Her Spirit Friend. The man she keeps seeing in her mirrors and other places. I think it's so exciting that she has decided to make contact, don't you? I had hoped that she would!"

"Make contact?"

"Yes. It is so important for her to communicate with him. She can learn so much from the Netherworld. It's wonderful that she's been given that opportunity."

Dan couldn't believe what he was hearing.

"I'm sorry, I'm not following you…"

"It will be the only way she'll get 'you-know-who' to leave. Though I am a little worried for her. From what she told me, he sounded like a dark source. You're going to have to keep a close eye on her, Dan. This may be a nasty sort she is dealing with. He may even put her in some possible danger."

"Danger? What? Listen, did you talk to her about all of this—this stuff?" he asked, feeling perturbed. It was suddenly clear to him where his wife was getting all of this garbage.

"Why yes dear. I told you she had called me."

"What exactly did you tell her?"

"Oh, we had a long talk about this spirit fellow. I told her not to be afraid and to make contact with him and that she should help him in any way that she could, but to be careful. I only wish I could be there to see him too. Hmmm, maybe I'll get a bus ticket and come out to visit you kids. I can guide her. You understand it's not everyone who gets such a chance to communicate with one. The spirit world only chooses and trusts certain people."

"Enough Lydia. Will you cut the bullshit?" Dan growled through clenched teeth.

"Pardon me?" The old woman sounded baffled.

Using extreme effort to control his temper and keep his voice out of Mia's earshot, he continued, "Listen, when she talked to you the other day, you had to have noticed that she's been under a lot of stress lately. She's having a hard time handling things with losing the baby and her dad and all of that."

"Why yes, she told me that very thing."

"Well, then, what you don't seem to understand is that she is going through post-partum depression right now. And lately, she's losing what little grip she has left on reality."

"But this *is* reality, Dan! This isn't the baby blues. Don't you see her speaking to somebody in the reflections? Just because you don't see him there yourself, doesn't mean that he doesn't exist. Mia has been chosen for a very special task to help him. And it is not going to be easy."

"Goddamnit! You're not getting this, are you? She's delusional! If you really want to know what reality is, she tried to take her own life! I found her freaked out with a loaded gun in her hand and she was serious. Okay? If it weren't for the therapy and medication, she probably would've gone through with it already. So you can see why she doesn't need anyone filling her head with a crock of shit right now! Understand?!"

There was silence on the other end.

Then Lydia spoke up in a small voice, "Mia told me how you won't open your mind to believe."

Dan knew there was no use in trying to get through to her. He took a deep breath trying to regain his composure.

"What? No. Listen, Lydia, I'm not going to lose her, not to something like this. She's going through a rough patch right now, but if she keeps up with her therapy she should rebound soon. So listen, I'm going to hang up, okay? I know that you care about Mia, but I really can't have you talking to her right now. She'll get in contact with you when this is all over with, all right?"

"Dan, wait! She needs guidance. This isn't someone she should be dealing with all by herself."

"I'M HANGING UP NOW."

The conversation ended abruptly with a click.

He clenched his jaw in fury. In a sudden, deft move he slammed the counter hard with his fist, his frustration boiling over. The phone jumped and rattled in complaint from the impact.

"Honey?" Mia called from the living room. "Is Aunt Lydia still on the phone? Seth decided to take off for now, so I can talk to her."

Listening to his wife's voice, he was amazed at the normalcy of her tone and words.

"No," he said, bottling up his temper. "She said she'd call back some other time."

Since that evening in the nursery, three days ago, when she begged him to believe, he had stood aside and given her full reign to do what she felt she must do without any interference from him just to see where she was going with this. And in these past few days, he had given it an honest effort: looking into the reflections, studying her as she talked to them, hoping to catch even the tiniest glimpse of whatever it was she was so fixated on. But nothing was there. And he knew that there never had been.

That evening after she had fallen asleep, he slipped out of bed and got dressed. He had been lying awake in the darkness for a couple of hours already and was feeling restless. As he stepped out into the cool night air, a light rain was falling. He breathed in deeply, hoping to clear his head swarming with thoughts and alternatives. He zipped up his jacket and walked down the street, letting the rain fall upon his uncovered head. The Wallingford neighborhood was empty at that late hour, his footsteps on the pavement echoing in his ears.

Images of her flooded his mind—her singing to music on the radio or proofreading a manuscript; her face smudged from gardening; her eyes inviting and seductive when she wanted to make love. Various scenes and memories from their life together collided with the overwhelming fear that had invaded his thoughts. Was he losing her?

As he cleared the first city block, he could feel his stride stretch, his pace quicken. His heart started to respond to the increased demand and his lungs filled with the moist air. He didn't know why but he couldn't slow down, his legs forcing him to move faster and faster beyond his control. He broke into a jog.

Within another block, he was in a flat-out run. He ran hard as if his body were possessed, his arms and legs pumping in perfect rhythm. The neighborhood passed by him in a blur and his feet pounded on the pavement. Dan felt as if he were back in basic training; running mile after mile, his drill instructor barking out commands, pushing him onward over obstacles and beyond his endurance.

He crossed streets and yards, splashed through puddles of water coursing alongside of the road. He had no idea why he was running or where he was running to, but he couldn't make his legs stop, either. With each stride, thoughts of her flashed through his head in rapid-fire succession. A painful stitch flared up in his side from his manic pace. Gripping it, he pushed on further, driving himself to go even faster and harder. He felt as if his legs weren't his own. They had captured and held him hostage on this wild flight.

Finally, after some miles, with his lungs burning and his heart beating wildly out of control, his body cried defeat and slowed to a stop. Bending over, he tried to force air into his oxygen-starved lungs. He walked in a wobbly circle and came to rest against the wet brick wall of a store, gasping and hacking. There for several more minutes, he panted heavily, looking up to the sky at the rain that continued to come down upon him. A thick, painful knot formed in his throat. Tears came to his eyes, but as they escaped, they mingled and were lost on his rain-wet cheeks.

Mia…Why?

Despite the run, he wasn't able to flee the thoughts of her crowding his mind. It was odd how he could hear her voice, her laugh, her quiet tones that soothed and comforted. He thought of the way he could tell her anything, the light touch of her hand, and her caring ways.

Lately everything had turned to tears and arguments, moods and depressions. That deep, never-ending sadness had enveloped her and took over her life. Their life. And now the sightings—those reflections she kept insisting on. He couldn't identify what they were or when they would ever end. There was an insidious change coming over her. Trying to fight it, he knew what it all was boiling down to, but he didn't want to have to make that decision.

How could he?

The rain continued to fall and his jacket was soaked through. Dan was on the move again. He was drawn to a pub that was still open, its neon light splashing red onto the wet sidewalk. There were only a few people left in the dark corners of the quiet bar. Like him, they had come in to get out of the rain falling upon their heads. He pulled himself up onto a stool, ordered a drink, and brushed the droplets off his shoulders.

As the scotch slid a warm finger down his cold throat he thought wryly, *I could do with a few more of these "visiting spirits" myself.*

He drained his glass and ordered another.

EIGHT

SHE NEVER REALIZED THAT HIS EYES WERE SO VIVID. The only time she had ever seen such blue-green eyes, they were staring back at her from models in the glossy ads of magazines such as *Vogue* or *Cosmopolitan*. Even then, she was never sure how much was airbrushed or PhotoShopped. Her own eyes were a dark walnut, Dan's a deep, dark brown, almost black. And her father's were the color of a leather saddle. Sure, co-workers and friends had blue eyes or green eyes. But she never had such close contact with eyes like Seth's. It wasn't just the color. They had the power to captivate and peer through to her very soul. It amazed her to think that those same pair of eyes had terrorized her just weeks before. They were strange and evil then, threatening and consuming.

What made her notice them on this day was that for once, they appeared lively and benign. Gone were the last of the angry red blood vessels that snaked across the whites. And he no longer stared with the look of a dazed sleepwalker. He now made direct eye contact and was very expressive.

The last of the dirt and mud were completely gone as well, and the ghastly gray pallor had faded from his skin. His complexion now, a healthy vibrant tan. His legs, strong and straight, allowed him to move with athletic grace and ease. Miraculously, even his fingertips had completely healed. The only trace left of his former appearance was the blood and mud stains that blotted his jacket and jeans.

His transformation had been nothing short of astonishing. However, the most noticeable change in Seth was that he looked alive and familiar, as if she were talking to someone she had known for a long time. A friend she could confide in and share with. The only thing that set him apart from any living, breathing person she knew was the pane of glass between them.

Mia saw now that he had rugged good looks and was lanky in build. The tallness of his frame and the shadow of a beard across his face made him look older than his eighteen years. She couldn't get over how much things had changed since she had been in high school, when the boys in her class had always seemed so underdeveloped and sophomoric. Surely, there must have been some girls in hallways in Seth's school who breathlessly giggled his name to confidants while clutching their books a little tighter to themselves, hoping to be the recipients of his shy charming smile.

Now that Mia was free to talk openly to Seth any time he appeared, communicating with him was no longer taboo. Dan's change in attitude and backing down on his scrutiny was unexpected but welcomed. She only wished that her husband could join in on these conversations with them. It had to be only a matter of time before Seth felt comfortable enough to appear before Dan. Her husband would have no choice *but* to believe then. She held that hope in her heart.

In the past week and a half, she and Seth had made huge strides in their talks. He grew increasingly coherent, and recalled and comprehended more with each passing day. She never lost an opportunity to speak with him wherever he showed up, whether he appeared on a shiny vase, a chrome strip on an appliance, a pot lid, or the numerous mirrors that she had purchased for around the house. She also had become quite adept at reading his jagged backward print, no longer needing to hold up the notebooks for deciphering anymore.

Through their many hours of "conversations," she tried to get the youth to explain why he was able to contact her out of all people. She didn't understand why he wasn't communicating with a family member or his girlfriend or even an experienced person that dealt with the paranormal instead. Seth, himself, remained unclear on how it happened at all. He only knew that Mia was there one day.

All he could remember was being scared, hungry, alone, and in intense pain for days on end. He was trapped in some kind of dirt cavern that was completely devoid of any light. He had become very weak and given up all hope of anyone ever finding him. From dehydration, lack of food, and pain, he lapsed off and on into a deep, dreamless sleep. After some time, it became very difficult for him to differentiate between consciousness and unconsciousness in the blackness of the pit.

One day, his sensitive eyes picked up a small light boring through one of the walls of his dark prison. He struggled to get to it, but it proved to be very elusive. Awaking from his sleep, the light would disappear. But it continued to beckon each time he slipped from consciousness, promising hope and rescue. Through the darkness, whenever fatigue and weakness overcame him, he learned to focus on the small light. It became a goal for him and freed him momentarily from his plight, even for only seconds at a time.

As he turned his full attention to it, the light grew brighter in intensity. Eventually, the seconds he spent turned into minutes. At one point, he found that if he concentrated hard enough on the light, he escaped his entombment to another world beyond the abysmal cavern. It was then that he found her.

From what Mia comprehended from his sketchy descriptions, when the light appeared, he was transported to a mirrored environment parallel of her surroundings. Once there, he was free to move about and access any object in whatever room or place she was in. He was there with her in the garage and kitchen, at the store, and in her car. Only he didn't see her as she did him, in the reflections of his world. Instead, he was there viewing her in her world but always through some invisible barrier that kept them apart. If he tried to go beyond wherever she was, he was instantly cast back to the dark, fetid enclosure with no way out. His existence was intrinsically linked to her but neither of them could fathom why or for how long.

Mia tried to gather as much information as possible whenever he appeared. Many times their talks were serious and intense. Gleaning from their conversations little by little, she learned of the numerous details that made up his life. She found out that he grew up in a small town. His mother and father divorced when he was about five and his mother remarried a couple of years ago.

Sometimes their talks were informal and fun. He played shortstop on the varsity baseball team. He was fixing up a '73 Chevy Malibu with his friends. And to her surprise, Seth had a sense of humor and he liked to use it. But she also learned that his moods were fleeting and on occasion, Mia saw flashes of his quick temper.

"You're looking good today, I hardly recognized you! But who else would be visiting me through my living room mirror?" Mia teased.

OH, I'M SURE THERE'S GOT TO BE OTHERS

"What do you mean?" she laughed.

WELL YOU'RE THE ONLY PERSON I KNOW OF WHO TALKS TO REFLECTIONS, SO THERE MUST BE OTHERS LINED UP WAITING FOR A TURN SOMEWHERE. MAYBE YOU SHOULD CHARGE ADMISSION OR SOMETHING—YOU'D GET RICH QUICK!

He laughed back.

She countered, "I should charge you. The overtime alone would probably pay off my car."

WITH THE CAR YOU DRIVE, IT SHOULD BE PAID OFF ANY MINUTE NOW, HUH?

"Funny! Oh, so you're not only looking good, but now you're a comedian, eh?"

Grinning mischievously, he sat on the sofa and tossed one of the throw pillows high into the air and caught it. She was amused by his boyish exuberance.

"And what's so bad about my car? You seem to think the back seat is pretty comfy," she countered. "You like to ride in it often enough."

NOT BAD. BUT YOUR HYUNDAI NEEDS MORE HORSEPOWER. IF I COULD, I WOULD TRICK IT OUT FOR YOU. PUT A REAR SPOILER ON, CHANGE THE TIRES, CONVERT IT TO DROP IN A TOYOTA 2.7 L WITH 5 SPEED MANUAL SHIFT, CHANGE THE SHOCKS. HECK - I'D MAKE YOU A REAL STREET RACER YET.

"Whoa! You may want to consider that I happen to *like* my car the way it is," she cried in defense.

UH HUH. SURE YOU DO. THEY ALL SAY THAT. BELIEVE ME, KNOWING YOU, I BET YOU'D BE A REGULAR SPEED QUEEN IN NO TIME

She picked up another throw pillow and chucked it playfully at the mirror, hitting his reflection square on the head. He flopped down in mock injury upon the sofa, holding his head, pretending to moan. They both shared a laugh at his antics. But after a few moments, he sat up, his bright smile starting to wane. He rose to his feet and paced the room a bit, then stopped to rock on his heels, and stretch.

I'VE GOT TO FIND SOMETHING TO DO TO PASS THE TIME. I FEEL GOOD. MY LEGS ARE GOOD AND MY HANDS ARE FINE. THE PAIN IS GONE NOW. ONLY WISH I COULD GET OUT OF HERE AND GO DO SOMETHING. IT'S FUN TALKING WITH YOU AND ALL, BUT I JUST FEEL SO TIED DOWN.

"Yeah, I know. We're working on it, okay? Just a little longer, so hang in there, Tiger. I think we have to keep doing what we are doing. We seem to be getting somewhere. You're looking great." Trying to encourage him, she continued, "What would you do today if you were out of there?"

DUNNO. GO FOR A HIKE , PLAY SOME BALL, SEE SHAYLA OR PROBABLY WORK ON MY CAR.

"Oh yeah? Work on your car? Well at least mine runs!" She teased again.
He gave a sheepish smile in response.
"So what are you doing with your car?"

ITS CARB NEEDS SOME WORK. BUT I'D REALLY LIKE TO SUPERCHARGE IT SOMETIME WHEN I GET THE MONEY.

"Supercharge? Would that make it go faster or something?"

OH HELL YES. I'D LOVE TO GET IT OUT ON THE HIGHWAY THEN AND OPEN IT UP. I COULD REALLY PUT SOME MILES BETWEEN ME AND THAT TOWN

"Did your dad teach you how to work on cars? I know my dad was handy like that. It seemed that he could fix almost anything."

YOU MEAN STEPDAD. NO HE DOESN'T DO MUCH WITH ME.

"Really? Don't you guys have anything in common—sports? Fishing? Camping?"

NO. NOTHING

She thought of the loving bond she had shared with her own father and found his response foreign. "Well, do you at least talk about things?"
When she asked, she noticed that Seth quickly lost the merriment from his eyes. It was replaced by a seething anger. His brows drew together and the corners of his mouth turned down.

TALK? HA. THAT'S A LAUGH.

IT'S MORE LIKE YELLING AND BLAMING

This intrigued Mia. "Yell and blame? About what?" she asked.

ABOUT EVERYTHING. NOTHING I DO IS EVER RIGHT WITH HIM

"I don't understand. You are a good kid and a smart guy, too. What could you possibly do that is so wrong?"

HE SAYS THAT I MAKE MOM CRY. THAT I'M SHIFTLESS AND LAZY. BUT IT'S ONLY BECAUSE I WON'T DO WHAT HE WANTS ME TO DO

"Which is...?"
He started writing fast and hard. The lines appearing in the notebook left heavy imprints in the paper from the pressure.

LISTEN TO HIS BULLSHIT. SAYS THAT MOM AND I NEVER HAD ANYTHING UNTIL HE CAME ALONG

Mia decided to press on although it was obviously a sensitive issue. This was a facet of Seth she hadn't seen before in their conversations. He was starting to open up and she didn't want to discourage him. The more pieces of information she could put together, the closer she felt she was to solving his mysterious presence.

"How were things between your mom and you? You know, before she remarried?" she asked cautiously.

WE MANAGED. MOM WAS AT WORK A LOT AND I TOOK CARE OF THINGS AROUND THE HOUSE FOR HER—COOKING, CLEANING, FIXING THINGS. I'LL ADMIT WE USE TO GET INTO ARGUMENTS SOMETIMES. ONE TIME I EVEN RAN AWAY. BUT WE ALWAYS WORKED THINGS OUT. THAT IS - UNTIL HE CAME ALONG

"Did you and your mom still talk afterwards?"

NO. HE WON'T LET US. HE'S ALWAYS GETTING BETWEEN US. WHENEVER SHE COMES HOME FROM WORK, HE'S ALWAYS THERE, DOMINATING HER TIME OR PICKING FIGHTS WITH ME SO I'LL LEAVE

"Doesn't your mom notice what's going on?"

YES. BUT I THINK SHE'S AFRAID TO SAY ANYTHING BECAUSE SHE
DOESN'T WANT HIM TO START IN ON ME. ONE TIME SHE SPOKE UP
AGAINST HIM, AND HE SLAPPED HER. I WENT TO STOP HIM AND THEN
WE REALLY GOT INTO A BIG SCRAP. HE ALMOST BROKE MY NOSE
THAT TIME. FUCKING BASTARD

Mia winced as she read the pain within the lines. "Did you talk to your teachers or counselors at school about this? How about the police? Have they tried to put a stop to this?"

MY TEACHERS SAW MY FACE ALL SWOLLEN UP. SONS OF BITCHES
DIDN'T CARE BECAUSE NOT ONE OF THEM ASKED ME ANYTHING
ABOUT IT. THEY'RE PRETTY USELESS. AS FOR THE POLICE, THEY'VE
BEEN OUT ONCE, WHEN HE GOT LOUD AND THE NEIGHBORS CALLED.
BUT THERE'S NOTHING THEY CAN DO SINCE MOM DOESN'T WANT TO
PRESS CHARGES. BESIDES, HE'S DOESN'T GO AFTER EITHER OF US IF
WE STAY OUT OF HIS WAY. COPS GOT BETTER THINGS TO DO THAN
TO WRITE UP A BUNCH OF REPORTS ON A FEW BRUISES AND FAMILY
DISPUTES

She took all of this in for a moment and wondered what he was going to do next. She wanted to give him some advice, suggestions to guide him through this harrowing time in his life. If she could even just hug him to give him some moral support, but sadly she remembered that his fate had already been determined for him. He would never escape. She knew that Seth always referred to himself as if he were still in the present, but in truth, he would not get a chance to grow up and live his life away from abusive stepfathers and small, closed-in towns.

"Oh Seth…" she said as her heart broke for the youth.

This was the first time they had ever shared so much. Overcome with pity, she reached out to comfort him. He watched her hand as it came near, but he didn't move away or retreat to the depths of the reflection as she expected.

Instead, he moved closer to the glass and stood very still. Her fingertips grazed the glass timidly, stroking the side of his face. Seth's eyes met hers. He responded by putting his palm against the mirror. Mia let her hand slide down to rest against his. It seemed so strange to be separated by such a thin piece of cold glass.

"I am so sorry for you. Why does life have to be so… unfair?" she whispered quietly, her breath held hostage by grief.

She could feel the old depression coming on once more and was taken back by its intrusion. It hadn't been around since she had started communicating with him. He looked sadly at her for a minute then managed a smile.

HEY—DON'T FEEL BAD. IT'S OKAY. I'M USE TO IT

"Well I'm not. There was so much ahead of you. So far you could have gone…."

NO REALLY. I'M FINE. THANKS FOR CARING. DON'T WORRY ABOUT ME.

Then Seth hesitated for a moment and wrote another line.

MIA—DID YOU EVER WANT TO HAVE ANY KIDS?

She was surprised by his candidness. "Wh-what do you mean?"

SEEMS TO ME THAT YOU ARE A COOL PERSON. YOU KNOW—KIND, HELPFUL. AND WELL—YOU'RE MARRIED AND ALL. IT WOULD BE ONE LUCKY KID TO HAVE YOU AS A MOM.

"Well, thank you Seth. I don't know what to say."

His innocent statement unintentionally sent a sharp jab through her, and she had to look away from his questioning face for a moment.

He must have noticed her reaction because he wrote,

DID I SAY SOMETHING WRONG? ARE YOU OKAY?

She wiped away a tear from the corner of her eye and tried to smile. "It's all right Seth. We tried to have a baby, but I—I lost him. I had had a miscarriage a couple of months before I met you. We *have* been trying to have a baby, all along. Ever since we've been married. We just haven't succeeded. I don't know what is wrong with me. Then when I finally got pregnant, I couldn't hold onto him."

Mia had never told anyone about her inability to conceive, partly out of her own shame and partly out of fear that there was something seriously wrong with her. Yet, she didn't know why, but she felt the need to divulge it to Seth. Somehow, she knew she could trust him to simply understand and completely accept it, without passing judgment or requiring any explanation from her.

He looked at her sympathetically.

I'M SORRY I BROUGHT THAT UP. IT WAS REALLY STUPID OF ME.

"No, it's all right. You know, you are about the only person I have trusted enough to tell that to."

He nodded his head in response, but still looked regretful. She tried to think of another topic for discussion, but none was forthcoming. She had a headache and queasiness settled in her stomach.

"Listen, I've got a headache right now. It's been coming on all day, but all of a sudden it's really gotten bad. Would you mind if I stop now and go to lie down?"

RIGHT NOW? LISTEN - I DIDN'T MEAN TO HURT YOUR FEELINGS OR MAKE YOU FEEL BAD—DO YOU HAVE TO GO? WE CAN TALK ABOUT SOMETHING ELSE. ANYTHING YOU LIKE.

"It's okay, Seth. I told you that I am not upset. In fact, I've needed to share that with someone for a while, now. But I really do need to lie down."

She looked at him standing there, looking lost again. She realized how young he still was and how much he needed to be reassured.

"I guess you can follow me if you want."

Mia went to her bedroom and closed the blinds. Her head was splitting and she was nauseated. It was the worse headache out of all the ones she had been having these past days. The cool pillowcase felt good to her hot face and she gladly sunk into it.

She really wished that she could have continued talking with Seth. They had covered a lot today. But the arrows radiating through her head told her otherwise.

Overcome with exhaustion brought on by pain, her last glimpse was of the small mirror she had placed on her nightstand. Seth was there, watching her with concern. As she faded off to sleep, those vivid blue-green eyes followed her into her dreams, searing an image against the black backdrop of her eyelids.

◊ ◊ ◊

"Mr. Labont? This is Dr. Rueben Gamez, head of mental services at PartnersHealth's Capitol Hill facility. I understand that you've been calling."

"Uh, yes sir. I've been trying unsuccessfully to reach Gerry Monroe. My wife is under his care," Dan answered.

After numerous attempts and no responses from Monroe, he was getting ready to pay a very near visit to the office and straighten out matters in person. Gamez's phone call to the editing room was quite unexpected.

"I apologize for us not responding to your calls more promptly. Mr. Monroe has not been in this week. I have been handling some of his more urgent calls for the time being. I understand you have questions concerning your wife, Mia Labont?"

"Right. Well it doesn't seem like things are improving with her condition. As a matter of fact," Dan looked up to see Hoason enter the room, then lowered his voice, "things seem to be getting worse."

"I see. And can you describe in what manner is it 'getting worse'?" Gamez asked in a tone that was clip and dry.

Hoason had seated himself at the monitor and was listening intently to the conversation, but quickly averted his eyes and started tapping away at the keyboard when Dan glanced over at him. Dan turned his back to his coworker and tried to explain, hoping to maintain some privacy. He considered stepping out into the hallway, but Greenlee might be passing by and personal phone conversations on company time were not tolerated well.

"Mia has been complaining about seeing things. We mentioned it to Gerry, but he said it was perfectly normal given the stress that she's been under. She's been taking her medication for about six weeks already, but it hasn't helped any. In fact, it's gone the opposite way, Doc. She's still pretty depressed and—"He cupped the receiver with his hand and lowered his voice even further. "—she's *talking* to herself in mirrors and reflections now. She swears that she sees some guy there and she needs to 'save him' or something like that."

"And can you think of anything that may have triggered this new behavior?"

"Well, to tell you the truth, I think her aunt may have put some ideas in her head."

"Her aunt? How so?"

"Mia's aunt is into all of that spiritualism and new age herbal stuff. I guess they've been calling each other and her aunt has her convinced that she's communicating with some kind of ghost or something. I'm sorry, I know it sounds ridiculous …"

"It's perfectly all right, Mr. Labont. There's no need to apologize. In reviewing her file, I see that Mr. Monroe increased your wife's dosage of sertraline."

"Yes. I guess going on about, hmm… three weeks ago."

"And she is continuing the diazepam as well?"

"Yes, sir. But she still has trouble sleeping at night. Sometimes she even has to take a little wine in addition to help her relax."

"I see."

Gamez sounded clinical. Dan had the feeling that they may finally get somewhere with *this* guy reading her chart.

The psychiatrist continued, "Taking everything into consideration—Mr. Monroe's notes here, your wife's complaints, and your input—I am inclined to believe she may be having an adverse reaction to her dosage."

"I'm sorry, come again?"

"Her sertraline level is on the high side accompanied by the diazepam. And you tell me she is taking alcohol in conjunction with them. She may be responding negatively to the medication. Infrequently, it happens with a few of our patients."

Dan perked up. "So, you're telling me that her medication could have something to do with all of this?"

"Yes. Perhaps. It has been known to happen."

"Okay, so all of these things she sees in the mirror and her fluctuating moods, it *is* because of the medication." He wanted, no, *needed* definite reaffirmation.

"It's possible. Although it is very rare, sertraline has been known to cause insomnia, anxiety, and hallucinations in a very small population of the patients tested in clinical trials. But you understand that each patient reacts differently. Some are more sensitive than others. A therapist could not know about a patient's predisposition until the symptoms have become apparent."

Dan could hardly contain himself, however he wanted to make absolutely certain that he was hearing the psychiatrist correctly.

"Okay, so what you are saying is that if she stops her medication, she should stop seeing all of these *things* that she is talking about?"

"Correct. In fact I want her to cease all medication for now. And I'd advise her to not ingest any more alcohol for the time being until her body has had a chance to adjust. A change in her symptoms may not be obvious immediately, but we'll see in a week or so if it helps to alleviate some of these hallucinations that she has been experiencing. At that time, if there is no improvement and she is still showing persistent signs of depression, we may switch her to fluoxetine. Some patients seem to tolerate that better."

"Okay, Doc! I'll be sure to tell her. Now what about Gerry? When should she see him next?"

"Mr. Monroe should return next week. At that time he will contact her to set up another appointment to evaluate her condition and to see if she'll need a change in her prescription. Now are there any other concerns I may help you with today, Mr. Labont?"

"No sir. Thank you very much for calling back. I tell you, this is a load off of my mind! I really appreciate it, Dr. Gamez," Dan answered, immensely relieved.

"You're welcome. Good-bye."

Dan hung up the phone and swung around in his chair.

He clapped Hoason on his shoulder and said happily, "It's her medication, Ho! Oh god! What a relief! Can you believe that? Her medication! That was the shrink on the phone. Not that jackass counselor, but an actual doc. Seems he looked over her charts and wants her off the meds."

"Hey, that's great, man! Are you going to call her?"

"I think I'll go home and tell her right now —that is, if you don't mind covering for me for the next hour or two?"

"No, blow on out of here dude. I think I can hold things down for now."

Grabbing his jacket, Dan said thanks over his shoulder and was out the door.

At home, he found Mia dressed in old sweatpants, t-shirt, and robe, sitting on the sofa, and talking quietly to the large tile mirror. She looked up at him and smiled wearily. She was a little off-color and there were deep shadows under her eyes.

"Hey Murph, how are you?" he asked affectionately, giving her a kiss on her forehead. "Are you feeling okay? You don't look so well."

"I'm not. I was just telling Seth that I can't seem to shake this headache. I even tried lying down and taking a nap earlier today, but it hasn't gone away. Say hi to Seth, Honey."

"What?" Dan asked as he looked over his shoulder at the mirror but saw only Mia and himself. He gave a half-hearted wave. "Yeah. Hey there, Seth," he mumbled and then turned back to her.

"So what are you doing home already? Did you forget something?" she asked, perplexed.

"Babe, I have great news for you. Dr. Gamez called today because he's filling in while Gerry's out. You remember Gamez, the little bald guy who's the big shot over at PartnersHealth? Well, he was going over your chart, and after reviewing your symptoms and dosage, he thinks that you are having a bad reaction to your medication."

Mia sat and stared at him, as if she couldn't follow what he was saying.

"Hon, are you hearing this? You are having an adverse reaction to your meds. He wants you to stop taking all of it immediately. He said that *that* should clear up these hallucinations you've been having!"

"Hallucinations? He's saying that these are hallucinations? But Seth is standing right there. I don't know why you can't see him." She pointed around him to the mirror.

He took her by her arms. "Please Murph, just stop taking the damn pills. Let's see what happens, okay? Maybe that's what's causing your headaches too! Now he says that it probably won't affect you immediately, but things should clear up pretty soon. Oh, and you should back off on the wine too."

"Okay," she shrugged and sighed.

He was dumbfounded by her apathetic response. He thought she would be just as excited as he was. Nonetheless, he was happy that there was some kind of plausible explanation for all of this. He took her up in his arms and hugged her, then kissed her. She resisted a little, trying to turn back towards the mirror, but he held onto her. Taking her chin in his hand, he redirected her attention back at him.

"We're gonna be okay," he beamed.

◊ ◊ ◊

SO DO YOU THINK THIS WHOLE THING WITH YOUR MEDS IS TRUE?

Seth asked the next morning as soon as he appeared.

"What, about them causing hallucinations?" she asked.

She had slept a little better the night before, and thankfully this morning, her headache had finally abated. But she wasn't prepared for his questioning. She overlooked how Seth witnessed everything going on in the house, including her conversations with Dan.

YEAH. I KNOW HE THINKS THAT I'M ALL SOME PART OF YOUR IMAGINATION AND THAT YOU'RE JUST TRIPPIN' OUT OR SOMETHING. BUT IT SOUNDS LIKE A BUNCH OF CRAP IF YOU ASK ME.

She sighed. It was obvious that Seth was in one of his moods again. After what they had shared yesterday, she felt a little disappointed by his surly behavior today.

"What's the matter, Seth?"

I DUNNO. I'M RESTLESS, I GUESS. HOW LONG DO YOU THINK THIS IS THIS GOING TO TAKE—YOU KNOW TO GET ME OUT OF HERE?

"I don't know. I wish I knew."

For a moment, the two of them contemplated his situation. There were so many pieces missing from this puzzle, yet. She still didn't know his last name or the name of the town or any other clue to his identity.

"I think that when you can recall how you got there—" she started.

He jotted down his reply quickly.

I STILL DON'T REMEMBER. WHY DO YOU KEEP ASKING ME?

"I'm just trying to sort this whole thing out and find out who you are and what happened. I think that's the whole key to this."

I'VE TRIED BUT I TOLD YOU, THERE ARE SOME THINGS I STILL DON'T REMEMBER, NO MATTER WHAT. BESIDES, WHAT IF IT DOESN'T WORK - WHAT IF I'M STUCK HERE FOREVER?

"We've got to keep trying. I know we'll figure it out," she offered encouragingly.

AND THEN WHAT?

"We'll just have to come up with something else. You're not supposed to be there. Somehow I know it. It can't possibly be that it was intended for you to be stuck here with me for the rest of my life instead of moving on to some place better."

A scowl darkened his eyes once more and threatened to spread across his face.

"Seth? What is wrong with you today?" she asked, perplexed by his terrible mood.

I LIKE TALKING WITH YOU MIA. I CAN'T TALK WITH SHAYLA - NOT LIKE THIS. THIS IS <u>DIFFERENT</u> - YOU'RE DIFFERENT. I LIKE BEING WITH YOU.

AND I THOUGHT YOU LIKED BEING WITH ME TOO. BUT IT ALMOST SEEMS THAT YOU <u>WANT</u> ME TO GO AWAY

"I'm confused. You don't want to be there, and I don't blame you. But are you upset with me now because I want you to be free?"

He stood brooding, not picking up the pen to write.

She continued, "I... like talking with you too, Seth. You are funny, and bright, and have so much to say. It's just that I can't keep going on like this."

SURE I'D GET OUT OF HERE IF I COULD. BUT IF WE <u>HAD TO</u> CONTINUE WITH THIS, WHY NOT? I'M <i>NOT</i> SO BAD, AM <u>I</u>? I MEAN I KNOW I SCARED THE SHIT OUT OF YOU IN THE BEGINNING AND I'VE APOLOGIZED FOR THAT

Thinking of his limitations, she tried to explain gently, "Well, before all of this happened, I use to have a job and friends. And it's been a while since I've gone out and done anything. Like you, I am starting to feel restless..."

YOU CAN DO THINGS WHILE I'M AROUND. IT'S <i>NOT</i> LIKE I'M GOING TO GET <u>IN</u> THE WAY OR ANYTHING.

He shrugged and smiled at his attempt to joke.

She smiled patiently at him. "It's not that easy. My husband and I need to work things out and get back to where we use to be. We've built a life together. And it's hard to live that life when we are at odds with each other."

His eyes narrowed at the mention of Dan and his mouth twisted sardonically.

YEAH—HIM. HE REMINDS ME OF GOOD OL STEPDAD. ALWAYS SHOOTING HIS MOUTH OFF, BUT NEVER LISTENING. I'VE SEEN HIM WALKING OUT ON YOU WHEN YOU TRY TO TALK TO HIM. HE SHOULDN'T TREAT YOU LIKE THAT.

"You haven't had the chance to get to know him. He's a good person. Really. It's just that… well this is hard for him to understand. If you would only appear to him, like you do to me. If only he could see you I know he would believe. He could even help."

She stopped short as he furiously wrote something down.

I DON'T NEED HIS HELP

"Why are you being so stubborn? We need all the help we can get. What if I'm overlooking something? I've never been good at solving mysteries or puzzles. It would be beneficial to have another person working on this with us. You say that you want to get out of there. But you are not going to unless we can understand how and why you are there in the first place."

He held the notebook closer to the glass and pointed to his previous message again. Then he added,

BESIDES, ACCORDING TO HIM, I'M JUST A HALLUCINATION, RIGHT? WHY WOULD HE WANT TO HELP SOMEONE THAT IS NOT REAL?

Mia closed her eyes and sighed, "All right, Seth."

They had reached an impasse. It was obvious they weren't going to get anywhere today.

Just then the phone rang. When she answered, it was Dan wondering if she felt up to going out that night. He wanted to take her to dinner at a restaurant they hadn't been to since they were first married. She felt relieved at his suggestion. It was just the thing she needed at the moment, to get away from the house for a bit. She told him yes and then returned to the mirror. Seth was waiting with a message.

ALL RIGHT - I'M SORRY ABOUT WHAT I SAID ABOUT WHAT'S HIS FACE

"It's Dan. You know that. And I forgive you. "

He exchanged his petulant scowl for a lonely look instead.

NO REALLY, MIA. PLEASE – JUST DON'T BE MAD AT ME.

When Dan returned home from work that evening, he was lively and talkative, a far departure from the anxious silent man he had become in the past month. Mia was happy to see him like that again. His enthusiasm was infectious and she began to look forward to their time out.

Seth had continued hanging about all day, following her from surface to surface as she tried to tidy the house and get ready to go. Looking at his expectant face, she knew she would have to ask him not to tag along tonight. She chided herself for not telling him earlier in the day. Instead she had put it off, not wanting to hurt him or make him feel unwanted. His mood was testy at best and she didn't know how he would respond. Now she tried to find a minute when she was alone with him. While Dan was in the bathroom, she had her chance.

"Listen, Seth, Dan and I are going out tonight, okay? It's been a while since he's been in such a good mood and we've gone anywhere. We need to spend some time together. So you and I will talk some more tomorrow, okay?" she smiled reassuringly into the mirror.

I THINK I'LL GO ALONG. I HAVEN'T BEEN 'OUT' FOR A WHILE, MYSELF.

SHOULD BE INTERESTING

She couldn't be sure if he was being sarcastic, but she did note that he had a sour look on his face.

She tried again. "Well, it's just that I told you I'm trying to patch things up with him. It would be better if you wouldn't show up. You know I can't really talk to you openly when he's around. He doesn't say anything about it, but I can tell he's not too comfortable with this whole situation."

Seth looked at her stubbornly, then rolled his eyes, and tried to act disinterested.

SURE THING. I CAN HANG OUT HERE BY MYSELF AND HAVE SOME 'FUN' OR

MAYBE I'LL THROW A PARTY AND INVITE MY WHOLE GRADUATING CLASS OR SOMETHING

"Please? C'mon Tiger. I promise you we'll talk first thing in the morning, okay?"

By then, Dan had come back into the room.

"Ready to go? God, you look great!" he said, looking her over and giving her a kiss on the cheek.

She threw one last begging look at Seth, hoping he would understand and acquiesce. But to her dismay he persisted, appearing in the car's side mirror, the glass doors of the restaurant, serving trays, and dishes on the table. He settled on the polished bowl of her soupspoon so he could contemplate her directly. She glanced at him from time to time, but tried to keep her attention fixed on Dan. It was one thing to talk to Seth at home, but she wasn't going to embarrass her husband or herself by talking to him in inanimate objects in public. It would appear as if she was crazy.

At one point, Seth made the sign they used when he needed something to write with. Mia tried to ignore him and focus on her husband, until Seth caught her eye by motioning big. She decided to take a chance. There might be something important that he finally recalled.

"Now where did I put my tissue? I hope I packed some along," she said casually as she fished around in her purse.

Dan smiled and watched her. When he directed his attention to their waitress who had just approached, she dug out a pen and an old receipt and then placed them discreetly under the edge of her plate out of her husband's view.

DOESN'T HE LOOK 'NICE' TONIGHT. REMINDS ME OF AN ASSWIPE

She knew she had made a mistake.

Dan reached for her hand across the table. "You know, I was thinking that when my vacation comes up we should get away somewhere. We can go back to Hawaii and see all the things that we didn't get to when we honeymooned or maybe we can do something really different, like take a cruise or something."

"Oh, that sounds nice! But can we afford it? I know we don't have my paycheck anymore, but I hope to find another job."

"Nah, I think we can manage. It may be tight for a little bit, but hey, we can count it as a Christmas gift to each other this year."

YEAH RIGHT. HE'LL FIND SOME EXCUSE AND NEVER TAKE YOU. YOU SHOULD TELL HIM WHERE TO GET OFF. HE'S NOTHING BUT A LOSER

"So, what do you think? Hawaii or maybe a cruise somewhere?" Dan asked her again. She realized that she hadn't answered him.

"Oh, I'm not sure yet. They're both tempting," she said, acting as if the patrons at the next table over had distracted her.

She grabbed up the scribbled receipt and pen and shoved them back into her purse. Seth glowered at her, his face distorted and out of proportion in the rounded bowl of her spoon. She placed her napkin over it, blocking his stare. She most definitely would address his rudeness and ugly remarks, but for now, she and her husband would dine undisturbed by his presence. Although she knew Seth was still there, skulking about and probably waiting for another opportunity to intrude.

As the evening went on, she relaxed once more and dismissed Seth's misbehavior to the back of her mind. She missed her husband and was enjoying this time they were having together. It had been so long since they had acted 'normal' toward each other.

Dan looked very handsome in the black sweater he was wearing and his easy laugh and lopsided grin brought back the old feeling from when they had first had dated complete with dancing butterflies in her stomach. She delighted in his flirting and the attention he was lavishing upon her. Once again, their conversation rekindled itself and they were lost in each other, oblivious to everything else.

They ordered dessert and a round of margaritas and reminisced about when they were first married and the people that they had known. After another round, they discussed the places they had visited and places yet to go.

Then to Mia's surprise, Dan stood up and reaching out his hand to her, asked unexpectedly, "Dance with me?"

"Dance? You don't dance," she said, amazed.

"Well, there's always a first time for everything, isn't there?"

He led her out to the dance floor in a small dark corner of the restaurant where they were the only ones under the mini-mirror ball. Although he ended up accidentally stepping on her toes, he held her tenderly and close. Mia knew he was trying his best at dancing. She felt really touched by this gesture.

"Hon, you know, we don't have to dance if you really don't want to. I mean I appreciate the offer, but we're the only ones out here," she whispered self-consciously as she looked about.

"One of the things I regret is never taking you out to dance. I know you've asked me plenty of times and I've always been such a mule. It's such a simple request. And don't ask me why, but I couldn't bring myself to do it. But I've been thinking about a lot of things lately, Murph. Mostly about you. I may not have told you this enough, but I love you. I am hopelessly, desperately in love with you and I think I always will be. Do you want to know the first time I knew?"

She thought about it for a moment, but couldn't honestly answer. She looked up at him and shook her head.

"You're not going to believe this, but remember the day we met?"

"It couldn't have been love at first sight. I can't believe that!" she laughed.

"No. There were too many people around, the food line was too long, and your mother was too mean looking," he teased.

"Well, then when?"

"How about four hours later when it was just the two of us looking out over the Bay on the bench in my parents' backyard. You were so beautiful, I had to kiss you."

"And you did."

"Yes, ma'am, I sure did. But I don't remember you fighting me off either."

"Nope, that's what my mother was there for."

He laughed as they swayed in time with the music, but then grew serious.

"I know I've been acting like a real jerk lately and I want to tell you that I am sorry. I couldn't ever think about losing you. I don't know what I would do," he said.

He stopped dancing and took a long look at her. Then he kissed her deeply. She yielded and kissed him back.

As they drove back home, Mia was very careful to avoid looking at any reflective surface. She didn't want her evening with Dan to end, and seeing Seth in one of his dark moods would spoil it. She would deal with him tomorrow and get down to the bottom of those nasty messages he had written. Tonight, was only for her husband and her.

When they entered the house, Dan came around behind her to slip her jacket off.

She started to say, "It was fun seeing that old place again. You know, it really hasn't changed much since we first went there. Just some of the things on the menu were—"

But Mia stopped short when he deliberately turned her to face him and studied her for a moment in the half-light from the kitchen. His dark eyes, shining, searched hers.

"God, you are beautiful," he murmured in a low soft voice.

His hand caressed her cheek then lightly trailed down her neck. It came to the top of her blouse where it lingered. Mia could feel her face flush and her breath quicken. She didn't want him to stop, so she reached up to find his warm lips with hers. Encouraged, he slowly unbuttoned her blouse and opened it to reveal the soft curves of her breasts peeking out over the lace edge of her bra. He pulled her close and planted small, gentle kisses at the base of her neck and worked his way down. Breathing heavily, she trembled with pleasure at the feel of his lips on her skin and rolled her head lazily back. He opened the front clasp of her bra and started kissing her breasts. Moaning softly, she half-closed her eyes and glanced off to the side.

Seth was there, watching them.

He wore a strange and twisted expression on his face, while a thin scarlet line of blood ran from his nose. He was the last thing she wanted to see just then. In her interlude with her husband, she had forgotten all about him. Quickly pulling her blouse together she shot a dirty look at the mirror. Confused, Dan raised his head and backed off immediately.

"I'm sorry, I thought that you—" he started to apologize.

"No, I do. I do. But just not here," she reassured him.

She gave one last look to the mirror to see Seth's eyes intent on her. Unexpectedly, she could also see the letters W—G, AZ for the first time emerging from the bottom of the crusted insignia on his jacket. Not wanting to take the time now, she made a mental note to ask him about it tomorrow.

As her husband took her hand and led her to their bedroom, the teen pressed his palm up to the glass and said something, watching her until she disappeared beyond the door.

Dan turned on the lights in the bedroom, but she immediately turned them off again. She took the vanity mirror from her nightstand and stowed it in the drawer. Having secured everything, she then turned back to him. Wrapping her arms about him, she kissed him once more, pulling him onto the bed. Tonight, as she determined before, was just for them alone.

◊ ◊ ◊

"So will you see him anymore this month?" Dan asked as they dug up the weeds and expired plants in the backyard garden.

"No. This should be it for a while. As long as everything is going like it is, I should be fine," Mia answered.

She reached over and pulled up the last of the crab grass and tossed it into the pile with the others.

"And you feel pretty good about it? I mean, are you sure?"

He put his foot against the heel of the shovel and sunk it deep at the base of the diseased rhododendron.

"Yeah. I think I'm going to be all right this time," she said with a tiny spark of confidence.

Her sessions with Gerry had now been tapered down from the bi-weekly schedule they had followed since her very first therapy session so long ago, to only once a month. She was feeling better although still a little weak yet, as if she were recovering from a physical illness. And her headaches had finally diminished.

It felt good to be outside working in her garden once again. It felt even better with Dan beside her. It had been a long time since she had felt this complete. She embraced and reveled in reclaiming her life. So much had changed from where she had been only a few weeks ago, and so rapidly. Thinking back, she couldn't get over just how deep and dark of a hole it was that she had fallen into with her depression. She had really gotten off track. It was a wonder that she could have ever emerged intact.

Looking back objectively, it frightened her to think that she had ever thought some person was appearing to her, lurking in reflections. She couldn't believe that she, out of all people, could have ever become so delusional. She had always thought of herself as a logical, sensible person and yet, her imagination had concocted an entire person, complete with identity, emotions, problems, even hobbies! Although he remained a mystery to her, she didn't want to think of his name or face or any other detail about him ever again.

She had stopped taking her medication the very afternoon that Dan had spoken with Gamez, and remarkably, within a couple of days, everything—

the images in the reflections, the shadows, the writing in the notebook—had ended. Her hallucination named Seth, was gone. She and her husband both questioned if the cessation of medication could have taken effect that quickly, but they didn't want to disclaim it either. It was the final solution to the madness they had suffered through for the past few months.

When she considered how her meds were increased, she realized how much they correlated with the frequency and severity of her hallucinations. The more she hallucinated, the more medication she took. It had become a cycle of destruction.

Since then, she refused to take any more pills. She even refrained from wine. And when Gerry offered her a standing refill as an alternative to stave off any residual depression, she flatly told him no. Instead, she decided to take hold of her life on her own, looking into other natural remedies of diet, exercise, and meditation.

Her recovery began the morning after their night at the restaurant three weeks ago. Dan left her to sleep late with a kiss on her cheek. She slept for a half an hour more and then awoke again, reaching out for him. She was disappointed to find his side of the bed empty. Grabbing up his pillow to hug and hold close, she wished he would come back to bed so she could exchange the pillow for him. But she knew that once he was up for the day, he didn't usually go back to bed.

That is, unless I can persuade him, she thought wickedly, remembering their night of passion.

Going over the events of the evening, the sulky look on Seth's face suddenly forced its way into her thoughts. She was going to have to set the teen straight. Although she had agreed to help him in any way possible, he could not attack her husband. She definitely felt annoyed with him, but before she could grow too irate, she reconsidered his circumstances. She sighed, knowing that he probably wouldn't be so bitter and angry if he weren't trapped there.

Mia fished out the vanity mirror from her nightstand drawer.

"Hey Seth, now about last night.." she started as she held up the mirror, only to stop short when she faced her own image.

She was sure that he would be waiting there—angry, petulant, and ready to continue his verbal assault on Dan.

Perplexed, she rose and went to the bathroom where she pulled down the towel from the mirror that she had covered for privacy. Seth was not there either. Clad only in her nightgown, she walked out to the large mirror in the living room where she knew he would be waiting smugly after making her play his little game of hide and seek.

But it too, was empty.

He must be really upset with me, she decided.

She was certain that he would reappear given a few hours or so when he had time to cool off. He had nowhere else to go. In the meantime, she took up their notebook and opened it to their last discussion. There she jotted down what she had seen on his jacket the night before: W - G, AZ. It would be a good topic to switch to after she talked to him about the crumpled receipt with his remark. She closed the book and waited.

The morning passed. She returned to the large mirror after he still had not appeared on any surface about the house. Apprehension filled her.

"Seth? I know you can hear me. C'mon, we've got a lot to talk about last night. I know you are upset, but it's not going to help if you keep hiding. Let's discuss this and get it out in the open," she said patiently. "You know, I don't even know why you are mad at me. After what you said, I should be angry with you. But I'm not. So come on, already."

"Honey, what are you doing?" Dan asked when he discovered her talking to the mirror again.

"It's Seth. He isn't anywhere around today. It's really unusual because he would have shown up by now."

"So there's not some guy in there looking back at you anymore?"

"Well not right now. He'll probably show up again eventually. There's nowhere else for him to go."

"He's not there at all? In any of the reflections?"

"No. I've waited all morning. He's not anywhere. And I don't know where he could be. I think he may be upset because we went out last night. And he was there when we came home and started to make love."

Dan relaxed and smiled broadly. "Don't you get it? You've stopped taking your medication! I know it's a little early yet, but maybe, in addition to knowing it is going to make a difference, it has started changing things already," he said.

She continued to search about in other reflections. "Hmmm, I don't know…I think I'll give it some more time. I'm sure he'll show up sooner or later. He's probably just doing this to get back at me," she answered, not convinced.

Seth never reappeared again.

The mirrors stood empty and their notebook remained closed. She waited expectedly, carefully surveying all the places he used to show up. Mia couldn't help but worry about him and how he was doing. She thought about him being alone in that cold dark place.

Yet, another part of her wanted the possibility that this all could really be ending. By the end of the week with no other sightings or odd occurrences, she had no choice but to face it. It had been the medication all along. At first, she couldn't help but feel the loss of Seth. Their close interactions had really become a part of her. Perhaps he was just a manifestation of some longing. Or possibly the mental state that she had been in. She found it odd that her mind had selected the persona of a teenage boy as a conduit for the jumbles in her mind. But the promise of finally making her way out of her *own* darkness and chaos prevailed. She was free herself, and her survival and the survival of her marriage won out over anything else.

Now with the bright sun warming their backs as they worked the back yard, she reached for the pony-packs of marigolds while Dan hauled over a large bag of compost and set it down. He took out his pocketknife, sliced it open, and spilled out the fragrant contents in a pile beside her. Squatting down next to her, he watched her hands working the compost around the plants for a few moments.

"I was thinking about us visiting your Pop today. Would you feel up to that?" he asked carefully, heedful of her recovery.

Mia turned to face him and smiled. "Yes, I think that would be great. This time I want to bring him some flowers. Maybe even a few of these little marigolds would be nice there."

"Okay," he said. "Sounds like a plan. Anything else you'd like to do while we are out?"

"As a matter of fact, I wanted to stop by the farmer's market down at the Square and then go to grocery store. I'd like to make a beef stew dinner for you tonight. You know, we should get some fresh French bread from the bakery to go with it and how about homemade chocolate cake?"

"Stop it! You're torturing me," he said, wincing and clutching his chest in pretend agony. "Man, we haven't eaten like that in a while, huh?"

"Yeah, I guess it has been a bit," she admitted feeling a little ashamed.

When she stood to stretch her back and dust the dirt off her knees, the pyracantha bush by the fence caught her attention. Walking over to it, she peered carefully about its branches to find the house finch nest to show Dan and to tell him of the family of birds that lived there. Within a few seconds, she located it. It surprised her to see that it was abandoned and forgotten. Apparently its tenants had all flown away.

◊ ◊ ◊

Being on probation was a new experience for Gerry and he did not tolerate it well. It was hard enough to catch up on all of his work without having to answer to Gamez for every dotted 'i' and crossed 't.' Okay, he knew his one day of sick leave had extended to the remainder of the week. And he knew that Gamez had to cover for him. He also knew that if it weren't for the fact that PartnersHealth was currently beating the bushes for therapists, he'd be searching the Internet for a new job.

Still and all, with all the other custody and lawsuit problems he had to endure, it was just another pain in the ass to be monitored all day. Lately, he determined, his ass was beginning to feel like a pincushion.

There was word that the Childresses were planning on filing a separate civil suit against him since their little Ashley (*ol' Twiggy*, he referred to her smugly) was now suffering from ulcers in her trachea as a direct result from her bulimia, and was facing possible corrective surgery. They construed that it was his fault for not curing her sooner. Those vultures were unbelievable.

PartnersHealth was likely going to settle out of court for some undisclosed amount already. Why were these bloodsuckers coming after him? If they hadn't let that skinny bitch continue sticking her finger down her throat every time she wanted an increase in allowance, a laptop, or permission to boink her boyfriend under their noses, all of this crap wouldn't have happened. He was only her therapist for Chrissake, not some trained watchdog.

He was tired of bending over backwards for everyone only to get it right up the ass. He made up his mind never to take the short shaft from anyone again. If what they wanted were pills to forget all their troubles, he'd serve them right up. If they wanted to hear that they were nuts, he would be just the one to tell them that they were. If they wanted results, then *by God* he was going to give them results. He would tag and bag them as they came.

The custody battle over Austin wasn't going much better. His son had told him directly that he did not want to live with him, and Amy was threatening to move out at the prospect of having a teenager in her life. Alysse had the audacity to petition for an increase in child support and his new attorney wasn't aggressive enough to hold her off. Even the '68 Corvette he was hoping to get with unpaid child support had been sold off to someone else. Life didn't look like it could get much worse for Gerry at this point.

His interoffice line lit up.

"Monroe? I need to see you in my office immediately,"Gamez commanded.

Then he hung up, not waiting for any reply. Obviously, he assumed that Gerry would drop everything and report immediately because his commander in chief ordered him to do so.

Oh yeah? Well watch this, you son of a bitch. No little balding king shit is going to order me around, he mused to himself.

Gerry looked up at the clock as his eyes fixed a bead on the minute hand. He defiantly folded his hands behind his head and leaned back, savoring his insubordination, and did absolutely nothing. Three minutes later, he slowly rose from his seat, straightened the knot on his Knicks logo tie, and headed to Gamez's office down the hallway. He gave the door a couple of short knocks and then entered.

"Hey Rueben! I heard that you were looking for me? What can I do for you?" he said brightly, feigning his best smile.

"Be seated, Mr. Monroe."

Against his will, Gerry's legs betrayed him by folding and depositing him into the chair.

"I've been reviewing your patients' files and they all appear to be in order. There is one, however, of particular interest."

He picked up a chart, opened it, and scanned through a few pages.

"Go ahead and shoot, Big Guy," Gerry said amicably.

Monroe stared hard at Gerry from over the top of his reading glasses, a predatory owl surveying its next meal. He was far from being amused. Then he returned to the chart and flipped through a couple more pages.

Finally he said, "Mia Labont. It seems that she has made tremendous progress in a relatively short period of time. And she has been taken entirely off of all medication. There are no withdrawal problems reported. No current episodes of depression or delusions to speak of. What exactly do you account for her rapid recovery?"

Gerry had to think for a second until the patient in question came to mind. "Oh yeah, the Postpartum. Well, we've been—"

"*Mrs. Labont,*" Gamez emphasized.

"Okaaay. *Mrs. Labont* and I have been in constant communication and I think we've made some terrific strides together. She's finally opening up and seeing that this was all a chemical imbalance from the get-go. And I have been showing her some excellent therapeutic exer—"

"I spoke with her husband while you were 'out' and he was convinced that she really believed she was seeing something tangible. Has he reported any more of this or any other unusual behavior on her part since the termination of her medication?"

Gerry shook his head. "Nope. Not a single boogey man."

Gamez initialed the page then shut the file.

"You will keep me posted on any changes. We need to continue to monitor her very carefully. This is a case in which we don't want to act too hastily."

"Oh, I'll keep my eye open for anything. But it looks like she is doing fine."

"We *don't* want another situation like the Childresses. Do I make myself clear?"

Gerry locked eyes with the serious little man he despised so much.

"Crystal."

As he returned to his office, he yanked at the knot on his tie that was now choking him, all the while kicking himself for letting Gamez do it to him again. Gerry made yet another promise to himself. There was no way he was going to let Gamez gain advantage over him like that again. He needed to strengthen his defense and the only way he saw how was to make sure that the head doctor couldn't cry foul or error on any shots. He would make sure that there would *not* be any more situations.

As he passed the MA's station, he noted the assistants were busy working on their charts and phone calls and whatever the hell it was they did there. He did not have to deal with any of those bitches at the moment.

But when he took the corner in the hallway, Doreen called out smugly to him, "Hey Gerry, how's Dr. G doing today?"

At this remark, she and her cronies erupted into unified laughter, obviously at his expense. He flipped them a bird over his shoulder as he continued to his office.

They mockingly cried out, "Ooo!" and "Uh oh!" and then started into another round of laughter.

Oh yes, Gerry told himself as he shut his door to their cackles. *From this point on, there will be no more "situations."*

NINE

THE END OF OCTOBER AND APPROACH OF THE HOLIDAYS brought to her a mix of anticipation and sentiment. It would be the first time she had ever experienced the season without her father. Last year, she would not participate in any holiday celebrations, still mourning and reeling in the wake his absence had left. This year already had its own fill of heartbreak, turmoil, and having to get by. It would have been easy to refrain from the preparations and traditions once again. But she endeavored, forcing herself to take part in life once more.

The damp morning air slowly yielded its coolness to the sun as she sped walked around the neighborhood, her walking shoes passing over colorful leaves wallpapered to the sidewalk from an early rain. Mia worked through the details in her mind as she strolled. Though it was almost a month away, she knew that she had better start planning for their Thanksgiving dinner.

She wanted everything to be just right. This would be the first year they would be hosting the meal. Usually, it was held at the senior Labonts' or her parents' home. But since her mother remained in the Holy Land and didn't give any indications of an immediate return and the Labonts were still on their road trip, everyone decided to let the "kids" have a try.

It would be nice to be surrounded by family again. The Labonts would be passing through town by then and Jenna was flying in from Vermont where she attended college. Dan was getting equally as excited and kept reminding her to buy the biggest turkey as soon as they arrived in the stores. He had also invited Hoason to join them after taking pity on his friend's current state of singleness.

It was a good season for her with plenty of activities and events to keep her mind busy, although she continued her regimen of taking vitamins, exercising, eating comfort foods, and meditating whenever her thoughts started to stray too much. In addition, she started to look through the want ads again. Now that they had finally been reunited with their repaired computer, she cruised job websites and posted her resume. She had an interview this very afternoon with another small magazine. It didn't look like it would pay as much as her position with Loren, but it would feel good to be productive in the real world again.

Her nights were devoid of all nightmares and sleep brought her peace once more. As time went by, she quit looking at reflections, boxed up the numerous mirrors to sell in a yard sale, and tucked away the communication journal in her desk. At first, she was going to throw the notebook away, but at the last minute, she decided to keep it. She figured that when she was strong enough to handle it in the future, she planned on doing some research into her past "condition" to find out where she could have gone so wrong. It would be good to know more about herself and her weaknesses.

Living day to day felt completely different this time, as it did anytime one returned from a hard and perilous journey. But she was feeling good and going in a positive direction. She appreciated things so much more—simple things. Instead of watching TV, she and Dan took walks at night, both of them enjoying this new activity together. She rekindled her friendships and interests. And her final appointment with Gerry took place a week ago. There was nothing more to tell him.

Mia turned the block and stopped at the donut shop. After having a short but entertaining conversation with the proprietor, she splurged and bought a dozen donuts and headed home. Dan was going to like this small surprise.

It's a good thing we are walking at night, she thought to herself with a smile.

Lately, it looked like he was putting on a few pounds. But that was okay by her. They had both dropped weight during the Ordeal.

She could hear the phone ringing inside as she unlocked their front door.

"Hi Babe. Just wanted to see how things were going with you today," Dan's voice greeted her when she picked up.

"I can't complain. I just got in from walking. It's beautiful out today, isn't it?" she answered breathlessly as she placed the donuts on the counter and kicked off her shoes.

"Yeah. Wish I could be home spending it with you instead of being cooped up in this hole with my slack ass partner over here. Hey speaking of whom, would you mind if Ho brought along a date for Thanksgiving? I told him it would be okay, but I thought I had better mention it to you since you are the hostess."

"That's right, I am," she said with authority and satisfaction. "Sure. It's not a problem. And good for him! It's nice to hear that he's dating. Poor guy needed a break."

"Yeah, old Ho is getting to be a regular Romeo these days. What-?" his voice broke off to address his co-worker. "No, I don't need any lessons. I taught you everything you know. Hey, would you mind if I continued my conversation with my wife?"

Mia laughed, "Yes that would be nice, especially since you were the one who called *me*. Get back to work Hoason!" she called playfully over the line.

"He says goodbye too. Anyway, I wasn't just calling about that character, the real reason I called was to wish you luck today."

"Luck? What for?"

"For your interview. You remembered you had an interview today, right?" he teased.

"Oh that. It's really nothing big. I'm not too worried if I don't get it."

"You'll get it. They'll take one look and fall in love with you just like I did. You have that affect on people, you know."

"Oh get out of town," she blushed. But it was nice to hear anyway.

"I'm hoping that we both can 'get out of town,' as soon as you look over those vacation brochures I left on the dresser. There are millions of things to see. I found cruises in Alaska, safaris in Africa, ecotours in Costa Rica. There's even a dude ranch in Arizona where we can rope steer if we want. We'll plan for right after Christmas, okay? But listen, Hon, I've got to get going. We've got work piled up to our ears and we haven't had a break all morning. So, good luck! And remember that I love you. Call me and let me know how things went, okay?"

"Okay, I will Murph," she said happily. "I love you too."

The rest of the morning was spent on making her many lists for Thanksgiving Day, looking through the travel brochures, and working in her garden. She prepared dinner in the Crock-Pot and caught up on her emails to Jenna and friends. Before she knew it, it was time to get ready for her interview.

She carefully laid out the clothes she had selected on her bed and searched around for pantyhose and shoes. She showered, and then styled her hair. Happily humming one of her favorite tunes, she applied her makeup.

In her underwear and slip, she walked down the hall with her clothes in hand to the large dressing mirror still hanging on the nursery wall. Even though she didn't consider this a really important interview, nevertheless, still liked to make sure that everything was coordinated and tucked in for the best impression. She picked up her blouse and looked into the glass.

The mirror was streaked in blood.

Gasping, she squeezed her eyes shut. She took several deep breaths.

Am I feeling anxious about this stupid interview? she questioned herself. *I've got to calm down. When I open my eyes, it will all be clear.*

Taking one big breath and blowing out determinedly, she lifted her eyelids.

The blood had begun to run down the smooth surface of the glass. It had already reached the floor in the reflection. She cried out as she looked about her, only to find all the reflective surfaces in the room trickling the scarlet fluid and looking as if a grisly crime had taken place.

Clutching her things to her, Mia started to shake at the horrific sight. She stepped back slowly, moaning, "No... No, No, No..."

She ran from the nursery and retreated to the safety of her bedroom. *This can't be....* Everything was going fine. She had finished her therapy and was pronounced sane. *I am not delusional...*

It was the medication that was the culprit. The depression.

But I've been cured....

She spoke out loud to herself, "I -I am okay. There is nothing there. I need to get this under control... I AM okay!"

She looked about her bedroom to confirm her sanity. Everything was in its place and all reflections were clear.

She repeated, "I am in control. I am okay... I am in control. I am—"

Long red stains began seeping through to appear on the glass panes of the pictures on the walls. Within seconds, the blood pooled and ran down the glass. Terror gripped her.

"This can't be happening... NO! This is NOT happening!" she shrieked willfully, praying it would all stop. "Not again! Not again!"

The bright fluid ran jagged lines to the floor, trapping her behind crooked bars of crimson. The madness was starting all over. A scream escaped past her hyperventilating. All of a sudden, the walls seemed to move in on her, crowding her. The floor beneath her feet felt as if it were pitching and rolling.

She bolted from the room and ran blindly through the house, barging through the front door. She stood for a second on her front walkway not knowing which way to go, but her only instinct was to escape as quickly as possible.

Sobbing hysterically, she ran to her Hyundai, and pulled at the door handles to get in. But the doors were locked, the keys forgotten inside the house. In sheer panic, she frantically pounded on the car window, desperately needing to flee. There reflected on the glass, she saw his familiar silhouette, framed by the glare from the sky.

"No! I am not seeing this! You are not real!" she shrieked at him, backing away from the car. But his image remained, appearing on all of the windows.

"You are not real...not real. Go away...I'm begging you... I can't...not again. Please... go away...." She wailed at the reflections, her hands hanging useless and limp.

The world was caving in. She could feel its cruel weight bearing down upon her but she was too weak to hold it off. This could not be happening. Everything was going just fine. She had held her life firmly within her grip. Within that instant, it ran out of her grasp like water through her clenched fingers.

"Please...Oh God! Noooo."

Mrs. Lopez had emerged from her house and was walking towards her minivan, but spying Mia, ran to her.

"Mija! What's wrong?" she asked as she quickly checked over her neighbor for injuries.

Then she looked around for someone to assist them, but they were the only ones home at that time of day for the entire block.

"Are you hurt? What is the matter?" she asked again.

Mia did not hear her. She continued to cry and point to the window of the Hyundai.

"You are not real... I can't... Not anymore...I'm not suppose to see you!.... GO AWAY!"

Mrs. Lopez wrapped her arms around Mia's bare shoulders. "Come, come inside. You're trembling! It's too cold for you to be standing outside dressed like this! Ai, Mija, you have nothing on your feet. You are going to get sick. Come on now...."

She helped her back towards the house. Mia was reluctant to return. But it was inevitable; there was nowhere else she could go. She knew, with a bitter certainty that *he* would be there inside, waiting for her. She felt like a fish, hooked and thrown upon the hard dry land, gasping desperately for a saving breath. The last shred of her sane normal world was unraveling, against her will and out of her control. There was nothing she could do to get it back.

Defeated, she resigned herself to being led through the doorway and to the sofa. There, she wept convulsively while Mrs. Lopez wrapped a throw around her. The older woman stepped back and wrung her hands, not knowing what to do for her distraught young neighbor.

"How can I help you, Mia? Did something happen to you? Do you want me to call your husband?"

Mia continued to weep, not saying anything. She didn't know how was she going to break this to Dan. He wanted their life back to normal just as much as she did and had worked so hard in seeing her through all of the madness. How could she face him and tell him the reflections were back? This time, they could not blame the medications. This time, they would have to face another reality.

As Mrs. Lopez went to the kitchen to call and make some hot tea, Mia despondently faced the mosaic tile mirror. Seth was clearly there, expectant as always. But what she saw now shocked her. His healthy tanned complexion was gone, his skin dull, contrasting with the bright blood that ran from both of his nostrils. He looked worn out and sick—all of his renewed vitality and strength gone. A pathetic, debilitated creature had replaced the cocky energetic teen she had come to know.

Mia forced herself to objectify him. He was only a figment of her imagination. This must be a reoccurrence of her hallucination. Maybe it was residual from the antidepressants. She held herself steady and slowed her breathing back to normal. She would not react. There was a logical explanation to all of this.

He looked at her with affection and anticipation, and then tried a smile. All of a sudden, he held himself tight and shuddered violently, gripped with pain. He threw his head back and clenched his teeth. At his apparent agony, she gasped and sat up straight.

What has happened to him? her thoughts cried.

His blue-green eyes were glassy as he returned his focus to her. Then he slowly lifted his contorted hand to the glass and placed his palm against it. As her eyes continued to survey him, she saw that his fingertips were mangled again. His hand slid slowly down, trailing a scarlet and mud stained smear. His lips clearly pleading, "Mia, please…Mia…"

At this sight, her heart broke for the teen, melting away her fear and revulsion of his return. She suddenly recalled the hand of her unborn infant lying still in the blue surgical cloth. With instant remorse, she realized that she had failed Seth too.

He was imprisoned, all alone and forgotten, dependent upon her. How could she have possibly turned away from him? He was no hallucination. He never had been.

"Oh Seth, I am so sorry! Ohmigod! Please forgive me…" she cried, reaching out to him.

Clutching the phone to her ear, Mrs. Lopez peeked nervously around the corner of the kitchen at Mia, wondering to whom she was talking to, but she didn't dare come any closer.

"Yes, I need to speak with Mr. Labont… Hello Dan? This is Anita Lopez. You need to come quickly! It's Mia… No, she is right here. But come home now! She is acting very strange. Hurry!"

She hung up the phone and stood watching her neighbor but remained by the doorway, her hand to her mouth in amazement.

Mia continued to beseech the mirror, "What happened to you? … I'm sorry I got angry. I knew you were all alone there, but I left you anyway! I waited for you to come back but you never did. So I forced you out of my mind…I let myself believe what everyone was telling me… please forgive me…"

Any terror she had felt was replaced by overwhelming guilt. How could she ever believe that he was not real? Here he was standing before her once more. And it was evident that her lack of faith had brought this misery upon him.

In the next instant, Seth doubled over again and holding his stomach, vomited a vile mix of blood and bile. He continued to wretch repeatedly until it was finally reduced to a violent, hacking cough. Feebly, he looked up at her and made a slight motion with his hand. It had been over a month already, but she recognized in an instant what he wanted.

Throwing off the wrap, she leapt from the sofa and ran to the bedroom. There, she immediately dug out the communication journal from her desk and rushed back to the living room to hold it up for him to see. Then she carefully placed it and a pen upon the shelf nearest to him and stepped back to wait.

He could barely hold the pen in his battered fingertips. He looked dazed and seized up momentarily as waves of pain racked his body. A new round of tears flooded Mia's eyes as she watched the young man's labored movements. She couldn't bear to see him suffer so.

I should have never given up on him. My body killed my baby… what have my actions done to Seth? she thought. Then she said, "I promise you that I will never leave you again. Just tell me what you need… What do you want me to do?"

He slowly wrote:

CROSS

Unsure of his message, she asked, "What does that mean? Do you want me to look for a cross...? Or is it a church? A graveyard? I don't understand..."

At the mention of this, Mrs. Lopez sucked her breath in sharply, then hastily made the Sign of the Cross and piously kissed her fingertips, whispering, "Ay mi Dios! Ay Papa Dios!"

Hearing Mia continue with her monologue, curiosity coaxed her out a few steps from the safety of the kitchen doorway for a better look at the macabre scene playing out in the living room.

Not paying any attention to the older woman, Mia begged, "Please Seth, I need a little more than that. What do I need to do? Do you need me to find a cross? Where?"

His dull bloodshot eyes beseeched her. She remembered those eyes last when they were vivid and full of life and her heart leapt for him again.

HELP ME

What Mrs. Lopez saw was enough to make her run, screaming from the house in terror.

◊ ◊ ◊

When Dan received the phone call, he only managed to exclaim, "It's Mia!" to Hoason before sprinting out to the Jeep. Running red lights and weaving in and out of traffic, he raced through the streets, his thoughts racing even faster. Waves of nausea, prompted by fear, churned through him. He didn't know what to expect. He reasoned that physically, she must be all right or Mrs. Lopez would have called an ambulance or said something, but she hadn't mentioned anything like that.

What could be wrong?

He prayed that Mia hadn't suffered a relapse. The depressions, the crying, the hallucinations —the last time was too long of a fight for her to see her way through. She almost didn't make it.

Driving up their street, he spied Mrs. Lopez waiting outside their open front door. He could see her peer into the house then look back down the street, anxiously awaiting his arrival. As soon as she caught sight of him, she waved frantically and called out. When he pulled into the driveway, she bustled down to meet him, talking excitedly.

"Dan! Thank God you are home. I don't know what's the matter with Mia. First, she was out here in the driveway, crying and screaming and pounding on her car. She wasn't even dressed! She's inside now."

"Is she hurt? Where is she?" he asked as he bolted for the door.

But before he could enter, Mrs. Lopez had reached out and hooked his arm, anchoring him with her weight and pulling him back.

"Wait! There is something going on in there! Something evil. I don't know what It is saying to Mia, but she's talking back to It. And crying. She keeps crying. You need to get her out of there, Dan. It is evil," she said ominously, clutching at his arm.

Breaking away from her grip, he entered the house. Mrs. Lopez cried after him, "The notebook! Look at the notebook!"

When he found Mia intact, sitting on the sofa, his captured breath escaped in relief. She didn't respond to him as he entered the room, but remained mesmerized by her reflection in the mirror, her face streaked with tears and running mascara, her slender body still clad only in her slip. He rushed towards her, but then caught himself and moved more slowly, not wanting to startle her.

"Mia? Are you all right? Come on, Honey, look at me," he said cautiously as he approached.

He took her by her shoulders and pivoted her to face him, but she fought and twisted back towards the mirror.

"Mia, look at me. It's not real. Come on, Babe. You have to get control. Get it under control," he insisted.

"He wants me to understand the numbers. I need to help him. I should have never left him alone like that. Oh my God. I didn't mean to... I didn't mean to..." she whispered over and over again.

"Aww, Hon, don't do this again. You've worked so hard..." he begged her. "Get control, Babe. Come on. Look at me... Mia?"

She would not respond, remaining fixated with her reflection. "I'm sorry I ever did that to you Seth. Forgive me..."

Dan flew to the phone and dialed it frantically, then waited for a response.

"I need Gerry Monroe now! This is an emergency... I don't care if he's with a patient! I need to speak with him immediately! ... No, I don't want to speak with his goddamn nurse. You either get him on the phone right now or I'll personally make sure that you are fired, now GO GET HIM!!" he screamed into the receiver.

A few seconds later, the therapist was on the line. "Hello? Who is this?"

"Monroe, this is Dan Labont. You've got to do something. Mia's freaking out! I mean totally freaking out. She's back to talking to the mirror again. But this time she's not responding to anyone or anything else."

"Now calm down, Dan. We—"

"I don't want to calm down! She's right back to square one! Like nothing has happened. You've got to do something, now! I'm bringing her in."

"Well, I have other appointments that I—"

"You better cancel those appointments because we'll be there in about twenty minutes!" He slammed down the phone.

Mia stood sobbing by the mirror, her hand pressed against the glass. Dan tried to move her to the bedroom to get dressed, but she resisted saying, "NO! Don't! I can't leave him alone! Something's really wrong with him. He's sick and in pain!"

He scooped her up instead and carried her to their room. She reached back for the mirror and struggled.

"Put me down! I can't fail him again! He's trying to tell me something," she cried.

In the bedroom, she broke away and ran to their closet. There, she ripped open the box marked 'for yard sale' and snatched out one of the several small mirrors.

Cupping it protectively in her hands, she said, "I'm here, okay? Can you see me?"

"Please, Hon, tell me what's going on," Dan asked.

"He's been here all along. I was wrong to forget about him, wrong to shut him out. His existence depends upon me. Do you understand? Upon *me*, and I can't lose him."

She robotically dressed with the clothes Dan handed her, but her eyes and attention stayed fixed to the mirror. He led her out past Mrs. Lopez who stood on the lawn wringing her hands to the Jeep. There Mia sat, still clutching the mirror and saying, "I'm right here, Seth. Can you see me? I won't leave you. I promise."

On the way to PartnersHealth, Dan tried once again to get to the bottom of this new scenario.

"But I thought you didn't see anything in the reflections anymore. You knew that it was all hallucinations from the start. And your medication was off. You haven't started taking them again, have you?"

She continued to cry and stroke the mirror, remaining unresponsive to him.

"Mia? Stop looking at the mirror and look at me. What is going on?" he asked her again slowly.

She gasped and jumped in reaction to something she saw in the reflection. "He's in so much pain… so much pain. I'm sorry I don't know what to do for you, Seth. I don't have anything to write with here. No. It's all back at the house. I've got to figure something out."

His questions ignored, Dan retreated to his own thoughts. Way back when, at the beginning of all of this, he had blamed the miscarriage for all her bizarre behavior. However, she had had counseling and time to recover. Then he shifted the blame to the medication. But she has been off all medications for a while now.

What was happening then? Was there something else yet? She was fine this morning and had been for the past couple of months already. *Now this.*

He had prayed that this would never come to pass again. It appeared now that he was faced with the same heart-wrenching conclusion he had wrestled with before. He hammered on the steering wheel in frustration then gripped the side of his head as it swam with thoughts. Fear, like a cold stream, coursed through him.

What if this is incurable? He looked to his wife.

She sat unfazed by his outburst, but continued to stroke the looking glass and soothe, "It's all right, Tiger. I'm right here. I won't ever leave you again…."

◊ ◊ ◊

"Mia? Hey how are you? Dan's been telling me that you are having a rough day," Gerry said when they entered his office.

Mia chose not to respond to him, but sat down instead.

"Hey. It's Gerry. Now tell me what happened today," Monroe said as he crouched in front of her and looked up into her face.

She wouldn't return his stare, keeping her eyes trained on the mirror and weeping.

"Come on Mia. Look at me," he insisted.

"May I please have something to write with?" was all she said.

Gerry ignored her request and instead tugged at the mirror in her hands. "Well, I guess we're going to have to take *this* for now."

"No!" she exclaimed. "You can't!"

"No, no, no. It's okay. It'll just be for a minute," he reassured when she resisted, closing her grip on it. "Really, it'll just be for a minute, I promise," he said as he struggled with her.

Finally he pulled it out of her hands and laid it on his desk.

"Give it back! I need it!" she said as she jumped up out of her seat to retrieve it. Gerry firmly pushed down on her shoulders, forcing her back into her seat. Dan, who was standing off to the side watching everything, moved in quickly.

"Hey! Watch how you're—"

"It's okay, Dan. I'm not hurting her. I've got to get her focus off the mirror." Keeping her pinned, he looked her directly in the eye. "Okay Mia, what's going on?"

"Everyone thinks I'm crazy. That I'm imagining things. Hallucinating. I've tried to tell you that he is *real*. But no one will believe me. He is right here, with us right now. Whether you can see him or not, he's here. And now he's sick, and I don't know what to do."

"Who's sick?"

"Seth!"

"Okay. Why is Seth sick?"

"I don't know. He was doing so well. He was back to normal. We were so close… I should have never given up on him, but I failed him, like I failed my baby," she said forlornly.

"How did you 'give up' on him?"

"I should have never let him go. Never left him alone. He was upset, I can see that now, but I should have never tried to push him away. I *wanted* to forget. I purposely turned my back on him! At the very least I could have continued to pray for his soul, but did I? It was my own selfishness and now he's paying for it. He would have been free already if I hadn't left him. Please let me get back to him. He's in pain and he's trying to tell me something important!"

"You said that you needed to help him. Why do *you* need to help him?" Gerry persisted.

"Because I'm the only one who can. There isn't anyone else. I can't explain it. He's all alone there and all he has is me. He trusted *me*, and I failed him." She struggled to rise, but he held her firmly in her seat. She protested, "I'm not some child! Now let go of me!"

"Okay, so how do you intend to help him?"

"I don't know yet. He gave me a number," she said, then suddenly struck her head. "But I left it at home. Damnit! I'm so stupid! How could I have forgotten it! But I still don't understand what it means. A phone number? Social security? But that can't be! There weren't enough numbers..." she dropped off, lost in thought.

"Numbers? What do you mean?"

"Maybe it's his student ID? Or an address? Coordinates? It doesn't make any sense. Please, I need my mirror back and something to write with! He could probably give me the rest of them. I know he's trying to tell me something right now!"

"And what happens if you don't help him?"

Mia's eyes opened wide. "He'll be lost forever! And I could have prevented it! I could have prevented all of this if I wasn't so selfish. I was only thinking about myself, but I never considered what effect it would have on him... Let me go!" She struggled against Gerry's hold. "What is wrong with you? I need to see if he's all right!"

"Mia," Gerry continued, "What about Dan? He's very worried about you."

She looked at her therapist and begged, "Please give me the mirror, Gerry...Don't you understand? It's the only way he can talk to me. He's having so much trouble. If you could, just for a moment, open your mind and believe. Please. Give me my mirror."

When he released his hold on her, she sprang forward and grabbed up the precious item. Then she searched around the top of Gerry's desk.

"Hey, wait a minute! What are you looking for? You have your mirror," he reacted.

"Paper—anything. And something to write with. Where do you keep your pens? I need one now! ... No! Seth, hang on. Please. I am so sorry..."

While she whispered to the mirror and stroked it gently, Monroe approached Dan who was visibly shaking and whose expression had turned dark.

Monroe confided in a low voice, "Don't worry, I keep everything locked up. But this doesn't look good, obviously. She's really regressed. I don't think she is going to respond to the previous treatment again. I can call my supervisor in to evaluate, but he's probably going to say the same thing."

While they talked, Mia went to the bookshelf and took out a book. Laying it open on the desk, she ripped out the front page.

Both men pivoted their sights back at her. Dan yelled, "Mia! What the—?" while Gerry exclaimed, "Hey!"

"Don't worry. I'll pay for it. I told you he needs some paper. Now where can I get a pen?" She continued her search.

Gerry moved himself in front of the door just in case she thought about leaving. Then he looked at Dan for an explanation.

"I don't understand it. She was fine this morning! Making holiday plans, getting ready for a job interview. I talked to her on the phone. Everything was normal! I *swear* she was acting normal," Dan stated, perplexed and frustrated. "Goddamn it! Everything was *fine*. She gave no indication. I would have seen it!"

"I hear you, Dan. You know, sometimes these setbacks happen out of the blue and blindside us all without any forewarning," Gerry explained. "It's just one of those things."

"There isn't *anything* that you can do?" Dan asked.

"No, I'm afraid that this is way beyond me. It looks like she's going to need more help than our office here can provide."

Suddenly Mia cried out, "Are you okay? Oh god, Seth. Can't both of you see? We're wasting time here. Please, we've got to help him…I need a damn pen!"

"Well, what then?" Dan continued, growing more agitated, more so at himself than at the situation. How could he have let her slip? She must've been showing some small sign.

"There's an excellent facility that I'm going to refer her to. It's within the PartnersHealth network, so you don't have to worry about payments, just make co-pays or deductibles or something like that. But I think they could really help her there. It is fully staffed with experts who are trained to deal specifically with this kind of situation."

Gerry realized that word had come up, again. He was relieved that this time he was on top of it, ready to sink the shot.

"I'll need you to sign some papers if she happens to resist, okay? So listen, I'll be back in a moment. I have to get the forms and the head honcho, so hang tight."

Alone in the room, Dan studied his wife. She seemed totally unaware of what they had been discussing, or even where she was. She had returned to weeping and whispering to the mirror. He went to her and knelt by her side.

Taking her hand, he implored, "Babe, c'mon now. You've pulled yourself out of this once before. You've got to be strong, Murph, and do it one more time. I know you can do it. Okay? I am here for you. We can do this together.

Please Mia, just one more time…" His eyes searched for hers, hoping she would make contact.

She returned her gaze to the mirror. "But I can't leave him, Dan. He's getting worse. And he has no one else. He is so utterly alone there in all of that darkness and pain. Oh, why can't we just help him? That's all I'm asking of you. Really, it's not difficult. We just have to follow the clues he gives us. He shouldn't be suffering so much now. I caused all of this. Isn't it only fair to give him a hand?"

"But don't you hear yourself? It's a mirror you're talking to for Chrissake!" he said in exasperation.

"Take deep breaths, Seth. That'll help with the pain. I know it's hard, but try…" she said, ignoring him.

Had the time come? Dan wondered.

His mind retraced the events of the past month, searching for any clue or sign that she could have possibly been giving off, signaling her return to madness. With tremendous guilt, he knew that he so desperately wanted her back, that he had hastily insisted that all was better again. Had he missed something?

It was all the medication, he had invariably concluded. In doing so, apparently he overlooked a more serious underlying condition that may have been there all along. Perhaps it existed before he even knew her.

The woman in Texas. The loser husband.

He had fallen for delusions of his own and at her expense. Now neither she nor he had any choice left in the matter. With heart-wrenching sorrow, he realized that the decision had finally been made in spite of them. There was nothing he could do.

Gerry returned with the paperwork and Dr. Gamez. The psychiatrist acknowledged Dan with a nod as he entered the room, then approached Mia. Dan rose and stood aside.

"Mrs. Labont? Are you willing to answer some questions?" Gamez asked in his measured voice, crouching by her.

At first, she did not seem to notice that he was there, concentrating instead on the mirror and breathing sporadically as if she was watching something shocking.

"Mrs. Labont?" Gamez asked one more time.

She turned to face him and implored, "Dr. Gamez, I hope you understand that I am not crazy. Seth is real and I need to help him. There is no one else who can. I don't know why I was chosen, but I was. All I need is a pen. That's it. So please, do you have one? It's how we communicate."

He extracted the pen from his pocket and handed it to her. Mia eagerly took it from him, showed it to the mirror, and then placed it on the desk in front of her.

"Go ahead Seth. They are watching. Show them."

Gamez studied her intently over the top of his glasses.

Suddenly, her face turned ashen. She looked at the psychiatrist with bewilderment and grief.

"Maggots…. He just vomited up maggots… Oh dear God…." she said in disbelief and let out a throaty cry.

"Mrs. Labont?"

She broke down sobbing. Getting no further response from her, Gamez stood up straight and nodded to Gerry who produced the form. Then he picked up his pen off the desk, made a few notations, and signed the paper. As he turned toward the door, Dan caught him by his arm.

"But can't you do something, Dr. Gamez? You're a psychiatrist, why won't you help her?"

"We are simply not provisioned for the level of treatment your wife is going to require, Mr. Labont."

"What are you saying?"

"These clinics are designed for more routine matters. Anything above that is automatically referred to specialists that determine the most effective measures."

"So you are saying you're *not* going to help her."

"I am saying we are not provisioned for it here. If you care to discuss this further with me, please make an appointment at the front desk so we can schedule time for a conference. In the meantime, I highly recommend that your wife go to Meadow Brook. There is nothing further we can do for her here." With that, Gamez left the office.

Gerry held the form up to her. "Mia? There's a place we'd like for you to visit. They'll help you with that person in the mirror there. If you'd sign right here, you could go right now and get help for him," he said patronizingly.

She remained sobbing, "Why won't anybody help him?"

He repeated, "Mia, here's a pen and a form for you to sign to 'help' Seth, just like you want. All you need to do is sign ri—"

She snatched the pen out of his hand and held it up to the glass. "Here Seth, here's a pen and paper." She took the form out of Gerry's hands and placed it on the desk beside the pen. "Please, quickly, tell me what you need." Mia looked expectantly at the pen and paper. "That's right, go ahead...." she encouraged in a trembling voice.

Gerry watched the paper and pen on the desk, and then Mia. He glanced at Dan who was taking everything in, and gave him a nod. Then he plucked the pen and form off his desk.

"Listen, Dan, the sooner we do this, the better it will be for Mia."

"Nooo!! He was about to write something! You took the pen away from him, you bastard!" she screamed in fury as she turned around in her seat to face him, her eyes blazing.

Gerry soothed, "You need to calm down Mia. No one is trying to do anything to him."

Dan ignored the therapist as he knelt before her one last time.

"Mia? Please Hon, do you understand what is going on? They want you to go somewhere else to be seen. I think it's some kind of mental hospital."

"It's okay, just as long as I can—Wait a minute! Quick, give me back the paper and pen." She turned her full attention to the glass again.

Dan's head dropped and he studied the floor. Then looking up one last time, he asked, his voice breaking, "Honey? Do you understand what is going to happen?" He hastily swiped at his eyes. "Do you understand what they want to do with you?"

She looked past him, scanning the desk. "Please Dan, get me that pen from Gerry?"

Dan patted her leg and angrily wiped away the tears on his cheeks with the back of his hand.

"You're going to have to sign the form Gerry gave you..."

"If I do, can I finally be left alone? I can't waste anymore time."

"Yeah. Sure."

He didn't dare hold onto her because he knew if he did, he would grab her up and flee the office and what was about to befall her. Instead he rose and reluctantly went to Gerry who stood holding out the form and pen for him. He scanned over the paper with unseeing eyes and then held it out for her. Mia immediately signed it without reading it. Then she placed the pen carefully beside the torn book page on the desk in front of her.

"Now please. Give him a chance to write," she said.

Gerry snatched the form from her hand, dashed down a few notes, double-checked the signatures and then signed it himself.

"Okey-dokey," the therapist said with a brief smile. He picked up the phone and dialed. "Monroe here. Uh-huh, we're ready… Yes. In my office." Then he and Dan watched Mia. She appeared to be waiting anxiously for something to occur.

"Go ahead Seth," she repeated, "Tell me what you want me to do."

Within a few moments, there was a brief knock at the door and a man and a woman entered the room. They surrounded Mia on either side from where she was standing by the desk.

"Mrs. Labont, you're going to come with us right now, okay? Your husband will follow along later. We're taking you to talk to someone," the woman said reassuringly, but firmly.

She and the man latched onto her arms and started moving her. Mia suddenly looked up from the mirror.

"What? Wait I can't go now. Hey—" She turned to her husband. "Dan? What's going on? Who are these people? Wait… I can't go! I have to help Seth. Dan?" she called out to him in confusion.

"Go with them, Honey. It's all right. I'll meet you there, okay? I'll be right there," his voice was choked and thick.

He guiltily averted his eyes as the nurses took hold of her. She let out a startled cry and started to resist and struggle. The trained nurses easily overpowered her and lead her out of the room.

The door closed behind them. Mia's voice trailed off down the hallway, crying out, "Let me go!" Where are you taking me? Let me go!!!…Help me!.....Daannn!!!"

The two men remaining in the room listened to the turmoil outside the door.

With a bemused look on his face, Gerry turned to Dan and half-chuckled, "Don't worry, they always put up a fight, but they usually calm down once they get there."

Dan was upon him in an instant, gripping the therapist's throat and instantly pinning him down upon the desk with one hand, while the other hand drew back and clenched. He was grim and determined as his fist trembled inches from Gerry's face, poised to strike any second, held only in check by extreme control and effort.

"Whoa, big guy!" Gerry managed to squeak as his air was choked off.

His fingers pried uselessly at Dan's rock hard hand encasing his throat. He knew he had better negotiate—quick.

Using the rest of his air, he managed to whisper through clenched teeth, "I know... you're upset. Don't take... anger out on the wrong person!"

After a few more tense seconds, Dan's grip slowly relaxed and the fist recoiled just as Gerry's face turned from beet red to purple. The therapist rolled off the desk onto the floor where he gasped for air. He drew in several deep breaths, coughed violently, and rubbed at his throat. Then using the desk to pull himself up, he slowly stood holding up a hand in surrender, while Dan backed off.

Gerry swallowed a few more times, coughed some more, then continued hoarsely, "Listen. I'm sorry if I said something wrong. I was only trying to lighten things up a little. She's fine! Perfectly safe. Nothing is going to happen to her. They will take good care of her at Meadow Brook. The important thing here is that Mia is going to get the help she needs. I've seen cases worse than this and they usually have really good outcomes."

He knew he was lying. In fact this was the first time he had ever been involved in the committal of a patient. However, he also knew that at the moment it was more imperative to diffuse this upset husband than to worry about his integrity.

He took out a brochure from his desk drawer. "Here's the place. Look at that. I hear it's an excellent facility. Top notch. They've got everything there. Don't worry, you'll be able to see her during visiting hours. And I'll be checking up on her too, okay?"

Spent from rage, Dan sullenly took the brochure and left. The door shut behind him without another word. Gerry rolled his head around on his shoulders, trying to get his cramped neck muscles to relax. He swallowed a few more times, and rubbed, assessing what he felt would surely develop into a deep bruise that would look like he had had a noose about his neck. Despite the fact that he was very near to being benched by that maniac, he had to admit that Labont had quite a grip. He straightened his Flags of the World tie and sat back down behind his desk, clearing his throat repeatedly, and massaging it.

Gerry considered calling the police and reporting the incident. But he decided to be generous this time and conceded not to charge the big guy with assault, thinking that Labont was already having a bad enough day.

But next time, if that asshole even attempts it, I won't even think of holding back, he promised himself. *So many of them demand results, but results really suck when they're not the ones you are looking for,* he concluded as he opened Mia's chart to receive the signed release form.

Situation: handled.

◊ ◊ ◊

There was another round of paperwork to fill out once he got there. More release forms, insurance forms, privacy disclosures, medical records retrieval. He read the established diagnosis on all of them: Postpartum Psychosis. He couldn't believe that it was his wife they were referring to. She was the smiling, happy girl he had left this morning, the one with the plans and dreams and the rest of her life awaiting her.

When he finished in Admitting, he was forced to wait in the lobby for another two hours before being allowed access to her. By that time, visiting hours were almost over. It wouldn't have mattered much anyway. Mia was heavily sedated when he finally got in to see her. She looked small and frail in the hospital bed. He smoothed back her tousled hair, pulled up her blankets, and contemplated her in her unconsciousness. For now, although her face was puffy from crying and the corners of her mouth were turned down, she looked peaceful.

Putting his lips to her forehead, he whispered, "I'm sorry, Murph. I'm sorry I let you down. I was supposed to be there for you, but I wasn't…I let you get away. I didn't try hard enough. All I wanted was for things to be back to where they use to be, that's all. Can you forgive me, Honey? Please forgive me…"

He dropped and clung to her, his tears spotting her hospital gown. His fists clutched the blankets and drew them up, covering his face. Her soft warmth enveloped him as he opened up and cried bitterly.

"I'm so sorry…."

He remained holding onto her until the attending nurse appeared in the doorway and told him that visiting hours were over.

It was late when Dan returned home. He turned on the lights in the dark house and sat in his chair, feeling numb except for the headache ringing in his head. The house seemed unusually quiet. Mia's absence left a void that was very obvious. His eyes drifted to photographs of them on the wall and to the mementos around the house that she cared for. He had never been apart from her since they were married. And until now, he never knew how alone he would feel without her.

He was weary from the day's events. The smell of the dinner in the Crock-Pot reached his nose, but he wasn't hungry. Suddenly overcome by impulse, he got up and switched to the sofa where he sat down directly across from the mirror. Looking at the glass, he could see himself in it—every line that creased his face, the shadows under his eyes, the stubble of beard growing in.

What is it that she keeps seeing there? The thought persisted in his head.

Remembering Mrs. Lopez's ominous warning from earlier in the day, he rose and looked around for the notebook. It still lay open on the shelf. Written in that foreign longhand, he read:

SSORC

EMPLEH

360148682

None of it made any sense. Why was their neighbor so insistent on him seeing the notebook? He flipped back to the previous page where in Mia's handwriting he read:

W - G, AZ - *Under the insignia on Seth's jacket. Be sure to ask him about this*

On the preceding page there were more lines of barely legible letters and numbers. He thumbed through the book only to find page after page of the same confusing code. Mia had certainly added a lot since he had last seen it. He thought about showing the book to Gerry, but then thought otherwise.

It would definitely be way over that shit-wad's head. Maybe there would be someone at Meadow Brook who could make sense of it.

As Dan got ready for bed, he noticed the colorful travel brochures that were scattered across the top of the dresser. *Mia must've been looking through these today, right before she started to regress.* He stopped the thought cold.

Instead, he picked up a cruise brochure and looked at it, regret aching within him. He never should have waited so long before taking her on a vacation. Maybe she needed to get away from all of this earlier.

What bothered him more were the questions, *Was I too hard on her, asking her to fix the problem herself? What was I thinking when I told her that?*

She had shown so many signs during her depression. Maybe he should have listened more, instead of arguing with her.

He recalled one of the last conversations he had had with Pop Pappas. It was on a lazy Sunday afternoon a week before Pop's fatal heart attack. Dan had just finished installing a satellite dish for him when Pop brought over a couple of beers, pulling them out from under his shirt. They sat down in the shade of the towering trees in the backyard, hidden away from Margaret's disapproving eye for alcohol.

"I keep these in the small fridge in the garage. Margaret never goes in there. Mind you, they are only for special occasions," he confided to his son-in-law with a wink and a laugh.

As they leisurely enjoyed the cold brew, they watched the kids across the street tackle each other on the lawn.

"Pretty soon, you'll be having a few of those yourself," Pop nodded towards the kids and then back at Dan.

Dan smiled and shook his head. He knew how eager Pop was to be a grandfather.

"You've really done a fine job. I'm proud of you. What's more, I'm even prouder of myself for picking you," Stephanos said, smiling happily, first admiring the dish, then his son-in-law.

"Aw, Pop. It's only a satellite dish. There's really nothing to it. I'm sure that you wouldn't have had any problems installing it if your arthritis wasn't acting up."

"Yeah, it is only an old satellite dish. But I was talking about you and Mia. You've made her so happy. The look on her face says it all the time. There's nothing more that I can ask for beyond that. I just wanted to thank you, Dan."

"But I love her, Pop. And she's incredible. So it's easy to do for her."

"I can see that, son. But you'd be surprised. Regardless of how much you care for a person, there may be—no—there *will* be times when it will be very difficult to keep loving her and doing for her. It'll take a lot of strength. Yes, sometimes physical strength, but more mental strength, emotional strength, and endurance too. And it'll take a lot of patience. Especially if that person should ever change and not be the same person you once fell in love with..."

Pop grew quiet as he slipped off into his own thoughts for a moment.

He took another sip and then continued, "So many people enter into marriage thinking, 'so what if it doesn't work out? I'll get a divorce.' Sadly, too often it's a self-fulfilling prophecy. It takes a whole other sense of commitment to stick it out and be there for each other through good times *and* bad. When things are not going so well."

The screen door squeaked open and Margaret stood in the doorway. "Steve, if you and Dan are finished with the dish, I have some lunch waiting for you," she said. Then she looked disdainfully at the beer in their hands. "But you better be sure to get rid of *that* before coming in or you can stay outside." She turned a sharp eye towards her son-in-law, "And that goes for you too, Dan."

"Yes, ma'am," he answered respectfully. They watched her return into the house.

"Did I tell you that a sense of humor is important too? Better drink up, Son, or you won't get fed," Pop chuckled, and then drafted the remainder of his beer.

Dan had taken Pop's advice to heart, but wished he had used it more. Not only did he let her down, but he let Pop down as well. Summoning up his resolve, he made a promise to both of them to do whatever it was going to take to help Mia beat this thing, no matter what, and no matter how long it took.

As he scooped up the brochures, he glanced at the one on top. It featured the Flying J Dude Ranch. According to its copy, it was a vacation designed for 'city folk' complete with a big ranch house, trail rides, barbecues, and square dances all under the sprawling western sky. At the very bottom of the cover, below the colorful photographs of horses and desert hills, and under the ranch's flamboyant golden logo, something else caught his eye: Wickenburg, AZ.

It suddenly occurred to him where he had seen that before. Taking the brochure and dropping the rest, he grabbed the notebook to read Mia's notes of W—G, AZ once more. What he saw made his heart jump. Did this mean anything? It fit the letters in her notes, now he needed to find some kind of connection. It might possibly shed some light on what was going on in her head, or maybe it could lend a clue to deciphering all of that code on the pages. It was a long shot, but he knew he had to find out.

A couple of hours later, the Internet disappointingly yielded little following this lead. A handful of websites featured the Flying J Ranch, realty companies, the Wickenburg Chamber of Commerce, a photo tour company, and the Wickenburg High School Alumni.

It was a disheartening search although Dan wasn't sure about what he was seeking anyway. He was hoping that something, *anything* would jump out and solve this whole mess instantly. But nothing seemed likely. He rebuked himself for being so simplistic.

Did I really think it was going to be that easy or was I just reaching for another rushed conclusion?

The clock read 1:27 a.m. and he knew he had to get some sleep. He wasn't sure what tomorrow would be like but he was certain he would be facing an uphill climb.

◊ ◊ ◊

It felt as if her head had been hammered in. As she roused herself awake and started to move, her muscles were sluggishly heavy. She desperately needed a drink of water to get rid of the horrid taste in her mouth and her tongue felt thick and fuzzy. Her eyes focusing on the mint green walls of her room, she became aware of the starchiness of her pillowcase and the medication-disinfectant smell in the air.

Sitting up, she looked about her. The room was modestly decorated, but sparse in furnishings. Aside from the bed she was in, the only other things present were a table and a chair by the window and an armchair by the foot of the bed. The fabric of her clothes felt foreign against her skin and when she looked at them, she saw that she was dressed in a hospital gown. There was no closet, so she wasn't sure where her own clothes were.

Her recall of the previous day's check-in went only as far back as the Medical Assessment and Stabilization Area where she had been given a general exam, asked a few questions, then ordered to take a couple of small white pills handed to her in a plastic dosage cup. Aside from that she had no recollection of ever being brought to this room, undressed, and put into bed. She felt oddly violated.

Still groggy, it was hard for Mia to get her brain to pull the pieces together, but suddenly, she remembered her mirror. Looking all about her, it wasn't anywhere in the room. The nurses in the MAS had taken it from her when she persisted in trying to talk to Seth.

She remembered getting agitated and struggling with them when they tried to make her hand it over. *That's what probably led up to the pills*, she deducted, and then felt stupid for being so gullible. They had told her she would get her mirror back once she took the pills.

How was she going to communicate with him now? Taking a quick scan of the room, there were no other reflective surfaces about her. Feeling anxious, she wondered how he was doing today. Was he still in pain and retching and convulsing, or… worse? Suddenly the thought struck her— he was losing some sort of battle. But a battle against what?

Searching her heart, it told her that he was dying, if that was possible. His *soul* was dying. She may very well lose him after all. It was time for her to find some way to get back to him.

Pulling back the tightly tucked in blankets, she got out of bed and stood up. The room pitched and swayed for a moment, but she managed to take teetering steps on rubbery legs, making it to the door. It was locked.

She peered out the door's small rectangular window that was impregnated with wire mesh. There was no one in the hallway except for an elderly woman sleeping in a wheelchair. She knocked loudly on the door and called out to her, hoping to get the woman's attention, but the woman slept on.

She crossed the room to look out the window, but she was on a second floor that faced a lush canopy of treetops. There was not much to see but their leaves and a sidewalk below. Returning to the bed, she sat down and pulled her knees up. With frightened eyes she looked around at the four walls that imprisoned her, the comprehension of her predicament fully sinking in and becoming reality.

I've really done it this time Mia thought, fear growing within her. *I've been locked away. Oh God, They think I'm insane!*

She contemplated on what could possibly happen to her next. The harsh realization of it all heightened her senses and shook her body with adrenaline. She felt completely overwhelmed. She would have to find a way to save them both now…

A few seconds later, there was a rap on the door and then keys in the lock. A stocky woman with graying braids and large glasses ambled in. Mia opened her mouth to ask her about what had happen, but she closed it. Her instincts immediately told her not to ask this strange woman anything. Instead, she stared at her with the wary eyes of a hunted animal.

"Hello Mia. Welcome to Meadow Brook. I'm going to be your nurse. My name's Lynnette. I need to check your vitals for a moment."

The woman took out a digital thermo-scan and put it against Mia's temple. A few seconds later when it beeped, she took note of the temperature and clucked, "Temp is normal at ninety-eight point six." Then she picked up Mia's wrist with two fingers and studied the minute hand on her watch as she took a pulse. "How are we feeling today?" she asked amiably.

"Okay, I guess…My head hurts."

"Yeah, well that can be expected. It should go away after a little bit. Can I get you anything? Do you need to use the restroom?"

"Uh, yes. I do," Mia answered feeling self-conscious. "Where is it?"

"Right down the hall. I'll take you there. Here, up you go." The woman's hands were surprisingly strong as she helped Mia to her feet. "There's some slippers under your bed. If they aren't the right size, just let us know and we'll get you some others, but we're pretty good at guessing sizes around here."

She opened the door and they entered into the hallway, walking past the sleeping old woman and down the corridor in silence. Lynnette knocked at the restroom door and then unlocked it with her keys. Once inside the small room, Mia immediately did her business much to her relief. As she stopped to wash her hands, she looked into the polished plate of stainless steel affixed to the wall mirror over the sink. Although it wasn't as clear as a glass mirror, she could still see a blurry reflection of herself.

"Seth? Are you there?" she called.

Within a few seconds, he slowly came into view, his image just as unfocused as hers. She breathed a sigh of relief upon seeing him. However, it was hard to tell how he was doing because of the lack of details. She could barely make out the features of his face, and his movements seemed to be slow and full of effort.

"Hey, Hon. I'm here, okay?" she said gently to him. "I don't know how well you can see me. I can hardly see you at all in this polished metal." Trying to fight against the hopelessness that filled her, she continued, "They really think I'm crazy this time. We ended up here. I don't know what we are going to do. And they took away our mirror."

He made a familiar gesture to her.

"No, I don't have anything to write on. Not here. The room I'm in doesn't have a lot either. We're going to have to find some way to talk. I'm going to try to look around, if they'll let me."

"Mia?" Lynnette's voice called from outside.

There was a short rap on the door again, followed by her keys instantly in the lock. The door swung open.

"Is everything okay in here?"

Her eyes did a quick sweep of the room and then settled on Mia standing in front of the sink. A look of knowing came over her face.

"Were you talking to Seth?"

Mia's eyes opened wide in surprise. "How do you know about Seth? Can *you* see him?" she asked incredulously while pointing to the metal sheet on the wall.

"Your therapist sent over your file. Come on. We're going to take you back to your room now. Breakfast will be served in about a half an hour. But don't worry. It's announced over the PA for anyone who doesn't pay attention to the time," she said.

Mia took one last look at Seth, afraid to say or gesture anything to him in front of this woman. Nothing seemed to escape the nurse's eye.

Back at the room, Lynnette continued, "I don't know if they told you in Admitting, but you will be staying in this room for the first twenty-four hours until you are settled in. Looking at the roster, we'll be moving you to room 315 with Agnes, probably before breakfast tomorrow. That's a couple of doors down. I think the two of you will get along. She's pretty nice.

"During the day, your door will be unlocked. You are permitted to go to the lounge, the visitor's area, and the sunroom. For all other areas, you must be supervised. You are assigned to restroom C which is located at the other end of the hall to your right. There are showers there for bathing and you'll find clean towels there too. If you need anything, including any toiletries or feminine hygiene products, you can ask at the nurses' station that's located directly across from the lounge area. That's where you can find me too.

"You are married, correct?"

Mia nodded.

"Visits are by appointment only and no longer than thirty minutes, so be sure to remind hubby. I'm sure that they told him in Admitting, but we get so many misters and missus that seem to forget. You get three telephone call privileges a day and no longer than ten minutes apiece. We have to make sure that everyone gets a turn around here. Tomorrow after lunch, you'll have your first visit with Dr. Churosh at three-thirty, but don't worry, we'll remind you." She glanced down at her clipboard. "Okay, any questions?"

Mia shook her head that continued to spin and float and drift while toggling between worry for Seth and despair.

"All right then, Mia. Again, welcome to Meadow Brook," Lynette ended.

As soon as she left, Mia searched around for her clothes. As there was no closet or drawers present, she resigned herself to wearing the gown. More pressing to her at the moment was to locate paper, pen, and a place where she could see Seth more clearly. He seemed to be declining at such a rapid rate, she had to get as much information out of him and try to piece things together quickly before he lost all ability to write. The thought of Aunt

Lydia's words mingled with those of her mother's: *lost soul, eternal damnation.* It hurt her to think of Seth being sentenced to somewhere horrible and frightening forever.

Venturing out into the hallway again she hunted for reflective surfaces. To her dismay and frustration, there weren't any. She slipped past the sleeping old lady and made her way to the lounge area, feeling self-conscious about being so underdressed. There were only a handful of women patients of various ages sitting about the room. Most of them barely noticed her as she entered. Some looked at her briefly with vacant, sad, or hostile eyes and then returned to their own business and musings. One woman wept quietly in the corner.

Mia couldn't help but feel intimidated and a little terrified of them. She had never been around any mentally ill people before. All she knew were the extreme examples she had seen in movies or read about in books.

Passing timidly by them, she located the nurses' station. There she could see Lynnette holding a chart and talking to two other nurses. Upon her appearance, the three of them stopped to look at her and exchange knowing glances with each other, and then resumed talking amongst themselves.

Oh, they think I'm nuts all right. To them, we all must be considered crazy in one way or another if we've been put here, Mia concluded. As she looked around at her fellow residents, she wondered how many of them were simply misunderstood, just as she was.

She wandered into the glass-enclosed sunroom off the lounge. It was a pretty terraced area overlooking the lawns and parking lot below. There were live plants on shelves and a potting bench in the corner although there were no potting tools in sight. A parakeet chirped brightly in a locked cage in the far corner of the room. The colorful creature distracted her momentarily from her search, reminding her of the only pet she had ever had. Smiling, she went over to it.

"Hey there little guy. What are you in for?" she said half-heartedly as she held her hand up to the bars. The bird chirped and landed on the perch next to her hand. "You look just like my Abraham," she said softly to herself. Suddenly, she felt a jostle from behind.

"Stand aside and get out of the way! I need to feed her." The woman who had been weeping in the corner rudely pushed past her and unlocked the little luggage lock on the door. Her puffy cheeks were still wet from tears and her nose was running although she made no attempt to wipe it. "I get to feed her because it is my privilege."

"Okay…" Mia said as she stood back. Maybe this woman would know where she could get some things to write with. Not knowing how she should address her, she ventured, "Uh, hi. I'm Mia. What's your name?"

The older woman ignored her as she filled the seed cups and water tube from supplies she had carried in a little tote.

Mia tried again, "Would you know where they keep paper and something to write with around here?"

The resident did not respond. She continued her task, changing out the soiled newspaper at the bottom of the cage while making kissing noises at the bird and wiping her hands down the front of her shirt.

Mia was about to give up and looked around for someone else to ask when the woman abruptly answered, "There's paper in that drawer there. Any pens or pencils you have to get at the nurses' station. But the bird privilege is *mine*," she said possessively.

"All right. It's okay. I was just saying hi to her. I use to have a bird like that when I was a little girl."

The woman went back to murmuring baby talk to the parakeet and paying her no attention. Mia went immediately to the drawer to retrieve some paper with even more of a sense of urgency. She had to get out of Meadow Brook as quickly as possible. Inherently, she knew there was no way neither she nor Seth was going to make it if she had to stay here.

A nurse named Cathy checked out a pen to her, although Mia had some trouble explaining what she intended to do with it. She wasn't sure if she should just tell the truth or if that would work against her here. Her instincts kicking in once more, she finally made up a lie that she wanted to write poetry.

Next she combed the lounge and sunroom for reflective surfaces. It was a lot harder than she ever thought it could be. Most everything was made of plastic or wood, veneer, stainless steel, or vinyl. Finally, in one area of the sunroom, with the sun hitting at just the right angle on the steel meshed window pane, she could see her own image reflected clearly on the glass.

"Seth? I'm here. Hurry. We don't have much time," she said in a low voice, taking occasional glances over her shoulder to make sure she was alone. The parakeet woman had left and the other residents remained in the lounge.

He appeared in an instant. Mia held her breath to keep from gasping. The gray pallor had returned to his skin, and numerous sores had now erupted all over his face. His eyes were sunken and red-rimmed once more. He managed a tired smile and a slow wave of his hand.

"Hey, Tiger," she said tenderly, choking back tears that instantly welled up upon seeing him again. "It's going to be really hard to talk here. The light is just right, but I don't know how long it's going to last. And they are watching me all the time."

He nodded and then picked up the pen she had placed in front of the glass by the paper.

IM SCARED

"Me too. But we'll get through this. We'll just have to put our heads to—" she stopped short as he added:

FOR YOU

"For me? I'll be fine. It's *you* that I'm worried about."

NOT MCH LNGER FOR ME

GETTING DARKR

ITS ALRITE - ILL BE OK

This alarmed Mia. Her greatest fear for him was affirmed. He was slipping away from her.

In effort, she choked her voice to a whisper. "What! No Seth! You have to hang in there. Please, for me? Now think hard. What were those numbers that you gave me?"

PHONE

"Are you sure? There weren't enough numbers for a phone number. You must have left one out. Come on, try to remember."

Seth turned away for a moment. When he looked back at her, she noticed that tears were starting to fall from his eyes and run down his cheeks. It was the first time she had ever seen him cry. He looked so young and vulnerable.

3? 9? CANT REMBR CANT DO IT NT THNKIN CLRLY ANYMR

"Okay, three or nine. We can work with that, but I can't remember what the rest of the numbers were that you gave me. I only saw them briefly yesterday. It's written down in the notebook I left at home. Can you tell me again? I can call from here… C'mon, hon, try not to get upset."

He shook his head miserably. Then suddenly, he struck himself hard in the head out of frustration. His tortured skin broke open at the site of impact and started to bleed.

"No Seth! Don't do that! Stop it!" she whispered hoarsely. "Please don't hurt yourself anymore."

NEED TO HELP U GET OUT OF THR BUT IM USELES

"You're not. You are in so much pain….We'll help each other, okay?" she said as her own tears ran freely.

SRRY I GOT U PUT IN THER

"No… shh. You didn't. I did. I was too stupid to think that—"

AND SRRY 'BOUT WHT I SD 'BOUT DAN

"It's okay Seth. It's okay. Now think more about that number."

A cold, measured voice interrupted their dialogue. "Mia? Is everything all right? I can hear by your voice that you are starting to get upset. And Dahlia here told me that you were being rude to her. Let's calm down or you will have to return to your room."

Lynnette, Cathy, and the parakeet woman stood in the doorway. She looked up in surprise at them. Was she talking that loudly? How much had they heard? She was unsure if they would let her continue.

"Can I talk, if I keep my voice down?" she asked innocently.

"I'm sorry, but that will not do. You are too upset already and any unkindness to your fellow residents will not be tolerated around here. We are to respect one another," Lynnette answered.

"But I am calm and I will remain calm. And I wasn't being rude to Dahlia. I just said hi to her and asked if she knew where the paper was kept. That's all. Now please, if you would just let me continue what I am doing. It is very important that I—"

"Mia," Lynnette started again in a patient tone, "You are not listening. I think it would be best for us to take the pen for now. When you stop being upset, we might be able to give it back to you. Now come on. Breakfast is going to be served and you're probably hungry by n—"

"But I wasn't being rude!" Mia stared incredulously at Dahlia who stood between the nurses, looking smug. What had she done to provoke the woman? "Please, I'm right in the middle of this. May I have some more time? You already know about Seth. Well, he's in bad shape. And I need to help him before it's too late. I'm going to lose him and this is the only place I can see him clearly. I had a mirror, but they took it from—"

"Give us the pen and come away from the glass. Since you are not cooperating, now you will have to return to your room. We'll bring your breakfast to you."

"No! I just need a few more minutes. Fifteen more minutes, okay?" she implored, taking a few steps back. Her back bumped up against the glass. She immediately realized she was cornered.

"Mia. Give us the pen," Lynnette demanded as she held out her hand and approached slowly.

Mia turned back to the glass. "Seth! Start writing! Show them!" she demanded and put the pen back down on the ledge for him. Then she faced the nurses and held out her hands defensively, guarding their advances for the pen.

A crowd of patients had gathered around the door, hoping to get a peek at what was going on. It was always an exciting event when any of the nurses got worked up, being better than any reality show they could catch on TV. Some clapped and called out. Others cried and pulled their hair. Still others stared at the spectacle with no expression on their faces at all.

Lynnette said to Cathy, "Go get it, quick. I think she may J-54 on us." Then she turned to the other residents and commanded firmly, "The rest of you need to go back to what you were doing. NOW!" With some reluctance, they obediently dissembled and went away.

"The jacket?" Cathy asked for confirmation.

"No, the two of us won't be able to manage. Get the other," she nodded, obviously talking in a code they understood between themselves. Lynnette focused her attention back on Mia.

Mia felt apprehensive over what these two women could possibly do to her. Her adrenaline was flowing and she felt panicky.

She tried to explain, "You have to give him time to write. He's having such trouble—"

Before she could finish, Cathy returned almost instantly, producing a needle in which she injected into the top of a small vial. Withdrawing it and checking the volume, she depressed the plunger and flicked the side with her finger, removing all the air bubbles.

Frightened by the sight and with her voice quavering, Mia asked, "What is that?"

Cathy approached, ignoring her question and holding up the needle. "Okay Mia. We'll give you one last chance. But there are two conditions: number one, you *have* to calm down, and number two, you *have* to give Lynnette the pen and return to your room without a fuss. You can talk all about this to Dr. Churosh tomorrow. But we need your full cooperation now."

"But I am being calm! And tomorrow may be too late! If you would just give me some more time, I might be able to figure this out today! Please. You don't understand. He's dying!" She tried to explain once more. When Lynnette took another step towards her, Mia scooped back up the pen and held it tightly to herself. "And this is the only way that I can communicate with him."

They rushed her. Mia clutched the pen with one hand and with the other, reflexively shoved back hard in defense. Lynnette caught the full force and flew back, landing on her rear on the floor. Her mouth was open round in shock, but then closed in determination as she rose. She nodded to Cathy, and then in a quick, deft move she tackled Mia.

Mia was knocked to the floor and was completely stunned by the impact and strength of the older woman. Lynette expertly rolled her onto her stomach and then sat upon her with her full weight. Mia could feel her ribcage flex and compress, as her rapid breath grew short. With strong hands, one of them pinned her head to the cool linoleum, while the other pulled up her gown and plunged the needle into her hip. A burning sensation flared up under her skin.

"Arrghh," Mia squealed in pain. Then she gasped, "Nooo!! Please—"

The nurse continued to sit on her for the next few moments while Mia struggled and kicked, clinging on to the pen. She couldn't draw in a full breath and grew weak, her muscles feeling as if they were filling with liquid lead as the sedative invaded her bloodstream. While she remained pinned down by the nurse's full weight to the hard floor, Cathy and Lynnette started talking to each other as if she had somehow floated out of the room and was no longer present.

"You know, I'm about to give Churosh a piece of my mind. It's bad enough that we have to contend with the nursing shortage, but his idea of giving new admits free roaming on the floor within their twenty-four hour adjustment period is a bunch of bullshit," Lynnette said as Mia gasped and flailed beneath her. "Look at her. If Kimberly was still here, we would have been able to get the restraint jacket on her instead of sedating, poor thing." She stroked Mia's hair. "Mia, if you'd stop struggling, it would be much better for you."

"No! You don't understand. Please… it will be…too…late," Mia mumbled, her mouth, tongue, and throat felt as if they were acting independently of each other. A thick cloud rolled over her eyes. She could no longer hold up her arms. The pen rolled out from her clenched fingers.

"I know," Cathy agreed with an impatient sigh. "It's gotta give somewhere. Either keep them locked up until we know what they are capable of or give us more backup. I've already spoken to Dr. Pullman about this, but he says his hands are tied. Churosh has pulled seniority and he wants his pet program with new admits to be a success. And you know, I hear that he's thinking about cutting back the twenty-four hour adjustment to only twelve! Meanwhile, we're the ones on the frontline while he's safe in his office…. Huh. I guess this is the poem she was writing." She picked up the paper from the window ledge.

"Oh yeah? What does it say?" Lynette asked, still stroking Mia's hair.

"Looks like we got another one that likes to write backwards. Remember Bonnie? Here. Take a look." She handed to paper to Lynnette.

The nurse glanced it over. "Hmm. If this is a poem, it doesn't make much sense. Oh, but did you read the last line? It says 'I am real.' Huh, well at least I think that's what it says. Her handwriting is terrible. Interesting. We'll just have to give this to Churosh."

"So anyway, do you want to do the paperwork on this little episode or do you want me to…"

To Mia's ears, Lynette and Cathy's conversation sounded as if it was being held at the bottom of a pool of water. She fought with all of her dwindling strength to simply lift her head, but mind and body were completely detached. The last thing she remembered before it went completely dark was her mouth falling open to scream.

◊ ◊ ◊

Trying to make up the time he had been taking off, Dan left earlier for work the next morning. It suited him anyway. He hardly got any sleep the night before and waiting out this twenty-four hour adjustment period to see Mia or even call her was driving him nuts. As he headed out the door, he scooped up her notebook as a last thought, hoping to have some time at lunch to study it some more.

However, it was the first thing he opened as he sat in front of the monitors and found he couldn't concentrate on anything else. Some of the longhand was too scribbled to be legible, but other pages showed some improvement. He scoured it to find some kind of pattern or logic to it like any other puzzle.

Or maybe not he thought recalling Mia's bizarre behavior. *Maybe it's some kind of imaginary language that she had concocted.*

He shook his head. What did he think he was doing? He was no psychiatrist.

"What is that? Sanskrit? Wait…Hey! Word puzzles! I love those things!" Ho said as he entered the room and immediately snooped over his friend's shoulder. "Those look pretty good. Did you do them yourself?"

Dan knew there was no point in holding back much longer. He held up the notebook for Ho's inspection. "No. This is Mia's notebook."

"Uh huh, uh huh," Ho nodded as he scanned over the page. "Okay, very clever, but very simple."

Dan sat up straight and looked at him. "What do you mean? You understand this?"

"Sure. We use to do this stuff in Boy Scouts. It's the secret code!"

"Secret code? Well, what does it say?!"

"Don't tell me that you were never a Boy Scout! Well dude, I can't just reveal the code," Ho joked.

His coworker shot him a no nonsense glare.

"Okay! I don't know. It's backwards. You have to hold it up to a mirror to read the secret message," he explained.

Dan looked at the page again and did a double take. The foreign script suddenly transformed itself into familiar patterns of words and phrases.

Of course! It made perfect sense. Her fascination with mirrors—why hadn't he seen it before? Perhaps he was just too close to the situation. *Or did I really want to see it?* he doubted himself.

"Did Mia go to Girl Scout camp or something? My buds and I use to write the code to each other all the time." Ho stopped as Dan leapt up from his seat and left the room. "Hey? Where are you going? Can I play too?" he called after him.

Dan held the notebook up to the large mirror in the men's room. "I'll be damned," he murmured to himself in amazement at the discovery.

There was all sorts of information he could easily read now—lines describing school, a stepfather, a car, a girl. It was all one sided, as if they were responses to questions from another person.

The questions that Mia kept asking herself in the mirror...

He poured over each page, searching for answers when his friend came in behind him.

"Whoa! Look at all of that... Boy, Mia really got into this, didn't she? Man, her handwriting's just as bad as mine," Ho remarked, leaning in for a closer look.

"This is her notebook, but she claims that there's someone else who has been writing all of this. Look at the difference. Here's one handwriting... And see, here's her handwriting here," Dan explained distractedly as he read through the lines.

"Oh. Who? You mean that dude she talks to in the mirror? It would explain why it's all backwards," Ho asked as he studied the pages.

Dan felt a little annoyed to find out that his coworker had been eavesdropping on all of his phone conversations with PartnersHealth, but also relieved to be able to finally share this with someone.

"Yeah, supposedly. But I can't find anything here that would explain what it is she's doing now. What made her so upset? And why did she totally revert? I think I'm too close to this. I can't even think straight anymore."

They both read through some more pages.

"Well, maybe she's imagining that she *is* him. Kinda like role-playing or something. How about starting with all the stuff about him instead? Find out what *he's* all about. I mean, you know her side of the story, now what about his? Wait, wait. Go back to the first few pages. Okay, now go slow."

"You know, Ho, there's a lot more to you than what meets the eye," Dan said as he eyed his insightful coworker, and then carefully read through the notebook.

Following this new perspective, he scanned the pages for any clues about Seth's description, condition, or location.

He started reading out loud, "All right. Here. This is supposed to be what 'he' wrote: dark place, strange smell. Deep...cold... damp..."

"Uh huh. And here—mud, steep sides...can't climb out. Man. It sounds like that dude's in..." Ho's voice trailed off as he read more.

"A grave," Dan finished somberly. He could hear Ho make a shuddering noise beside him.

"That's freaky, man."

They both studied it some more. Then Dan spoke up, "Yeah. But this is supposed to be the journal where Mia writes down her personal thoughts and feelings. Why would she come up with all of this? Did her imagination go that berserk? Maybe she never recovered from the loss of her dad before we lost the baby."

"Yeah, but can you be absolutely sure it was her who wrote it?"

"What, you mean like Mia and not the 'role' she was playing?"

"No, I mean like the actual dude in the mirror."

Dan looked at his friend in disbelief. "What? Weren't you just giving me all the psychoanalysis of how she was role playing and all of that?"

"Yeah, but what if—"

"Aww, don't tell me *you* believe in all of that ghost stuff too. I don't want to get started into all of that bullshit again."

"Hey, I remember my great-granny and my grandma and my ma sitting around and talking about ghosts from the old country all the time. From what they said, there were all kinds of them, for everything. Good ghosts, bad ghosts, evil spirits. Charms to entice them, talismans to keep them away. Everything on our side of the world had some kind of link to them on the other side. And they would visit people here whenever they damned well felt like it. You know, sometimes to help out, sometimes to do evil… Man, I haven't thought about that stuff in years. I use to think that the old folks made it up to scare the shit out of us kids, you know, to make us behave and all."

"But this is reality, Ho! Sure, my sister and I told ghost stories to each other around the campfire every time we went camping, but we didn't take any of that crap seriously. We just did it for fun."

"Well, I don't think Mia was looking for any entertainment value *here*," Ho said resolutely, looking back at the script.

Reluctantly, Dan had to agree.

The door to the restroom opened a crack and Bill from Graphics poked his head in. "Hey dudes. Heads up. Greenlee is looking for you guys," he announced, breaking up their detective work.

Getting back to their workload, they were too busy to discuss the writing anymore between them and spent the rest of the morning mixing and editing footage for a documentary on disappearances. It was slow tedious work as they cut and mixed interviews, visuals, and graphics. Dan tried keeping his mind on task and the notebook closed, but the morning's revelations played and replayed in his head.

By lunch, he knew there was someone he had to call. Maybe she could shed some light on what he and Hoason had been looking at. In the past, he had always listened to Aunt Lydia's oddball opinions patiently and respectfully, but he never put much stock in what she said. Now he was willing to try anything.

Although he was grateful for his friend's input, Dan drove home to call her instead of calling from work. He needed time to think and sort it all out. Once home, he pulled out Mia's phone book and ignoring the four messages waiting on the answering machine, he started dialing. The continuous ringing on the other line matched the nagging questions in his mind.

"Hi? Aunt Lydia? This is Dan," he said when she picked up.

"Ohhhh!" she cried into his ear, "I've been trying your number all morning! I keep getting your answering machine! It's terrible Dan, oh, just terrible! Mia is in danger!"

"Wait, wait—What are you talking about? Have you spoken with her today?" he asked with alarm.

Aunt Lydia's voice was nearing hysterics. "Nooo! I had nightmares about her all night. AND that spirit fellow. And then this morning, when I went to fry eggs, all the yolks were broken! A terrible sign… I tried the phone, then I tried getting a bus ticket to come over there, then a plane ticket, but my credit is all run up and I don't have any money in the bank and it's—"

"Nightmares? Eggs? So you didn't talk *to* her."

"Ohhh, *horrible* nightmares. She was trapped and couldn't get out and there was someone trying to kill her and that spirit was talking to Satan himself!"

"Lydia. Listen to me. Calm down. Mia is totally safe," he told her reassuringly.

"She is? Where is she? Let me talk to her!"

"Uh, you can't… We had to…" he broke off, not wanting to go on, but then continued, "She went to a mental care facility yesterday. But she is under excellent care. I'm going to see her just as soon as I—"

"No Dan! You've got to get her out of there! I know that you told me you think it's all a bunch of trash, but PLEASE, trust me and trust her too. What she tells you is true! Open your mind and believe!!" she shrieked into the phone.

"But she's under the care of a psychiatrist and nurses and other professionals," he explained logically, confused by her fear.

The old woman broke down and sobbed, "Pleeease, Dan! Please. She doesn't belong there. She's not crazy. If you say you love your wife, then trust her. Just this once, trust her…she's in danger…" she lamented pathetically.

Dan remained silent, helpless in knowing how to console her. Oddly, he didn't know why, but her pleas touched him in a strange way.

Considering Mia's rapid regression and Hoason's folk tales, and now Aunt Lydia's ominous warnings, Dan reluctantly allowed some reasonable doubt to surface through his careful rationale. Should he allow this as a very small, very remote possibility? At the very least, he felt that Mia believed it enough to get herself confused. He reminded himself that he would try anything to help his wife.

After a few moments, he quietly acquiesced, "Okay. All right. I'll see what I can do."

"Listen to her. She'll tell you what she needs. She's helpless in there. You'll have to be her eyes and ears and hands. In the meantime, do everything to get her out of that place!"

"Okay, okay. Now what about her 'visiting spirit'? She wrote about him in her notebook. That's why I was calling in the first place. I couldn't make any sense of it. There are descriptions of people and places written in there. Are they symbolic or is it some kind of lingo in, you know, the 'spirit world' or something? I thought that you might know."

He felt really stupid in asking, but if it yielded even the tiniest of insight to Mia's condition, it would be worth it

"That spirit…" Lydia's voice grew cold. "I believe he is already lost."

"Huh? What do you mean 'lost'?"

She remained silent.

"Aunt Lydia, are you still there? I said, what do you mean he's lost? And what about the writing?"

"Please Dan. If you love her, you will get her out of there immediately!" she ordered, and then abruptly hung up.

Confused by her behavior, Dan couldn't help but wonder, *What was that all about?* But more so, *what was she so afraid of?*

Next, he dialed the number on the card they had given him in admitting. He asked to speak to Mia, but they reminded him that she was still in her adjustment period and couldn't use the phone. When he asked how she was doing, they told him that she was sleeping at the moment.

He looked at the clock and thought that was peculiar. Why would she be sleeping in the middle of the day? The first appointment they could offer to him to see her would be tomorrow morning at nine-thirty. He knew he would be there no matter what, even if he had to quit his job.

As he drove back to work, he worried about her. She had to be frightened and confused there. As far as he knew, she had never been in a place like Meadow Brook before. He knew how much she valued her privacy and the comfort of her own home. Aunt Lydia's warnings of danger overlapped with images of Mia being led away from Gerry's office, crying and betrayed. It only heightened his worry.

For a brief moment, he let his guard slip and considered, *What if this spirit business was true? At this point, maybe it wouldn't make a difference if he would just let himself believe....*

No. It was ridiculous. Logic and reason and reality said as much. If he went that route, he might as well join her in Meadow Brook. However, against all of what he believed in, he finally concluded that maybe he could indulge Mia's wishes and requests. *Help her in any way you can...* Aunt Lydia's words rang in his ears. After all, she was already under psychiatric care. Under their watch, he could at least try to give her some happiness and support, he argued with himself.

But what if I end up misguiding her?

By the time he reached the parking lot of Pryus, he had reasoned himself weary. He would do it—anything she asked for, he was prepared to try. He hoped to God that this time, he was making the right choice.

When he entered the edit room, Hoason had already returned from lunch and had more footage cued up. There was a news reporter talking on monitor one, and monitor two held an interviewee in freeze frame. Dan sat down in his chair, his head still swimming with possibilities.

He mechanically went through the motions of adjusting the sound levels and flagging certain special effects for the doc they were working on. The journalist continued with her report, her voice droning on in the background. When the right frame came up on the counter, Ho hit the pause button, returned to the exact insertion point, and then started up the cue from the other file.

"Wait a minute. Go back! Go back!" Dan ordered suddenly.

Something she had said in the very last second caught his ear. He abandoned what he was doing and pulled himself over to that counter to get closer to the screen.

"There!" he said when it counted back. "Roll it."

The woman, frozen in pause with her eyes half-closed and an odd expression on her face, instantly came to life when the play button was hit. "This is Carol Mendoza, 12 Nightly News, reporting live from Wickenburg, Arizona."

"Which story was this?" he demanded.

"I dunno, it's about some old dude who had disappeared while hiking with his touring club in the desert. They found out that he had had an accident and was killed. I wasn't really paying attention. We're not up to sequencing it out, yet. I was just loading the raw footage," Ho said.

"I need a rewind," Dan said as he impatiently reached over and cued the file to the beginning himself.

They both listened as the reporter explained, "A sixty-seven-year-old man was killed earlier this week when he accidentally fell while hiking. Members of his group reported him missing since Monday evening and local authorities have been searching for him ever since."

"Okay… What are we looking for?" Ho asked as she went on with the details.

"I'm not sure yet. Let it roll."

The reporter continued, "The search focused on a region about twenty-seven miles southwest of Wickenburg. The area is known for its numerous abandoned mine shafts. The man apparently had fallen."

Ho looked at his co-worker. "And this is important because?" he started to comment.

"Watch this," Dan answered as he grappled at the mouse and clicked until he scanned the edit cursor to the exact scene. "Think about it: Wickenburg, Arizona; muddy, steep sides; can't move legs; dark and cold …" he rattled off the clues as he found the point and hit play. He turned up the volume.

The reporter repeated, " … area is known for its numerous mine shafts."

"There," Dan said definitively.

"Hold the phone! Do you suppose our boy…?"

"Yes. I do."

"Whoa," Hoason answered and whistled under his breath.

◊ ◊ ◊

Gerry skimmed over his schedule for the rest of the week on his computer's calendar. Everything looked pretty routine although he noted the Thursday, four o'clock at Meadow Brook with interest. He was required to meet with the psych over there in charge of the Labont case.

Not only would this mark his first time dealing with a client who had been committed, it would also be his first time seeing the inner workings of an actual psychiatric hospital. The prospect gave him a small charge. He was finally doing genuine therapy work.

Giving his imagination the freedom to expand on the concept and fueled by Hollywood plots, he pictured himself driving up a curved concrete driveway to the institution, past the rolling security gate and expansive manicured lawns. Patients dressed in pajamas and bathrobes strolled about the grounds or sat in wheelchairs, accompanied by strong young orderlies in crisp white uniforms. He would step out of his BMW, looking smart in his suit and carrying a brief case full of important charts and records on the mental patient he was about to confer on.

The head psychiatrist would greet him at the door, shake his hand, and offer him a cup of coffee. He would wave it off, knowing they had more immediate matters to attend to, such as saving a person's sanity. Gerald Monroe, Licensed Therapist, would discuss psychiatric profiles and diagnostic scenarios with his colleague as he was given a guided tour through the facility making their way to the patient's wing.

They would pass the hopelessly insane and catatonic. Better yet, the criminal psychopaths locked away in padded rooms and wrapped up tight in straight jackets, snarling at anyone viewing them through the bars on their doors. He pondered if there was any way he could finagle this upcoming experience onto his resume.

Still daydreaming about his new role, he walked over to the supply closet to retrieve some sticky notes and rubber bands. His appetizing dream of institutional psychiatry was edged out by his growing irritation on how Marcia never deemed it necessary to keep his office stocked.

On his way back, he stopped at the back office desk and browsed through a box of donuts that one of the MA's had brought in. Snagging one, he looked up at the checkout board and noticed that Gamez had already left for the day. That was enough to pique his curiosity.

"Hey Doreen. Where's Dr. High and Mighty this afternoon? Wait, don't tell me. He went home sick? I don't believe it. I didn't think that gods suffered from mere mortal calamities," he said while feigning amazement.

Doreen looked at him with mild annoyance. "If you're talking about Dr. G, he and his son were drawn for bighorn in California. He's taking today and tomorrow off to go. He won't be back until Monday."

"You're shitting me—bighorn sheep? As in hunting?"

"No, for a truck commercial. What do you think?" she snapped, wagging her head. "Why? What's it to you?"

"Oh nothing. Listen, has anyone ever told you that you are absolutely *charming* as well as *helpful?*" he said sarcastically. "I really don't know what they would do here without you. But I'm gonna make it a point to look into it."

Smirking, he picked up his mail and thumbed through it, the chocolate donut with rainbow sprinkles held firmly in his mouth. His imagination still active, his mind entertained images of little Dr. G scrambling up a mountain side with an Elmer Fudd hat on, then fleeing back down the slope as a big ram charged him. All the while his plump little wife galloped after him lugging a huge backpack filled with sandwiches and thermoses of coffee...

The phone rang. Gerry listened in as Doreen explained that Dr. Gamez was not available until Monday and that she would be happy to pull the chart and leave it on his desk. He was turning to leave, when he heard her mention the name, Labont. Throwing down his mail and supplies for a moment, he motioned frantically to her. It was just the opportunity that he had been waiting for: Gamez, remiss of duty, while Gerry carried the team.

With her face now radiating extreme annoyance, the MA put the caller on hold and glared at him.

"*What*, Gerry?"

"I'll take that. Labont is my client."

"They didn't ask for you. They asked for Gamez."

"Transfer it to my line. Now!" he said as he gathered up his donut and mail and started jogging down the hall to his office. Over his shoulder he yelled, "And I need that chart too!"

The line was blinking for him when he entered.

"Monroe here," he spoke into the receiver as he sat down at his desk and took up pen and pad.

"Excuse me, who are you?" the caller asked.

"Gerry Monroe. I'm Mia Labont's therapist. Do you have a question concerning her?"

"I was really hoping to speak with Dr. Gamez."

Doreen entered, carrying the chart. He snapped his fingers impatiently until she handed it to him.

"He won't be in for the rest of the week and Labont is *my* patient. What's up?"

"Well…" The caller sounded somewhat unsure, but then went on, "This is Muriel, Dr. Churosh's nurse. He wanted me to call Dr. Gamez because we've been experiencing some trouble with Mrs. Labont. It's still a little early yet, and she may settle down in a few days, but she is having a very hard time with her adjustment period. She's been sedated twice already. We've reviewed yours and Dr. Gamez's notes, but it seems her outbursts are getting more severe in duration and intensity, and within a short period of time, than what was indicated. Dr. Churosh will be treating her and monitoring her meds, but PartnersHealth doesn't show any coverage for her for more invasive measures, that is, if needed."

"Invasive measures?"

"Well yes, you know, some of the MAOI's, hypnosis, ECT, et cetera." She rattled them off like a shopping list.

Gerry had to stop himself short from uttering "Wow" over the phone. He had hit the big times.

"Not that we may ever need to utilize any of those. But we like to be prepared just in case an emergency arises."

"Yes, of course," he composed himself. "So you're asking…?"

"For an override on benefits. We need authorization to provide these services to your client, if needed. Since you are her PCP we have to run everything by you. Or I mean, Dr. Gamez."

"Of course. Yes, he, uh, *delegated* me to handle this case for him personally. You know, since I've had a lot of close personal contact with Mrs. Labont, I know her better than anyone here. He trusts me and he trusts my opinion to treat her implicitly. He's just merely overseeing the case. And being that he's out of town at the moment, I am acting as interim. So if you have any questions, you've come to the right person. I'm the one to ask."

The nurse was silent for a moment. Then she continued, "Okay, Terry, would you—"

"It's *Ger*-ry."

"Oh, right. Would you mind holding a moment?" He could hear her confer with someone else in the office about it for a few minutes. Then she was back. "Okay. I'll put you down as the PCP for the time being, at least until Dr. Gamez gets back. So then, we have authorization?"

"Yes, do whatever you think is necessary," he said, full of self-importance. "To help the poor woman," he added to top it off. "And keep me posted on her condition."

Setting the phone back into its cradle, Gerry couldn't help but feel quite satisfied with himself. He leaned back in his chair and sunk his teeth into the rich chocolate donut and chewed thoughtfully.

Now that wasn't so difficult... Bighorn sheep... Huh.

Maybe Gerald Monroe was cut out to be a therapist after all.

TEN

He was there before visiting hours began, partly because his watch was always set a few minutes early and partly out of his own eagerness. But visiting hours at Meadow Brook began promptly at nine-thirty and NOT at nine-eighteen, leading to a twelve-minute stare-down with the receptionist who had been quick to correct him on the time. It was obvious that she was use to this; she didn't flinch or redirect her gaze regardless of how impatient he appeared.

After a few halfhearted attempts to read the magazines scattered on the end tables, he ended up staring out the window instead while he waited. Eventually the lumbering minute hand moved onto the half-hour mark and he looked over to the receptionist once more. This time she put on a bright smile and hit the button to open the big double doors that permitted entry to Dan and a handful of other visitors.

She greeted them cheerily, "Welcome to Meadow Brook."

Navigating by the instructions given him by the clerk in Admitting, he passed the physical therapy center, the arts and crafts room, the counseling room, the auditorium, crossed over to the elevators, and eventually found his way to the third story visitor's lounge. It was a large area divided into four smaller "living rooms," each containing its own sofa set and area rug. Several pairs of overstuffed armchairs were tucked away in the corners and lined up along the large window that overlooked the pond and lawn below.

The warm glow of the morning sun lit the room and fresh coffee brewed on a side table set with napkins, cups, stirrers, and fresh flower arrangements. Dan thought about helping himself to a coffee, but decided he was just too nervous to drink anything. He parked himself with her duffel bag of personal belongings beside him in one of the armchairs by the window.

Within a few minutes, the residents began to file into the room one by one. Attendants accompanied some, while others walked independently or rolled in on wheelchairs. He watched as each patient paired off with their respective visitor resulting in various greetings of joy, self-conscious hellos, or resentful sullenness. Dan peered around anxiously and wondered what had happened to his wife. He rose from his chair and started towards the doorway, looking for an attendant to find her, and hoping that someone had told her of their appointment.

Just then she walked in, supported by a nurse who kept a firm grip on her arm. Mia looked bedraggled and weak, taking slow unsure steps. Dan was shocked to see how fragile she looked in this place. Keeping his guilt in check, he ran over to assist her, but uncertain of how she was feeling towards him after what happened the last time he saw her in Gerry's office, he hesitated and only reached out to her instead.

"Hey there…" he said shyly.

She looked into his eyes. Her thin face was drawn and her eyes had deep shadows beneath them.

Oh here it comes, he thought to himself, *and I deserve every bit of it.*

Without saying a word, she suddenly threw her arms around him and clung to him. He hugged her back, holding her close and feeling relieved that she wasn't angry with him. He nodded thanks to the nurse and showed Mia to where he was seated. To afford them a little more privacy he positioned the chairs around to face the window with their backs to the room. When they were settled, she looked at him and smiled, saying a quiet "hi." But when he took up her hands, her smile melted into tears.

"Hey, Babe. How are you holding up?" he asked her gently.

"Please Dan, get me out of here!" she whispered urgently to him. Then casting a furtive glance over her shoulder and leaning in even closer, she went on, "I'm not insane, Murph. You've got to believe me. I know what it must've looked like, but it wasn't that at all. I'm sorry that I frightened you."

She spoke so earnestly her words ignited an instant spark of encouragement within him. *Maybe this was a horrible mistake after all,* he thought.

"I know, Honey, and no one is saying that there's anything wrong with you. It's just that, well, you went way off. I don't know if you remember, but it was like you weren't responding to anyone or anything. I didn't know what to do. And I wasn't sure if you would hurt yourself. It seemed that you needed more…'help' getting on track, that's all. Are you feeling any better? Have you gotten to talk with any of the docs here?" he asked.

"I feel fine. But nobody here understands what I must do. We can't stay here. He's really sick. I don't know why, but for some reason he's losing ground each day and rapidly too. It feels like we're running out of time, but I don't know how much time is left. I'm no good to Seth at all here. We need to be able to communicate freely with each other, but they won't let us."

"Oh," Dan answered, trying to hide his disappointment.

There obviously was no mistake. But he couldn't keep his mind from turning back to his phone call with Lydia and the writing in the notebook. Most of all, he remembered his vow to help Mia in any way he could. *But could he help her? Or would it harm her even more to try?*

Looking at the face of the woman he had known, trusted, and loved for the last four years, he wanted to give his wife at least the benefit of a doubt. He had to give her one more chance.

Summoning up courage to continue, he offered, "Mia, you know if there's anything you want me to do for you, I'll do it. But you've got to realize that these people here are trying to help you too. You've got to let them."

She pressed the knuckles of her fingers tightly against her lips and gritted her teeth, trying to hold back words. "But they keep blocking me. They're forcing me to bend. Forcing me to leave him. All I need is for them back off. If I can talk to him, it's the only way I know I can help Seth be on his way. That is all. There is so much we have to still figure out and there's not much time left. Don't you understand? Once he is there, I'll be okay and life will return to normal for you and me. I know it will. Now that's not unreasonable, is it? Just a little bit longer is all I am asking."

"But how much longer? And why is it so imperative that you help him? Can't you just ignore him and he'll vanish or something? Like he did before?"

"I can't. I promised him that I'd help. If I don't, his soul could be lost forever. Maybe limbo, or purgatory, or someplace worse. His short absence away from me this last time really caused a lot of damage. He had been improving up until then. I really felt like we were on to something."

"But how is that going to affect us? So what if he's lost! Why is it such a big deal? He's in some 'other world' anyway, right? We're not going to know any difference. Maybe *then* we can put this whole thing to rest and you can concentrate on getting well."

She shook her head. "I've told you that there is nothing wrong with me now! I was extremely depressed, but that was before. And I understand what I need to do to get through it now. Besides, you know me better than that. I can't just forget about him and act like nothing ever happened. I couldn't live with knowing that I could have done something to save him but chose not to.

"He is only a kid. What short life he did have on this planet was a terrible and abusive one. It's not fair that his afterlife should be the same. I know if there were someone depending on you, you'd do whatever it took to help. Well now, I'm depending on you to help me help *him*. It will only be for a short time longer. We are so close. PLEASE Dan, try to understand. I know you don't believe in all of this stuff, but don't force me to abandon him too," she implored.

Although he knew her argument was pure fantasy, it was persuasive. He tried not to let her pleading eyes capture his heart like they always did. Yet they nagged him of that commitment he had made to her long ago. In search of some respite, he made himself tear away from her gaze for a moment and look out over the green expanse of lawn outside. He wished that she and he were out there instead, strolling past the grounds as mere pedestrians on their way to anywhere else, but here.

He turned things over in his head. In a way, she was asking him to play with her own sanity. Was keeping his word worth that? Pop's advice echoed in his ears. This was definitely one of the hard times he was talking about.

After a few more moments of agonizing deliberation, he finally decided to concede. He would let her see this thing through and assist her. *Just this one last time…*

With his eyes still trained on the lawn, he said in a tired voice, "Okay Murph. I can't say that I can necessarily get you out, but I'll talk to the doctor. Now, you've asked me 'to help you help him,' so what is it you need me to do?"

"What? I- Hon, I know that you don't—"

"No, I said that I would, so I'm asking you, what is it? What can I do to help you?" he said, turning to her.

"Do you mean it?" she asked in surprise, but looking a little skeptical.

"Yeah. Go ahead… You know I'm still trying to make sense out of all of this, but if you say that this will all be over with soon then I'll give it a shot. BUT if it doesn't work, then you have to promise me that you'll let the doctors here treat you without any argument, okay? And also, you've got to cool it with talking to him around these people. I don't think that's helping your case any. Okay?" he said resignedly.

He couldn't believe he was doing this, but he reassured himself that it must be something she had to work through to get it out of her system. Once she did, he would have to see what would develop next. In the meantime, he secretly hoped that should this be a mistake on his part, the psychiatrists would catch her in time.

"Okay," she said, her face brightening. She reached over and gave him a squeeze. "Well, I'll need a mirror. All they have here are those pieces of polished metal in the bathroom in place of mirrors. I think they don't want anyone to injure themselves if they go berserk and break any glass, but I can't see him clearly in them. Did you bring one in my stuff?" she asked covertly.

"Um, no. I wasn't expecting this. Didn't you have one with you?"

"It was confiscated. The best I did yesterday was a reflection off a piece of glass in the sunroom. But they caught me talking to him. I need a small mirror that I can keep on me and talk to him in private."

He was amazed at her resourcefulness and tenacity. "I'll look around home and see what I can find, okay?"

"Oh, that might take too long! He's losing ground even as we speak. If you could only see him! He's so tired and his complexion is turning and getting worse. I think he's dying." She stopped abruptly. Dan could see her visibly shudder as she drew in a breath. Then she continued, "But I'm also going to need something to write with."

Wasn't this guy supposed to be dead already? Dan pondered her inconsistency.

He thought of questioning her about it and all of the other things he had found in her notebook, but then decided it would be better if he didn't hear the details. If he heard enough of them and they were crazy enough, it just might end up deterring him and changing his mind. *I'm going to see this through,* he focused.

He asked, "I passed an arts and crafts center downstairs, couldn't you use something there?"

"No. They sedated me the last time I used one of their pens."

He exclaimed "They did *what*? Who—" This was all new to him.

"I just need my own stuff," she insisted.

"But Hon, they sedated you? For what? Tell me why."

"There's not enough time right now. I'll explain later. Don't worry, I'm all right. Did you bring the Jeep?"

"Yeah, why?" He still felt uneasy about the sedation. Someone was going to have to answer some questions around here.

"I'm pretty sure that there's a little pocket mirror in the glove compartment and I think there's some old pens there too. I can keep them under my mattress or in my clothes or somewhere they can't find them. Would you mind getting them right now?"

He had intended on spending the entire thirty minutes of visiting time with her and this would cut into it. He started to object, "But I thought that we could talk some more."

"Dan, I really need them now. *Please.*"

Reluctantly he left to retrieve the items. On his way to the parking lot, he knew this was his last chance to ditch this whole crazy scheme. And he knew he would in a heartbeat if he really took the time to analyze it. He could drive away and then call to apologize later. But he cleared his mind; he was determined to keep his promise, no matter what.

When he returned, she looked up at him with a big smile of relief despite the rings under her eyes and disheveled hair. A small gleeful giggle escaped from her when she received the mirror and pens and held them close, then she quickly concealed them in her robe pocket before the nurses could spy them. Seeing her excitement he imagined what she must've looked like as a little girl at Christmas.

"So, is there anything else I can get for you? I'm going to have to leave in a few minutes."

"Please tell me that you packed my journal notebook in here?" she asked as she rummaged around in her duffel. "I need a number that is written in there."

"What, you mean that phone number on the last page?"

She looked up at him. "Yes. Wait a minute—how did you know?"

"I've been reading through your notebook. I hope you don't mind, I was only trying to get a handle on what was going on... Anyway, does Wickenburg, Arizona mean anything to you?"

"Wickenburg? No....Why?"

"Well, it seems to fit what you have written in there—you know, about the insignia on his jacket or something—a W, several spaces, G, comma A, Z? If he's wearing anything like a school varsity jacket, it might be the town he's from. And the town of Wickenburg only has one high school, Wickenburg Union."

He watched her reaction carefully, trying to read any subtle changes in her behavior should he happen upon something significant or strike a nerve.

She looked at him with amazement, and then burst out, "Oh my God! That's probably it! He told me he lived in a small town. How did you figure it out?"

"Oh, just a little deduction, that's all," he said modestly.

"You're a genius!"

"Uh, before you go too far with all the flattery, I forgot your notebook at home," he ventured.

Her mood swung to disappointment. "All right, but could you call me later with at least that phone number?"

He nodded.

"Did you figure out anything else?" she asked, perking up again.

He debated whether or not to tell her, but then went on. "Did he ever mention anything about a mine shaft?"

"No. He hasn't…A mine shaft? Why?"

"It fits the description of the place he's in. And the outskirts of Wickenburg are littered with abandoned mine shafts. There've been a lot of accidents and deaths attributed to them. We saw some footage on it at work for a doc that we are editing right now. Anyway, just thought you might find that interesting," he said.

"You know, it seems to fit. Yes, come to think of it, it would explain a lot. You're incredible. Thank you so much honey. I need all of this information to piece everything together, and hopefully it will all be enough in time," she said giving him a kiss and a hug. Holding him close, she whispered in his ear, "And thank you for believing in me. You don't know how much I have wanted to share this all with you."

When she pulled away, her eyes were shining. For some strange reason, he couldn't help but feel as if he were deceiving her in some way.

The sound of soft chimes filled the room. An attendant opened the door, signaling that the nine-thirty to ten o'clock visiting time was over. They looked at each other, not wanting to part. He held her hands.

"So Murph, you've got the stuff that you needed. Now remember your other promise, okay? Give them a chance."

She gave a small nod. "Okay. I'll try. I know that I'll be able to get him on his way quickly now and then I won't need their 'help.' And please be sure to get that number for me, it's really important."

"I'll bring your notebook tomorrow. I just have to arrange times at work to see you, but I'll call you later on today, okay?"

The chimes sounded again and the attendant announced, "Visiting time is now over."

"By the way," he added quickly as they stood up, "Did you know that the area code for Wickenburg is 928? I didn't know if you could use that too."

"I love you," she said, kissing him and hugging him tightly.

Before he left through the doors, he took one last look at her. She waved to him, and then started to dig around in her duffel. At least for this brief moment, he had made her happy.

On his way out, he saw a nurse with gray braids talking with a tall well-groomed man in the adjoining hallway. As Dan passed by, the nurse appeared to point him out to her colleague. Abruptly finishing their conversation, the man thanked her then jogged over to catch up.

"Hello. Are you Dan Labont? Mia's husband? Hi, I'm Wade Churosh."

Dan stopped to address him and shake the man's outstretched hand. "Yes sir. Is there something I can do for you?"

"I'm her attending counselor. Do you have a few minutes? I'd like to discuss some things with you," the man said amiably. He motioned towards his office down the hall.

Cognizant of what he had just agreed to do for Mia, Dan felt an uneasy feeling worming its way into the pit of his stomach. As he was shown a seat in the spacious wood paneled office, he glanced at the wall lined with various diplomas and certificates indicating that Churosh was a licensed doctor of psychiatry. That uneasy feeling mushroomed. Dan was never comfortable with any of these types, whether they were therapists, psychologists, or psychiatrists, and always wondereg if they were analyzing his every word and gesture. This guy might even figure out what he had just done in aiding Mia. Facing the soft-spoken counselor from across the polished mahogany desk, he waited for Churosh to continue.

"As Mia's attending counselor, I oversee all of her treatment here. As you may know, when residents first enter Meadow Brook, they undergo a twenty-four hour adjustment period. During this time we carefully observe and monitor each of our residents to see how they are receiving their surroundings. We note any signs of distress or maladjustment on their part and then try to treat and room them accordingly. Let me say that it's common for some of our residents to react negatively at first. This can be quite an adjustment for them, but they usually settle down fairly easily.

"But some never do adjust and we have to re-evaluate their own individual level of comfort and trust that is necessary for progress. It has been approximately forty-two hours since Mia has been admitted, and while there's no need for excessive worry, her reactions are still quite strong, and in fact, getting more severe. We reviewed her files sent to us by Dr. Gamez but they didn't give any indication that she would behave in this manner. Our information gathered by our admitting staff and triage didn't shed any light either," Churosh explained.

"She told me that she was sedated. For using a pen?" Dan questioned as he eyed the older man warily.

"Yes. Unfortunately, it became necessary after the nurse asked her to return the item because it seemed to be over stimulating her. At that point, Mia became physically hostile and the subsequent sedation resulted after a long negotiation had failed to placate her. We had to prevent her from harming herself or any other staff or resident. And this is precisely the kind of unanticipated behavior that is the cause of my concern."

Dan was puzzled by this news. This didn't sound like Mia… but then again, lately, who was she? "How *has* she been acting otherwise?" he ventured with curiosity, but remained guarded.

"Well permit me to show you a portion of our talk yesterday afternoon. We video record all of our sessions for review and accountability, and your wife was well aware that she was being recorded at the time." The doctor got up, unlocked a file cabinet drawer, selected a DVD from the neatly shelved row of others, and then continued. "Mia shows an unusual fixation with reflections, as I'm sure you are aware." He loaded and started the DVD player.

There on the screen, Mia and the doctor were seated across from each other in a couple of armchairs. After all the thousands of hours Dan had logged reviewing interviews, it was odd to see his wife as the subject of one. At first, the doctor led her through a series of preliminary routine questions in which she answered with ease. There was the person Dan knew—cooperative, friendly, and articulate.

But when Churosh mentioned her conversations with Seth, Mia became excited and asked to see him. The doctor offered her a mirror, which she snatched up immediately. From that point on, she no longer paid any attention to the counselor and spoke with Seth exclusively. It was a scene that had become all too familiar to Dan.

He continued to watch as the doctor tried to question her about Seth or her behavior, but she politely apologized to the doctor and told him that she couldn't speak th him at the moment. When he persisted, she ignored him and continued to talk to the mirror instead. The session progressed and the only time she interacted with Churosh was to ask him for writing materials. He gave her a pencil and paper, but she only laid them upon the desk, asking her reflection to write something. For Dan, it was reminiscent of the scene that had played out in Gerry's office. Finally, at the end of the session, the doctor asked for the mirror back, but she refused. When he demanded it back, she alternated between outrage and pleading with him. All the while, Churosh remained patient, but firm with her.

The psychiatrist stopped the DVD there. "A short time later, she became very agitated and tried to leave the floor without permission. Another struggle ensued, resulting in her being placed in isolation."

At the mention of these words, Dan closed his eyes and shook his head. His jaw clenched and that initial uneasy feeling was now a snake writhing inside of him. There wasn't going to be any way he could ask Churosh for her early release. He doubted he would let her go while she was acting like this and it would be pointless anyway. It would be better and safer if she was closely supervised. He thought of the mirror and pens he just gave her. *Am I making this worse?* he worried.

Churosh snapped him back from his thoughts. "Are there any anomalies in her family history that you are aware of? Any relatives that behave abnormally? She did not indicate any family mental illness on her admission forms but sometimes our residents don't paint the most accurate picture."

Dan thought immediately of his mother-in-law awaiting ascension into heaven in the Holy Land and Aunt Lydia with her delusions of psychic powers. He shook his head and held his tongue. Although it took extreme effort, he was going to hold resolute to his promise to Mia. He would allow her at least the rest of the week to get this thing together. However—if things hadn't changed by then or started going downhill, he was going to have to shift gears and divulge everything to this shrink and hope that he hadn't wasted too much precious time on her part.

"I hope that you will call me if there is anything you may recall or need to discuss regarding your wife's condition. We do our best to keep spouses and other family members involved at all levels and most times, they are our best resources. In the meantime, we may have to investigate diagnoses other than post-partum psychosis. At this point, we are considering the possibility of schizophrenia."

The words blindsided Dan. "Schizophrenia? Are you sure? Can it be anything else?"

"There is no need for alarm, Dan. I was merely stating that it might be a possibility. However, we must consider *all* possibilities given her behavior and symptoms so we can be prepared to deal with them, immediately if necessary, and get her the treatment she needs."

"But shouldn't you get to the source of why she is doing this first? You realize that she is still grieving over her father and our child."

"We must focus on the treatment first. Only then can we get to the core of the problem to resolve it," Churosh answered resolutely.

Leaving the office, Dan felt as if he were going to vomit. The severity of what Churosh had said rang in his head as he recalled how just moments before he had easily handed over the mirror and pen to her. A small panic flared up within him. But he held himself in check once more as he fought the urge to go back into the office and confess what he had done. I will see this through. I will give her one more chance. He ducked into the lobby's restroom to splash some cold water on his face to battle the unrelenting queasiness. As he dried his face with the paper towel, he stared at his own reflection in the large clear mirror.

It occurred to him that he had never gambled on anything before in his life. Why did he choose to take a chance with his wife's sanity now?

◊ ◊ ◊

Mia returned to her new room that she had just been moved to that morning. She was eager to shed the hospital gown and get into the clothes that Dan had brought for her. It felt good to slip into her own jeans and jersey. Looking through her duffel, she was grateful that he had included her favorite sweater. It had just the right pockets to carry the mirror close to her, out of sight, and without having to risk crushing it in a snug pant pocket.

When she slipped the glass out of its case, Seth's eyes caught hers immediately. Red rimmed and deeply bloodshot once more, he was starting to hold them half-closed. The sores that pocked his face were much more numerous and large; some had begun to seep lymph fluid and pus. His nose was bleeding constantly now and a fine layer of dust had covered him once again. It made her heart heavy to think back to the lively handsome youth she had come to know months before. He managed a weak smile when he saw her.

"It's going to be all right, Seth. Dan brought this mirror for us and pens to write with…"

He slowly nodded his head yes.

"But I can't talk to you when anyone's around. Okay? So please don't think I'm ignoring you. If they catch me talking to you, they'll take everything away and probably sedate me again. Do you understand? I don't know if you saw what happened last time."

He nodded once more.

"Now, Dan is going to call me with the num—"

Just then the door opened and Agnes, her roommate, walked in. They had been briefly introduced to each other earlier in the day. Mia wasn't sure if the older woman was going to become 'upset' at her conversing with a reflection, as the other residents had the day before. But Agnes merely looked at Mia and smiled, glancing at the mirror in her hands. Saying nothing, she shuffled over to her bed instead where she picked up an old issue of *People* magazine and started to read, her pale blue eyes never leaving the pages.

Mia took another peek at the mirror. Seth was moving so laboriously. His breathing was heavy and he started once more to mouth those strange repetitive words from long ago. This regression disturbed her. He could, at any moment, be reduced unwillingly to that grisly phantom he had been once before.

She looked about their room, hoping to find some privacy to continue their discussiom. As she gathered up her writing things, there was a short knock on the door. She was able to cram everything into her sweater pocket just as Lynnette popped in to tell her it was time for Group. With relief, Mia saw that the nurse hadn't caught her, but she knew she was going to have to be more alert.

Begrudgingly, she went to the session led by Dr. Churosh. While the other nine residents attending the session took turns griping, venting, or sharing, she sat sorting through her thoughts instead. The mirror, concealed in her sweater's pocket, could have been alive. It was as if she could feel warmth radiating from its weight resting against her. When she reached in to reassure herself of its presence, her seeking fingertips could almost feel its pulse. So eager was she to get to it, to be able to talk and confide with it in private, the mirror became a living thing to tend to. Every time she touched it, she knew Seth was there and she wanted to offer him any possible comfort and consolation she could, wishing he could feel the warmth of her hand through the glass. Despite the pain he was in, however, he would have to endure the morning crawling by, just as she.

The leads Dan had given her were encouraging. A town in Wickenburg, Arizona! She tried to recall any details Seth may have mentioned that would substantiate the claim. Arizona was a desert state. But she knew it also had pine forests and the Grand Canyon. Where could Wickenburg be in that huge state? And a mineshaft…she didn't know anything about mineshafts, but she knew from what he had told her that he was in some large deep enclosure with no way out. The pieces were falling into place now and each one drew her emotionally closer to him.

She suddenly became aware that the room around her had grown quiet. She glanced nervously about to see Churosh and her fellow residents looking at her.

"Mia? I asked is there anything you'd like to contribute to Group today? We are all here to listen and we hope you'll feel comfortable enough to share with us," Dr. Churosh repeated patiently.

A little embarrassed about being caught, but also annoyed that she had to be here, she shook her head and passed. She noticed that Churosh immediately wrote something down on the notepad that he carried. *Was there some kind of point deduction for not participating?* she worried. Her thoughts returned to Seth as her fingers closed around the mirror in her pocket. The youth didn't know that she drew just as much support from his presence as he did hers.

Next, they were moved to the art room for another unbearable hour on some craft in sculpting clay and then to the lounge area where a young, newly trained psychologist taught them various deep relaxation techniques. It was difficult for her to concentrate as the lesson dragged on. She had burned up so much valuable time already. Some of her fellow residents were just as unwilling to be there but were more vocal than she—grumbling, wailing or yelling whenever the mood hit them. It was growing contagious. Although she was feeling more agitated and frustrated herself, she carefully held in her own urge to scream, not wanting to catch another needle from Lynette or Cathy again. She knew they were monitoring her behavior very closely. After lunch, she finally found the break she had been waiting for. The nurses were gossiping in the nurse's station, and the hallway and lounge were relatively quiet. Residents were left to nap or have some individual time. There were no other scheduled activities for the afternoon.

Agnes took off on her daily walk, taking advantage of her open campus privileges. The spry older woman liked to go outside to pet all the trees she had named and to visit her old cocoon site from where she allegedly had emerged.

Mia crept back to her room. She felt at last she could have some privacy, but there wasn't any way for her to lock the door. The nurses had the keys. She tried propping the desk chair against the knob to deny entry, but it was no use. The knob was purposely set higher on the door for that very reason. As a last resort she pushed the chair up against the door instead. At the very least it would act as a crude alarm system to give her the few seconds she needed to hide everything.

She sat by the window and set out the pen and precious scraps of paper including a shred of clean newspaper stolen from between the bars of the parakeet's cage when no one was looking. When she took out the mirror, she found Seth waiting for her.

"Sorry, Hon, it's been a long morning, hasn't it? I couldn't wait to get back to you. There's so much to go through. Are you ready?" she asked, keeping her voice down regardless of the closed door. She was taking no chances.

He nodded his head, but looked dazed.

"Okay, first, do you know anything about Wickenburg, Arizona?"

He appeared to have trouble concentrating at first. Mia knew it was a long shot, but they had run out of options. She was prepared to try anything at this point. Seth puzzled over it for a few more seconds, but suddenly his head snapped up with wide eyes full of recollection. He snatched up the pen and wrote, gripping it between his torn fingertips.

<u>YES!</u> ITS TOWN WHR I LV

"Oh my God! Really?" she said enthusiastically. "That's incredible! So you remember it now?"

He nodded again, a faint smile beginning to emerge from under the blood and dust.

"All right, let's see if that has helped to trigger your memory some more. You gave me a phone number. Whose is it? Do you think you can remember that now?"

Once more, he pondered the question. Then he printed quickly and held up the paper, pointing to it with an imploring expression on his face while mouthing the word, *please*.

MY MOMS —TLL HR WHR I AM

"I will, Tiger, but we're going to have to wait until Dan calls with the number later. He'll get it to me as soon as he can. Unless…do you think you can you recall it now? You're doing great so far."

He looked off into space, concentrating hard, but then dropped his gaze and shook his head sadly.

MY MEMRY CMES AN GOS

"It's okay. We'll get to it soon… All right Seth…" She hated herself for having to ask the next question, but she knew she had to. "…do you recall anything about where you are? Could it possibly be any kind of mineshaft? Are there any close to where you live?"

He closed his eyes for a few moments in recall and rubbed his brow.

Is it possible for us to solve all of this so quickly after all we've been through? Mia wondered as he pondered the question.

Her thoughts were interrupted when Seth started to tremble violently. Within seconds, his whole body quaked. His eyes flew open wide in alarm. A silent scream fled his mouth and his hands started to claw wildly at the air. His body twisted and writhed about in bizarre angles as he frantically thrashed about the room in a mad frenzy, crashing into things as if he were blind. Mia squelched her own scream with a hand clapped over her mouth as she watched in horror. She knew his panic could only be caused by sheer terror. In the next instant, his legs buckled beneath him and he dropped to the floor, clutching his ribs.

Trembling herself at the sight, she nearly lost grip of the small glass in her hand. "Seth? What is the matter? What is going on?" she asked him. But seeing him as he cried out and clawed at the air some more, it occurred to her that maybe Seth had just brought forth from his memory his own desperate attempt for survival. It was apparent that he was—or had been—in a mineshaft.

She tried to console him. "Seth! Seth, Honey! Please, listen to me! I'm right here. Shhh, shh, calm down. I'm right here. Shhh, Honey. I'm here. I'm here…"

He was panting rapidly from his exertion as tears coursed down his hollowed out cheeks. Rivulets of blood ran from his nose and into his mouth and down the front of his throat. A few moments later, he clutched at the footrest of the bed and with extreme determination, pulled himself back to a standing position once more. Hands forming fists, he threw back his head and howled in anguish, then broke into spasmodic sobs that racked his dwindling body. Seth lifted his eyes in a plea to her and started saying those puzzling syllables again, his lips moving rapidly in secret code.

"Please Seth. It's okay. It's okay," she repeated in a hoarse whisper, fighting back tears. She knew she had to press on. "What happened? Can you tell me now—how did you get there?"

He shook his head slowly, and then picked up the pen.

NO. ITS

But he trailed off, sobbing despondently.

"It's what?

CANT WRT. TOO MCH TO SAY. GTTING WEAK

"We have to find a way, Seth. You have to tell me what happened. It will help us. I know it will… it's…I can *feel* it," Mia said.

He dismally shook his head again.

She thought hard for a moment. "Is there any other way you can reach me besides writing—I don't know—gestures? Moving things?" Feeling defeated, she repeated to herself, "I don't know… there's got to be some other way…"

For some reason, Aunt Lydia suddenly came to mind. It instantly gave her an idea. *Could it possibly work?*

"Do you think that you could communicate with me through some kind of séance? Or even through a dream? I remember, in the beginning, I use to dream about you all the time. Could you do that?"

Her question made him look away. She stared at how his jacket hung limply on his thin frame, and his shoulders were curving inward.

This has to work she told herself, *we don't have much else.*

He rubbed his face and then slowly, turned back to her.

WE CLD TRY DRM

"What? A dream? Okay, let's—" she stopped short when he wrote:

DON'T KNW IF ITL WRK

NVR HV TRID THIS BEFR

She answered him gently, "Well neither have I, Tiger, but I'm willing to try. Are you?"

He shrugged again and then wrote,

GO TO SLP. C U THR

She sat back in the easy chair and closed her eyes, trying to will herself to sleep immediately. Her heart was still pounding from his tumultuous struggle and collapse, and her mind was racing with millions of thoughts and concerns.

This has to work. It's the only way her mind repeated.

Minutes passed and she was nowhere nearer to sleep. Squirming in her seat, she scrunched her eyelids down hard and gripped the armrests. Her raw nerves made her feel jumpy. She tried to concentrate on him, but her brain toggled back and forth between worry and fear for him. Feeling anxious, she knew she wouldn't be able to go to sleep and they'd run out of time again. She gritted her teeth and pounded an armrest with her fist out of frustration. If only she could just relax….

She suddenly remembered the deep relaxation techniques that she had been shown that very morning. If she could recall everything the young psychologist had instructed, she might be able to do it. Murmuring a quick and sincere thank you to him, she settled back and started going over each step in her head.

For the next couple of minutes, she picked a focal spot in the room to clear her head, while drawing in a series of slow deep breaths. As minutes ticked by, she could feel her body respond to the tension release and wind down just as it was suppose to, permitting her to slowly regain control. She felt encouraged by the progression. Continuing the deep breathing, she moved onto the next step as she closed her eyes and imagined an ensuing blackness enveloping her. Next, she concentrated on making each part of her body feel light and free. Bringing her pulse rate down and emptying her mind, she re-centered her focus and meditated just as he had taught her.

Whether it was remnants of sedatives still floating in her system or her own exhaustion, within a few minutes, she was there.

◊ ◊ ◊

The two sat side by side on the ground in the shade of a craggy boulder, their fingers inter-laced and their legs outstretched. The cloudless, sprawling sky rested heavily upon the rolling desert hills. The dry air was still, with only the sound of an occasional fly flitting by or twittering bird on the wing.

"Are you feeling any better today?" he asked her.

"Not really. I was throwing up all morning. How long is this supposed to last anyway? It's already going on three and a half months and I still can't keep anything down," she moaned.

"I don't know."

They looked out across the heat-soaked earth.

"I wish I could get a new phone. Mine's a piece of junk," she said as she woke up her phone, glanced at its screen, and then shut it down again. She was obviously fidgeting.

"What's the point? Service out here sucks anyway."

"Yeah. I guess. It'll still be nice to get a new one sometime."

Seth was already breaking a sweat in his varsity jacket, but he had just received his pin for baseball for his senior year and he wanted to be able to display it properly, even if the warm climate wouldn't comply.

Although it was cooler in the shade of the rock in the September early evening, any parts of them exposed to the bright Arizona sun warmed up rapidly. He scooted his feet in when they started to get hot while Shayla left hers basking in the light. The days were already moving into autumn, but she still wore her summer flip-flops so she could show off her toe rings and bright pink nail polish.

"What does *he* want to see us about anyway?" she asked shifting her petite frame uncomfortably on the hard ground.

"I don't know. He wouldn't tell me," Seth replied as he scuffed some sand with his boot at a big black ant crawling toward him.

He felt uneasy about this whole setup. Something didn't feel right. But he didn't want to alarm Shayla by mentioning it. Looking at her, he could see that she still displayed a slight green shade from the morning sickness.

No, he told himself, *I will deal with this.*

"I don't like him, Seth. He creeps me out. Aside from being a total asshole, he just seems, I don't know, dangerous or something. Like one day he's going to go totally ape shit. It's just a feeling I get whenever I see him. We'll probably see his picture on the news someday saying that he's wanted for an ax murder or something," she said moodily.

"Well, it's not that I like him either. I hate that bastard," he answered with disgust.

"Why did you listen to him then, and show up here?" she asked, her voice rising.

"'Cause basically he told me that I had better meet him here with you and not say anything to my mother about it or he was going to kick me out of the house."

"What's wrong with that? You want to leave home anyway. You could finally get out of there and come live with me at my house."

"Yeah, right. And have your old man blow my head off for knocking up his daughter? No, that's okay. I'll take my chances with Mr. Psycho-Whack-Job. I can handle him. Besides I told you it'll only be until I get some work. That way we can find a place of our own and I can support the three of us. Whatever we do, we have to look out for our baby. We both agreed to have him. We're going to have to do our best for him then," he said decisively.

Trying to ease the tension that flared up between them, he tried an optimistic tone. "C'mon Shayla, maybe we can even find a place out of this dump, like in the Valley or something. We could rent an apartment in a complex with a swimming pool, and maybe close to a big mall and restaurants and movies. I know you'll love that! We'll get a stroller for the baby so we could take walks to the park and do stuff with him." He flashed her a bright grin of encouragement, hoping she'd put her fears aside.

She reluctantly smiled back and nodded her head in agreement.

He went on, "I've already promised the little guy that I'm not going to be like my old man and abandon my family to whatever sleaze-ball comes along. I've already got three hundred and fifty dollars saved up, but we are going to need a lot more than that."

"How much more?" she demanded, the smile fading. "Three hundred and fifty bucks is a lot already, isn't it? Won't that be enough? I mean, we don't need anything fancy."

He explained patiently, "No, most apartments will want us to put down a deposit and at least first month's rent. Some of them want two. Then we're going to have to start up all of our utilities. It's going to take a lot more than what I have. I really need to get a full time job, quick."

"But how much longer is that gonna be? You began looking for work three weeks ago and you still haven't found anything," she whined, turning up her small nose.

"Just a little bit longer, Baby," he said as he kissed her forehead. "I've asked around and put in applications, but there are no jobs here. I'm gonna try Phoenix this weekend."

She pulled away quickly. "Uh Seth—you're doing it again." She held up her fingertips and smeared a drop of blood around in them to show him.

"Aw, shit, I'm sorry. Did I get any on you?" He recoiled, pinching the side of his nose with his finger and holding his head back.

"Just a little. I'm okay. But it looks like you got some on your jacket... What's up with that anyway?"

He swallowed and then said, "My jacket? I told you that I'm not hot."

"No! Your nose and how it bleeds and all."

He swallowed a couple of more times, choking down the salty blood coursing down the back of his throat.

Then he replied, "Ever since that freak almost broke my nose, I always get these friggin' things. They seem to come on whenever I'm nervous or I get worked up about things. I was suppose to get it cauterized, but the doctor never wanted to do it because he didn't know what caused them, and Mom's afraid to tell him how it all happened."

"Oh," she said as she wiped her fingers off on her jeans.

They settled back against the rock, neither of them having much else to say. His nose continued to bleed. She leaned her blonde head against his shoulder, and he put his arm around her. Their apprehension mounted of not only what the future held in store for them but what awaited them within the next hour or so.

A half-hour later, they heard heavy footsteps crunching up the dirt path behind them. The young couple looked at each other with uncertainty at the approaching sound.

"Now where the fuck are those kids?" They could hear his voice softly swearing.

Shayla's eyes were big with fear as she looked at Seth and shook her head no. She tugged at his arm, hoping that he would join her in keeping quiet and out of sight behind the rock. But Seth mustered enough courage to smile reassuringly at her.

We're here already. I might as well get this over with and see what he wants, he told himself.

He waved his hand out from around the rock and called out casually, "We're over here, Ed."

Shayla scrunched up her face and silently mouthed the word "Shit!" then hunkered against her boyfriend.

The big man moved around to the other side of the rock and glared down at them. He breathed heavily from the effort of his hike, invoking his smoker's deep hacking cough until his face grew even redder. Sweat beaded on his forehead, throughout his thinning hair, and stained his dirty shirt collar, as well as leaving a belt of wetness around his bulging middle.

The three of them regarded the other with wary eyes.

"Listen, it's hot out here and I still have to go home and wrench on your mother's piece of shit car, so I'm gonna cut through the crap right off. I know she's pregnant, dumb-ass," he accused, pointing a thick finger at Shayla while looking at Seth. "And I know that you're the prick that's been screwing her, so that must make it yours. You better know right off that I have enough supporting your mother and your dead lazy ass. I'm not going to be supporting any mistake of yours too!"

Shayla gasped and looked at Seth.

Ed turned his attention to her. "What? You don't think everybody knows? First you go around spreading your legs all over the place. Then you start puking your guts out. You didn't think anyone could put two and two together? They're talking about it all over town, even at the garage. I think the guys are pissed because your ass wipe boyfriend here beat them to the action."

"Hey, watch how you talk to her," Seth growled.

Ed's lips formed an ugly sneer. "Like you're gonna do anything about it, you little prick? I'll tell you what you *are* going to do: take your slut here down to Phoenix this weekend, find a clinic and get an abortion. I'll loan you the money to do it, but you are gonna pay me back. *With interest.* Understand?"

"Yeah, well you can go shit yourself then. We're keeping our baby," Seth answered in a calm but measured voice.

"Not at my house you're not. As a matter of fact, you can pack your shit and move out now. I've had it up to here with your bullshit."

"It's my mother's house! She owned it before you ever moved in. And you can't tell me what to do."

"The hell I can't. I'm telling you one more time so you better get it straight. She gets a hanger job this weekend or you're going to find your fuckin' ass out on the street! And if your mother opens that goddam hole of hers, I'll kick her fuckin' ass out too. I don't need any of this goddam shit." He coughed again, then snorted and spat a wad of phlegm into the dirt by them.

Seth was on his feet in an instant, his eyes narrowing. "Don't you ever threaten my mother," he said in a low voice.

"Like I said, what do you think you're going to do about it you little cock sucker? You useless piece of shit. I'm the one who is bringing in the paycheck, so you better keep your fuckin' mouth shut!"

"Shayla is not getting any abortion, so I guess I'll be packing my shit this afternoon. But you better keep your filthy hands off of my mother," Seth growled defensively.

For a moment, Ed looked at the teenager in disbelief. "What the—?" he started. Then, as if he got the punch line, he laughed coarsely and taunted, "Oh, I get it. You want to be the big man in front of your bitch!" He then hunched down in a threatening position, his fingers motioning Seth to approach. "Come on, jerk-off. This is gonna be sweet. I've been waiting to take you out without your goddam 'mommy' always being around."

"Seth! Just leave it!" Shayla begged.

She was on her feet now and positioning herself between them. Seth looked at her and shook his head tying to motion for her to get out of the way.

"Yeah, Sethie-boy. You had better listen to your cunt, you fucking coward. She knows what I could do to you. As for you," he said as he reached over, took Shayla by the wrist, and twisted it hard, "I wouldn't mind a little piece of you myself," he breathed low in her ear, "But that'll be later after I kick your boyfriend's ass." Shayla squeaked in pain.

Ed was knocked off his feet in an instant when Seth charged him, toppling him to the dirt. The big man landed hard on his back, but his hands reached up, one holding Seth back by the throat, the other pushing back his head. They grappled around in the dust, each trying to get a grip or land a hit on the other. The youth's lanky frame was no match for Ed's hardened and heavier muscles. Seth's lack of fighting experience also played to his disadvantage. He managed only to land a couple of body blows, before the older man grabbed a fistful of dirt and threw it in his eyes.

As the teenager recoiled back, Ed struck him with a heavy roundhouse punch to the side of the head. Shayla screamed as Seth tumbled to the ground and lay there stunned, trying to regain his senses. Ed got to his feet, still wheezing and coughing from being tackled. When he saw an opening, he hauled off and viciously kicked Seth hard in the ribs.

As the teenager clutched his side and groaned, Ed vehemently spat out, "Just who did you think you were messing with, you stupid shit!"

The big man savagely kicked at him several more times, aiming for any unguarded spots about his head, back, and stomach. Seth writhed in pain. He tried to rise, but the constant assault kept him down, trying to protect his face and head from the heavy boot.

"Do you think I was kidding with you, you shit ass little prick? I'll show you not to—"

Ed stopped, mid-sentence when Shayla came up behind him and struck him in the head with a large rock. It was enough of a blow to disable him for a few moments, making him stagger about while giving Seth a chance to get up.

As the teen rose slowly to his feet, Ed shook his head a few times and then touched the palm of his hand to the back of his head. He drew back his hand to see the fresh blood from the blow. Upon spotting this, he turned his full fury upon Shayla, who had since dropped the rock and was backing up in terror over the man's rage.

"Why, you fuckin' little bitch!" Ed growled as he lunged after her.

Seth charged him from the side and tackled the man to the ground once more. In the scuffle a Colt revolver slipped out from Ed's pant leg and tumbled into the dust. Seth stared wide-eyed at the weapon as he realized Ed's dangerous intent.

His stepfather made a grab for it, but Seth did not allow Ed to overtake him again. Instead he pounded away at the big sweaty face, over and over again, not giving the man a chance to regain dominance.

"I hate you, you bastard! I hate you! I hate you!" the youth growled through clenched teeth as he continued to strike.

Years of bottled up frustration and fear came pouring out from Seth's balled up fists. The big man absorbed each jarring hit spraying saliva, blood, and sweat in every direction. With each frantic blow, Ed's face quickly mutated to a bruised and bloody pulp.

Then Seth grabbed Ed by the ears and slammed his head hard against the ground a few times. The man's eyes fluttered, rolled back and then closed.

"Seth! Stop it! You're killing him!" Shayla screeched, running over and pulling him back by his shoulders.

The big man lay very still upon the ground, while Seth knelt above him, panting wildly and holding his aching ribs. He could still feel his rage burn within him, but hearing Shayla, he managed to bring himself under control.

She moved in closer and stared in horror and disbelief. "Ohmigod! Is he…? I think he's dead," she whispered.

Wiping away the sweat and blood that was dripping from his own face, Seth stared in disbelief at his stepfather. Fury gave way to shock, and then fright as the realization of what he had done started to sink in.

No. His mind stated resolutely.

Then he grasped Ed by his jowls and gave him a tentative shake. The man's large mouth gaped open slightly, but there was no response.

No, please God, no.

He felt around the sweaty rolls of the man's neck for a pulse, but couldn't find any there or on his thick wrists.

Oh Christ! NO!

Seth couldn't believe what had just occurred. Could it happen so quickly? There had been no choice, he reasoned. Ed was trying to harm them. But he hadn't intended on killing the man. He only meant to subdue him so they could get away.

NO! NO! Could I have done this? This can't be happening.

Shayla whimpered as Seth leaned his ear by Ed's gaping mouth in hope of catching any escaping breath. There was none. Repulsed, he pushed himself away from the lifeless body and stood up, wincing as his cracked ribs and bruised kidneys burned with pain. He could also feel Shayla's eyes upon him.

"I-I didn't mean to…" he said slowly, backing away.

"But he's *dead*, Seth!… Ohmigod! What did you do?!" Shayla lamented, clutching her stomach.

Terrified and sickened by the deed he had just committed, Seth turned to her, "But I didn't mean to! You hear me? I didn't mean to!"

She sobbed, "But you killed him!"

"He was trying to harm you... the baby..."

"He's dead! What are we going to do, Seth?" Shayla hid her face in her hands and shook her head.

Waves of panic flooded Seth and his heart raced wildly. He focused on his attacker. Just seconds ago, Ed was dangerous and diabolical. He had to be stopped. Now he lay motionless and quiet.

Seth's knee-jerk response was to flee. Run away from the body of his stepfather lying in the dust. Run away from Shayla's face, stained with tears and dirt, her cries echoing in his ears. Run away from this small town closing in on him with no possible escape.

Run!

He turned and bolted, answering the instinctive order given to him from his panicked brain. In his mad flight, his long legs covered ground quickly, hopping over rocks, crashing through creosote bushes, and slipping on loose rocks and gravel. He moved swiftly, putting as much distance between him and the scene as was possible; his girlfriend and the slain falling quickly behind him.

No matter how far or fast he ran, Seth could still hear Shayla's cries in his ears and see Ed's lifeless face flash before his eyes. The teen roared loudly at the top of his voice as he ran, "I didn't mean to!" his shouts echoing off craggy boulders and the surrounding hillsides. Someone or something had to hear him and believe.

He suddenly veered in his flight, his only impulse to head home, get his car, and grab some things. He would come back for Shayla and the baby as soon as he could. And then they would call his mom from wherever they ended up. But first, he had to get out of here.

Breaking through cholla and brush, he lost his footing tripping over a large rock. He scrambled to his feet and took off again in his mad dash across the desert to the direction of his house. The setting sun was intense and blinding, obscuring his vision, its harsh light creating a haze through the dust hanging in the desert air.

As he ran, his foot struck upon something hard like a curb, and suddenly Seth found himself in a free fall, going straight down. His heart crammed into his throat and his stomach lurched upward from the rapid descent, arms and legs flailing wildly as he plummeted through the air. It became instantly dark about him, as if someone had shot out the light.

In his tumble, his right leg struck against something hard, shattering his tibia upon impact and shooting excruciating pains through him. He tumbled downward some more, his body tossed like a rag doll, skipping off of crumbling walls. To him, it seemed endless, but in the next second, he landed upon something narrow and hard. He managed to hold on, his fingers recognizing wood as they dug into it. He realized he was hung up on a piece of timber, jutting from a wall of this gaping pit.

Gasping, he strained to get a better grip, but the beam groaned, then made a loud cracking noise under him, and lurched downward. Seth's hands slid along the rough surface as he tried to hang on. The timber splintered and broke under his weight, bucking him off its back.

He felt himself falling again, when suddenly he slammed into the ground, knocking the air from him. With a snapping sound his other leg had folded in an odd angle underneath him. Another hot, immense pain seized his ankle. He screamed out in agony.

When he opened his eyes, he saw nothing. The pit he had fallen into was completely and totally devoid of all light. He blinked a couple of times, but could only feel the peppering of dust and dirt still raining down on his head and back from his descent. The settling dust filled his nostrils and mouth. He coughed and spat, trying not to breathe in the particles that continued to coat him.

Squeezing his eyes shut, and then opening them once more, he knew instantly there was nothing wrong with his eyes. He held up his hand until it was almost against his face and could not see even its outline. As he felt the ground beneath and about him, his hands became slimy, wet, and cold. The air was dank and foul smelling.

When he attempted to get to his feet, his broken leg blasted piercing arrows of torture through him, nearly causing him to faint. Summoning up the rest of his strength, he clawed at the walls, trying to pull himself up. But he fell back into the slippery mud and foul puddle beneath him. His heart was beating out of control, adrenaline pumped through his veins, and pain wracked every inch of his body. Yet none of it could stem the tide of encroaching fear and panic that seized him.

"Help!!" he wailed upward to the direction from which he came. "Help me!!!" he screamed over and over again into the black tunnel above his head.

There was no one there to answer his desperate pleas. He was totally and utterly alone in the darkness.

◊ ◊ ◊

There was a bump, and then a slight scraping sound. A harder bump, and metal feet screeched across the linoleum floor. Agnes pushed her way in. She looked behind the door and spotted the chair that blocked her progress. She persisted by pushing the door open until the chair slid into the room. At the noise, Mia sat straight up in the easy chair, gasping for air, her cheeks wet with tears. Agnes studied her for a moment then entered the room.

"Why is there a chair behind the door, dear?" she asked.

Mia couldn't answer her. She was in shock by what she had just seen. All she could feel was shaky and cold. She had never experienced a dream so graphic and realistic. It was as if somehow she had been magically transported to that faraway place.

But she *was* there—a witness to brutal, horrific events; every last detail perfectly clear behind her closed eyelids. She smelled the creosote and dust in the air, and felt the sun's heated rays on her back. She even felt the unevenness of the rocky ground beneath her feet.

And he was so alive, there in the sunlight, in the outdoors. Seth had been right in front of her. She could've reached out to touch him, he was so close. She saw the breeze tousle his brown hair. She saw his dark gray varsity jacket with the yellow insignia: Wickenburg Union High School Cougars, Wickenburg Arizona. The sun splashed across his tan face, and caught the silver of the lone earring he wore.

She heard his voice for the first time, recalling its low timbre and its soft southwestern accent. And revealed to her for the first time was his concern for his unborn child and his bravery in protecting Shayla. Mia had witnessed his commitment and courage, but above all, his humanness.

He was *alive*.

However, a cold truth sunk in and shook her, swiftly unlocking the door to grief. She had also witnessed his death.

Visions of Seth being savagely brutalized by his stepfather, then alone and dying at the bottom of the mineshaft replayed in her memory, breaking her heart. Before, she had always held a spark of hope that he could possibly be alive somewhere and was somehow communicating with her telepathically. There was no denying it now. The dream had dashed any of that possibility. He was dead.

With the tragedy so fresh before her, she couldn't bear it. Grief-stricken and dazed, she remained in the armchair, trembling and holding herself tightly.

"I visited my old cocoon spot today," Agnes told her pleasantly from her perch on her bed. "And Trudy's leaves are all yellow, and Jonathan's still have a little green on them, while Charles has lost all of his already! He's always been an early bird."

Catching a ragged breath, Mia picked up the mirror with shaking hands. Her eyes searched the glass. He wasn't there.

"Seth? Where are you? Seth!" she asked anxiously. Had the dream ended it all?

"And Lacey looks like she has a robin's nest in her top branches and Cynthia may have some bark beetles. Or you know? Maybe they are termites. Yes. That's what they probably are. I should really speak to the groundskeeper about that."

Slowly he came into view, looking disheveled and worn out as he wrote his next message:

DREM TOOK IT OUT OF ME. SO TIRED

With overwhelming affection for him, Mia viewed his tortured face and lightly stroked the glass. She broke down and cried, "Oh God, Seth! I am so sorry. How did you... were you..."

She couldn't go on. If only she could have him here beside her. She wanted so much just to hold him close.

DON'T CRY MIA. IM OK

"But I put you through all of that again. I didn't mean to—"

"That's all we need. To have everyone catching Cynthia's termites. You know the saplings will be the first to go. Have you met the saplings? They are the cutest things. Why, there is Amelia and Geoffrey..."

"Please forgive me...." she asked of him as she wiped at her tears.

He offered a smile in attempt to reassure her. Although she accepted it, she caught herself—she should be comforting *him*.

She sighed and then gathering her composure, tried to continue, "You have a baby... Why didn't you ever tell me?"

DIDN'T KNOW WHT YOUD THNK OF ME

"I wouldn't have thought any different about you. You're a good person, Seth, and you would have made a good dad and husband too."

"…And there's Martha and Raul. You know, every time you turn around those two are always getting their branches entwined…" the old lady giggled naughtily.

A SON. DON'T KNOW WHT THAT WOULD BE LIKE

They both were silent, separated by their thoughts. Agnes' chatter filled in the void, providing a steady rhythm in the quiet room.

Seth looked wistful and wrote,

WNTED TO SEE HIM AT LEAST ONCE

Her heart leapt at this all too familiar wish. "You will Seth. Once we get you where you are going, you'll be able to see him any time you want and watch him grow. I promise you," she reassured him.

Oddly, upon saying the words, she felt a touch of envy. She would she never have that opportunity with her own lost child.

UR GONNA BE A COOL MTHER, MIA.

UR KIDS WILL BE LUCKY

She looked at him with gratitude. He still managed to be kind, though he had been through so much. She imagined if she had a brother, he would he have been like Seth. Decent and kindhearted like her father.

She swallowed hard and gathered up her resolve. "We have to keep going, Tiger. We have to figure this out…There's got to be something else that is holding you still. You are *not* supposed to be there."

BUT I KLLD MY STPFTHR. DON'T MRDERERS GO TO HELL?

"It was self defense! You did what you had to! He would've killed you. And Shayla and your baby too!"

"… Josephina has gotten so big! Why, she doesn't even need supports anymore," Agnes babbled on happily to no one in particular.

Just then, there was another short knock on the door. Brenda, the evening nurse, came in holding two dosage cups. She took a moment to glance briefly at the chair out of place against the wall and then scooted it back to its position in the room. Then she resumed her mission.

"Hello ladies. Time to take your medications," she said cheerfully as she handed a cup to Agnes.

"Thank you, Brenda. Did you know that Cynthia has termites?" Agnes asked as she took the cup and swallowed down the pills inside of it.

"Oh really? Well, that doesn't sound too good, now does it?" Brenda answered patronizingly. Then she turned to Mia who was trying to avert her tearstained face. "Mia! Hey, what's up, hon? Not feeling too good? It's probably because it's time for your medication. Here, take these. They will fix you up in a jiffy. Oh, also, your husband called about ten minutes ago. He said he couldn't talk to you at the moment, but he left this number." She held out both the cup and slip of paper to her.

Mia reached past the medication, snatched up the slip and eagerly poured over it. Then realizing that Brenda was still standing there, she turned back to the woman.

"Um, thanks. I've been, uh, waiting for this number," she explained quietly.

Then she self-consciously took the cup, swallowed the pills inside, and handed it back to the nurse who was now evaluating her.

What was she thinking about me? Mia worried.

She knew she had to be very careful around all of these people. One wrong gesture, move, or statement could end up with her being sedated or isolated.

Brenda let a critical eye wander over Mia from head to toe for a moment more. "You're welcome," she finally said.

Mia sighed inwardly. The cat had released the mouse.

The nurse reminded her, "If you are going to call anyone, remember to keep your phone privilege to ten minutes so that everyone has a turn." With that, she took one last look around the room to make sure everything was in order, then left.

As the door closed, Agnes pouted, "I bet Brenda doesn't even care that Cynthia has termites. Not one little bit! That nasty-nellie. They're all cold and heartless, I tell you. Cold and heartless."

Thoroughly put out, she picked up one of her magazines and thumbed through the pages with disdain, mumbling to herself.

Mia waited a few seconds to make sure the nurse didn't return then resumed where she and the teen had left off. "Okay, Seth, I've got the number! Is it your mom's?"

He nodded yes.

"All right. I'm going to call right now. The bad thing is that we don't have a private phone in this room. I'll have to use the one in the sunroom."

She slipped the mirror back into her pocket, opened the door, and cautiously looked up and down the hallway. Then she stealthily made her way to the sunroom. No one was present aside from the parakeet woman who was there caring for the bird.

Mia casually walked over to the window and pretended to look out on the grounds below, waiting for her to finish and leave. She didn't know what to expect on the phone when she talked to Seth's mother and she didn't need an audience if she needed to confer with Seth.

Five minutes later, the parakeet woman was still whistling and talking to the bird and wasn't any closer to feeding it. Mia was growing impatient. Soon it would be time for dinner and the staff would start rounding them all up. She decided to apply a little pressure by walking over to the cage. The other woman eyed her suspiciously but continued her baby talk to her little charge.

Holding her hand up to the bars, Mia remarked, "You know, I use to have a little parakeet just like this when I was growing up. In fact he looks just like *my* Abraham. Do you suppose I could have a turn in feeding him? You're such a pretty bird, yes you are," she cooed to the parakeet.

"It's a her! And it's MY privilege to feed her. No one else's," Dahlia said possessively.

"But you take *such* a long time to do it. I'm sure if I tell Brenda that I can feed her faster, she'd probably let me. You know everything is on a schedule around here. In fact, they'll be calling dinner soon. They can't have anything or *anyone* holding it up," Mia said innocently. Then she made kissing noises to the bird, and said condescendingly, "Hey there, little girl. I'm sure you're starving by now, aren't you? Do you want me to feed you? I know, I know. Dahlia is just too slow, isn't she? Let me talk to the night nurse right now so you can have your dinner, okay? Brenda is right outside."

The woman roughly shoved her aside. "It's MY privilege! And I can do it just as fast as you. Even *faster*. That's because I do it every day because it is my privilege." Giving Mia a dirty look, she unlocked and opened the door, flung in some birdseed, then quickly slammed the door shut and locked it once more. Having done the deed, she turned back to Mia with a smug look on her face. "There! See? Bet you couldn't keep the time. And I know something else. I bet you don't even know what her name is. *I* do. But I'm not even going to tell you."

Looking satisfied in having had the last word, the parakeet woman scooped up the feed and cleaning supplies and haughtily left the room.

Relieved at her departure, Mia waited another agonizing minute to make sure she wasn't going to return with a nurse in tow, and then dialed the phone. The 928 area code fit easily with the rest of the number and she waited anxiously while the line rang. Her heart skipped a beat when it finally picked up.

A recorded voice informed her, "You must first enter a personal access code for all long distance phone calls. Please hang up and try your call again."

Gritting her teeth and slamming down the phone, Mia remembered that all residents had to sign out for access codes. It was the way Meadow Brook kept tabs on outgoing long distance calls.

She immediately went to the nurses' station where she signed the clipboard and handed it to Consuela, the attending nurse. The nurse then signed out a personal code to her and warned her to make sure that no one else can get to it, or otherwise she would be charged. Impatient with all the bureaucracy, Mia raced back to the sunroom, hoping against hope that no one was using the phone.

It was clear.

She dialed the number again, her pulse building to a crescendo once more. The phone rang six times before it was finally answered.

"Hello?" The woman's voice sounded hurried as if she had just gotten home to find the phone ringing.

Hearing a live person on the other end, Mia didn't know what to say. She had been so focused on getting the number and calling, she hadn't prepared herself for this moment. She realized she didn't even know the woman's name.

Stammering, she started, "Uh, yes, hello. You don't know me but I—"

"Are you selling something? Because if you are I can save us both the time. I am not interested."

"Uh, no, ma'am. Please don't hang up. I am not a telemarketer. Really. I need to talk to you about your son, Seth," Mia tried.

"Are you the police? We've been through this a million times about his stepfather already. I don't know where Seth is. He hasn't called or emailed or anything." The woman started sounding agitated.

It was painfully evident that his mother did not know what had become of her son.

"I-I am a, friend of his," Mia began, not knowing how to explain what she knew.

"Oh my God! Do you know where he is? Tell him that he *has* to come back home! Please! He's in trouble with the law and the more time he spends away, he'll be in even worse trouble. I've already found him a good defense attorney. He told me that he should be able to get him off or at least a reduced charge... I knew I should have divorced Ed long ago. It should've never come down to this..." the woman moaned, guilt saturating her voice.

"Would you mind if I ask what is your name?"

"My name? I guess Seth didn't tell you. Cross. Juanita Cross. At least it's my maiden name. I've gone back to it."

It was falling into place now. C R O S S. *Seth Cross!* Mia inwardly kicked herself for not being able to figure out that he had been writing out his last name, not a clue to a location.

His mother continued, "This is not like him to stay away so long. The school has called to drop him already. Tell Seth he can't stay away for three months without *any* kind of contact. I've been worried to death about him..."

"Ms. Cross? It's going to be hard for you to believe what I am about to tell you, but—" Mia paused, feeling queasy, then took a quick breath. "I'm sorry. There was... an accident. He's ... Seth was killed."

"What?! My Seth? No..." There was a sound on the other side of the line not unlike the sound of a wounded animal. "You must be mistaken. He can't be...not my boy... no... not my son..." Then silence.

"Ms. Cross? I'm really sorry..."

"Who are you? Where is he! How do you know this?" Ms. Cross returned, her voice now strangled and high.

"My name is Mia Labont. After the fight with his stepdad, Seth was cutting across the desert to return home when he accidentally fell down a mine shaft."

"Where you there? How do you know all of this?!" she repeated.

Oddly, Ms. Cross started to sound as if she was drifting away, her voice growing tiny and echoing down a long passage. A sensation of weightlessness pitched the floor beneath Mia. At first, she didn't know what was happening when suddenly she recognized the effects of the medication that Brenda had given her.

No! Not now. Hang in there... Mia told herself. This was not the time for her to be woozily incoherent. *Why didn't I spit out that damned pill?*

It was becoming harder to concentrate and she hoped was choosing the right words. "No- no. I wasn't there. He told me...in a dream."

"In a dream? Who are you! Where is my son? What have you done to him? Tell me!!" she shrieked. His mother's shrill pitch echoed and reverberated in Mia's ear.

"He's dead. I'm sorry... He fell through a mineshaft. In Wickenburg... He comes to me in reflections in mirrors, pot lids, knobs.... He talks to me all time..."

Mia knew she was slurring her words and wondered if she was making much sense. She squeezed her eyes shut and focused hard.

"He showed me everything in a dream..."

"Where are you calling from?!" the woman demanded.

"Meadow Brook Mental Health Clinic," Mia admitted, not knowing why she did.

"I don't know who you are or what kind of sick twisted game you are playing, but I'm calling the police... Oh god...My Seth, no..." his mother sobbed.

There was the sound of the phone hitting the floor, but the line stayed open.

"Ms. Cross? I'm sorry.... I had to tell you like this. Please try to understand... Juanita?"

She was no longer there. Mia stayed on the phone for the next minute or so calling to her, but his mother did not return.

Mia dropped her head in her hands. How could that have gone so wrong? The medication was fogging everything. She couldn't think straight or make the words come out right. And of all times when she needed to be the most concise and astute.

What a horrendous way to find out about your only child...

She felt horrible having to break the news to Seth's mom in the manner that she did. But reconsidering it, there wasn't any other way that would have been much better.

The woman had lost her son...

She made her way back to her room and threw herself down on her bed feeling disconcerted and sick to her stomach. Agnes wasn't around and had probably taken off for dinner.

Pulling out the mirror, she shamefully faced Seth.

"Seth, hon, I tried… This medication—it's screwing with my brain right now. I'm really sorry. But I did talk with her…"

YU TOLD HR ABOT ME?

She rubbed her temples and shook her head yes. Seth closed his eyes and breathed deeply at her reply while blood fell in large heavy drops upon his boots. But when he lifted his eyes to her once again, they were filled with gratitude.

THANK U

Through her drug-induced haze, Mia studied him carefully. His skin looked worse and his shoulders sagged with fatigue and suffering. Even with the recent disclosure of his stepfather's murder and his own accident, his condition hadn't improved miraculously like she had expected. She had hoped there would be some kind of change by now. They had made such huge strides in solving this mystery. Seth had killed Ed in self-defense. She knew he wasn't a murderer, yet he was still losing ground. It was baffling.

In the next moment, she saw something in the mirror that made her blood run cold. She wasn't sure if it was it some kind of drug-induced vision. A rush of adrenaline suddenly cleared her head of the medication fog and made her stiffen. She sat up in bed and scrutinized the room in the mirror.

Tilting the small glass at different angles, she asked in a hushed voice, "Seth, what is that? Behind you?"

A mysterious inky black shape was present in the corner behind him. At first, she thought it was only his shadow, cast by the lamp in the room. But this thing moved on its own, despite the fact that Seth was sitting still.

IT SHWD UP WHLE U WRE CALLNG MY MOM. ITS WAITING

"Waiting? For what?"

Seth lifted his hand and calmly tapped his chest.

Confused, she asked, "For you? Why?" Then suddenly overcome with a fearful realization, she told him, "No! You can't! Tell it to go away! Don't go near it, Seth, whatever you do. We *have* to try harder. Now think—there's got to be something else we still have to do. We've contacted your mom and told her. How about Shayla? Does she know what happened to you?"

DN'T KNOW

"Well how can I reach her? Do you remember her number? Think Seth!"

CANT REMBR

"You have to! Now think hard!" she demanded.

To her alarm, he rolled back his head and screamed. His eyes fluttering and turning white, he grimaced at her like he did the first time she had beheld him so long ago. Then all of a sudden his grimace turned into a dark scowl, and he lunged at her like an animal, baring his teeth. Letting out a gasp, she flinched and dropped the mirror.

Shaken, she looked at the glass on the floor. A third of it had broken off and shattered. She knelt down and apprehensively peered into the remaining piece, not knowing what to expect. But Seth—her Seth—was there once again, looking drawn and apologetic. She picked up the mirror once more, but this time, she felt on guard. Would he do it again?

IM SORY. DN'T KNW WHT JUST HAPPND

As she tilted the broken mirror to read his message, she could see now that the shadow was directly behind him, cloaking his shoulders.

"Seth! It's right behind you!" she whispered urgently.

He reached out a trembling hand to her.

DN'T WNT TO GO—PLESE HLP ME MIA

"I am trying, Honey—"

The door opened abruptly and Lynette and Brenda came in.

"Is everything okay in here? We missed you at dinner—" Lynnette stopped mid-sentence when she spied the broken glass on the floor and the mirror in Mia's hand. "Where did you get that from?" She reached out and plucked the mirror out of her grasp. "No. I'm sorry Mia. That is not going to do. You know you are not permitted any glass without supervision."

The sharp edge of the broken glass sliced through Mia's finger, but she ignored its sting, as she demanded, "Give it back He's dying! I need it back!"

"Oh look now at what happened to your finger. That is exactly why you can't have—" Lynnette was cut short as Mia reached out to snatch back the mirror.

She grappled with the nurse for a few moments while Brenda moved around to the back of her and looked for a grip on the flailing arms.

"Mia? We are going to have to isolate you if you don't calm down. Don't force us to do that to you," Brenda threatened as she succeeded in securing Mia.

Mia howled with frustration. She broke the grip that Brenda had gotten on her and pounced once more on Lynnette. The two of them went sprawling down onto the linoleum.

"I thought you gave her her medication!" Lynnette yelled to Brenda from the floor, holding the mirror out of Mia's reach while pushing back with her other hand.

"I did! I can't believe she is still this active! She was fine when I saw her just a bit ago," Brenda said through gritted teeth as she pulled Mia's arms back again.

This time she deftly pinned her face down on the floor. Mia kicked and screamed and tossed about while Brenda's knee pressed into her shoulders.

"Please! Give it back! He's dying! LET ME GO! I've got to help him!"

Brenda held on and puffing hard, asked Lynette, "So—do you still want to try to move her into isolation?"

Lynnette rose from the floor, straightened her glasses, and tried to smooth back her ruffed-up hair. She slipped the mirror into the pocket of her scrub top, and then examined her own hands for any cuts she may have received from the sharp edge.

She replied tersely, "No. I'm tired of screwing around. She already gave Cathy and me trouble yesterday. And I'm tired of her and her antics. She's going to get it. I don't care what Churosh has to say about it."

"But will Agnes be okay with her in here the way she's acting?"

"With this, I don't think she'll be doing anything to anyone for a while."

A sharp painful sting in her hip told Mia they had sedated her again. With her last ounce of dwindling strength, she strained against the restrictive weight of Brenda, and then passed out.

◊ ◊ ◊

Dan had just finished topping the sandwich with the last piece of bread in the bag when the phone rang. He looked at the clock and wondered who could be calling so late. He had just gotten home from an eleven-hour work day. Hopeful that it would be Mia, he picked up the receiver.

"Mr. Labont? This is Dr. Churosh. Hello. I hope I'm not interrupting your evening."

Dan looked down at the cold sandwich sitting on the counter then pushed it away.

"It's okay. You're not," he said. "What can I do for you?"

"It's Mia. We had somewhat of an incident after dinnertime. Nothing serious I assure you, and she is all right, so don't be alarmed. Somehow, she got a hold of another mirror. We're still unclear on how it came to be in her possession. Our residents are not allowed to keep any form of glass with their personal belongings, for their own well-being. I'm sure you understand. And with Mia's own fixation with reflections, it's best that she does not have access to a mirror, unless she is being directly observed or supervised by myself or one of the other therapists or nurses."

"Did she do something?" Dan swallowed hard, not having considered the possibility that she could have harmed herself with the contraband he had provided her.

"Well, she became extremely excitable and upset when one of our nurses discovered her with it. The nurse reported that Mia apparently had been trying to cut herself with a broken edge and she succeeded in cutting her own hand. Unfortunately, she put up a struggle and attacked one of our nurses when they tried to take the glass away from her. It resulted in her being sedated. She will be closely monitored when she wakes up. If she returns to her agitated state, we will probably have to confine her and medicate her again."

"Attack? A nurse? Mia… Is she all right?" Dan asked with alarm.

"Your wife is quite all right. And luckily the nurses were not injured either."

As the psychiatrist's words caught hold, Dan grew so angry with himself, he found it difficult to speak at the moment.

"She has a four o'clock session scheduled with me tomorrow afternoon, but I think it is necessary for us to try to arrange for an earlier meeting. Dr. Gamez and Gerry Monroe from PartnersHealth will be attending as well. At that time, we will discuss and revise her treatment strategy. If she continues on this current course of uncontrollable excitability and growing hostility, we may have to move her to a more secure ward where we will have to counter with a higher level of drugs or employ other measures."

"Other measures?" Dan asked, hesitatingly.

"We may consider utilizing electroconvulsive therapy or ECT. Of course it would be an informed consent, so Mia would have a choice in the matter and—"

"Hold on, hold on—ECT? Electo-what?"

"Electroconvulsive therapy. You are probably more familiar with the term 'electro-shock' therapy. I know most of us have heard about it from movies and books, and unfortunately the accounts have not been the most favorable, but in reality, it is a highly effective and harmless treatment that has shown tremendous results with behavior such as Mia's," Churosh spoke rapidly, but reassuringly.

Dan felt panicky nonetheless. "But you *will* try other medications and treatments first, right?"

"Certainly, Mr. Labont. Yes, we definitely will. But there is much research to substantiate that, in many cases, ECT is quicker and more effective than standard drug therapies, and with far less adverse side effects. I fully advocate it. I hope that you will be supportive should we choose that course. If you have any questions or would like more information on it, I will gladly answer any questions you may have and provide you with materials. Please call to arrange a time when we can talk this over in person.

"In the meantime, Mia is resting comfortably. We have even let her remain in her own bed and in her own room under close supervision. As long as she can contain herself and doesn't pose a threat to staff or any of the residents, we'll let her stay there."

Dan couldn't let them think that she was entirely to blame for the incident. He had to confess, "Okay. Listen, she asked me for the mirror. I gave her it and some pens. But I didn't think that she would go that far."

"It has been dealt with Mr. Labont. But please, for her sake, DO NOT let it happen again," Churosh said sternly. "She could have caused serious injury to herself, another resident, or one of the staff. As a matter of fact, refrain from giving her *any* items from home unless our staff approves them first. You should have been told that in Admitting. Now, do you have any questions that I might answer or other concerns?"

Dan jumped to his wife's defense. "Dr. Churosh, you haven't had a chance to get to know the real Mia. She's not this way! It's totally unlike her to be aggressive and violent. In fact she is a loving, gentle and sensitive person," His voice broke for a moment, but he swallowed hard and then continued, "Try to understand that she has it in her head that she's helping someone, that's all. Just keep that in mind. She wouldn't have been this way if she hadn't lost the baby... It's my fault she has gotten so far off."

"I think I understand, Mr. Labont. But don't worry. We're doing everything possible to help your wife and we keep her best interests always in mind."

Two hours later, the sandwich was stale and untouched on the kitchen counter. Dan added another empty beer can to the seven he had stacked on the table as he browsed through the scrapbook Mia kept. Throughout the various photos of vacations, celebrations, house projects, and other occasions, his wife's face beamed at him from the busy pages.

He studied her every feature and expression he loved. He lingered on her soft brown eyes and the bright smile that had lit up every room he was in.

"Mia, honey... where are you headed with all of this?" he asked out loud.

He remembered how excited she had been when she first broke the news to him about the pregnancy. She had thrown her arms about him and led him in a zany happy waltz around their bedroom floor, laughing and hugging him.

How are we ever going to get through this? His fingers gently caressed her photograph as his heart felt heavy.

"I'm sorry, Murph... I really screwed things up for you..."

Dan reached for another beer, but the case was empty. Exhausted from the day and the most recent news on her, he decided to go to bed. But after his shower, he lay there sleepless, feeling the air drift off the fan blades spinning slowly above his head in the darkened room.

Contemplating his promise to her and Pop, he knew he was going to have to put a stop to it all. Mistakenly, he had given her the mirror and those idiotic clues to the gibberish she had written in her notebook, thinking that somehow, it would help her out in some possible way. Now it was time to face reality. It was time to divulge everything to Churosh and let them fully treat her.

Her life and sanity depended on it.

Feeling cold and empty, he reached for Mia's nightgown that lay upon the bed in the place where she had last laid it down. He held it up to his face. Her scent was faint, but lingered still within the cool soft folds. Curling up onto his side, he tucked the nightgown partway under his chin and held onto to it. He longed to have her here, safe beside him. As he lay there, he was surprised to find himself praying—he had never relied on that before—until he finally drifted off into a fitful sleep.

ELEVEN

"Oh no no no. That just won't work. Caroline wouldn't be very happy if I were to try *that*. She likes to be the one who coordinates everything. And it wouldn't do me any good at all if I were to attempt it behind her back. She would be most upset and I've told you before that when she's unhappy ..."

Gerry inhaled deeply and opened his eyes wide in effort to stay awake. Bob Bowles' whiney, nasally voice droned on and on making the counselor wish that he had remained at home under the blankets with his sleep number dialed down to twenty. He forced himself to focus on Bowles, his patient, but all he could see was a talking head. At this point, Gerry wasn't even listening anymore.

"... she makes me unhappy. It's a lot easier on me if I keep her happy. Do you understand? Don't get me wrong. Caroline is a fine woman. She cooks for me and shops for me. I don't know what I would do without her. But I don't think that I could—"

When the phone line lit up, Gerry jumped to answer it. He didn't care who or what it was about as long as it rescued him from this descending, spiraling pit of bone-numbing boredom. He held up an index finger. Bowles instantly clammed up in mid-sentence and obediently receded into his seat like a well-heeled dog. Gerry snatched up the phone and swung away in his chair from the mosquito-like man.

"Monroe here."

"Mr. Monroe? This is Muriel, Dr. Churosh's nurse at Meadow Brook. Good morning. Dr. Churosh was wondering if there was any way we could possibly move up this afternoon's four o'clock with Mrs. Labont to sometime this morning instead? Her behavior shifted erratically yesterday and he wants to see her and meet with her team as soon as possible. We'd like for Dr. Gamez and you to be present. That is, if you have any openings in your schedule. If you don't, we understand this is a very short notice."

Thank you, God. Gerry looked at his watch and calculated that Bowles would be babbling on for at least another three-quarters of an hour more. And following that, there was a two-hour review with PartnersHealth's legal staff over the Childress case. Thinking of his limited options, there was nothing more he would like to do better than skip them both.

"No, no, it's quite understandable. I mean, who can foresee emergencies, right?" He raised his voice, hoping that Bowles was eavesdropping as usual.

"Well, it's really not an *emergency* per se. We just need some input from her PCP before we proceed and—"

"No, it's no problem at all. I can make it. What time are we looking at?"

"Could you be here by eight-thirty?"

Thank you thank you thank you.

"Eight-thirty it is. Fine. We'll see you then," he answered. Then without delay, he immediately rang the MA's desk. "Marcia?"

"Yes, GERRR—*RY.*"

"Yeah, hilarious. Cancel all of my appointments for this morning... actually until after lunch. There's an emergency at Meadow Brook that I must attend to."

"Oh, are you talking about Mrs. Labont? You know, just for your information, you're really not supposed to go by yourself because you're *only* a counselor. Dr. Gamez needs to go with you. But unfortunately he's not here today. His son injured himself while they were hunting and Dr. G decided to stay for a couple of more days to be with him. So Gerry, I guess you're going to have to wait until then. I'm so sorry. I can call Muriel back if you'd like," she said condescendingly as if she were explaining to a kindergartener.

"Listen, just cancel my f–" The following obscenity stuck fast on his tongue as he remembered his stooped-shouldered client was still patiently sitting there. "—appointments."

Bowles straightened up in anticipation as he hung up the phone.

"Sorry about that. Hey listen, Bob, that was just a call from Meadow Brook *Psychiatric* Hospital. You know the big one about five miles from here?" he said carefully with emphasis.

His client nodded.

"It seems they are having a big problem with one of the patients there and were wondering if I could come over for an assist."

"Yes, I heard you mention an EMERGENCY," Bowles said, his eyebrows rising in alarm. Then he added quickly, "Not that I was listening in or anything."

"Yeah. Uh huh, well as a matter of fact, it is not a very pretty situation. And it's *critical* that I get over there right away. You know how things can go when people exhibit irrational behavior. One minute they're fine and the next, they could snap—just like that."

The loud snap of his fingers made Bowles flinch and his eyebrows raise even higher. Gerry knew if it had been Mrs. Lattimer, it would have been an entirely different story. She was not so easily impressed.

Monroe laid it on thick. "I knew you, out of all people, would understand how I like to give my all to each one of my patients. So I'm really very sorry, but I'm going to have to cancel the rest of our session so I can hustle on over there. They're counting on me. You know I would do the same for you, Bob. Any day."

"Oh, yes, Gerry, I understand. That's quite all right. Should I reschedule for next week?"

Bowles stood up immediately and readied himself to go. Gerry took note that Caroline had done a swell job in making sure her husband was an imposition to no one.

"Righty-O, Bob. Catch you later. And thanks a million, man," he said gratefully as he shook the thin man's hand.

Out of all the patients to be seated across from him at this minute, he lucked out with Bowles. The man was so hen-pecked, he'd acquiesce to just about anything.

Within the hour, Gerry was swinging his BMW into Meadow Brook, his pride swelling with the idea of being called in specifically to consult on a patient that was out of control in a psychiatric hospital. The psychiatrist had asked him in for *his* opinion and he was just the person to give it.

Gerry Monroe had arrived.

As he drove in, his excitement was immediately quelled. Scanning the grounds, he rechecked the sign to make sure he had the right place. To his surprise it looked more like a resort than an institution. There was no steady parade of patients being wheeled about by orderlies, only a handful of people walked by. And oddly, they were dressed in regular street clothes. Where were the bathrobes and crisp white uniforms? There was also no Dr. Churosh anxiously awaiting him by the curbside. And searching about, there wasn't any place to park his BMW except in the crowded visitor's lot, where it was sandwiched between an old rusted Chevy pickup and a minivan.

Gerry entered the large modern lobby where the receptionist checked him in with little more than a bored glance to his ID and pointed him through the double doors. Walking down the brightly-painted hallways decorated with residents' accomplished artwork, he kept his eyes and ears open for any monkey children scurrying about or bloodcurdling screams emanating from within padded rooms. But neither was forthcoming.

Instead he only heard music playing softly overhead from the built-in speakers. He passed by residents and staff holding normal conversations, laughing at jokes, gossiping. He took in the atriums and sunny sitting areas and large picture windows.

He felt, intuitively, that there had to be more here than was obvious. This couldn't be what a bona fide psychiatric hospital was like. Within a few more steps, his curiosity overtook him and he impetuously opened the next door he passed hoping to catch something exciting. He ducked his head into the room and ogled. To see anything that resembled a person in a straight jacket or hooked up to some kind of electrodes would have satisfied him. In contrast, only a few attendees out of a roomful of people glanced up briefly at him from their potter's benches, unphased by the intrusion. They returned to their mounds of clay while their instructor didn't miss a word.

Meadow Brook was a disappointment. The place echoed a college campus instead of a mental ward for the insane. From what he could see, there were smiling, normal, well-adjusted people here. *Complete with happy faces and potted plants for god sake,* he grumbled to himself. This so-called 'hospital' was more befitting of some ho-hum bore like Gamez.

Deflated, Gerry trudged the rest of the way to the nurses' station where they instructed him to take a seat in the easy chair by the window. There, he couldn't help but wonder if it was a mistake to come after all.

Within a few minutes, the nurse informed him that Dr. Churosh was ready to speak to him. Straightening up his tie, he went in, a shred of hopefulness still clinging to him. Maybe there was still a chance the doctor would give him the guided tour of the *real* story behind the façade of Meadow Brook and at least an offer of a lousy cup of coffee.

"Hello. Come in," Churosh called cordially from behind his desk.

Gerry entered the psychiatrist's office, taking it all in through his periphery vision while trying not to appear too obvious. The large room was tastefully decorated with abstract prints, rugs, and sculptures. A huge shelf of books occupied an entire wall. The neat stacks of files and papers situated on the desktop were organized in designer chart racks. Churosh appeared to be busy working on some kind of spreadsheet on his computer that sat upon the huge polished mahogany desk.

I bet this bozo never has to get his own sticky notes and rubber bands, Gerry mused to himself.

"I don't believe we've met. I'm Wade Churosh," the psychiatrist said as he came around the desk and extended his hand. "It's a pleasure to meet you."

"Hi—Gerry. Uh, Gerry Monroe," he answered as shook the doctor's hand.

His eye fell upon Churosh's Italian silk tie and Rolodex watch. Suddenly he regretted that he had selected his rubber ducky tie to wear that morning.

"Hey, thanks for shifting your schedule around. I apologize for such short notice," Churosh continued good-naturedly.

"Uh, sure. No problem."

"I was sorry to hear that Rueben couldn't make it today. Tough news about his son, Mark. I think this is the first time, eh?"

Feeling surprised about being included in on his supervisor's personal life, Monroe answered confidently, "Bighorn? Yeah. I believe it was."

"No, I was referring to his hunting accident. They're usually pretty careful out there. Well, I hope his recovery is quick."

"Yeah, well..." Gerry cleared his throat. Recouping his blunder and adjusting his tie, he said, "Hey, this is quite the facility you've got here. It's a lot different than what I expected."

"Oh really? Different? In what way?"

He chose his words carefully and then lied, feigning aloofness. "It's... just *smaller* than what I'm used to."

"Right. You've noticed that too? Luckily we've just been awarded another generous grant to expand. We are so excited! Now we'll be able to add the new wing as well as a second indoor therapeutic wading pool. Construction should start this spring."

"Oh," was all Gerry could think of to say.

He shifted uncomfortably in his seat. He was beginning to dislike this man.

"But I'm sure you're really curious about what has been going on with Mia. We'll meet with her in the conference room shortly. Here's a report outlining her behavior, drug schedule, and progress at Meadow Brook thus far. I was just printing out the latest update when you came in." He handed the detailed report to Gerry, and then continued, "She's somewhat of a baffling case. I really can't say she is exhibiting true symptoms of post partum psychosis, nor does she show classic symptoms of schizophrenia either. What's more, she isn't responding to the risperidone as well as expected."

The PartnersHealth therapist leafed through the impressive report, trying to decipher all the medical terminology and dosaging that was so pervasive throughout it. He couldn't make heads or tails out of most of the diagnosis and hoped Churosh couldn't see it on his face as he pretended to read with authority and know how. His forehead and armpits were starting to feel damp, adding to his discomfort.

"It's early yet, but you know, she is showing such persistent akathisia. Now according to your notes, this behavior has all been fairly recent. It would have been ideal if you had established a baseline so I could gauge how her reactions are progressing. But I wasn't able to find one in her records that were sent over.

"So I called this conference hoping that you and Reuben could expound on your experience with her instead. It's unfortunate that Reuben couldn't be here. He and I usually come to the same conclusion on many of the cases we've collaborated on. But Muriel tells me that Mia has been under *your* complete care all along," Churosh explained.

With instant regret, Gerry wished he had never opened his mouth on this Labont case. What was he thinking? If he had played it cool, Gamez would have been here doing the Dance of the Stupid, instead of him. He cleared his throat again and took a shot, hoping that by some miracle, he could pull this off and save face in the meantime.

"Uh, yes, well she was okay, I guess at first. I mean, not *okay* okay. You know, since she had lost her baby, she seemed to be showing post partum depression. Well, I mean, at least at first she did. Even Reuben agreed."

The psychiatrist looked at him, his brow creasing slightly. He jotted down a quick note and then returned his full attention to him. "Okay, go on."

"She was… doing the typical post-partum thing. You know, crying, not sleeping, and well, basically driving her poor husband crazy." Gerry forced a laugh in a half-hearted attempt at lightening this stiff up.

The other man did not join in, maintaining his analytical demeanor and intensifying Gerry's discomfort.

Monroe shifted in his seat once more.

What was this guy after? He had all the files from PartnersHealth already. Why couldn't he just accept what was written there? he thought.

He tried again, "Well, we talked a lot. Really, I should say, I talked a lot. It was like pulling teeth to get her to open up. She was very uncooperative. I gave her some things to work with to help her along."

"Some 'things'?" Churosh asked, raising an eyebrow.

"Well, yes. I provided her with positive affirmations to practice. Uh, you know, affirmations that she could say to herself… And we discussed stress management, too."

Wade nodded his head a couple of times and then sat back in his chair, still listening intently. He propped up his elbow on his armrest as his thumb cupped his chin and his index finger lay alongside of his clean-shaven cheek. Monroe could not get a read on what the man could possibly be thinking. Was he convinced? Or merely being polite?

"I mean, uh, you know how, um, *resistant* some clients can be. I don't think she ever carried through with the stress management classes though, although I urged her to. I believe that was what constituted most of her problem." Gerry fidgeted, coughed, and then smiled nervously. This was beginning to be nerve wracking.

"Yes, I think I'm beginning to understand," the psychiatrist said, regarding Gerry carefully. He paged through the file on his desk. "And your notes here also say that she started seeing 'things.' Can you elaborate?"

"Oh, yeah. I mean, she had been seeing things all along. You know, here and there—inanimate objects, imaginary people. But I can't say she was ever really clear on her descriptions, in fact, she was vague and evasive. Then, uh, as a result of our sessions and drug therapy, she recovered and things quieted down. She stopped her delusions and her life returned to normal. Not one problem for a couple of months. And then one day, out of the blue, she has a total relapse. Except now, it's even more extreme. The guy she had been seeing in the mirror has a name all of a sudden and now something was wrong with him and she's the only one who can help him. She became uncontrollable. I just attributed it all to the post partum," Monroe explained but then added quickly, "Reuben did too."

"Uh huh." The psychiatrist nodded slowly.

Gerry had the sinking feeling of déjà vu; he was in Gamez's office again. How did he always end up on this side of the stick?

Churosh jotted down a few more notes when his intercom beeped. "Would you excuse me for a moment?" he asked politely.

"Dr. Churosh? The Estrella Conference Room is open now. Would you like for us to send for Mrs. Labont?"

"Yes, if you would please, Muriel. Thank you." Then standing up, he redirected to Gerry, "If you're ready, we will go to meet with Mia now."

As they walked to the Estrella room, Dr. Churosh greeted a few patients as they passed and paused to sign a few forms that nurses offered him. Gerry noted his confident stride and poise.

Oh, he's the king shit around here, all right he thought enviously, wondering how some people could be so goddam lucky in life.

Churosh unlocked a door to a comfortable space filled with natural light and plants. It was a peaceful, welcoming room with the soft sound of running water from a desktop fountain in the corner.

It's just a regular fucking paradise here, isn't it? Gerry mused scornfully to himself as he adjusted his accursed tie again.

Dr. Churosh showed him to an overstuffed easy chair and then both settled down to wait for their client.

◊ ◊ ◊

"Mia? Mia dear, it's time to get up."

She was being beckoned from a cozy world of black. This blackness muffled sound and filled her eyes, completely insulating her. She was an animal coiled up in a deep dark burrow, waiting for the disturbance to be over with so she could yawn and stretch and settle back into torpor once more. But she faintly detected a distant noise and sensation intruding in on her safe haven.

The disturbance continued. Her body swayed lazily as someone rocked her shoulder.

"Mia, honey. C'mon sweetie pie. It's time to get those lazy bones up. Rise and shine."

Her limbs felt massively heavy and she couldn't turn her head. She became aware of another sound—rasping and repeating somewhere off in the distance. Another shake from the outside source, and she realized it was the sound of her own breath rattling down her dry throat. Concentrating, she cracked her eyes to permit the morning light.

Seth's face immediately flashed before her eyes, masked in blood and dirt, his mouth twisted in torment, his eyes rolling about in their sockets uncontrollably. But as consciousness prevailed and she propped herself up, Seth's face morphed into that of her roommate, Agnes, looming only inches from her own.

"C'mon dear. It's time you got up. You can't spend the whole day in bed. You've got places to go and people to see," the old lady said sweetly.

From her close proximity, Mia could see that Agnes had painted her thin lips with a crooked line of red lipstick and dabbed on some pink cheek rouge. It was obvious that her roommate had fixed up to go somewhere.

Mia rubbed her face and tried to clear the fog in her brain. "Huh? What are you talking about?" she slurred. She was having a hard time shaking the effects of the sedative Lynnette had jabbed into her hip the evening before.

"You have to get up. The termites are coming. In fact, it looks like they're already here," Agnes said with a little more urgency.

"Termites? Wha-?"

When Mia sat up straight, all of a sudden her head was filled with intense noise, like millions of tiny feet were on the move. Her vision faded for a second and was replaced by numerous flashing lights firing red, white, and yellow. She held her temples tightly and squeezed her eyes shut as the head rush passed.

"Ohh dear. First Cynthia, and now you. We've got to get you out of here before it's too late. They were just in here checking on you a minute ago, but your lights were still out."

The older woman was surprisingly strong as she pulled Mia to her feet. Mia swooned and started to fall back to the bed, but was caught and steadied once more. Before she had a chance to think otherwise, Agnes started dressing her, rolling a sweatshirt over her nightgown, followed by her sweater pulled around her. It was everything the younger woman could do just to keep upright.

Mia felt a tapping at her ankles. She looked down and parted her heavy eyelids enough to see Agnes holding open one of the legs of her jeans for her to step into, as if she was dressing a toddler. Too groggy to put up any kind of resistance, Mia obediently raised her feet, one at a time, and let Agnes pull up her pants, button, and zip them. At this point, Agnes could sail her out the window and she wouldn't care.

"There you go. Now that's a good girl. We have to keep moving. Now your shoes. Oh, these *are* cute," she said as she stopped for a second to admire Mia's footwear. "We don't want you to catch a cold. It's a bit nippy out and you don't have any more of your leaves left. Now, I know that you're probably getting hungry and you'll want your breakfast, but you are going to have to skip it today and wait for lunch. These termites are very nasty and quick. You'll have to slip away before they notice you are gone."

"Wait a minute, when you say, 'slip away,' what do you mean, Agnes?" Mia mumbled, grasping at coherence.

"What do you think I mean? *Leave*. Escape. Get away. Vamoose!"

"From this room? Wha…?"

"No! From Meadow Brook, you goose! It is time for you to go."

"But how am I suppose to do that?" Mia asked finally coming around to full consciousness only to become leery of this strange woman's intentions.

"I'll take you, silly, and I'll open the door and set you free. How else are you going to leave? Through a window? You are definitely not a bird, dear."

"But Lynette will be—"

"Oh screw Lynette. And Cathy, and Brenda, and all the rest of them too. I've been watching them very closely and I see how they are with you. You might think I haven't, but I have! It's definitely time for you to go. I don't want you getting all chewed up. You're too young and pretty. They like chewing on sweet things."

Trying to understand her reasoning, Mia questioned, "But what about you? Aren't you afraid of being 'chewed up'?"

"I can't be chewed up, you goose. I'M a BUTTERFLY," she said haughtily, tossing her head back and smiling grandly.

"Oh, okay..." Mia responded.

Her head continued to spin and Agnes' gravelly voice rang in her still sensitive ears. She sized up her roommate. The old lady was obviously delusional. However, Mia didn't possess the strength to put up much resistance at the moment.

"Ah ha. You don't believe me, do you? Well, it's absolutely true!" Agnes smiled knowingly.

"But how are we going to do it? We can't just get up and walk out of here. They'd catch me and I don't know, sedate or restrain me or maybe even worse...."

"Ohhhh, but you see? That's exactly what they *want* you to think. Don't you understand that you can walk out of here any time you ple-ease?" her roommate sing-songed as she strolled her fingers through the air.

"But I tried leaving a few days ago. They locked me in isolation!"

"That's only because you didn't know you *could* leave," Agnes resolutely stated.

"I can? I don't understand."

"Was there a judge that committed you? Or was it *you* who signed some papers when you first got here?"

"No, there wasn't any judge. And yes, I signed something at the doctor's office, and then at Admitting, but they told me that I had to, and I... just did," Mia said slowly as she thought about it.

That day had been so distressful. She realized she hadn't paid much attention to what was written on the forms that she was signing her name to.

"Well, you see, you committed yourself. And now you are going to *un*commit yourself. Simple as pie."

Could it be true? Or was it the drugs still flowing through her veins that made this all sound possible? Although Mia wasn't sure she comprehended the words correctly through the buzzing that still resounded through her skull, she could feel the lure of Agnes' proposal, however crazy it seemed. This might be the only chance at escape that she would ever have.

"Simple as pie, but not easy, mind you. We're going to have to be VEH-WEEE SNEAKY," Agnes said in her best cartoony voice. "But first, you have to call the Groundskeeper and let him know that there's a termite problem and that you are coming down with them yourself. Come on."

She opened their door and glanced both ways to make sure no one was around. Mia debated whether or not to follow her, but before she could make up her mind, she was grabbed by the wrist and led down the hallway.

The old lady seemed to be having a good time of it all. Mia wasn't sure how much further she should encourage her in this strange game. It made sense that she possibly *could* 'uncommit' herself, but she didn't want to risk the fact that Agnes was probably wrong. After all, the woman was crazy wasn't she? But then again, Mia thought, any casual observer on the outside would say the same about *her*. Still, she couldn't help but feel anxious at the thought of being sedated again should she be caught.

When they arrived at the sunroom, Agnes opened the door and peered in. The parakeet woman was there feeding the bird its breakfast.

Mia quietly moaned, "Oh no. Not her again. She's always in there. It'll take forever for her to quit messing with that bird."

Agnes gave her a sly wink, then stood in the doorway and barked, "Dahlia! Leave Xanadu alone and SCRAM. Do you hear me? Come now. Pronto."

To Mia's surprise, Dahlia jumped at the order and hastily threw some seed in the cage. Then she nervously gathered up the supplies and hurried to exit the room. Tears filling her eyes, she scowled at the two of them.

"You're an ugly horrible butterfly! I hate you!" she snarled at Agnes as she passed.

Agnes wriggled her fingers in a friendly wave back and said innocently, "Bye-bye dear. Have a nice day!" Then she pushed Mia into the room. "I'll keep watch. You call the Groundskeeper."

"But I don't know who—"

"Just call him. Hurry," she said as she shut the door.

Mia stood for a moment in the middle of the room. This couldn't actually be happening, could it? Was there a possibility that she could escape this place? She thought back to Agnes' extensive roaming privileges throughout the facility. Maybe she knew of a secret way out?

If they were caught, it would most likely result in Mia being medicated again. She might even loose her semi-private room privilege to permanent isolation. But if she stayed, neither she nor Seth would survive here.

Deciding to take a chance, Mia pondered Agnes' instructions as she went to the phone. She wondered who the Groundskeeper was that the old lady kept referring to. She couldn't possibly mean the actual groundskeeper of Meadow Brook, could she? Did he aid in helping patients escape to the outside? Keeping in mind her roommate's odd references to termites, leaves, and cocoons, she picked up the phone and decided to dial home instead. She desperately needed her husband at the moment. Not sure of what time it was, she prayed that he hadn't left for work already.

"Dan?"

"Babe! Hey, how are you? Everything all right?"

To Mia, his voice sounded so far away. She became instantly homesick.

"I don't have time to talk but I need you to listen carefully. Agnes, my roommate, is arranging to get me out of here somehow, right now."

"What! Mia you can't just—"

"Dan, please listen. She knows this whole facility and I think she knows a way out. I'm going to need you to pick me up."

"But how is that possible? Where's Churosh and the nurses? Do they know what—"

"Of course they don't!" she said, trying to keep her voice down. "If they did, they would confine me and who knows what else. I *have* to get out of here. I am not insane, but if I stay here, they will make me insane. Agnes is waiting for me right now. I don't know how she's going to do it, but I'm going to take a chance. Just please, come pick me up! I don't know how long it will take us to get out of the building, but I'll meet you at the turnoff for the driveway up front. I'll only be able to wait there for about ten minutes, tops. If I don't see you, I'll head—I dunno—east, I guess."

"East? Hold on. I think you should just stay there and we can talk and—"

"I've made up my mind. Seth desperately needs me now and this might be my only opportunity to get out of here. If you and I don't meet up, I'll give you a call wherever I end up. Just come for me! Please, tell me that you'll be there."

"Honey, you're going to get yourself into even more trouble. They are trying to help you figure out all of this if you would just—"

"PLEASE Dan! They sedated me again last night. I can't keep going through that. If you love me you'll do this for me!"

He hesitated for a moment. Then he said quietly, "I can't, Mia. Churosh told me what happened last night. I've already caused enough problems for you by giving you the mirror. I love you and I won't be helping you get any better by doing this. But listen to me, I want you to stay right there, okay? Don't take any chances. I'll see if I can make an appointment to come see you this morning."

Hearing a noise outside in the hall, she lowered her voice and whispered into the mouthpiece. "Hon? I've got to go. There's someone coming! Just be there! Please!" she insisted.

She could hear his voice calling to her over the line as she pulled the phone away from her ear. But she had to resist the temptation to talk to him for any longer. She was running out of time.

Agnes popped her head in. "Aren't you finished yet? Come on. The nurses are making their rounds! Hurry!"

Mia quickly hung up the phone and ran to the door on legs that still felt rubbery and weak. She felt so uncertain about what Dan had said. What if he was right? Maybe she shouldn't risk it.

No, she told herself resolutely. *I have to at least try.*

"We have to be extra careful. They are going to closely supervise you after what happened yesterday. They know the medication will be wearing off and you should be coming around about now, so they'll be checking on you shortly," Agnes whispered covertly as she led Mia once more.

They scurried down the hallway, spying frequently over their shoulders. Mia couldn't believe that they were doing this. Her heart pounded and her ears strained at every sound. At any minute, she expected Lynnette to step out from a corner in front of them.

Agnes continued, "Normally, they would keep our room door locked, but since I pretended to sleep a little longer this morning, I could hear them unlock it for me. They know how much I like to take my morning walk to greet my children. Now, Dear, did you get to talk to the Groundskeeper?" Agnes asked.

"I called Dan, my husband," Mia admitted.

"Yes, but you spoke with the Groundskeeper? You told him about the termites?"

As they past the restroom, Agnes tried the doorknob to find it unlocked.

"Oh, this is our lucky day! See? It was meant to be!" she whispered excitedly.

Then she opened the door and shoved Mia in. Hunkered down with her back against the wall, she put a finger to her lips, motioning for the younger woman to stay quiet.

Breathing rapidly from excitement and nervousness, Mia could feel the bruises on her back and ribs from Brenda's overbearing weight the night before. The injection site on her hip was also aching. While they waited, she looked at the metal mirrors on the wall. There, she could make out Seth watching them. She held up her hands to him, indicating for him to wait as well. He nodded back.

Agnes studied the watch on her wrist for about twenty seconds, then cracked open the door and peeped out again. All of a sudden, she seized Mia's arm once more with her strong bony fingers and led her back out. They hugged the wall and spied down the hallway just in time to see Cathy's back as she entered the sunroom. The nurse had just missed them.

"The Groundskeeper?" Agnes repeated as they moved along.

Mia gave it a try, "Uh yes. I spoke with the Groundskeeper."

"Good. You're in safe hands now."

They turned a corner and came upon a locked door that led to another wing. Mia had never been this far before. From the pocket on her housecoat, Agnes withdrew an employee's ID badge complete with magnetic strip. Lynette's face stared blandly from the small photo on it.

"Where did you get that from?" Mia whispered in amazement as her roommate swiped the card through the magnetic reader on the doorframe.

They heard a click as it unlocked. Agnes opened the door slightly, spied around, and then motioned for Mia to follow.

"Why, I see you recognize our dear 'friend' Lynette! A couple of weeks ago while she was wrestling with Marie to make her take her medication, it accidentally came unclipped and was kicked under the sofa in the lounge while she wasn't looking. I just borrowed it," she said innocently.

They continued on their flight, passing several rooms. Mia glanced through some of the small, reinforced windows on the doors. From a few of the limited views afforded her, she could see various occupants standing, sitting, or lying about despondently in their cubicles.

She couldn't help but think, *Is this where I would have ended up?*

She stepped aside as one angry resident wearing a straight jacket surveyed them menacingly as they passed. The patient's hot breath left a cloud of steam on the glass as she mashed her nose against it.

"Didn't Lynnette notice her ID was missing?" Mia asked, nervously watching the woman.

"Oh, I'm sure she couldn't help but notice at one point. But this would be the second time this fall that she's lost her ID, and her third time this year. She would be in really, really hot water if she reported it gone. You know, I think she will probably get the boot this time."

"But how does she get around? I saw her wearing an ID yesterday."

"It's counterfeit, sweetie. Probably got it made at a Walgreens or somewhere. But it has no magnetic strip. She and Cathy are an item, don't you know, so Cathy opens any of the doors with the magnetic readers for her. I say she had better keep tickling Cathy's fancy, if you know what I mean," Agnes giggled wickedly.

Mia was amazed at the old woman's savvy. This was no feeble butterfly.

Just then the blue light on a panel of several paging lights lit up above their heads. Looking down the hall, Mia could see all the units lit and flashing their same blue lights. She froze in place.

"Uh oh," Agnes frowned. "Looks like they found out one of their chicks has flown the coop."

"What do we do? Does that mean they are after us?"

"No. Not yet. It's only the blue light. That means one of us loony tunes is unaccounted for. They're doing a room-to-room search of our wing right now. Now when you see that light go red, then we've really got to scram. In the meantime, let's get on the hot foot and keep moving. We're almost there," she said cheerily, leading the charge.

They paused at another door leading to a stairwell. Just as Agnes swiped the card again and the lock clicked open, one of the doors down the hallway opened. They could hear a male nurse talking to an occupant in the room. Apparently, he hadn't noticed them when they had passed the room's window. They dashed into the stairwell and tried to get the heavy door to close fast behind them, pushing with their weight and fighting against its pneumatic door closer. In what felt like an eternity, the door slowly bumped shut. They sat with their backs against it, holding their breaths and praying that the nurse didn't hear anything. He would be on alert now, seeing the flashing blue light.

A moment later, they jumped as the doorknob rattled above their heads. They pulled their feet in close, knowing that he would be spying through the small window on the door as he checked the lock. After a few seconds they heard him turn and walk away, the squeak of his shoes' rubber soles receding down the hallway. Only then did they let out a collective sigh of relief. Recovering, they got back on their feet again and started down the stairs.

"How do you know about all of this?" Mia asked on the second story landing when they stopped to let older woman catch her breath. "You know— these stairwells, the entrances, the security systems, and, well, everything?"

"Well, cutie pie, I was one of the first residents to check in when Meadow Brook opened their doors over twelve years ago. My cocoon used to be where the rose garden is now. Would you believe that I lived in that cocoon for fifty-two years? .... *Fifty-two years...*" Agnes said, trancelike, melancholy veiling her face. "Yes... Charlie... and my girls...so many memories... so many memories," she murmured, lost in reverie.

She sighed sadly and shuddered, her eyes becoming moist. Her spunky demeanor vanished, leaving behind a weary, pathetic old woman. Mia looked sympathetically at her roommate and reached out to squeeze her hand in comfort.

The controversy surrounding the construction of Meadow Brook had happened before she and Dan were even married and had moved to the Northwest, but Mia knew about it from an article that had run in the local magazine she had worked for. The article was about preservation of historic neighborhoods, but had featured the case of Meadow Brook versus the Willow Neighborhood as an example. The neighborhood had fought, trying to stop the developers, only to lose their houses in the end. The general public lacked any interest in getting involved in the dispute between the owners of the antiquated houses and the shareholders of a new, state of the art mental facility.

Looking at her roommate wiping at her tears with a shaky hand, Mia thought Agnes was abandoning their plan to escape. Her heart sunk.

I guess I shouldn't have expected to get this far. How are we going to get back? she wondered in despair.

However, in the next instant the older woman perked up and smiled broadly, saying brightly through her tears, "But look at me! I'm a *butterfly* now, and I live here. Oh yes. Indeedy, I do." The blue light in the stairwell continued to flash. "Well, come on, sweetie. You're not free yet! And we've only got a little ways left to go. You're almost there," Agnes said, giving Mia's hand a pat back, her eagerness returning.

"Are you sure you're okay?" Mia questioned.

"Sure as I ever will be my dear. Now smile, honey, you're going home today," Agnes cackled.

One more flight of stairs and they finally reached ground level. The older woman gestured for Mia to stand against the wall, while she took a peek through the door's window. Then she opened the door a crack and surveyed the area.

When all was clear, they stepped out into a small corridor that led to the vast kitchen. Several workers toiled in the noisy room, preparing and serving the morning meal that would feed hundreds for the next hour and a half, but not one of them noticed the two residents huddled against the wall.

The blinking blue light switched to red.

Mia tapped on Agnes' shoulder and pointed to it. Within seconds an alarm sounded. It shrieked in the kitchen as well, but none of the workers seemed to pay any attention to it over the din.

"Time to go now!" her roommate whispered urgently.

The women jogged the last few feet to the exit, pushed against the heavy door, and finally found themselves outside of the building. The massive door swung shut behind them and latched shut with a loud click. It was suddenly quiet all around them.

"Halleluiah! Wasn't that something? We just about got our buds nipped in there!" Agnes laughed, thoroughly enjoying their adventure.

Mia soaked in the vivid sights and sounds of outside and breathed deeply, feeling the air fill her lungs. It felt different than on any other day of her life. She wanted to jump up and yell with joy at just getting out of the building, but she knew they had to keep moving. She started to quicken their pace, but the old lady slowed her down after a few yards, trying to make her walk more casually.

"You don't want to look too conspicuous," she reminded her young roommate.

Mia heeded her advice and tried her best at a leisurely stroll, although her heart was still racing. When a couple of cars turned up the driveway and approached them, Mia gasped and froze in place. She quickly searched for a place to hide.

"Just look ahead, like you are taking your morning constitutional, and pay them no never mind," Agnes coached. "They conduct a thorough search of the building before they start looking out here. Since they like to believe that Meadow Brook is 'inescapable' they'll concentrate in there first. Besides, those cars came from outside. They have no idea of what is going on in *there.*"

The cars continued on their way, without the drivers even so much as looking at them, much to Mia's relief. As they strolled, Agnes took the time to introduce Mia to each tree they passed as if she had somehow forgotten they had just broken out from a mental hospital.

They were only twenty minutes into their escape, but to Mia it seemed like hours had passed before they finally reached the end of the driveway. Taking one last look over their shoulders to make sure no one was on to them, they took the corner and found themselves outside of the looming hedge and fence that marked the property of Meadow Brook. There they stood on the busy street out in the world once more.

"And here you are, honey-pot. See? Didn't I tell you it would be simple as pie? Now run along and be free," Agnes said with satisfaction, suddenly shooing her away as if she were a wayward puppy.

"I don't believe it! We did it! I don't know how I can ever thank you, Agnes, but THANK YOU, so much!" Mia said, giving her a warm hug. "I can't believe we did it!"

The old woman chuckled and hugged her back. "Oh, it was nothing dear. It was completely my pleasure. Now be sure to say hi to the Groundskeeper for me. Oh, and also that nice boy that you talk to, Seth? You know, just between you and me and the fencepost, he's a real cutie-pie, so tall and broad shouldered! If only I was fifty years younger… I sure hope he will be okay. He was looking a bit sickly, poor dear."

It was the second time she astounded Mia.

"Seth? You mean - you can see him?" she asked incredulously.

"Why, of course! Plain as day! Why wouldn't I? It was hilarious that Lynnette and all those other ninnies didn't have a clue. While you were 'sleeping,' I decided to have a visit with him with my own mirror. He was just standing there looking so forlorn. So I decided to cheer him up. We've had a couple of tête-á-têtes since then. Poor sweetie was somewhat shy. Sometimes he held up messages he had written, but I couldn't make heads or tails of them. Tell me, is he foreign dear?"

Now it was Mia's turn to chuckle. "No, no he isn't. I wish I had time to tell you about him, but I am going to have to go. He needs me."

"Yes, dear. I understand. You better go now. The poor boy looks like he's in real trouble. And in a few minutes, the Looney Tunes brigade will be out here looking around for you. Well good luck, honey, I'm going to head back in. It's time for breakfast and it smelled like they were cooking omelets. Mmmm, they're my favorites."

"You mean you're going back? In there?" Mia was shocked. She thought this escape was for Agnes' benefit as well as her own.

"Why yes, sweetie. I live here. But I know that you don't and can't. That's why you must go." She hugged Mia one more time and grasping her hands said, "Now wasn't this fun! I wish I could break someone out every day. You know? I just might do that."

Then she turned and meandered up the driveway without any further farewells, patting and talking to each tree as she passed. Mia called goodbye to her, but Agnes did not look back.

Mia stood alone on the corner. She had no cell phone or even money to make a call.

How am I going to make it back home from here? she wondered as she pondered what her next move should be.

Looking at her surroundings, the nearest stores that could possibly have a pay phone were about a mile down the street.

Besides, if I went back home, would they be waiting there to take me back?

Her heart sunk a bit when she thought about Dan. She knew he didn't believe that Agnes could ever get her out. And besides, he felt that the best place for her was at Meadow Brook to be 'helped' anyway.

She heard a car horn behind her. Surprised, she asked herself, *Could it be him?*

Turning expectantly, she was greeted instead by a teenage boy hanging out of the window of a pickup truck being driven by another teen, both yelling and jeering at her as they passed.

"Ooo baby! You're making me so hot!" he said as he rubbed his chest and puckered his lips, then laughed coarsely.

She suddenly became aware of how she must look as she touched her disheveled hair and gazed down at her nightgown flaring out from under her sweatshirt. It was too long to tuck up under her top or into her jeans, so she pulled her sweater more tightly about her, trying to cover up. She felt cold as she turned away from the street in embarrassment.

The wind had picked up and the clouds promised rain at any second. She kept spying over her shoulder, back to Meadow Brook. So far, it remained quiet by the front, so she hoped they weren't combing the grounds yet. She recalled how she told Dan that she would wait for ten minutes by the front for him to show. Now she realized that she wasn't thinking clearly when she had called him. There was a chance he decided to believe her and had come and gone already. She wouldn't ever know. He could still be on his way... What if he wasn't?

She agonized over her dilemma until she grew too anxious to wait any longer. As the morning light increased and the traffic pulling into Meadow Brook grew, she knew that someone from the hospital would eventually spot her outside of the fence.

She did not know where to go and had no money or ID. She wasn't even sure exactly where she was on the map. She decided to try to make it to the stores down the street. As she started on her way, she felt as if she had just emerged from a cocoon herself.

◊ ◊ ◊

In the Estrella room, Gerry stole a peek at his watch once more. It read 8:47a.m. He was hoping to get on with the session with Labont and not give Wade the chance to fire any more questions at him that he couldn't answer. His well-groomed colleague, on the other hand, looked completely comfortable and composed as he set up the video camera, placed out a few items, and jotted down some notes on a pad.

"Hmm, I wonder what is taking Mia so long? She should be with us shortly. It's possible she is having some ill effects from the sedation last evening in addition to the risperidone," Churosh remarked casually.

Monroe noticed the blinking blue light that had lit up in the corner of the room a few minutes before, but he declined to ask about it. Churosh didn't seem to pay it any attention and Gerry did not want to show his ignorance. He had had enough of that already. Instead, he tried to formulate in his head what he would say to Labont before she arrived. He knew he had to come up with some half-way intelligent sounding questions and remarks for her in order to redeem himself in front of this clown. After all, she was his patient.

There was a knock at the door and then Muriel entered and approached her boss. "May I speak with you for a moment, Dr. Churosh? Outside?" she asked him covertly.

Wade looked a little perplexed. "Would you excuse me, Gerry?" he said and then left the room.

At first, their voices were too muffled for Gerry to make out what they were saying. But within a minute, the psychiatrist's voice rose, and Muriel's sounded apologetic. Gerry could recognize irritation altering Wade's tempered voice as he distinctly heard, "And *how* long has she been missing?

Didn't anyone do an early round this morning? ... What about the search of the wing? ... Well they had better find her immediately or someone's ass is going to be in a fucking sling. This incompetence will not be tolerated!"

A moment later, Churosh returned. Despite looking a little agitated, he managed to regain his cool composure. "I'm sorry about the interruption. Mia should be joining us shortly," he repeated.

They waited a bit longer, neither man saying anything. The sound of the desktop fountain cascading and bubbling happily suddenly sounded out of place against the tension building in the room. As they sat, all of a sudden Gerry connected the blinking blue light to Mia's tardiness.

Could there possibly be a flaw in this perfect system? he wondered with glee.

He settled back in his chair and waited anxiously to find out. The morning was indeed looking up as he thought about the good fortune of having a front row seat to the toppling of this stiff before him. He would have paid to see this.

Finally the phone rang, breaking the standoff. Answering it, the psychiatrist said, "Churosh... Uh huh. I see. Are you certain? Okay. Has the Rapid Response Unit been called? Very well, then. Keep me posted. Thank you." He hung up the phone with great restraint and then faced his guest, folding his hands before him. "It seems that Mrs. Labont will not be joining us today."

The blue light switched to red.

◊ ◊ ◊

Dan had tried telephoning Meadow Brook immediately after he had hung up with Mia, but the recorded message said that the facility did not open until nine o'clock. Looking at the kitchen clock, there was still another twenty-five minutes to go. He left a message on Churosh's voicemail instead and hoped that the psychiatrist answered his calls early. In the meantime, he paced restlessly, her phone call just a few minutes ago resounding through his mind.

He hated what he just did to his wife. It was one of the toughest things he ever had to do. How could he ever tell her no? She had begged for him to come to her aid, but he had to turn his back on her. Mia asked for so little and yet, he would not comply.

There was no other way possible. He was forced to do it in order to help her. He needed to entrust her to Churosh's care and let go. Nevertheless, he found it increasingly difficult. Something was still holding him back.

Maybe it was because Churosh's care included her being continually sedated or locked up like some kind of animal, he reasoned with himself.

He squeezed his eyes shut trying to block out that image as he inwardly despised himself. He relied on the fact that her roommate couldn't possibly get her out. It couldn't happen in a place like that— so secure, well staffed, and supervised.

But what if she did get out? Where would she go? What would they do if they caught her?

His brain cranked through the endless scenarios. If only someone would answer the damn phone over there. It would put a lot of his worry to rest.

His stomach growled loudly, reminding him that he hadn't eaten anything since grabbing a bite at a hot dog cart the day before. He reached into the refrigerator and took out the carton of milk. Taking it to his lips, he chugged hungrily, only to spit out the milk the immediately into the sink. Rinsing his mouth and watching the sour curds go down the drain, he couldn't help but feel it was a befitting punishment.

My just desserts for what I did to her, he thought wryly as he took the milk carton outside to throw into the recycling can. *It should have been shit instead.*

As he dumped the container in the can and closed the lid, he could hear Mrs. Lopez's high voice calling to him over the fence.

"Dan? Dan? Is that you?"

Her eyes and nose peered over the edge at him, her short stature aided by the crate she stood on for such occasions.

"Good morning, Mrs. Lopez," he answered a bit tersely.

He hoped this wasn't going to take long. Waking up late from a restless night's sleep, detained by Mia's phone call and trying to get through to Meadow Brook, he was going to be late to work already. He usually would have taken the time to chat with Mrs. Lopez, she was a pleasant enough woman, but today he wasn't in any mood for it.

"Oh Daniel! I'm so glad I caught you. How is Mia?"

"Uh, she's doing okay, Mrs. Lopez, thank you."

"Pobrecita! I've been saying novenas day and night for the both of you. Living in that house… I don't know. You two should think about moving out or at least getting it blessed."

"It's been blessed already, ma'am, when we moved in. Mia's mom called a priest in to do it. But listen, Mrs. Lopez, I'm late for work already and I—"

"Ohhh," she said apprehensively. "Then what is going on? I tell you, there's something evil in your house. I saw it!"

He sighed with impatience and shook his head. He had no time for this nonsense. Was everybody going crazy?

"What do you mean?" he asked, trying to mask his annoyance.

"Last week, after I had called you about Mia and while we were waiting for you to come home. I saw it with my own eyes! It was pure evil! There are no other words for it."

Her voice was rising higher than the fence. Dan guessed that the whole neighborhood could probably hear this conversation by now.

"Okay, calm down. You keep saying 'it.' What is that, exactly?"

"El cuaderno—the notebook! Writing appeared on it. All by itself! First Mia would say something, and then the letters would start appearing! Like someone was writing, but there was no one there! Ai Díos mio!" she whimpered and then blessed herself with the sign of the cross.

He couldn't help but feel skeptical of her report. "Wait a minute. You saw this?"

"Yes! That is what I am trying to tell you. I tried to warn you before you went in that day. Mia was in front of the mirror. Talking to it. Crying. Aí, that writing. It gave me chills to watch it. Look at my hand. It's trembling just from thinking about it." Over the fence she reached out a pudgy hand that was obviously shaking. "I think it was the writing of 'you-know-who.' Aí Díos mio!" she exclaimed and then blessed herself again.

He couldn't believe what he was hearing. "Who?"

Suddenly, she turned completely calm and said with authority, "*El Diablo*, of course. Who else would do that?" Then she lifted her chin and nodded slowly in confirmation of what she had just revealed to him.

Dan had to wonder if his neighbor had been sucked into all the hype. He grew uneasy with all of this talk of the supernatural. First it was Aunt Lydia, now her. Why, out of all the times he needed rational solutions, this kept coming up? There was nothing substantial here to help him right now. Still, he decided to hear her out. At least it would put one of their minds at ease.

Trying to comprehend all of what she was trying to tell him he asked, "Okay, so Mia was in front of the mirror. Could you see her hands? Was she holding the notebook?"

"Yes, she was in front of the mirror, but no, she wasn't holding the notebook. She was standing— Wait! Hold on! I'll come over and show you."

Mrs. Lopez's face disappeared behind the fence in an instant. Within what seemed like seconds, he heard the doorbell ring before he could even reach the door. He never knew his plump neighbor could move so fast.

When he opened the door, she hesitated before entering, peering cautiously around the room. Then she made another sign of the cross and whispered a quick prayer. Crossing herself once more, she slowly placed one foot inside and then the other. Watching her go through this ritual, he started to feel impatient.

"Okay, so could you show me where she was?"

Mrs. Lopez turned, and then sucked her breath in sharply when she saw the mirror. She was obviously frightened, but she steadfastly held her ground. Checking out the placement and position of everything, she reached up and grabbed Dan by his shoulders.

Pushing him to the exact spot, she said, "She was *here*." Next she looked around the room until she spied what she wanted. "And el cuaderno was *there*," she said pointing to the shelf a couple of feet away from him. Then she positioned herself by the kitchen doorway. "And I was over *here* watching the whole thing. She would say something and cry. Then the writing would start. She would say something else, and then more writing. All by itself! The printing would appear on the page, out of nowhere! There was no one there to write it, I tell you!"

Dan surveyed the distances. There was no physical way that Mia could have written the messages herself. He took a second to analyze the lighting, the angle. Mrs. Lopez was completely in clear view of the whole scene. Although she was excited at the moment, Dan had known his neighbor to be a sensible, caring woman who always had her wits about her, and a person they had trusted since they had moved in.

Taking into account the odd heavy handwriting, Mia's irrational, inexplicable behavior, and the mysterious clues written in the notebook, it all added up definitively in some bizarre way, despite what reality and his own reasoning told him.

Trying to quell the alarm that was quickly mounting inside of him, he asked once more, "And you are absolutely *sure* that you saw all of this happen?"

She nodded emphatically. "I swear on my LIFE! I saw three pages of writing with my own eyes! Three!" She held up three fingers for clarity. "And she *never* touched one!"

Dispatching all logic and relying on what his instincts were screaming instead, he jumped into action. Grabbing his keys, he dashed out the door leaving the confused woman behind while yelling over his shoulder, "Thank you Mrs. Lopez! I've got to go. Thanks again!"

The Jeep accelerated and jockeyed through traffic as he raced to Meadow Brook.

She said she would only be there for ten minutes, he turned over and over in his mind as the miles zipped by. *This is absolutely nuts.*

He had to agree that everything ultimately had led up to this. And now there was a reliable eyewitness to it all. While he didn't think it could be "El Diablo," there could be some possibility in this Seth guy. Although it sounded insane, it was the only explanation that made all the pieces fit, and at this point he didn't want to take the time to analyze it. Not while she was waiting for him with her very life.

He should have listened to Mia. Why did it take the testimony from someone else to make him believe? He remembered his voicemail to Dr. Churosh and cursed himself for leaving it. If he hadn't called, it could have given her more time to escape… Or maybe they caught her? He imagined her held down by some kind of restraint, looking frightened and confused as a needle plunged into her vein. Or worse yet, what if Churosh felt it was time for electro-shock therapy? Cursing himself once more, he made a resolute promise: *One way or the other, she is coming home today.*

As he approached the turn-in to Meadow Brook, he slowed down and started scanning the sidewalk, hoping to spy her somewhere.

If she even made it this far.

He drove down the street past the entrance for a few hundred yards and then made a sharp U-turn and came back. Again, he searched as well as he could while trying to keep his eyes on the road, but she was nowhere in sight. He turned the Jeep into the institution's parking lot and slowly cruised through while studying every pedestrian he passed.

They probably caught her. She didn't have a chance.

He wrestled with the decision whether to take the time to park and go inside to check, or continue searching out here, before she got too far away.

He stopped for a moment in front of the complex and looked at it. If she *was* in there, how was he going to get her out? He determined that he would march in and demand her release. But at the very last minute, he relied once more on instincts alone as he swung away and drove out of the parking lot. He was going to give it one last try.

Remembering her message, he headed east, slowly cruising up the road while irate, impatient motorists pulled out from around him and tore past. He searched both sides of the street, but didn't see her. Seeing more people up ahead he sped up to search. When he considered all that she would have had to do to get this far, he knew it was highly improbable that she even made it out of the building. Yet his foot stayed on the pedal, ignoring his rationale.

In the next moment, right before he was about to turn around again, he saw her, as if she appeared out of nowhere. She was walking quickly, tugging her sweater about her thin shoulders, her long hair pulled back into a messy ponytail. The lower hem of her nightgown stuck out from underneath her sweater and her ankles were bare. She looked as if she could be any one of the transients or homeless on the street. His remorse grew tenfold for what he had subjected her to. Honking the horn, he pulled up alongside of her.

She jumped and looked about nervously, preparing to flee at any minute, but didn't manage to see him. She instead, walked on even faster. He honked again, but this time she wouldn't even turn around. She was apparently intent on getting where she needed to be.

Dan double-parked the Jeep along the crowded street and scrambled out after her. He caught up to her in a few easy strides and grabbed her by her shoulders. Mia shrieked and stiffened. Then she turned around, swinging.

"Mia! Hon—" he said, releasing her and backing up from being hit.

Her haggard face lit up when she recognized her husband. "Oh my God, Dan. You're here! Oh thank you!" she said as she embraced him. "I thought you weren't coming, so I started walking."

"I know, Babe. I know. I'm sorry I was late," he said as he kissed her and held her tight. Then he checked her over from top to bottom. "Are you okay? You're not hurt or sick or anything? Your hands are freezing!"

"No, I'm okay. Really. Where's the Jeep? I need to get off the street before they see me."

"Sure thing, Murph."

She raced to the SUV and climbed inside. Reaching over and embracing him once more, she said, "Thank you, thank you, thank you honey, for believing."

"No, don't thank me. I'm just so sorry for what I have put you through."

"But you're not taking me back there, are you? To Meadow Brook?" she asked in a small voice, looking apprehensive.

"What? No! Oh God, no," he said holding onto her and then kissing her forehead. "You should have never been there in the first place. I was dead wrong in ever thinking that you should have been. Please, I hope you'll forgive me, Mia."

"I do, Honey. But could we please just go home?"

At her request, he swung the Jeep around and accelerated quickly. They passed Meadow Brook on the way back, but this time rapidly put miles behind them. As he drove, he kept taking glances at her to make sure she was all right. Her eyes had deep shadows under them and her face was creased with worry. All in all, she appeared to be in relatively good shape, taking into account what she had just been through.

"How on earth did you ever get out of that place?" he asked.

"I told you, my roommate, Agnes. She knows the entire facility. We literally walked out the back door!"

"You're kidding me! That fortress?" he laughed with amazement.

She pulled down the visor on her side and opened the vanity mirror to view the backseat.

"Hey, Seth. How are you doing, Hon? I'm sorry about last night. They got me again. Don't worry. We're going home. Did you see us? Agnes got us out! Isn't she amazing? ...Seth? ...Hang in there, Tiger." Her voice alternated between soothing and concern. "C'mon... Hold on. Don't slip on me. We're going home."

Dan glanced up at his rearview and scanned the empty backseat. But this time, before his mind could start nagging with doubt, he returned his eyes to the road and kept quiet. He was going to see this thing through, no matter what. It was good just to have her by his side again.

"Oh Dan, he's in such bad shape. I don't know how much longer he can hang on. It's so hard for him," she fretted.

"It won't be too much longer. Just a few more miles. Hey, when was the last time you had something to eat?"

She continued staring at the mirror, apparently having not heard what he asked.

He put his hand on hers and asked again, "Mia? When was the last time you ate? Are you hungry?"

She broke her gaze away from the mirror for a moment to face him. "Huh? I'm sorry. No, I'm not hungry right now. As soon as I get home, I'm going to have to try to contact Shayla."

"Shayla? Who's that? Another resident at Meadow Brook?"

"She's Seth's girlfriend. She doesn't know what has happened to him. I guess no one did. Not even his mother. They all thought he ran away after he got into a fight with his stepfather. You see, he accidentally killed him."

"No shit! Really?" He looked at her with astonishment.

"Yes," she answered sadly. "But it was completely in self-defense. The bastard was going after him and Shayla and their unborn baby."

"And he told you all of this?"

"He did. Really! I'm not making this up."

"No, I know. At least I know now. So wait a minute, then what happened to Seth?'

"Remember what you speculated about the mine shaft? It was true. As he was running from the fight, he fell down one, and was trapped. There was no way for him to get out and no one ever found him," she said quietly, looking down at her lap.

"Sweet Jesus," Dan muttered under his breath and shook his head. He continued, "Listen, I know it took a little bit for me to deal with all of this. I apologize about being such an ass about this whole thing. Maybe if I had listened to you in the first place, you would have never ended up back *there*. It's just so hard for me to believe in this stuff. I never have. My parents never did, so I guess I wasn't raised to think from that kind of perspective.

"But I'm really sorry that you had to go through all of this for me to finally come around. If anything would have happened to you back there I—"

She squeezed his hand. "But it didn't. And that part is over. Don't ever blame yourself. You did what you thought was right for what you knew. I can't say that I even believed in all of this myself before it happened. My Aunt Lydia would talk about it when I was little, but I never understood what was going on. As I got older, I always thought it was all some kind of put on."

When they pulled onto their street Mia prompted, "Okay Seth. We're just about there. Have you been thinking about Shayla's number? Anything. We need something to go on." She looked up into the mirror, and then sat forward in alarm. "Seth? Are you okay? Seth! Oh God, Dan, I think we're losing him."

◊ ◊ ◊

As Gerry eased his BMW through the crowded lanes of mid-afternoon traffic, he could not help but feel cheated. The morning had turned out to be a complete and total waste of time. He should have never gone. In retrospect, he would have had more satisfaction running rings around PartnersHealth's legal staff as they tried to get him to take the heat for the Childress case. Moreover, he could have finished out his session with Bowles. Now he was going to have to reschedule with that moron.

No. Instead, he had chosen to go to the Alpha and Omega of mental institutions, be grilled by a Dr. Freud wanna-be, and watch while a depressed housewife escaped under their very noses. The least they could have done for making him come all the way over there for nothing was to include him in on the search for her. He was really hoping to see her in a straightjacket or bouncing off the walls of a padded cell. She or any of the patients there, for that matter. That would have been worth coming for. But that Labont woman proved too slippery for those idiots.

As he ground through the morning's events in his head, he could at least glean some satisfaction from having watched the demigod Churosh break a sweat. That over-inflated king shit deserved to be taken down after the grueling inquisition he had subjected him to: "*It says she was seeing things. Can you elaborate on that?*" and how about "*And what makes you say that?*" Yeah, it was clearly the high point of the morning to watch ol' Wadey-boy squirm after pulling the superiority attitude on Gerry Monroe.

Thinking about how the Meadow Brook psychiatrist and Gamez both treated him, Gerry longed to have the tables turned. Just once he would like to be the heavy hitter making some poor minor leaguer drool. What made them so worthy to be granted that role in life, while Gerry had to slog through it all and take it up the ass? Didn't he work as hard as them?

Well, to hell with them all, he thought bitterly. *And to hell with Labont too,* he added when he considered how much trouble her case had caused him.

She had better not come sniffling back to PartnersHealth. He'd gladly toss her ass back into Meadow Brook just to keep her out of his hair. He didn't need another Ashley Childress mucking up things for him.

The traffic was snarled and had slowed down to a crawl due to a car accident. As a result, he reached PartnersHealth over an hour later. As he entered through the back office area, he could hear the MAs cackling away as usual, but once they spotted him, they all shushed each other and spoke only in low tones and giggles. Marcia approached him, holding out a stack of slips.

"Here are all your messages. You've also got Mrs. Lattimer sitting out in the waiting area for you for over forty-five minutes," she said matter-of-factly.

"You were supposed to cancel my appointments," he said indignantly.

"No. You told me to cancel your appointments up through lunch. It's *past* lunch already, Gerry," she shot back.

"Oh great. What did you tell her?"

"I told her that you weren't in yet," she answered with a smug look.

"Oh geez. Is that it? Well thanks a whole hell of a lot, you fat bitch. You mean you couldn't think of anything more creative than that?"

Marcia glowered at him down the end of her nose, and then turned to walk back to her desk. She bit her tongue and waited long enough for him get to his office, timing it so that as soon as he sat down, her voice trilled over the intercom.

"Oh Gerrr-rrry."

He jabbed at the button. "Eat shit!"

"No Gerr-rrry. I didn't get to tell you, but Dr. G's son Mark is doing remarkably better."

Completely irritated now, he replied, "Well, why the fuck should I care?"

She giggled and then said, "Because he is doing *so* much better, Dr. G switched tickets and caught an early flight this morning."

It took a moment for him to fully digest the medical assistant's information. "Gamez is back?" Gerry asked with a twitch in his stomach.

"Why yesss. He got in, oh, about an hour ago. *And* he wants to see you in his office *immediately*. I've already sent over the Labont file for you and now I'll let him know that you are back from Meadow Brook. You don't need to thank me."

Gerry sat back in his chair for a moment, the color draining from his face. The circumstances leading up to this moment flooded his brain, but they were all precluded by a singular thought: *Maybe now's a good time to start investigating a career in sports therapy.*

◊ ◊ ◊

The large mirror in their living room stood empty save for the reflection of their own faces staring back. Mia moaned low under her breath with anticipation.

"I don't see him, Dan. Where could he be?"

Reflexively, Dan started searching about the reflection in the mirror, but then caught himself. He cleared his throat and stepped back, feeling a bit foolish.

"I thought that when we came in, he would be here, waiting for me as usual. Maybe I should go back out to the Jeep," she said.

"You think he's still out *there*?"

She took another glance about the living room. "I don't know. He could be. He was pretty weak. Maybe he couldn't—wait a minute—there he is! In the corner!" she exclaimed as she studied the mirror once again.

Dan whipped around to face the empty corner in the room. He shook his head as he turned back muttering to himself, "I'm never going to get use to this."

"Oh Dan, he looks terrible! Seth, honey? Here I am. We're home," she said. "C'mon, Tiger. Fight! We can do this. All we have left to do is call Shayla. That's got to be it."

Seth viewed her through half-closed eyes. He slowly shook his head no, looking completely spent. His breathing was labored as he sat with his back against the wall and his legs sprawled out before him. Much to Mia's dismay, the black shadow that had showed up at the hospital apparently had followed too. It draped about him now, trailing wispy tentacles across his face and body.

"Yes. Come on! Get up. Maybe it will help if you keep moving around. You have to try," she pleaded to the mirror.

The teenager again shook his head. Even the motion of that simple act was arduous for him. All of a sudden, he doubled over as if he had been pierced by something sharp. His head flung back as he cried out. Blood and mucus dripped from his mouth, hanging off his bottom lip. The shadow grew excited with his anguish, encircling him in a threatening cloud.

"Seth. Get away from that thing, please. Just try. Please… For me?" she begged.

Hearing her, he opened his eyes wide for a moment, determination coming over him. He slid one leg up under and used it to leverage himself up, as he braced himself against the wall. His hands slid upwards as he rose, leaving crimson smears from his torn fingers. Slowly he approached the mirror, leaving behind the shadow in a whirling frenzy in the corner.

As Seth staggered towards her, Mia kept her eye on the dark figure, feeling distrustful of it, when suddenly she saw two yellow eyes appear from within its billowy folds. They were pointed and cruel, filled with hate and rage. When they fixed their gaze upon her, a primal fear sprung up and overwhelmed her, making her want to flee the room immediately. She held her ground, forcing herself to switch her focus back to Seth instead.

"That's it, Honey. Come on. Please, just a little more…"

He arrived at the glass, panting heavily from the exertion. The ugly wounds on his face were large and seeping, and his complexion was now totally gray. He looked shrunken as if he were severely malnourished.

Although Mia felt panicky, she steadied her voice to encourage him. "You did it Seth! I know that was hard for you, but I am going to ask you to do one more thing. Have you thought anymore about Shayla's number? We don't have a lot of time."

Seth's eyes rolled back, his eyelids fluttering. Then he grabbed his head as if his very thoughts wrought pain. His eyes reopened slowly and he looked dazed. Within a few moments, he nodded in recall.

"Good. Just hold up fingers. I'll write the numbers down—"

He held up his left hand. Most of the flesh had fallen off, leaving the glistening bones exposed.

The sight stole her breath.

"Oh God, I'm sorry..." she apologized. When he made his motion for the pen, she ordered, "Okay—Dan, quick! He needs something to write with! I'll get the paper."

Having witnessed the dialogue between his wife and the mirror, Dan jumped at her request, snatching up a pen from the kitchen and running it back to the living room. Mia took up an old notebook and fumbled through it, looking for a clean page. Then pen and paper were placed in their old positions upon the shelf closest to the mirror.

"Okay, Seth? Go ahead, Hon..."

He began to write.

Dan's mouth dropped open in awe. "Holy shit!!" he exclaimed as he watched the dark lines appear magically on the paper. "Do you see that!? Oh my God... I don't believe it. I just don't believe it!"

Filled with amazement, he grabbed his hair and then slid his hands down to rub his face hard. Blinking and refocusing, he trained his eyes again on the pen lines continuing to form upon the paper.

"Ho-ly *shit*...it is true!" he said once more in disbelief, shaking his head.

Mia watched Seth carefully as he printed Shayla's number.

This HAS to be it. This is the last thing we overlooked, she reassured herself.

His girlfriend, the mother of his child, had to be contacted. She needed to know about his death. Then he could finally find peace. Mia wouldn't allow herself to think otherwise. She knew they were out of solutions and time.

When he finally printed the last number, she dashed past her astounded husband to the phone and dialed. All in the room waited anxiously while the line rang. But as she looked back to comfort him, the teen had collapsed to the floor.

"Seth? ... What's the matter? Seth!" she cried as she dropped the phone and ran back to the mirror.

He laid upon the floor, gripping his sides, and screamed pitifully, his agony unceasing. In that instant, the shadow flew out from the corner where it had been waiting and engulfed him. As Seth floundered about feebly, the dark figure transformed itself into the shape of a man. With its newly formed limbs, it tugged, pulled, and clawed at the teen. Too weak to fight it off, Seth curled up onto his side, his arms shielding his head and face from the shadow's frenzy.

"Stop it! Stop it!" Mia shrieked at the sinister apparition. "Leave him alone! Dear God in heaven help him!"

The shadow lifted its head and looked directly at her, its yellow eyes first blazing, and then narrowing down to two sharp sickles of red against the inky black of its face.

"What's going on!" Dan asked looking back and forth between the mirror, his wife, and the notebook.

"Get away from him you bastard! You are not going to take him!" she growled at the apparition.

There wasn't any way she was going to let Seth go. Recalling all the years upon her knees as her mother watched over her, she shut her eyes and resorted to prayer, the words flowing fast and clear, "Holy Michael Archangel, defend us in this day of battle; be our safeguard against the wickedness and snares of the devil. May God rebuke him, we humbly pray, and do, thou prince of the heavenly host, by the power of God, thrust into hell Satan and all wicked spirits, who wander through the world for the destruction of our souls!"

The shadow's shape reared back and withdrew. It seemed to be thwarted momentarily by the forceful words directed at it. Mia's confidence surged. Maybe she could beat this thing. But once she finished the prayer, within an instant, the shadow sprung up and to her amazement grew half again in size. The towering specter then alternated its form—sometimes a man, a snake, a beast. It sprouted tentacles once more and wrapped them tightly around the boy. Seth cried out as his chest was squeezed unmercifully. Then the shadow opened its face to reveal rows of needle sharp teeth in a cavernous, bright red mouth.

Mia screamed, and then frantically repeated the prayer. The words detained the shadow only for the duration that the prayer flowed from her lips. Immediately following, it enlarged even more, and tortured the youth again.

While staring dumbfounded at this one-sided drama between his wife and the mirror, Dan suddenly became aware of a tiny voice calling out over the phone. He held it up to his ear.

"Hello? Hello? Is anyone there? Hello?" a girl's voice said over the line.

Dan asked incredulously, "Is this Shayla?"

"Yes. Who is this? What's going on?"

"My wife Mia is—listen, I don't have time to explain. Do you , uh, did you know someone named Seth?" he asked hurriedly.

There was silence on the other end.

Hearing Dan, Mia cried out, "Cross, his last name was Cross!"

"Seth Cross. Did you know someone by that name?"

The girl answered, but it was obvious she had started to cry. "Yes. I did. He was my boyfriend. His mother… told me what might have happened to him. Nobody here is sure. The police are checking it out. Who are you?"

"Okay, now this is going to sound crazy, and it's going to be hard to believe, but my wife has been talking to him. I mean, she's been communicating with his, um, spirit," Dan tried to explain.

"Is that her in the room with you?" the girl asked, sniffling.

"Yes."

"Tell her that it's him!" Mia yelled. "Seth—fight it! PLEASE! ... Dear God in heaven…"

"And you say she's been talking with Seth? But I was told he may have been killed."

"Yes, I know it's really bizarre, but somehow she can. Listen, can you—" Dan attempted.

"I've seen things like that before on cable, on the Discovery Channel," Shayla explained, still sniffling.

"Yeah, sure, like that. But listen Shayla, she needs your help!" he tried again with urgency.

The girl hesitated and then asked, "*My* help? With what?"

"She's talking to him right now and—"

"She *IS*?"

"Yes! Believe me! And she needs to ask you some questions," he continued.

"Well, how do I know she's talking to *my* Seth?"

"Dan? Please! What is she saying? We need to hurry," Mia called.

"Well, he gave us your number. Is that enough?"

"No. I'm sorry, how do I know that you just didn't just find it on Google in a phonebook?"

"Hold on a minute," Dan said to Shayla. Then he cupped the mouthpiece with his hand and turned to his wife, and said, "She wants to know that it's her boyfriend, somehow. She wants proof. Can he say—er, write something?"

Mia looked at Seth. The shadow had loosened its grip on him and withdrew, but was circling him slowly. It reminded her of a predator, moving in on its prey, looking for just the right time and place to strike. Seth remained coiled up on the floor, coughing and gagging. She felt so frustrated and powerless, watching but not able to help him.

"No. He can't. He's in too much pain." She looked at her husband and shook her head, her eyes pleading.

Dan turned back to the phone. "She's asking him right now," he fibbed. "Listen, can't you just give us your cooperation?"

"Well I want to make sure that it's him, and not some other person, or something," the girl said cautiously. "Seth meant a lot to me. But he ran off and left me. How do I know that he's not still alive somewhere and you two are just a couple of freaks or something? His mom told me some crazy person called her from a mental hospital, asking about him."

He cupped the phone again. "She still wants more proof," he repeated, gritting his teeth with growing impatience at the caller.

Seth was barely clinging to whatever life he had left. For the moment, the shadow had moved back to the corner again, but its wicked eyes kept a fix on the youth, like a big cat guarding its kill. Mia wasn't sure why it had retreated. Was it because they had made contact with Shayla?

She thought quickly, then said, "Tell her that Seth was fixing up an old Malibu with his friends, Jose and Marcus and, um, Justin."

Dan held out the phone towards her as she talked and then he pulled it back.

"Did you get that? He was fixing up a Chevy Malibu with his friends, Jose, Marcus, and Justin."

"No, it's not enough. Everyone in town knew that. I need something more or I'm going to hang up," Shayla said, starting to cry again.

"No! No, don't hang up. Hold on…" Dan held the phone away and hissed, "Would you believe she needs more?" He shook his head and rolled his eyes with exasperation.

Why does she need so much convincing? Mia thought desperately as she tried to recall something significant for proof. *And what do we need to tell her to in order to save Seth?*

Dan brought the phone over to her. Mia took it and after a moment of thought told her, "You two were going to move away somewhere, but Seth had to save up some more money. He only had three hundred and fifty dollars in the bank but couldn't find any place to work in Wickenburg. He was going to Phoenix that weekend when Ed showed up and—"

"Oh my God, how could you know—"

"Seth told you that day, 'whatever we do, we have to look out for our baby. We agreed to have him, we're going to have to do our best.'"

There was a loud sob over the phone.

"Yes. Yes. That's what he said. But then he took off! He left me…. He abandoned me there with that son of a bitch Ed!" she lamented, and then continued to cry more. She caught herself enough to say, "Our baby was born. A son… Tell him. Would you do that for me? Tell him we have a son?"

Mia's tears sprang anew. The last images of her own baby flashed through her mind, her child that she never got to hold. And after all he had been through, Seth, like she, would never know his son.

She turned to the mirror. "Seth? Can you hear me Honey? It's Shayla. She's here, on the phone."

He managed to pick his head up slightly off the floor and tried to fix his eyes on her. They were glassy and dazed. He reached out a trembling hand.

"Hang in there, Honey," she said gently. "You have a son. Shayla had your son. He's all right."

For a second, the youth smiled weakly at the news. His hand went down to the pen and book lying strewn on the floor beside him. With tremendous effort, he scribbled out one last message:

TLL HR - FRGV ME

LV HR

LV BBY.

Seth went unconscious. The pen rolled from his outstretched fingers. As his blood dripped on the page of the notebook, it instantly appeared, wet and red, on the page before Mia and Dan.

Up until now the shadow had been waiting, almost patiently, in the corner. Now it saw the opportunity it had been anticipating. In a swift move, it pounced on Seth's lifeless body. The blackness fanned out, as dark as a pool of oil, and completely covered the teen in the middle of the living room floor.

Seeing the swirling mass obscure him from sight, Mia shrieked, "Seth! Oh God, no, please no…"

Not being able to get over his amazement of it all, Dan picked up the notebook with the spidery black scrawl across it and read it, letting his fingers glide across the writing, smearing some of the wet blood into the ink. With wonder, he examined his fingertips and the red fluid that stained them. Then he picked up the phone.

"Shayla? Seth said he loves you and he loves the baby," he told the girl on the other line. "He also wants you to forgive him."

"Can I talk to him? I want to tell him something. I've been needing to tell him all this time…" Shayla begged. "…and I couldn't tell anybody else…"

"She wants to talk to him," Dan said quietly to Mia who stood shocked and trembling.

The blackness no longer permitted her to see him. Even more so, both he and the shadow were beginning to fade, dissipating slowly into a fine mist.

"Don't go, Seth…" she implored and then buried her face in her hands unable to watch any more. She turned away from the mirror and wept.

Why, God? Why wasn't anything making a difference? The phone call to Shayla should have done it. It should have saved him…but why hadn't it? … I'm losing him, after all… Mia was drowning in remorse, racking her brain as to what else she could have possibly done.

"I think it's too late," she whispered to her husband, her voice cracking.

Dan started to relay the message, "Shayla, he can't—"

Suddenly Shayla burst out, talking rapidly, "Tell him that I-I did it! I killed Ed. I had no other choice."

Hearing the girl's abrupt admission, Dan pulled Mia close and put the phone between them so they both could hear her.

Shayla confessed, "After the fight, Seth ran off so I just sat there. I didn't know what else to do. I felt so sick, I couldn't move. I was hoping that he would return for me. After a while, I was getting ready to walk back home since Seth never came back. I thought Ed was dead and I didn't even know how to handle that situation, but then he started to wake up! I really thought that Seth had killed him. But he wasn't dead, like me and Seth thought. I totally freaked out. He sat up and kind of shook his head some. He must've still been dizzy from the fight. And then he told me he would make me and Seth sorry we ever tried to defy him and that he was going to start with me first.

"So I picked up the gun that was still on the ground from when they were fighting and…I told him to stop… and … I had no choice! I had to protect myself… I had to protect my baby…" she explained in ragged sobs. "Tell Seth that I … I took care of our baby just like we agreed. That's why I did it! And I couldn't tell anyone what I did, not the cops, not anyone what had happened. I even threw the gun down a hole. I couldn't go to jail. How would I have taken care of our baby? So when everyone thought that Seth did it, I just couldn't tell them any different. But he has to know. Please tell him for me…"

Mia looked to where Seth had laid. There was nothing left. He and the shadow had both faded away. She stared numbly at the reflection of herself and Dan sitting huddled together on the living room floor, holding the phone between them.

With her heart aching, she thought, *If only Seth could have heard those words….*

Mia could barely answer. "I will, Shayla. I will…" she muttered despondently.

The young girl sobbed on the line. A few moments passed yet no one could talk, each of them sorting through the loss and heartbreak in their own individual way.

Then Shayla said, "I got to go. The baby's waking up… If you talk with Seth some more, tell him I still think about him. And he will always be Daddy to little John Michael here, but I don't think I can talk with him anymore…"

When Mia heard the baby's wail in the background, her heart felt the same vicious stab it endured the day her father died.

"All right, I'll… tell him…"

The baby's cries grew more insistent, but Shayla had one more request, "Um, except for Seth, you won't tell anyone what I told you. You know, about what happened? Please don't…I don't think it makes much difference now, does it? And I'm the only person John Michael has now."

No, it doesn't now. Mia thought. Instead, she answered, "No. You have my word. And thank you, Shayla. For all that you've done."

They listened for a moment more at John Michael's lusty cries and his mother's soothing tones. Then the line clicked as she hung up. The room was silent.

It was over. Seth was no more. Mia's hands fell limp into her lap. She was physically and emotionally spent. It was all she could do to hold herself up. Her eyes returned once more to the place where Seth had last lain. "He's gone, Dan," was all she could manage to say.

Looking at his wife and how distraught she was, Dan pulled her close and tenderly held her.

"It's over," she said weakly.

"It's okay, Murph. It's okay..." he said.

This harrowing ordeal with Seth had left its mark on every aspect of her life—Dan's trust in her, their marriage. As for her, it had nearly taken her to the brink of insanity. And all for what? But the part that tore at her heart the most, that made her want to give up completely was she had lost him, just as she had failed her own child who was so similarly dependent upon her for his very survival. She couldn't save either one of them. In fact, she had only made matters worse. Why had she ever been chosen for this task, if it was all to be in vain?

"I thought I could help him," she tried to explain, but realized it was more for her own sake than her husband's.

"Shhh, you did all that you could. There wasn't anything else that could have been done. I think he knew that," Dan said trying to comfort her.

"But I thought once we got all the pieces to fit, he would be all right. I thought he could finally be at peace and his soul would be set free, away from that wretched place that he was in. Now he's damned to be there forever or maybe someplace... worse," her voice cracked. "He turned to me for help, but I let him down. I was too late. I was TOO DAMN LATE!" she growled as her frustration and sorrow mounted. "Although he is innocent, he's going to suffer perpetual torment! Oh God...Seth... I just can't bear it!"

She broke down and cried openly, clinging to her husband. They remained seated on the floor, the notebook and the pen lying close by, the only testimony of what had been.

Mia said, her voice barely audible, "I don't know how to go on from here... I don't even know why I should..."

"We can stay here for as long as you need. I'm not going anywhere," Dan reassured her.

With overwhelming guilt and grief, she looked to the mirror one last time through her tears. Would she ever be able to look at it again without thinking of him? He was gone. It was as if he had never been. She wiped her swollen eyes and blinked hard, her sobbing making her body shudder.

Then she blinked again. There was the faintest glimmer of light in the reflection.

What was that?

When she studied it, she could see it was only the reflection of the daylight through the window.

There's nothing there, she told herself.

It made her think of his last day in the bright Arizona sun and how he was now sentenced to a world of darkness, loneliness, and suffering. Angered, she felt the urge to destroy the mirror, to break it into a million pieces.

To her surprise, the glimmer of light persisted. It wasn't merely a reflection as she had thought and its presence disarmed her. As she stared at it, it grew brighter in luminance. She turned to query Dan, but found he was looking at it too. His eyes were wide and he remained stock still.

"Are you seeing this?" she asked him.

He replied incredulously, "Yes ma'am… I most certainly am."

The glow continued to intensify until finally it was as bright as an afternoon summer sun, but amazingly, neither of them had to turn their eyes away from it. Its glow streamed out from the glass and illuminated the entire living room.

"What in the hell? What's going on, Mia?" Dan questioned as his arm went up protectively around her.

"I—I don't know…"

The light grew in size and shape filling the entire frame of the mirror. Just then Seth appeared, emerging from the bright rays. He stood erect and tall, looking all about him as if he had just awoken and entered the room for the first time.

Mia gasped out loud. "Do you see him?! Do you see him!! Oh my God… Dan?" She excitedly tugged at her husband.

"I do! … Son OF A bitch! I *can!*" Dan answered, gaping in astonishment as they rose to their feet.

The youth stood before them. He took a deep breath and stretched his arms high above his head. He was fully restored—his face, hands, and body—wounds, broken bones, and sores were completely healed. All evidence of torture was gone. His skin was tan and his eyes were clear and bright. There was not a trace of mud, dust, or blood anywhere upon him. Seeing him so vibrant and full of life, Mia let out a cry of joy.

Thank you God! Oh, thank you… her mind screamed.

Becoming fully cognizant of where he was, Seth looked at his hands in awe, and then slowly felt his face. The skin he felt beneath his fingertips was whole and healthy. He laughed out loud with the discovery and exclaimed "Yes!" as he extended his arms and legs to look himself over again.

Mia's eyes opened wide in amazement. She *could hear* him. "My God! I can—" she started to tell her husband.

"Yes! I hear him too! I can't believe this is happening! Holy shit!" Dan laughed in wonder.

Mia went to the mirror. Seth saw her and immediately did the same, his face radiant.

"It's me, Mia! And I'm fine. Look at me! I can't believe this. And I can hear you!" he said with wonder.

They both reached out to touch hands against the glass. But to her shock and his, this time, there was no glass. They looked at their interlocked fingers and laughed. Then she embraced him and held him tightly, her heart so full, it felt as if it would burst.

"Seth —I was so afraid that I had lost you. But oh my God, you are here! You are here!" she said, awestruck.

"I *was* lost. I was falling again through the darkness. But this time even farther than before. I've never seen anything, *felt* anything so black. Not even when I was in the mine. And the pain was incredible—it just wouldn't let up. I was freezing and felt so…so empty. As if I was made of nothing. As if I had never been made of anything at all."

"What happened, then?"

"I don't know how or why. Everything came to a stop. It just *ended.* I never did reach the bottom. And next I am here."

"And you're all right…"

She looked him over again, marveling at how alive and whole he was. She had to hug him once more. New tears, this time of joy, came to her eyes.

"But I don't understand. How did you-?"

"It was like I had been stuck in some kind of perpetual nightmare. But I finally woke up! And the darkness is totally gone… I don't know what happened. But I'm okay!" he answered, his deep voice full of elation. "I feel I can do anything now, go anywhere. I'm free… I'm *free.*" He looked at her affectionately. "And you were the one who freed me, Mia. How can ever I thank you, for caring about me so much? For everything…you didn't give up on me," he said gratefulness mingling with tenderness.

Then Seth turned to her husband who was staring dumbfounded at the scene before him. The teen reached out his hand. "And thank you, Dan. You know, you're all right. I should have let you help me out long ago," he said as he shook his hand.

Dan nodded his head in response, still too stunned for any words to escape. When they released grips, Dan stared at his hand in amazement where he and Seth had touched.

Mia put her hand to Seth's cheek and gazed at his face. He was alive and free of pain. "Now that you are here, there's so much that I want to ask you. We can talk out loud now, and we don't have to use the notebook anymore. And I can see and touch you. It must be some kind of miracle."

He shook his head. "I won't be able to stay, Mia. I must go."

"What? But you just got here! And you're whole and everything's okay. I don't understand—"

All of a sudden, the light grew and started to encompass Seth. He faced Mia once more.

"How can I ever thank you enough? You saved me."

"Can't you stay for just a few more minutes," she asked, feeling confused and disappointed at the abruptness of it all. "I have you here now and I don't know if I can let you go..." she said dismally. It felt as if she was losing him all over again.

He took her hands in his and gazed at her. Just when she found herself starting to despair, she found that her yearning ceased and her longing put to rest. Instead, a deep solace came over her. She wasn't sure where this feeling was coming from, but she felt in her heart and soul that it was right. She searched her mind and *knew* things were as they should be. Seth had to go and she could let him. It was as if all her questions were answered in an instant.

All, but one.

She nodded in understanding. "Yes. I know now that you must go, Seth. It's what we've been working towards ever since we first made contact. But before you go, please, there's one thing I need to ask you."

"What is it?" he asked her with that shy smile she knew so well.

"I need to know what it was that you kept saying over and over. You know, when we first met."

He answered, "'I didn't mean to.' I was saying, 'I didn't mean to.'"

She looked into his lively blue–green eyes knowing it would be for the last time. "I guess neither of us has to say that anymore."

They shared a knowing smile. The light grew even brighter and he looked over his shoulder and nodded. Then he turned back to her for their farewell.

She drew forward and gave him a small kiss. Missing him already, there was a bit of sadness mixed with happiness when she hugged him one last time and said, "Go on Tiger. I'll always remember you."

He smiled and continued to hold her hand. "I love you, Mia," he said.

"I love you, Seth."

He vanished, taking the brightness with him. The brilliant light went out like a snuffed candle and Mia and Dan were returned once more to their living room, lit only by the midday sun. She held her hand to the glass, feeling Seth's warmth slowly fade away.

Just then the phone rang, jarring her and Dan from their dreamlike trance on the empty mirror. Dan reached down to pick the phone up off the floor and pressed the TALK button.

"Hello? Mr. Labont? This is Dr. Churosh at Meadow Brook. I am terribly sorry to disturb you. We—uh, have somewhat of a problem. Your wife—"

Dan grinned. "She's here, Doc." He looked over at Mia and winked at her. She smiled in return.

"Everything's fine. She's fine. And don't worry. She's NOT going back. Thank you!" he said, and then hung up.

EPILOGUE
EPILOGUE

ALONE IN THE DARK, THE CRYING BEGAN. It continued softly, but soon it erupted into a mild disturbance as it found its way down the hallway to their bedroom.

"Honey, do you hear that?" Dan said as he awoke with a start.

Mia came around slowly. She was exhausted from an extremely busy day.

"Huh?" She listened for a moment. "Wait, give it a minute," she mumbled as she turned over and snuggled into her pillow.

But the pitiful demands grew stronger and continued to call to her, threatening to fill the entire house.

"Uh oh, sounds like he's in trouble again," Dan said, sitting up and turning on his light.

"Yeah, I guess it does, doesn't it?" she said groggily. "I'll go see what he wants."

"No, no. I'll go."

"Are you sure? I don't mind."

"Nah, don't worry," he said patting her leg. "You look beat. I think I can handle it. At least let me give it a try. You've got to admit, I'm getting a lot better than I used to be at this." He rose from their bed and left the room.

She could hear him down the hall talking in low reassuring tones. Within a few minutes, the crying stopped and everything seemed to settle down. Whatever he told him, must have done the trick. She was proud of how easily Dan dealt with all of this now. It certainly made a difference to have a true partner to give her a hand.

Just as she started to doze off once more, Dan was at the doorway.

"I'm sorry Murph. I tried to talking to him, but he's definitely looking for you," he said sheepishly as he brought in their infant son nestled against his chest. The baby fretted and kicked his little feet. "I told Nathan that I didn't think the lunch counter was open this late at night, but he wouldn't hear anything about it."

Father and son plopped down upon the bed next to Mia. She sat up and although she tried to feign being put out, she happily received her chubby baby boy. She kissed and cuddled him, then put him to her breast. Dan put his arms around her and gave her a kiss on the forehead. Then they settled back to watch their child together. It was a happiness and sense of peace they thought they would never know.

A year had passed since she last saw Seth, yet thoughts of him still entered her mind almost daily as she went about her life. On occasion, odd reflections in shiny objects and mirrors around the house would catch her eye, only for her to find it was nothing but a play of light. She never did see Seth again, though in a way, she never expected to. Dan's and her days gradually fell back into place as they picked up the loose threads from their unraveled life. Eventually, her pregnancy and the arrival of their son fully engaged them both and they happily welcomed it.

Seeing other children in the playground when she took Nathan out for walks in his stroller, she figured that Seth's son must be a toddler by now. Early on, within the months following "the Occurrence" as she and Dan had dubbed it, she wrestled with the thought of calling Shayla again to let her know that Seth had truly found his way. One day, she made up her mind to do it. Hesitantly, she dialed the phone only to find that Shayla had changed her number and left no forwarding one.

Since then, she and Dan agreed to keep the Occurrence between them. Although Hoason, Aunt Lydia, and Mrs. Lopez begged for more details, they simply stated that it was over. And there were times that she passed by the mirror in the living room and gazed into it, feeling as if it had all been part of an inexplicable dream. She only had to look as far as the notebook to know that it was not.

When she reread Seth's words upon the pages, she reflected upon his short, troubled life. There were so many other kids who needed help out there with no one to turn to. How many other souls were lost and forgotten? When she visited her father's tree, she still envisioned her father and her firstborn together as she had when her odyssey first began. Now, she liked to think that Seth was with them. She prayed that it was true. And within time, her heart told her that it was so.

One afternoon after Mia had put the baby down for a nap, she wandered out to the garage to find Dan. He was there, carefully following the woodworking plans for a hobbyhorse.

"Hey Hon, there you are. Don't forget that your mom and dad and Jenna are coming over tonight for dinner. They're at the RV show right now. I guess they didn't want to miss it before they left next week."

"Yeah, I didn't forget. I just wanted to work on this a bit. Nathan's going to be in college by the time I get this finished, if I'm lucky."

"Well, maybe he'll be able to give you a hand with it then, huh?" she teased.

She went over to the dryer and emptied it, filling the laundry basket with warm, clean baby clothes. Mia selected one of the soft flannel sleepers and nuzzled her face in it.

"Mmm, I love the way these smell," she said to no one in particular. Then she lifted the basket and hauled the clothes inside for folding.

"I'll be in a little while. Just give me a few more minutes…" Dan called after her as he carefully measured and marked a piece of wood to cut.

"Uh huh, more like another hour," she chuckled to herself.

After taking a peek at their son to make sure he was settled, Mia put down the basket and took up her post on the sofa to start folding the pile of tiny clothes. There was so much to do once he went down for a nap and she had time to catch up on things. She was softly singing one of the lullabies she had learned from the baby's many CD's to herself as she went through each of his clothes.

Something in the large tile mirror caught her eye. This time she could not dismiss it as another odd play of light. Within seconds, that old familiar feeling came over her and her heart sped up.

It couldn't possibly be. Not after all this time…

With a bit of curiosity mixed with hope, she lifted her gaze and faced the glass.

A little girl, not more than eight or nine years old, stared back. Her eyes were wide and serious, and a bit of fear shaped her small face. Her chin quivered, as she was about to cry.

Mia was startled to see her at first but then she took a deep breath and sighed. So as not to scare the child, she picked up the next shirt and started to fold it, and casually said, "Hello there! Welcome to my home. I'm Mia. And who are you?"

More Stories from Tess Marset

Lest We Fall
(Book Two of The Mia Series)
978-1-7333609-1-3

Gothic Suspense, Thriller

What if you had a unique skill that you never asked for?
A talent that would endanger the lives of your family...

With the appearance of a young girl in her mirror, Mia Labont's odyssey into the supernatural continues in this sequel to *With My Little Eye*. She and husband Dan were settling in to a renewed home life after the birth of their son. But their time of happiness is short lived as the forlorn child in the mirror starts to reveal clues of her imprisonment. Mia is forced to call upon her intuitive powers to solve the mystery surrounding the girl's whereabouts in a race against tragedy. In doing so, she comes face to face with a much darker force that will not only test her resolve, but ultimately, her will to survive.

On Frogs and Princes

978-1-7333609-3-7

Contemporary Romance

When Stazie Royale sets her sights on something, she usually gets it. The pampered daughter of a successful defense attorney for celebrities is used to having her way. However, life begins to change for her one rainy night once she runs over Rey Natal while he is riding his bicycle during a blackout. Trying to come to terms with guilt and depression over a tragedy in his past, independent Rey is more than a challenge for Stazie's willful wiles. Encountering more mishaps, this unlikely pair must get beyond misperceptions to gain awareness for what they each had all along: love and appreciation for what they didn't think was possible. On Frogs and Princes is a story of abandonment, forgiveness, acceptance, and discovering that while all frogs aren't princes, even princesses can have warts.